SISTERS OF THE MOON

MOLLY BURKHART

Copyright © 2021 by Molly Burkhart

Cover created by Covers By Stella

All rights reserved.

No part of this book may be reproduced in any form or by any electronic or mechanical means, including information storage and retrieval systems, without written permission from the author, except for the use of brief quotations in a book review.

❦ Created with Vellum

SISTERS OF THE MOON

Wendolyn Eudora Cheney is a bit of a mess.

Forty, overweight, prematurely white-haired, and the victim of a messy marriage and an even messier divorce, Wen has had a rough time getting back on her feet. She's the last person in the world who would find herself mixed up in a paranormal mystery with a side of dangerous fairy tale.

But when Dex and Callum—two bounty hunter shapeshifters from the United Kingdom—find her in the middle of Missouri at a grocery store and inform her that she has "called" them, she's a Sister of the Moon, and they're her loyal guardians for life, her world flips on a dime. Suddenly, she's flying to Scotland to meet another Sister of the Moon, Brigid, to learn the ropes.

When the third and eldest Sister of the Moon, Thea, shows up to tell them that all of magic is failing and her spirit guides say the Sisters must fix the Veil, Wen has to learn ropes none of them have ever heard of before. She might even have to make up a few ropes of her own.

Will she learn to use her dormant power? Will she almost die on a sea voyage? Will she have to enter a portal into the Night

Realm to cross mental swords with energy beings from another plane of existence?

Brigid's tarot cards say yes, and they are never wrong. The Sisters of the Moon, a complete circle of three for the first time in a century, have work to do.

Wen's book is a slow burn, stand-alone, reverse harem love story about finding the magic in yourself at any age.

Warnings: anxiety, gaslighting recovery, past mental abuse.

For my beloved sister. Always.
Also thanks to Sherri, for the help and the flowers.

1

Most people thought working from home would be a dream come true. Pajamas every day. Snacks any time you want. No meetings that could've been emails or getting called into the boss's office because of catty office gossip.

No. Bras. Ever.

But Wen knew better. For Wendolyn Eudora Cheney, working from home meant isolation. And though she'd been at her at-home job for almost twenty years, the last three years of that isolation had piled up to almost break her.

She was alone. Painfully alone. Forty years old, overweight, divorced, childless, friendless, anxiety-ridden, and *alone*.

It wasn't like she hadn't tried, but she'd been shy and awkward even before the divorce. She'd married right out of high school to an Army grunt almost done with his mandatory service—one who'd been the anchor of the championship high school football offensive line five years before and spoke of little else when having beers with the bros. Thus, she hadn't been surprised when Tucker Lennon quickly and effortlessly overshadowed her. He had a big personality to go with all that beef.

Wen never had. Mama's little mouse, she'd been, until her

mother died of ovarian cancer during Wen's second year of marriage. Her father had long since been out of the picture, and she had no siblings. Her mother's sister hadn't spoken to Mama in years, mostly because Wen could've just as easily been Aunt Helen's daughter, given her relationship with Wen's father.

Yeah. The Cheney women really knew how to pick 'em.

So when Mama died, all Wen had left was Tucker. And that had been enough at first. She thought.

Shaking herself, Wen stood abruptly away from her tiny corner desk, saved her spreadsheet with a jab of her finger, and took a quick walk around the room. It was a pitifully short walk, given that the one room was her entire apartment.

Tucker hadn't taken the house, per se, in the divorce, but he *had* taken half of her well-earned retirement savings, half the marital assets he'd bought with her money, and half the value of a house she hadn't wanted and couldn't afford to keep after he all but cleaned her out. It was "fairness" in the eyes of the law, perhaps, and meant to help oppressed women who hadn't been allowed to work to retain some sort of life after being abandoned by their better-employed husbands. But it was all bullshit.

Tucker hadn't been oppressed. He just didn't care about working anywhere that didn't immediately promote him to manager. Not when he had Wen working from home, doing all the housework while making three times what he did. He didn't care about building his own retirement savings when he could "share" hers. Same with the insurance she paid for that he had blithely used until the court-ordered year had passed after their divorce.

He had, of course, had an expensive, semi-elective "preventative" surgery the month before she could legally drop him. Huge copay, maxed out the deductible, cost her thousands. But he haaaaad to get that gallbladder out. It was really griping him. So much pain, Wendy, and it wasn't his fault the ports got infected,

Wendy, and what was he supposed to do, wait for an emergency situation when he didn't have any insurance, Wendy?

Fucking Tucker. Tucker the Fucker.

Three years later, and she was still stuck in a studio apartment while he'd bought an overpriced house in a new subdivision with her money, blowing through it on new furniture—despite him taking most of the old furniture in the divorce—a huge truck, the meat smoker he'd always nagged her for—*"Think of all the money we'll save smoking our own meat, Wendy!" "Tucker, we do not eat that much meat! We'd have to run a restaurant to make back that kind of investment!"*—a huge entertainment center, and and and *and*.

A new woman every six months or so, of course. Most of them figured him out long before Wen had. They wanted nothing to do with him once they saw how he really was.

If only she'd been so smart.

Grumbling at herself, Wen stopped pacing in tiny circles and jumped in place for a moment, shaking out her arms and rolling her head on her aching shoulders. Tucker had blown through his half of her life's work in just over a year. He'd had to go back to work himself—because of course he'd quit whatever job he happened to be hating during the divorce and picked up ACA insurance (which he'd demonized bitterly until he needed coverage of his own)—to keep the new house. Rumor had it that he'd already borrowed money from his parents, his brothers, and even a distant cousin.

Okay, so she had a Facebook account she'd never bothered with, and he'd forgotten to block her. The universe would surely forgive her a little curiosity as to what he was spending her retirement nest egg on. And she didn't have anyone left to gossip with about it in person, so she had to get creative.

It gave her a mean little jolt of pleasure to see him failing to make anything of himself when he'd told her all those years that *she'd* never make it without *him*. She still had her good—if brutally isolating—job and was dutifully rebuilding her future. She could've probably gone into debt on a house just as new and fancy as his if she'd wanted to, but she stuck with the studio apartment to save up and spare herself the stress of a mortgage. Or to at least lower it with a large down payment.

He may be keeping up appearances for now, but she was doing the real work.

Story of their marriage, really.

Her computer dinged, reminding her that she was only allowed five minutes at a time away from her keyboard during business hours, so she sighed, sat back down, and got back to work. Those aged fund sources weren't gonna bill themselves.

That was her job. Her steady, reliable, but oh, so isolating job.

Wen hated going to the store. It wasn't so much that having to put on real pants and a bra sucked, although it so did. She just always felt... wrong. In the way. Going the wrong way down an aisle. Always needing something right behind where someone else was standing. Or standing where someone else needed to be.

She never knew whether to smile at people or mind her own damn business. Should she offer to buy the crying toddler the toy his harried mother made him put back on the shelf? Or would that be offensive, like the poor woman couldn't take care of her own kid? Should she try to chitchat with the cashier, knowing that her efforts would be excruciating at best, or should she just smile and pay and get the hell out? Should she use a self-check station, or had she somehow picked something that couldn't be either scanned or weighed and required a manager's intervention?

And how much of that was Tucker the Fucker telling her she

could ruin a wet dream? How much of that was her own shyness? Was there any way to ever know for sure?

But she did occasionally need groceries, and while she could shop online and pay someone to deliver them to her door, she told herself that she needed to get out sometimes. Be amongst the normals. Maybe even make a friend. She was hopeless at people-ing, but if she never tried, she'd never be any less alone.

So she made herself go. Made herself try to look like a regular, functional adult who hadn't just taken off her favorite footie pajamas for the first time all weekend.

She even ate a healthy, balanced diet in hopes of avoiding unwelcome judgment of her weight, Tucker the Fucker's insidious voice always in the back of her mind, whispering that no man would ever want a heifer like her, even as he swore he loved her as the fat, lazy, prematurely gray-haired mess she was. Vegetables and fruit wouldn't shut out those awful thoughts—memories—completely, but it turned out she actually liked fruits and vegetables, so she did what she could to stop anyone else from saying them.

And she eventually stopped coloring her hair, even though she was really too young for the full head of silver-white she sported. She'd been going gray since she was sixteen, and she'd just hit her fortieth birthday a few months back. It was a lot of gray.

But she had no intention of coloring again until she was eighty. She simply couldn't stand to buy one more Dark Brown #4 kit from Wal-Mart, because that was the only color Tucker thought suitable for her. Darker than her own mousy brown, but not slutty Goth black.

And God forbid she even think of adding a touch of red, like Mama had done. Wen had always wanted to try red, to see if it helped her look more like her beautiful, strong mother. But no. Tucker had a lot of opinions about redheads.

"Hon?"

She flinched, her shoulders going up without her permission. It was just a nice little old black lady, her close-cropped hair dusted with white—but less than her own—and her face a roadmap of wrinkles.

"Yes? I'm sorry, I didn't... hear you?"

Jesus, had the old lady even been trying to get her attention other than the one word? Why couldn't she be normal just once?

"I didn't wanna draw attention." The kind-looking stranger drew closer, shifting her eyes from side to side and lowering her voice to a whisper. "Don't look, but I've noticed that that fella over there seems to be followin you."

Her whole body tensed. How could she *not* look now? Indeed, her head started to turn without even consulting the brain inside it until the little old lady reached out and laid a knobby hand on her forearm.

"Honey, don't. Try to look like I'm just askin you for help gettin that can of soup on the top shelf, okay?"

A normal person could do that. But not Wendolyn Eudora Cheney.

Hand shaking, she reached up for the indicated can, but she couldn't stop her eyes from searching out the possible threat. Surely, it couldn't be Tucker. He surely wanted nothing to do with her after the second time he tried to adjust the divorce decree to get more money out of her, and the judge told him to knock it off or he'd find him in contempt and give him a night in a holding cell to think about his choices.

She caught a blur of dark clothes and dark skin before her trembling fingers fumbled the can she wanted, tipped it back against the one behind it, and started a fearsome clatter as all the cans in the back tried to fall down behind the shelf. Flinching, she reached up with the other hand to try and salvage the situation and somehow managed to knock cans off the front, too. Three slammed to the floor, the paper label on one snapping off and rolling down the aisle.

Toward the dark blur, of course. Dragging her eyes that way.

Tall, black boots. Charcoal jeans clinging to tight thighs. Wash-worn black shirt stretched over a wide, muscled chest under a black leather coat. Charcoal scarf against the November chill outside. Dark brown skin not much lighter than the dreaded Dark Brown #4 hair color had been, but rich and velvety-looking as a skin tone. Long black dreads draped over broad shoulders.

Amber eyes. She'd swear they were glowing like a bonfire at midnight. Was he standing directly under a fluorescent or something?

Frozen as those brilliant eyes caught hers, she felt her mouth dry out and her tongue stick to her soft palate. And that first, shameful thought. A Tucker the Fucker thought.

A man as beautiful as that couldn't possibly be looking at *her*.

"Oh, honey." The forgotten little old lady sighed. "I suppose that was a way to go, anyway."

The tall, dark, and handsome stranger—*Jesus, Wen, is that really the best you can do?*—took a few steps closer, all prowling muscle and raw appeal. So not fair.

"I am so sorry."

British. Accent. If she'd still had any working brain cells, they would've fainted on the spot.

"Here, please allow me to help."

"No thank you, son." The old lady, of course, had no problem being a functioning, rational adult. "This young thing was just tryin to reach me down the Italian weddin soup. We can take care of ourselves, can't we, dear?"

Incapable of response while soaking in mortification and anxiety, Wen jerked over at the waist to pick up the fallen cans, adding the label-less one to her own basket because... she couldn't just put it back on the shelf. But she couldn't step closer to Tall, Dark, and Handsome to pick up the stray label, either. She'd figure out something when her brain kicked back in again.

"You go on now, young man. We're just fine."

With obvious reluctance—why? maybe he just hated leaving an elder in need; although surely Wen herself was his senior by more than a few years—TDH backed a few steps, locked those blazing eyes with hers again, then slowly turned away and left the aisle.

"I'm pretty sure you're gonna need to breathe at some point, honey."

She coughed out the air she hadn't realized she was holding, then gasped in a whoop that almost made her choke. If there was a god, he should've intervened long before now. How humiliating! Why, oh *why* couldn't she just be fucking normal?

"That's alright, honey. Just take a few good, deep breaths. If I'd known it would tongue-tie you so, I'd have just asked you to walk me to my car instead."

But when Wen was finally able to meet the dark eyes set deep in their crow's-feet webs, she sensed a reserve that hadn't been there before. Her mind raced—in circles, but very fast for all that—as she tried to imagine what she could've possibly said to offend. Or was she just so freaking weird that she'd scared the poor old thing?

And then she realized. And blurted, because she was a walking disaster.

"Oh! No, it's not because he's black! I'm just—"

She closed her eyes and felt numbness sweep over her. She might as well have said "I'm not a racist, but—" No way in hell could she convince this kind old woman that the crazy white chick she'd just tried to rescue was anything but the garden variety Karen.

Something in her chest area clenched painfully, then went

back to quiet numbness. The lady had been so kind to try and help.

"I'm so sorry. If it helps, I have anxiety." A huff that sounded more like a dry heave caught in her throat. "No, that's not it. I'm just a disaster."

She couldn't bear to look at her rescuer. In fact, she didn't think she could manage to even pay for the few groceries she'd basketed before now. Definitely not the goddamn naked can of soup.

"Well." Still sounding reserved, the poor woman shuffled back to her cart. "We ladies do have to look out for each other."

"Yes. And thank you so much for your help. I probably wouldn't have noticed until it was too late."

"Mm." It was a noncommittal noise, at best, but it was something. "You look out for yourself in the parkin lot, now. He was pretty, but that don't mean he's not bad news. And he *was* starin awful hard."

At what? the little voice in her mind sneered as shuffling footsteps faded away. *Me?*

The thought would be hilarious if it didn't make her want to cry.

She wished she could apologize better to the woman who had brought her attention to the situation, but she had no intention of following the poor old lady around, hitting her with even more microaggressions, accidental or otherwise. She should just leave.

Probably safer that way. Though the strange man couldn't possibly have actually been following her.

Too wrung out to be anxious, she headed for the doors, trying to keep an eye out for TDH without being obvious about it and failing miserably. She could almost see herself, streaky gray-white hair pulled back in a frizzy ponytail, button-up oversize flannel shirt hanging down below her coat's hem, eyes dazed and face pale, old tennis shoes scuffed and shuffling on the floor tiles. She was pretty sure her old, paint-spattered jeans had a worn hole on one inner thigh or the other, but she was still too numb to feel which as her thighs swooshed together.

No one was looking at her. Even the door greeter she handed her pitiful basket to for reshelving didn't really *look* at her.

Such a useless trip. All she'd managed to do was offend a kind old lady, weird out some random hot guy who was probably just watching an awkward white weirdo stumbling around a store with her head up her ass and one shoe untied, and *not* buy any groceries. Forget whether or not she wanted to be out and about; she shouldn't be *allowed* in public.

A disaster. A shambling disaster.

Feeling a wave of despair—self pity?—well up inside her under the numbness, she blinked watery eyes and suddenly wondered where the hell she'd parked. She never parked too close to the front because people needed those spots, but she didn't want to be caught huffing and puffing all the way through the lot, either, so she also never parked all the way in the back. Fighting the urge to just sit down in the middle of the parking lot for a minute, she dug in her pocket for her keys and tried to at least remember if she'd come into the store from the right or the left of the big glass doors.

She pushed the button on her key fob and heard a soft, reassuring honk off to the right. When she looked that way, though, she dropped her keys to the asphalt, her eyes widening.

Tall, Dark, and Handsome lounged back against the front end of her car, one foot crossed over the other, arms casually crossed over that broad chest.

What. What the hell.

True to her disaster self, she just stood there, staring, hand poised as if she would eventually reach down and pick up her keys but completely incapable of doing so yet. The stranger glanced at the fallen keyring but didn't move to snatch it up. Apparently, he wasn't after her car.

Her ten-year-old, reliable but run-down Roger, who had over a hundred thousand miles on the odometer, two bald tires, and a stiff steering column. TDH could do better.

But he didn't make any moves toward her, and when he spoke, she really did try to make sense of whatever he was about to say.

"I truly didn't mean to frighten you in there." His accented voice flowed like warm honey, his eyes no longer blazing amber now that he wasn't standing under harsh store lighting. "That wasn't my intention at all. I only wanted to speak to you."

She blinked. To her? "To me?"

"Indeed. May I have your name?"

Another blink. What was even happening right now? "Uh. No?"

Maybe he'd think she was mentally challenged and lose interest. Leave her alone. But what if he was one of those sickos who took advantage of mentally challenged people?

What to do? She *hated* going to the damn store.

But he only quirked the tiniest hint of a smile at one corner of his mouth. "Fair enough. I'm Dex, if it helps put you at ease. I swear I am not here to harm you in any way."

Dex. The word slipped through the funk in her poor, over-stressed brain. A name. Dex. Short for Dexter, perhaps? Something more exotic? *Dexie's Midnight Runners?*

Wasn't that "Come On, Eileen" song about a sex worker? Jesus, maybe—

"Madam, please. I wouldn't harm a hair on your head. I only wish to speak with you. And show you something."

Finally, blessedly, self-preservation kicked in and her eyes narrowed, her head coming up and her shoulders inching down. Flight was no longer an option; if she had to fight, she would. Despite all the self-doubts and twenty-some years of gaslighting, she *was* actually capable of taking care of herself. She'd been doing so most of her adulthood. Tucker had certainly never felt the urge to defend her or help her or stand up for her in any way, which was why it'd taken so long for her to leave him.

The stranger's expression changed slightly, his eyes narrowing, perhaps, but she responded before he could change tactics.

"I don't think that's a good idea, sir. I'm sorry, but I don't know you."

"My name is Dex Talmadge. I hail from a little village in the Lake District in England. I'm a bounty hunter—"

Her eyes widened, and she took an involuntary step back, even though she'd never done anything deserving of a bounty on her head, but he hurried on.

"—which is what has brought me first to America and now here to Missouri. I only stepped into the store for a few frozen dinners for a work partner and I. Then... there you were."

Her eyes narrowed. "Me."

He nodded. "You."

She waited, but that seemed to be all he had to say. "And what exactly about me had you staring at a total stranger hard enough that another stranger tried to help me in case you weren't one of the good guys?"

To her surprise, his face softened into something almost like amusement. "Is that what that was? I couldn't for the life of me reckon what had you throwing that nice lady's soup on the floor."

She felt her cheeks warm, but now wasn't the time for Tucker the Fucker's voice to remind her of how clumsy and slow and generally messy she was. She'd been a hitched breath shy of a panic attack in the store, and this rando thought it was funny.

Gathering herself, she finally bent down for her keys, not taking her eyes off him. "Well, I'm glad you enjoyed scaring the crap out of me, but I need to go now. If you could just unseat yourself from Roger's nose—"

"Beg pardon?"

Her tongue glued itself to the roof of her mouth again. Why was she so useless at communication? How could she possibly explain that her reliable, trustworthy car that always got her where she needed to go was basically her only friend without sounding even more pathetic than she already was?

Suddenly tired, she waved vaguely at him and dared to take a step toward her car. He seemed to debate staying put for a moment, then sort of winced around the mouth and stood away from the hood. He even put his hands up to show he was empty-handed as he backed away enough for her to feel safe dodging around Roger's hood to the driver's side.

"Madam, If you would only—"

"Sorry, man. I really am." Oddly, she really did feel sorry. If nothing else, this catastrophe of a shopping trip proved all too well that she wasn't built for making friends and influencing people. "But I have to go."

In a movement too fast for her to react to, the stranger swept close enough to reach out, his palm up and fingers splayed only inches from her chest. She backed away, but the car brought her up short, and she tried not to panic. Again.

But he didn't touch her. He simply stared hard at her, jaw working, eyes burning with that same campfire glow from in the store. It... it wasn't the store fluorescents.

It was *him*.

Then, he looked down at his hand, dragging her gaze down with his. The paler skin of his open palm... rippled. Changed. Became... leathery? Hair sprouted, wiry and short and black, the leathery parts separating out into... pads?

Not... surely not... a paw?

The world fell away, all the noise in her head silenced with the depth of her shock. A man had showed up out of nowhere, stalked her through a store, blocked her from escaping in her car, and now... turned his hand... into a....

No. It was a trick. Some kind of... David Blaine... Chris Angel... *Britain's Got Talent* fuckery.

"You did that." His warm honey voice flowed around the numb silence in her mind, not quite penetrating but prowling around the edges of what remained of her rational thoughts. "You *allowed* that. You are a Sister of the Moon, and I am your guardian, my lady, your loyal black dog and fiercest protector, if you will have me."

After that, the white-out took her completely.

2

Wen had been a fiend for the supernatural almost from the start. Mama hadn't known any fairy tales or Mother Goose or other common bedtime stories, so she'd told little Wendolyn about Big Foot instead. The Creature from the Black Lagoon. King Kong. Godzilla and Mothra. The Loch Ness Monster.

Fascinated, baby Wen had begged for another story and another and another, learning more about mythological creatures in grade school than most kids learned about state names and which president was which. As it became clear that her anxiety kept her from developing socially, she identified with the so-called monsters more and more. Outcasts. Hunted and feared. *Not normal.*

But she had never, ever actually experienced anything supernatural. Never glimpsed a Bigfoot or a ghost. Never found herself standing in a fairy ring. Never felt the wind blow just right until she felt like she could fly right up with it.

Not once.

On rare occasions where she couldn't get out of a dinner party for Tucker's friends or family or business contacts, she would wait in a corner, grimace-smiling, until someone almost inevitably brought up that time they lived in a haunted house. Or that time their cousins got drunk out in the woods and saw a UFO. Or if anyone had heard about any Loch Ness sightings lately, hey, is Nessie okay?

She could join those conversations, could listen with interest instead of agonized attention so she wouldn't miss a question directed at her or answer incorrectly or just plain freeze up. But for all her yearning for a touch of magic, for a glimpse through the Veil, Wendolyn Eudora Cheney had never so much as walked through a cold spot that wasn't obviously from an air conditioning vent.

Until now.

No. Impossible. She'd been overwrought. Flustered and freaking out from the fiasco in the store, worried and nervous about the stranger leaning up against her car, waiting for her. It had made her... hallucinate. See something impossible. Something she'd always wanted to see but no longer really believed in.

If she'd really seen what she thought she had, the stranger would have never simply let her drive away. Though she had very little memory of how that had come about, now that she tried to think back. It was lost in the white-out.

All she knew was that she had pulled into her crappy little studio apartment's parking lot alone and unharmed, stunned but safe enough. But with the indelible sight of that changing hand, the skin thickening, hair sprouting—

No.

Impossible.

Shaking herself, she looked around the lot and wondered, dazed, how long she'd been sitting in her car, dissociating and probably looking in need of the nearest ninety-six-hour hold facility. Five minutes? Ten? Half an hour? Surely not longer than that.

But she was cold, the damp November chill creeping through Roger's various cracks and creases, so she needed to get herself together and go inside. Pour herself a big, ice-choked glass of Coke. Or a good, stiff drink. She still had that flask of bourbon left over from the time she tried to make bourbon chicken and set off all the smoke alarms in her studio apartment when she went flambé.

Yeah. A good, stiff drink. She'd had one hell of an experience and nothing at all to show for it but shaking hands and eyes that were a little too starey when she met them in the rear-view mirror. She looked... shaken. Shifted off her foundation. Fundamentally *wrong* somehow.

Because she looked the same as always, except for the pallor, and she shouldn't. Something should be different. After that experience, she should have changed.

She felt the image of that... transformation, for lack of a less crazy word, try to surface again and shoved up out of Roger's low-slung seat. Keys clutched in her icy fingers as if she would never put them down again, she tried to run across the parking lot, but her legs simply wouldn't move that fast. Instead, she slogged through the cold and damp, unsure if the fog she moved through was real or only in her mind.

Leathery skin. Black fur. Claws.

You did that.

But she didn't. She hadn't done *anything*. She'd just tried to get some groceries, and failed even at that. What could she possibly have done to make something like that happen?

If it had.

Which it hadn't.

A choked laugh coughed up out of her throat, and she tripped over the first step up to her second-story apartment, almost faceplanting on a ridged metal riser a few steps up. What the hell was she even doing?

Another rush of white-out swept over her, and then she sat

curled up in her ratty old recliner, a cold can of Coke in one hand and her other arm wrapped tightly around her torso, her knees drawn up as tight as her belly fat, chubby thighs, and thick calves would allow. She had to get her shit together. She couldn't afford to lose time like that. Yes, she'd gotten flustered and nearly had a panic attack, then had a truly bizarre encounter with a total stranger moments later, but that was over now. She was home. She was safe.

The doorbell rang.

She stared at the door as if she'd never seen one before. Why would the doorbell ring? Had she somehow managed to order some takeout while stumbling around in a daze? She didn't remember doing so. But who else would be at her door?

Not like she had any friends to drop by unexpectedly.

The bell rang again.

And she knew. Somehow, she knew exactly who would be on the other side of the door when she looked out the peephole. Blazing campfire eyes. Silky black coiled dreads. The heavenly, slightly oily smell of his leather coat. And she was right.

But she was also wrong.

This time, Tall, Dark, and Handsome wasn't alone.

Wen didn't open the door. Of course she didn't open the door. Two strange men stood on her tiny stoop. Both were objectively large men—broad at the shoulders—and took up most of the space. She'd be a fool to open her door, a single woman alone.

But her hand crept toward the doorknob anyway. She didn't unlock yet. Didn't turn the knob. Just touched it.

"I know you're there."

Tall, Dark, and Handsome. That honey-rich voice and glorious accent was unmistakable.

"I swear to you, my lady, we would never harm you. Quite the contrary, in fact."

Sure, they wouldn't. She totally believed that.

Although he *hadn't* hurt her at the store. Even in the parking lot, he hadn't so much as laid a hand on her.

And here was the thing that kept her hand on the doorknob when sanity said she should be calling the cops—well, security, not the police; she did not want a fatal shooting of a probably-innocent man on her conscience—and hiding in the bathroom, behind the only other door in her tiny studio apartment: what if... *what if* it was real? What he'd done?

What if his hand really *had* transformed into a paw right before her dazed, freaked-out eyes?

"Oi, lass, I know my mate made a hash of it, but if you could at least open the door so we can blether face to face—?"

Scottish accent. She'd been in love with Scotland since Mama told her about the Loch Ness Monster all those decades ago.

Biting her lip, she leaned close to the peephole again, getting a better look at the man standing beside Tall, Dark, and Handsome. Ginger hair—wouldn't Tucker have loud and stupid opinions about that—pale skin and freckles, hazel green eyes, a nose that had clearly been broken at some point, broad shoulders under a bulky fleece jacket.

"I know you're there, lass. I can feel it."

What could that possibly mean?

"No. I won't be shiftin even a bit to show you. Dex can do that shite all he wants. Just know that I know I could shift right now if I wanted to."

Shift. Shapeshifter, he meant. Lycanthropes. Werepeople. Why hadn't she thought of that before? Of course that's what they were claiming to be. Hell, TDH had even shown her.

If it had been real.

What if—

Numb fingers flipped the lock, turned the doorknob, pulled the door half-way open.

"There you are, then. Dex is tops for plannin and gettin shite done, but he's bollocks about puttin people to ease." The Scot put out a hand. A perfectly normal hand. "Callum McLaughlin, at yer service. And you?"

She looked from one to the other, wondering if she was really doing this. "Wen. Uh, Wendolyn, I mean. Cheney." Flustered and, as always, wondering why she couldn't just be normal for once, she shook her head and sighed. "Sorry. Wendolyn Eudora Cheney."

Reluctantly, she put out her hand and took the one offered. Then, she turned her attention to Tall, Dark, and Handsome. Dex. Put out her hand.

To her surprise, he actually smiled the tiniest bit as he returned the gesture. "Charmed. I suspect we have much to talk about."

"I guess so." Unable to believe she was doing so, she stepped back enough to open the door fully. "Don't make me regret this."

Dex dipped his head in a half-nod as he stepped inside. "Never, my lady. We are your guardians. We could never harm you, as I tried to explain earlier."

"Badly," Callum said, smirking as he strode inside behind his... friend? Colleague? Fellow bounty hunter? "But we'll get it all sorted, never fear. Let Dex make us all a pot o' tea, and we'll have a nice, friendly blether, aye?"

She paused just before closing the door, her awkwardness coming back in a wave. "I don't have a teapot." Her shoulders slumped. "Or tea. Or... like... cups." Less than a moment into hosting, and she'd already failed. "I could— Coke? Water? I don't even have, like, instant coffee."

The men exchanged a glance, and Callum rolled his eyes. "That's alright with me, lass, but Dex might have a stroke if he doesn't get his daily quoter o' the brown stuff. I've no doubt he'll nip out for a shoppin run at first opportunity. For now, I could murder a Coke, if you've a spare."

Not sure if he was joking or not, she hesitated, then remembered she hadn't even shut the door yet and did at least that. As if the decisive movement freed her, she moved with more purpose toward the fridge and pulled out three cans of Coke, then gestured at her... living room. Area. The few square feet she'd allocated as a living room.

Which only had the one recliner and her tiny office task chair. Jesus. She really didn't have any friends.

"Uh... I guess have a seat? I'll just stand."

Callum relieved her of two cans, handing one off to Dex who looked as if he didn't know what to do with it. "Nay, lass. Either of us would go right through that wee rolly chair, and the other is clearly yours. You sit right down before you topple over. We're here to protect you." He smirked. "Even from yourself."

She wanted to grumble, but she still felt shaky and unreal. Not like all of this was a dream, but like someone had told her gravity was a liquid and rainbows were made of multicolored fireflies that didn't blink and Earth itself was a gas giant and she should sink all the way through to the other side. Like everything she'd ever known was now suspect.

So she sat down. And remembered she'd already been drinking a Coke. Dammit.

Dex and Callum exchanged another speaking look, and then Callum apparently decided to take over.

"When did you start goin white up top, then?"

It was such an unexpected question that she reached up to touch her hair as if it had somehow betrayed her. "I'm sorry?"

He smiled and popped open his can of Coke. "Sisters o' the Moon always lose their hair color young. Most are fully gray or even white by their mid-thirties. And you've got a nice bit o' silver glowin through, there."

She blinked, stroking her hair lightly. "Uh... sixteen, I guess? I think that's when I first noticed a few white hairs. But I started coloring when I got—"

Her throat locked up. *Got married,* she didn't want to say. Because she'd inevitably have to say she'd also gotten divorced. Callum eyed her more sharply than was probably necessary, but didn't press her.

Clearing her throat, she tried to hurry past the hang-up. "Anyway, what does that have to do with anything? Are all white-haired thirty-somethings these Sister people?"

"No' at all." He seemed unwilling to rise to her awkward sarcasm. "No' all white-haired thirty-somethings are Sisters, but all Sisters are white-haired, and well before their time."

She frowned and looked at Dex. "Is that why you... ya know. Saw me?"

"No." He didn't sound angry or anything. Just matter of fact. "I felt a pull. A change inside. I realized I was seeing with my dog's vision instead of my own, as if I'd partially transformed right there in the store, even though the full moon isn't for another week or so."

Her face squinched up. "I guess don't get it. What does that have to do with my hair?"

Callum huffed. "They're signs, lass." Dex elbowed him, and he sighed. "Milady. Satisfied?"

"Be respectful."

"Mate, it's *me.*"

She watched the two bicker back and forth and suddenly realized they were more than just work colleagues, or whatever Dex had called them. They were friends, probably long-time friends.

Something deep inside her twisted painfully. She'd never had a friend like that. She couldn't imagine being able to snark at someone and them just... being okay with it.

"Anyway." Dex's pointed tone regained her attention. "I reckon you've realized we're shapeshifters, yes?"

She nodded reluctantly. If what they were saying was at all true, they were indeed shapeshifters. As crazy as it sounded.

"As most of the stories suggest, shapeshifters can only shift under a full moon. And most can't avoid shifting during the moon without massive precautions, like a windowless, underground bunker sort of thing."

He eyed her as if he required some sort of response, but all she could do was shrug.

"But once in a while—a *great* while; fewer than once per generation, even—certain shapeshifters find their Sister of the Moon. And when they do—" He paused, then stepped closer to where she sat and stooped down to one knee. His eyes glowed rich amber, and it definitely wasn't the lighting in her dingy little apartment causing that glow. "When they find their Sister, they can shift at will. Any time, any place, day or night, full moon or new. And they can do that because their destiny is to protect that Sister from shifters that refuse their duty and seek only to use her power for their own gain."

She blinked. It didn't quite absorb fully. "So... a Sister of the Moon can make shifters shift?"

"Nay, lass." Callum, too, stepped closer to kneel before her, ignoring Dex's immediate elbow at the less respectful address. "A Sister *allows* us to shift. Her power. Her magic."

"Magic."

She couldn't keep the skepticism out of her voice. She was the least magical person she had ever met.

But Callum only looked amused. "Aye, magic. How on Gaia's good and green earth did you think shapeshifting worked?"

She opened her mouth, closed it, opened it again, then admitted she had no rejoinder to that. Wasn't Gaia some mother goddess from millions of years ago? Like the Paleolithic era or something? Or was she thinking of some other goddess?

She wasn't an expert in religious mythology. Just cryptids.

"You all right then, lass? Milady?"

She blinked. "Magic."

He nodded, serious but with a twinkle in those merry hazel eyes. "Magic."

She looked at Dex. Surely, he wouldn't mess with her like this. He'd seemed the more serious one of the pair, even though he'd basically stalked her.

Wait.

"How did you find me here?" Her eyes narrowed in suspicion. "You didn't follow me home."

At least, she didn't think he had. She'd been in the fog, in a white-out, but surely even on autopilot, she'd been aware enough to see if a vehicle was tailing her. She was usually hyper-aware while driving, terrified of being in an accident.

Not because she feared being hurt, of course, but because... how would she react? Would she freak out and be useless and just make things worse for actual victims? Would she fall to pieces and embarrass herself? Would she wet her pants? She'd heard that some people wet their pants or, God forbid, pooped themselves, if the accident was bad enough.

She'd die. She'd just die. Of mortification. She'd beg the EMTs to just let her pass.

But none of that mattered, because Dex had tilted his head to one side, watching her think, and now he smirked.

It was devastating. Tall, dark, and so fucking handsome.

Not for you, idiot. He thinks you're some sort of magic charm.

"Really?"

Really what? Oh, right. "Yes. How the hell did you find me here?"

He exchanged an amused look with Callum, then smirked again. "Bounty hunter."

She looked to Callum, who shrugged and grinned cheerfully. "Bounty hunter."

Oops. She'd forgotten that part amidst the sea of other information they'd thrown at her since walking through her door.

Callum's grin twisted into a smirk. "Might be a help that we shifters have keener senses than regular folk." When she continued to look blank, he rolled his eyes. "He sniffed you out, lass. Tracked you. He's a dog, y'know."

Despite the ridiculousness inherent in such a statement, she couldn't help looking offended. They'd both been smart asses. She could only deal with one smart ass at a time, and they'd double-timed her. And also insinuated that she reeked.

The bastards.

But some of her awe of them, her disbelief about the situation—which was still ridiculous however they tried to explain it—flowed out of her when she realized that they weren't super-awesome phenomenal beings of power.

They were just jerks.

She cracked open her can of Coke and took a few sips until their smirks faded. For the first time, they actually looked concerned.

Why?

Her eyes narrowed. "So... say I believe any of this. That the hand and eyes aren't a trick, that you two think you're supposed to be a guardian for some all-powerful moon lady, and that I, of all people, am said moon lady."

"Oi, bit harsh, lass—"

"Say I did believe you."

Callum hushed. Dex looked serious and intent. She had their full attention.

No. Don't wobble and hide now. Now is not the time to be a social disaster.

She looked at one, then the other. "What then?"

Dex's head tilted—like a dog's, she couldn't help but think. Callum looked as if he'd never considered such a question. But she meant it.

What did any of this mean? What was she supposed to do? What were *they* supposed to do?

What happened next?

The pair looked at each other. Hesitantly, Callum posited an answer. "We... guard you?"

She huffed. "Okay, but what does that mean?"

This time, Dex hesitantly stepped into the ring. "It means one of us is with you at all times. Preferably both, but at least one. We cannot leave you vulnerable and alone unless you are on Sister business that we cannot interfere with."

He sounded much surer of himself by the end of his explanation, but she wanted to groan with frustration. They still weren't getting it.

"But what does *that* mean? Is one of you gonna stand here watching me work, just looking over my shoulder? I mean, I deal with private information. It'd be a HIPAA violation, at best."

"Yes," Dex stated, even as Callum said, "Quit, then."

Huffing again, she put aside her Coke so she could gesture along with her frustrations. "I can't quit. What would I live on if I quit my job? It's not like I'm Jeff Bezos and could live a hundred lifetimes without ever working again."

They shared another look, less confident than before. Then, Callum shrugged.

"We'll take care o' you. It's literally our destiny. Our pleasure," he hurried to add, hazel eyes wide and appealing.

"Take care of me how?" She touched her forehead, a headache starting up in her temples. Now was not the time for one of her migraines. "You're bounty hunters, right? What do I do when you're off on a job? Where do you even live? Dex said you had to come to America for a job, so—?"

Yet another shared look, both of them less and less sure of themselves by the moment.

"One of us can stay whilst the other works a job...?"

"Stay where? Look around, boys. You're definitely not living with me. You're already taking up my whole living room just sitting there."

Kneeling, actually, but... semantics.

And now slumping. Dex looked actively worried, while Callum looked decidedly stormy. Leave it to shapeshifters to have a destiny to fulfill without a plan for implementing it. Or thinking about whether or not she'd even want their help.

Not that she knew any shapeshifters to gauge from. Not that any of it mattered anyway.

She'd been fine up until now. Why would she suddenly need protecting? Hadn't she been this Sister of the Moon nonsense the whole time? Forty years, and no one had threatened her life besides her own ex-husband, and only that because she was so desperate to escape him that she might have done literally anything to do so.

But she didn't like to think about that time in her life. Especially not right now. Definitely not the time.

"Guys—" She sighed. "Maybe we should just call this whole thing off. Forget it ever happened and all go our separate ways. I don't see it working any other way."

To her shock, both of them scrambled closer on their knees, crowding up against her and into her bubble too fast for her to climb up and over the back of her chair for escape.

"No no no—"

"Milady, please, donnae-—"

"—no not that anything but that—"

"—send us away noo that we've found ye!"

"—don't send us away!"

She huddled back as far in her old recliner as she could, and it creaked alarmingly. It wasn't sturdy enough for all three of them, and they'd practically climbed into her lap. She was not okay with that. All her anxieties and doubts flared up until the white-out threatened again.

Do not have a panic attack. Do not have a panic attack!

She couldn't bear them fumbling around trying to help her through it and likely making it worse. She just couldn't.

"Sorry, sorry—"

Callum pulled back first, thankfully seeing her distress. Dex scooted back, but didn't release her fingers, which he stroked gently with his big, warm hands. One of which had turned into a dog's paw earlier.

It felt... nice, actually. Warm. Gentle. Tucker had never touched her like that, even in the beginning.

It steadied her until she was able to look at them and actually see them again.

"We're sorry, my lady." His voice was warm honey again, thick and sweet. "But please don't send us away. It's our destiny to keep you safe from all harm. We will never willingly leave your side unless—"

Her breathing returned to almost normal, and she let her fingers remain captured, gently stroked, waiting to hear the "unless" part.

He swallowed hard, his brown eyes not glowing amber but still warm and inviting for all that. "Unless you *send* us away."

Ah. So that was what had upset them. She could send them away, and apparently, they would have to go. But why would that matter? Why would it bother them? She was no one special that they would crawl across the floor on their knees to be in her glorious presence.

...Oh.

Of course.

They'd said that her power—her "magic"—allowed them to shift whenever. Without her, they'd be at the mercy of the full moon again, unable to shift when they wanted to or to not shift when the compulsion hit.

It wasn't her. It was her "magic".

Not even magic. Just some hypothetical mumbo jumbo that was probably far more scientific and based on pheromones or whatever than *magic*.

She was no magical being. She wasn't a Sister of the Moon. And they wouldn't want her if she wasn't.

Ergo, they didn't want *her*.

They were just as selfish as Tucker. He'd wanted a housewife —a house maid, really, with "benefits". He'd wanted someone subordinate to him, someone who did what he wanted and waited on his needs, but had none of her own. And if she *did* have her own needs, they were an irritant rather than a priority.

These two, for all their U.K. accents and lovely good looks and brawn, were just like *him*. They wanted her for what she could do for them.

Fuck that. She hadn't torn herself out of Tucker the Fucker's clutches to tie herself to two more fuckers.

So, despite the gentle, warm grip on her fingers, she pulled herself free. It wasn't as hard as when she'd dragged herself away from her ex-husband. She just had to take her hand back.

Their expressions went from worry to downright fear, but they both scooched back, sitting on their heels, when she moved to stand.

She didn't know if they'd leave when she asked, and she didn't know how to kick them out. A traitorous part of her didn't want to. They didn't want her, not really, but... wouldn't it be nice to have some friends?

But they wouldn't be friends, would they? Not really. Guardians, they said. And only that if she was this moon princess they thought she was.

She wasn't anything like that. She was awkward and weird and, dammit, that's who she was. It was high time to own it.

"Gentlemen."

Callum started to speak, but Dex put a hand on the arm of his coat. She closed her eyes and made herself say it, no matter how dumb it sounded.

"I regret to inform you that I must decline your generous, if weird, offer. I'm not currently in the market for shapeshifting bodyguards, nor do I have the funds to adequately pay you for such services. Nor am I looking for roommates, as (you see for yourself) I have no room. Thus, while I appreciate the offer, I must decline. Thank you."

She blew out a heavy breath, then winced open her eyes. Their expressions—fear, worry, even despair?—toppled her confidence, but she clenched her teeth together and refused to say anything else. She'd said what she knew was right for her. For them.

Dex looked devastated. "My lady, please. I beg you. Don't send us away. A new Sister hasn't come to Light since the eighties."

She wanted to ask about the odd emphasis he'd put on "come to *Light*", but he marched on before she could get her thoughts together.

"Now that we've found you, *sensed* you, others will, too. Not all of them will have your safety at heart. They will want to use you. You would be a slave, not an honored, treasured—"

But he paused, unable to think of an appropriate word, so she filled it in for him.

"Resource? Tool? Would you not be benefitting from my so-called power, too? How is that any different?"

Callum leaned forward. "Lass, milady, they wouldnae be guardin you. They'd be *usin* you. Your safety is *why* your magic allows us to change at will, but no' all shapeshifters still follow the old ways. It's been so long since the last Sister that plenty of us have forgotten."

She blinked. "Did you just 'not all shapeshifters' me?"

He blinked, too, then shrugged. "Might have done."

A snicker snuck out of her throat. He grinned, a devilish set of dimples making him both adorable and devastatingly attractive. Did Dex have dimples? Would he ever smile wide enough for her to see them?

Pointless thoughts, but she couldn't help smiling ruefully. Laughter was her secret Achilles' heel. It usually meant she'd actually relaxed enough in someone's presence to not be in a constant state of low panic.

A rare feat, indeed.

Seeing her walls buckle the slightest bit, Dex tried again. "My lady." His voice soft, his eyes warm, he implored her with every part of himself. Broad shoulders and tight thighs and all. "Please don't send us away. Allow us to protect you, and I swear —*we* swear—you will never know another moment's fear."

She snorted, but softly. "Don't make promises you can't keep, man. I have anxiety."

"Then we'll guard you from that, too." A hint of a smile flirted with the corners of his mouth. "All part of the package."

Oh, no. He had a sense of humor, too. The bastard.

What on earth was she going to do with them?

Apparently, she was doomed to find out.

3

They wouldn't leave. Even after Wen said she'd give the whole shapeshifter bodyguard thing a try, they insisted their guard duties started now. This afternoon. Immediately.

With her hand again pressed to her temple, Wen tried to explain to them that she could not go from zero to sixty on the "crowded house" scale in a single afternoon. Did she want friends? Yes. Did she want two large, handsome men clogging up what little space she had? Not so much.

What would they do tonight? Where would they sleep? Not only would they not all fit in her double bed, but she hadn't slept with anyone since—

Well.

"Simple enough, milady." Callum, perhaps unsurprisingly, felt no awkwardness at all. "Dex'll stay here whilst I nip out for our gear. I'll even stop for food on the way back if you're peckish." He grinned. "He reckoned you didn't get what you wanted at the store."

She gasped and glared at Dex, betrayed. If she wore pearls, she would have clutched them.

"I said no such thing." He glared at Callum. "I merely said you may be hungry, as you didn't end up buying anything because I'd upset you too badly."

Her eyes narrowed, but she chose to believe him just this once. "Uh-huh. Well, either way, you guys can't just stay here. I mean, where would you sleep? I only have the one bed—" She held up a single, commanding finger before either of them could do more than open their mouths. "—and I've been the only one in it for three years, and that's not changing tonight."

The men exchanged a look. Callum shrugged.

"I'll kip out on the floor, and Dex can have the chair. We'll be right as rain."

She huffed. "You can't sleep on the floor. Good grief."

Uh-oh. There were the dimples again. "Then I'm in the bed wi' you. One of us needs to be the last defense, and that means one of us needs to be right in close."

Her jaw clenched. She could not sleep with either of them. They were... *glorious*. She was not. At all. She was forty. Overweight. Gray-haired, though that seemed, at the moment, to be a positive for once.

She couldn't sleep with them. Either of them. She'd toss and turn all night and be absolutely useless.

"Fine. I'll dig out some old blankets for the floor."

"See?" Damn those dimples. "Sorted."

It wasn't sorted. Not at all. But somehow, with every exchange, she let them further and further into her bubble. Was this progress, or were they walking all over her?

Tucker had opinions about the sturdiness of her spine. Her own doubts had opinions on the subject. For once, she declined to hear those opinions.

"Okay, fine." If she was supposed to be so precious, she wasn't about to do all the work. "You said you'd go get your gear?"

Callum gave a little two-fingers-to-the-temple salute and headed for the door, brushing past Dex on the way because they both had such broad shoulders and there just wasn't any room. This wasn't going to work. But she supposed they'd have to see that for themselves, and they'd all figure something out when it became too obvious to ignore.

She could perhaps dip into her savings, but she really hated to do that. She had secret plans for it. Hopes. Dreams.

As soon as the door shut behind Callum and startled her out of her reverie, awkward shyness tried to worm its way back in, but she shoved it aside. Dex had literally begged to not be sent away. Whether that had anything to do with her or not, she shouldn't allow herself to feel shy around him. He *wanted* to be here.

"Can you help me get some bedding out for you guys?"

He smiled—actually smiled, not just a hint of one—and she melted, though she tried not to show it.

"Of course, my lady. It will be my pleasure."

Great. Now she was blushing and tongue-tied. "Uh, not—you don't have to—" She gestured, unable to find the words. "Just 'okay' is okay?"

He stepped closer, and she abruptly turned to the back of the little apartment, where her bed was tucked up in the corner across from the smallest closet known to man. When she'd first moved in, she'd stuffed two crazy quilts up in the top shelf like a shrine. Her mother had made them while sitting through chemotherapy, and Wen never, ever used them for fear of damaging them or spilling something on them. But they were the only other blankets she had besides what was already on the bed, so she pointed to them so Dex could reach them down.

"That one on the bed, if you don't mind. We'll get you set up in the living room first and save the floor for bedtime. I hate for all of us to stumble over the pile every time we need to go to the bathroom."

How embarrassing. They'd be using her bathroom. Would

either of them even fit? She'd bet real money that they'd have to turn those broad shoulders sideways to edge through the door.

What would they do about showers? Her tub wasn't big enough for a bath. She barely fit in there at 5'6", so there was no way the over six-footers who had taken over her life would be able to even sit down in it without kissing their own knees.

Sadly, they all three probably weighed the same. If either of them weighed under two hundred pounds with all that muscle, she'd eat her own hair.

Not the time to think about that. They're not here for anything like that.

The reminder actually cheered her this time, and she edged around him to lead the way to the lone sturdy chair. Dex carried the other quilt, though she could easily have managed it herself, but instead of putting it on the seat of the recliner, he laid it delicately down on the floor beside it. When she raised her eyebrows, he shrugged.

"Thought you might want to have a sitdown. You've had to absorb a lot today. I know none of this will be easy for you."

"It's... weird. That's for sure."

She did sit down, then shifted awkwardly as Dex moved to sit on the floor at her feet. It seemed like a lesser position. He definitely was no one's lesser. Especially not hers.

"It'll take getting used to for all of us, my lady, but we'll sort it out. There will undoubtedly be others like us who wish to serve, as well as those who would only use you, so I imagine we'll all be doing a bit of stretching for the next little while."

Others. More shapeshifters. More guardians. Where the hell would she put them?

His warm, heavy hand on her knee startled her out of her thoughts.

"Please don't worry, my lady. We promised you no more fret. Allow us to make good on that promise."

His hand felt very nice, indeed, but also very intimate. She was not ready for intimacy, nor did she think he wanted anything like that from her. But she'd barely even shaken hands since Tucker and hadn't been the most physically affectionate person before that.

Would they all be touchy feely? Could she get used to it when she'd been so alone for so long?

As if he could see every one of her worries written across her face, he sighed. "I do wish I could make you a spot of tea. Nothing better for calming the soul than that." He sat up straighter and took his hand back to pull out a shiny, new cell phone. "I've had an idea."

He tapped out a message, then put the phone away before she could figure out what kind it was. It was definitely new, though. If not the newest model, then the closest to it. Did they have money, then? Were bounty hunters well-off? Maybe she was worrying over nothing. Maybe they really would be like roommates, sharing rent and chores and such in a bigger place without stepping too much on each others' toes.

"Tell me about yourself, my lady?"

No question had ever inspired more dread than that one. She hated talking about herself. She was the most boring person she'd ever known. Her problems weren't unique. Her sorrows weren't more tragic than anyone else's. She didn't have a sparkling personality to make up for a ho-hum backstory.

She *hated* talking about herself.

Unable to even fake a smile, she shook her head. "You first? And please, call me Wen. Just... not Wendy."

That one brought back too much of Tucker. He was the only one who'd ever called her that, even when she asked him not to.

He seemed to understand at least that, but he still shook his head. "My story isn't important, my lady. Wen." He quirked his small smile. "As I said before, I come from a small village, I shift into a black dog, Callum and I were bounty hunters, and now we are yours."

She frowned. "There's so much more to you than that. What job brought you to Missouri? How did you become a bounty hunter?" The frown lightened. "How old even are you?"

"Ah." The smile deepened. "Would you believe me if I say I'm almost a thousand years old?"

Her eyes widened so far the sockets hurt. "You're *what?*"

He snickered. *Snickered.*

Such. A. Jerk.

"Shifters do age slower than humans, but not by that much." His eyes twinkled instead of glowing amber. "We are, none of us, immortals. I am, however, a hundred and two years old next March."

She tilted her head, eyes narrowing almost as much as they'd widened a moment before. "Seriously?"

"Yes, seriously." He adjusted his expression until he looked more sincere. "I swear I will always tell you the strict truth when you ask for it. I fear I've spent too long around Callum and his Scots sense of humor, but he, too, will never tease if you ask him not to."

Some of her suspicion faded. "How long have you two been... partners?"

It suddenly occurred to her that perhaps they were a couple. That would actually suit her quite well, as she'd never have to worry about developing feelings for them. She could perhaps come to love them as friends, instead. *Just* friends. Which would be perfect.

"We consider ourselves brothers in arms, my la— Wen. We've been through the wars together." He shrugged. "Literally. We both fought in World War II. I signed up at sixteen, Callum at fifteen. Then Korea, then the Suez Crisis. We decided humans weren't worth fighting for anymore, so when England wisely refused to join that Vietnam ruckus after that spanking in Egypt, we allowed ourselves to be retired." He reached out and touched her knee again. "Present human company excluded, of course."

All she could do was blink. A hundred and two years old. World War II. War hero. What the hell.

"My lady?"

She blinked again. "Just... processing."

He eyed her with concern, hand still warm on her knee. "Perhaps you've taken in enough for one evening. Callum should be back soon, and we can speak of the future instead of the past, if that pleases you."

A hundred and two. He looked, at most, in his thirties. *Young* thirties. But he was older than anyone she'd ever known personally. Even her oldest relatives hadn't lived that long. Died in their eighties, mostly. She couldn't even imagine such a passage of time.

And here she'd been thinking she was old to him. Hell, she was more than half his age. A veritable whippersnapper.

Two sharp knocks startled her out of her astonishment, but Dex was already on his feet before she could even begin to get up herself. Callum, of course. The Scot bustled in with duffel bags criss-crossed over his shoulders, plastic grocery bags lined up one arm, and a stack of pizza boxes oozing cheesy-tomato goodness smells held high with the other.

"Dinner is served, lads!" He winked at her as Dex relieved him of the pizza boxes. "And lasses, of course. Here, Dex, take your—" He stopped cold and eyed her, then glared at his friend. "Decimus Braxton Talmadge. What did you say to her?"

Decimus? How did that shorten to Dex? And yet, it somehow fit.

Dex of course, only put the pizza boxes down on her miniscule "kitchen" counter and headed back over for some of the plastic bags, rooting around for what he wanted. "We've only been getting acquainted. She's a bit bothered by my age, is all."

Obviously relieved, Callum started shrugging out of bags and baggage and coat. "Called him Granddad yet?"

She startled into a laugh. "Is he older than you, too?"

Hadn't Dex said there was just a year between them? Or was she confused because of all the new things thrown at her today?

"He's a Scorpio," Dex said over the rustling of plastic bags. "That ought to tell you everything you need to know."

It didn't. She knew almost nothing about the zodiac. Did she have to know that to be a moon princess? Moon sister? Whatever they called it?

Wait.

Wait just a damn minute.

"Guys?"

They both paused and eyed her with readiness, as if they'd do anything she asked of them right then. She didn't necessarily like that feeling, but she didn't have the mental capacity to wrestle with that at the moment. She'd just had a thought that needed confirmation or rejection.

"Am... am I a witch?"

Callum eyed her carefully, sifting through the bags as Dex turned to fiddle with whatever he'd taken out for himself.

"Would you have a problem with that, milady?" He shrugged, though he still eyed her almost warily. "You *have* become a creature of magic, then. Sister Moon has chosen to Shine through you. You have come to Light. You'll age as slowly as we shifters do. If that makes you a witch—?"

So many layers to that particular cake. She wasn't always a Moon sister or whatever? She wasn't born to be one or destined, but chosen? Who made that decision?

Although she supposed he'd answered that one already. Sister Moon had chosen her.

Sister of the Moon. Sister Moon. That was... nice, actually. She'd never had a sister before.

"I think—"

She paused, mulling the idea over. She couldn't say she'd never thought about magic before, because she was a loyal cryptozoologist who loved the mythology as much as the search. But she guessed she'd always assumed there was some scientific explanation for all of her beloved monsters and ghouls and ghosts. Not that they didn't exist, but that they were... mutations, perhaps. Different arms of evolution. Health conditions like porphyria, the "vampire disease", or hypertrichosis, the "werewolf syndrome".

Even aliens that called Earth home. Like octopuses. She was convinced they were from another planet and were just as intelligent as human life, if not more so.

But not *magic*.

But if they—Dex and Callum, not octopuses—were shapeshifters, and if shapeshifters really were creatures of magic and so was she—?

"I think... that's okay?" She looked at them, almost asking if that was alright. "I mean, they don't burn witches at the stake anymore, right?"

They looked at each other again, and she huffed a nervous laugh. They didn't return it.

"Guys?"

Dex forced a big smile. It looked about as natural as an elbow in the middle of his forehead.

"It has been some years since the last one, my lady." He squeezed behind Callum in her miniature kitchen. "Why don't you sit back down, and I'll bring you a nice cup of tea?"

She narrowed her eyes. "Is that what you got?" she asked Callum. "You seriously went out and bought... I don't even know. A teapot? Tea? Cups?"

But the Scot was unashamed and beamed at her, dimples on full display. "I found you a nice enough tea service, yes, but it wasnae my idea. Dex texted that you were in need of a cup o' brown joy, so find a good, sturdy set until we could get you one you'd like for yourself."

Out of nowhere, her eyes prickled. Puddled up. Her nose started to run, her lower lip to wobble. She blinked rapidly, but the waterworks escaped anyway, and she spun away so they wouldn't see her crying like an awkward loser who'd never had friends who bought her tea sets just because she was upset and needed some comfort.

Of course, they weren't having any of that. They scrambled around each other to get out of her kitchen and trotted across the few steps to where she stood, facing her own damn lonely chair and crying like an idiot. They hesitated only a moment before enfolding her in their big, warm arms, surrounding her in a way that should be overwhelming but somehow felt... safe.

She couldn't remember the last time she'd felt safe.

The thought only made her cry harder. With her face a mess and her nose running and the headache amping up in her temples, she felt like a complete waste of space, but they only held her tightly between them, rocking gently and stroking her hair or her arm, whichever they could easily reach.

They stayed like that for a long time. And in those endless moments, Wen decided she might be wise to keep them around, after all.

Callum hadn't just bought a teapot, cups, and saucers. He'd purchased several different kinds of tea, cookies and "biscuits" that looked like more cookies, honey, jams and jellies, half and half and full cream (the tea set he'd bought came with a cream pitcher, of all things), some kind of Irish butter and two loaves of bread (one dark brown and one sort of yellowy-colored— pumpernickel and brioche, their respective packaging said), and a set of tiny, fancy teaspoons.

She felt like a princess. A moon princess, she supposed. Except she was about to have tea and biscuits with two large, brawny men instead of the little girl squad she'd never had. She would've felt moved to put on a dress if she had one.

The set was bright yellow with little daisies painted on. It should have looked childish, but to her, it just looked happy. Yellow could be such an uplifting color, and what was friendlier than a daisy?

And, though she'd been braced to hate hot tea the way she hated coffee, once Dex had creamed with half and half and sweetened with a touch of honey, she almost swore she'd never touch another Coke again. It was warm and soothing and delightful. What she supposed Dex would call a proper cup of tea.

Of course he would. He made it.

The tea didn't exactly go well with the pizza, but it was perfect for literally everything else they'd spread out buffet-style on her corner desk, so she left the boys to their feasting and reveled in the new glory that was Kerrygold butter. It was divine on both the hefty, dark pumpernickel and the soft, sweet brioche. She was discovering all sorts of new things today.

Grinning at her obvious enjoyment of the treat, Callum tipped his cup her way. "We'll have to take you back home for a clotted cream tea, lass. You'll never eat regular butter again."

Her nose wrinkled without asking for permission. "The word 'clotted' doesn't sound very appealing. Sorry."

He rolled his pretty hazel eyes. "Clotted as in clouted. Whipped with a paddle, like for any butter." He only winked when she blushed, feeling ignorant. "But with a high enough fat content to taste like a melty mouthful o' heaven. I swear it on me ol' mum's grave."

She stopped mid-bite, her blush fading. "Your mom's dead?"

Heartache. Sympathy. So many feelings that she put down her treat, no longer hungry.

"Aye. Nigh on half a century now." He shrugged. "Unfortunately, shapeshifting doesnae always run in families, so she lived a purely human lifetime, and then she was gone."

She closed her eyes, fearing another stormburst. They did prickle, but she thought she might be safe for the moment. If she was careful.

"My mom's been gone almost twenty years. Almost longer than I had her alive."

"I'm sorry, lass. Wen, I mean."

She'd asked them to just call her Wen, but they both had trouble with it in their own ways. She didn't want to be "milady" or even just "lass" to them. She wanted to be friends. Comfortable. All on the same level.

It was a work in progress.

Shaking her head once, she forced a small smile. "Anyway. Does Sistering run in families? I don't know anyone in my ancestry who had any shady, witchy roots."

Dex shook his head, gnawing on a massive bite of double-pepperoni pizza until he managed to swallow it all down. *Rather like a hungry dog,* she thought but would never dare to say.

"Heritage has nothing to do with whom the magic chooses. There are only ever three Sisters at a time, and we've been short one for nigh unto forty years now." He smiled softly. "We were waiting for you."

A very sweet thing to say, but not particularly helpful. But she grinned wryly, anyway.

"It's funny that you two besties somehow found the same Sister to shift you. Allow you to shift. Whatever." She paused, tilting her head. "Although, now that I think of it... is that weird? What are the odds?"

Callum abruptly looked a bit sheepish and put down his cup. "Honestly, lass, I'd no idea you'd call me until we were standing outside your door. Dex brought me to explain the Sisters to you because my cousin, Brigid, is one. He thought she and I could convince you to come to Culloden Moor to meet her and let her explain some o' the lore to you. That you'd be more likely to accept his protection that way."

She huffed. "What the hell kind of coincidence—?" Shaking her head, she picked up a tidbit of bread smeared with Kerrygold and fig jam. She'd never had figs before, either, but they were definitely going on her list of favorites. "So what do you transform into?"

"I'm no' a GoBot, milady."

Dex choked on a bite of double pepperoni.

"We donnae transform. We *shift*."

She raised an eyebrow, her lips twitching with the urge to snicker. She bit the lower one to keep it still.

After a moment's glare, he huffed. "I'm a war horse. Which is why I cannae shift to show you. I wouldnae fit in this wee box."

Dex grunted. "Shire horse, he means."

"War. Horse." Affronted anew, the injured Scot shoved up to refill his plate at the corner buffet without asking if anyone else wanted seconds. Or thirds. "Might as well call me a draft horse and be done with it. Rotten sod."

Eyebrows raised, she looked at Dex and mouthed, *Is there a difference?* Unfortunately, his only answer was a smirk.

Both of them were children.

"So you're a war horse," she said instead, treading carefully to avoid his injured pride. "And Dex is a black dog." She frowned. "What *is* a black dog? I guess I assumed it was just a dog with black fur, but if the 'war' is important, does that mean the 'black' is, too?"

Dex stood up for his own refill. "Ever hear of the Hound of Baskerville?"

"Sherlock Holmes?" She nodded. "But wasn't that just a Great Dane with phosphorescent paint or something?"

He looked back over his shoulder, his eyes glowing amber. "Sir Arthur Conan Doyle believed in fairies, but he didn't believe in omens and portents and creatures of the night. He should have switched the two."

Putting aside her plate with a few neatly-cut squares of bread and a smear of Kerrygold still waiting use, she pulled her feet up to cross her legs in the recliner instead of kicking the footrest out. If she did that, she'd be asleep in five minutes flat. Tea, snacks, conversation—had there ever been such pleasant riches before?

"Does that mean fairies aren't real?" She fake-pouted. "I was looking forward to meeting Queen Mab and joining the Wild Hunt."

Callum, who'd been stuffing his face to soothe his pride, finally rejoined the chat. "If there are, they've likely gone back to Underhill, or wherever they're truly from. No reliable sightins for hundreds of years, lass." He shrugged. "I'm no' sayin they're no' real. Just sayin they're no' here."

"Huh." She shook her head. "Seems a shame. Magic is real, but there aren't any fairies." A yawn threw her out of her reverie. "Ugh. I feel like I ran a marathon today, and I've barely done anything at all."

Dex shoved to his feet, though he'd just sat back down and clearly wasn't done eating, and held out a hand. She took it, confused, then scrambled out of the chair when he tugged gently.

"You've had a lot of shocks today. That takes a toll. Perhaps you should rest." He led her, gently clasping her hand, the few steps to the back of the apartment. The flat, as they called it. "I could run you a nice, hot bath? Would that help relax you?"

Awkwardness came rushing back and flared in her cheeks. "Oh. Ha. Um, not necessary. My tub is really too small for a good soak, anyway. I mostly just take showers. But... thanks?"

Wen, thy name is awkward. As it will ever be.

But Dex frowned. "A Sister of the Moon should have access to all the water she could want. Callum's cousin has a black pool on her grounds, just for swimming in Sister Moon's loving light. She pulls the tides, you know."

"Callum's cousin?"

He chuckled, his frowny face put aside for the moment. "No, Sister Moon. The moon controls the tides, effects Earth's gravity. Her phases echo the changing of seasons and the internal cycles of both humans and animals. Her shadows create liminal spaces where the Veil is thin. Only She can eclipse the necessary but harsh glare of the sun." He gently squeezed her hand. "Her energy is feminine, but She has never feared overtaking the masculine sun when Gaia asks it of Her. Neither does She submit to being eclipsed by the sun, instead turning to blood and tearing aside the Veil completely."

Blinking, she tried to take all of that in. She knew about the tides, of course, but she'd never really thought about anything else. She vaguely remembered hearing about Blood Moons and Wolf Moons and Super Moons, but she had no idea what the terms meant.

Apparently, she had some astrology homework to do. Or was it astronomy? Or both?

"Later, my lady. Wen. For now, a hot shower and bed. Everything else can be put aside for tomorrow."

"Everything what?" But she moved along when he gently shoved at her back, yawning again as she went.

"Tomorrow. I promise."

He shut the door between them, leaving her alone in the bathroom. Alone. It was so strange how quickly that had become an unusual state. Only a day—an afternoon/evening, really—and she had to remind herself what it felt like to be the only person in her space.

Because of two random guys. Two men who thought she was something special, even if only because she helped them somehow.

And there may be more shifters out there somewhere,

waiting to be called, as Dex and Callum referred to it. Or already called and on their way.

She couldn't really imagine such a thing. All she could imagine right now was a shower, bed, and maybe calling in sick to work in the morning because no way could she focus on aged charges and new invoices with all of this on her mind.

So, making sure the bathroom door was locked for the first time since she'd moved in three years before, Wendolyn Eudora Cheney stripped, gave herself a good look in the mirror without fully disapproving of what she saw, then turned on the water as hot as she could stand it.

A shower, she could do. Everything else, as Dex said, was for tomorrow.

4

She had to pee. The older she got, the more often she woke up in the middle of the night needing to pee. Or worse, having the dream where she's trying to find a functional bathroom literally anywhere but all she could find were clogs, broken seats, empty holes in the floor, etc., until she woke up with her bladder screaming at her.

Thankfully, this wasn't one of those nights, but she did feel more of a sense of urgency than usual, so she sighed and tossed off her heavy bedspread to claw her way out of bed.

And put her foot down on something soft and yielding instead of the floor.

Something that jerked up with a pained shout and flailed around in the dark, pulling her covers off the bed and making an even more tangled mess. What the—

The lights went on, and she suddenly realized what had happened. Dex and Callum. Dex in the living room. Callum on the floor next to her bed. Most of a pot of tea making an urgent plea from her bladder.

And from the awful groans from the floor, her foot right on the poor guy's junk.

Mortified, she covered her face with both hands and jerked her feet back up onto the bed. "I'm so sorry! I forgot you were there and I just had to—*I am so sorry!*"

Dex started to laugh. Chuckles, at first, but it built and built until the formerly stoic Brit had to bend over and brace his hands on his knees. Of course he knew what had happened. And of course he found the whole thing hilarious.

"Callum, can I help? Jesus, I'm so sorry, I forgot, I just forgot, do you need an ice pack or—?"

"'M alright," he wheezed, sounding about as far from alright as he could be without a bleeding wound. "Gimme a bit. Go on 'round me, then."

Face practically on fire, she crawled over the foot of the bed instead of rolling out from the side as usual, then fled into the bathroom and shut the door. Would she even be able to pee as wound up as she was now? Dear lord, she'd stepped right on his unprotected package. Luckily, she hadn't put down her whole weight, but... ow.

Would he forgive her? Would he be mad? If she so much as brushed Tucker's penis or testicles, he'd roared like a shot bear and called her every name in the book. She couldn't even imagine what he'd have done if she'd stepped right on him like that.

Callum won't hurt me, she reminded herself desperately. *He won't yell. He's here to protect. He won't hurt me. Won't call me a clumsy jackass moron. Won't shout that I did it on purpose until I believe him and apologize for trying to hurt him. Won't tell everyone about it later like it's a joke, knowing the public shame is more devastating to me than any physical blow he could deal me.*

Callum won't hurt me.

"Wen?"

Oh, shit, it was him. He didn't sound angry, but—

"You alright in there?"

She tried to say she was okay, but her throat refused to make the sound. She wasn't okay. She hadn't even tried to pee yet. Instead, she sat on the edge of the tub, arms gripped around herself, wishing she had the balance to pull her feet up so she could clasp her arms around her knees, too. Roll herself up into a little ball and flush herself down the drain.

The doorknob turned, and she froze, suddenly terrified. She hadn't locked the door. She hadn't needed to lock the door until now, and she'd forgotten. She really was an idiot.

The door opened a crack, and a ginger head poked through. "Wen? Ah, lass."

He opened the door all the way and hurried over to her, dropping to his knees on the cold tile at her feet. He wrapped himself around her, warm where she felt carved from ice.

"You didnae hurt me, milady. Startled me a bit is all, and a wee bit of a jolt. I'm fine now, aye? You didnae do anythin wrong."

Why was he being so kind to her? She'd stepped on his unprotected crotch.

"No more tears, lass. Please donnae cry over me." His big hands cupped her cheeks, his thumbs brushing away tears she didn't even feel. "I shouldnae been so close to your bed when I know you're no used to havin someone right there, aye?"

She swallowed hard, her throat aching, and finally hitched in a shaky breath that came back out on a sob. And the words followed.

"I'm so sorry. I'm *so* sorry. Please don't be mad at me. I'll be more careful, I promise. I'll never do it again."

He stared at her for a long, aching moment, and she waited. Waited for the gaslighting. Waited for the shaming. Waited for the awful names, the reminders of how ignorant and naïve she was.

"Oh, Wen," he sighed instead. "What did he do to you, lass?"

5
———

She woke up groggy, eyes burning, nose chapped, head throbbing like she'd thrown back a six-pack of Tucker's gross, watery beer. She wasn't hungover, though. She didn't even have a migraine. She'd just cried herself to sleep with Callum at her back, hugging her tight, and Dex on the floor, bravely placing his own junk in the danger zone of her clumsy hobbit feet.

She needed some ibuprofen. A cold wash cloth. A warm bath. Her favorite footie pajamas. A bottle of cold water. Instead, she tried to unwind herself from Callum's careful but close grasp and scoot down to the end of the bed so she didn't make The Mistake all over again.

Turned out, she shouldn't have bothered. Dex wasn't on the floor beside her bed, and the quilt he'd used was folded neatly square and put considerately up by her half-dresser so she wouldn't trip over it. She blinked and scrubbed at her gunky, bleary eyes.

Food. She smelled food. Eggs. Cheese. Jesus meek and mild, was that bacon?

Practically drooling, she finally managed to untangle her

pajama bottoms from the sheet she'd somehow wrapped around her calf and stumbled over to where she could see that Dex had managed to make himself right at home in her miniscule kitchen and was cooking up a big country breakfast.

Were those tomatoes? Who ate tomatoes for breakfast? And why were there baked beans?

Swallowing against the sandpaper in her throat, she grunted. "Where did you get breakfast stuff?"

"Morning, sleepyhead. I was about to wake you before your alarm could do the job. Reckon you don't need any rude surprises today."

She blinked, hair a mess, in desperate need of a face wash and a nose blow, pajama pants crooked, part of her pajama shirt tucked in and the rest unbuttoned to an almost scandalous degree. He looked immaculate, his faded black t-shirt molded to his form, dreads pulled back a bit from his face so he could cook, looking like he knew exactly where everything in her kitchen had been stashed.

Was he a magician? Like, he was a shapeshifter, but was he a wizard, too?

He chuckled. "Go on, then. Bathroom first so you can wake up a bit. I'll have a pot of Irish Breakfast ready for you when you're out. Bolder than English, but not as harsh as Scottish."

"Blasphemy," a groggy Callum said from the bed, scruffing a hand through his ginger muss. He yawned spectacularly, then stretched so hard the hollywood frame creaked. "You just have to be tough enough for Scots' blend to no' punch you in the face."

"As I was saying." Dex grinned wryly at her. "Anyway, my lady, feel free to do what you'd normally do in the morning. Though I suspect calling out sick might be in order?"

Yes. That, too. She absolutely could not imagine working today. But right now, she'd give her right arm for a toothbrush and a hairbrush, preferably in that order. Knowing herself as she did, she worried she might use the toothbrush on her hair and try to scrub her gums with the stubby bristles of her old nylon hairbrush.

Shaking her head, she dug the heel of one hand into her eye and turned for the bathroom before Callum got any big ideas of going in ahead of her. Once safely inside with the door locked, she stared at herself in the mirror and tentatively allowed herself to remember what happened the night before. She winced, then bent down to turn on the tap and splash water on her face. It was icy cold, but it woke her instantly and left her gasping.

After a few sips from her cupped palms, she ran wet hands up and into her frizz, wishing she could smooth down some of the curl. They weren't gentle, sexy curls, of course. In fact, Tucker had been known to say her hair felt like pubic hair when he touched it.

Nothing she could do about that now except run a brush through it and hope the water tamed it a bit. She never wore make-up, but she did like to put on some SPF. The sun was a cancer-slinging jerk that tried to kill humanity every day—or at least she thought so, given how being outside without sunglasses gave her a brutal migraine more often than not—and she had no intention of letting the big, shiny jerk get a permanent foothold on her face or neck.

The moon, though... Sister Moon... maybe she should be more acquainted with this new sibling. She hated daylight, anyway. She should become a creature of the night. Run with the pack.

Although her current pack consisted of a black dog and a war horse, neither of which she could keep up with in her wildest dreams.

Huffing, she shook her head, opened the medicine cabinet, and considered her migraine meds. They would likely help with the cried-out headache, but if she developed an actual migraine later—possible with all this emotional upheaval—she wouldn't be able to take another one for twenty-four hours. So, grumbling, she pulled down the big bottle of ibuprofen, shook four into her palm, and downed them with another gulp of water from the tap.

Finally feeling more put to rights, she pulled her hair back into a low ponytail and brushed her teeth, then actually washed her face with a cloth instead of just splashing it. The cold water and scrubbing left her pale skin blotchy and red, but it was the best she could do. She wasn't very good at pampering herself. She'd never learned the knack. Dammit.

Giving up, she straightened her pajama pants, buttoned the shirt all the way up and untucked the entire hem, then unlocked the door to go back into the main area. Callum had joined Dex in her shoebox of a kitchen, and she was again reminded of how large they were. Broad-shouldered, sturdy-waisted, tight thighs. They each looked to be carved from solid muscle.

And handsome, of course. In different ways, but neither less appealing.

Not for you. Not like that, anyway.

She squared her shoulders and strode barefoot across the worn carpet to see if she could make herself useful. Callum intercepted her, though, and led her by the hand—his fingers gentle around hers, so it wasn't as if she couldn't just tug her hand away—over to her recliner to sit her down. With a dimpled grin, he left her for only a moment before bringing over a steaming cup of tea, the bottle of honey, and the cream pitcher.

Full service breakfast, then. She'd never known such a wonder.

She sipped the brew straight, winced, and added cream. Another sip, and she hemmed and hawed before adding just a drizzle of honey. Perfect. Irish Breakfast may be her favorite beverage from now on, so long as the cream and honey supplies lasted. And the little yellow cup with friendly white daisies painted around it felt so cheerful in her hand. Like a miniature sunrise and a surprise bouquet, all in one.

She'd only had a few sips before Dex brought her a plate heaped with a truly ridiculous amount of food. She did well to have a slice of toast in the morning, considering she hated to cook and only grudgingly dragged out of bed in time to brush her hair and teeth before logging in to work.

This was like a five-course dinner, but for breakfast. Fried eggs, bacon that looked almost like ham, two sausage links split down the middle, the weird baked beans, a tomato cut in half and roasted. Mushrooms, for some reason. Some of the lovely brioche bread from the night before with fancy butter and something that looked like orange jelly with bits of peel in it. Cup of tea.

She couldn't possibly eat all this, but Dex looked so pleased with himself that she decided she'd give it her best shot.

"Is this your first Full English, then?"

Mouth full of meaty bacon, Wen paused and raised her eyebrows. Dex grinned.

"Technically, it's not a Full English without blood pudding, but I didn't want to push you into the deep end of British cuisine right from Day Dot."

She gestured down at the feast, and he nodded. Full English. Interesting. She felt like she was learning a whole new language.

Then Callum brought over her old, battered cell phone. "Didnae want you to forget in the haze of bliss you seem to be under."

She eyed him, but dutifully swallowed the wonderfully rich bacon goodness and scrolled down to her supervisor's number. She could call, but she wasn't an actress. It'd be easier to say she was sick for the day if she just texted that she, say, had a sore throat and couldn't talk. Less explanation needed.

She had no idea how to even begin to explain Dex and Callum.

Soon enough, the boys joined her, sitting on the floor at her feet and arranging the tea tray and a few extra saucers with toast and extra bacon around themselves so they didn't have to get up again.

"What's this orange stuff?"

Callum, mouth full of toast smeared with exactly that, swallowed quickly and replied, "Marmalade. D'you like it? Some people don't care for the peel."

She didn't keep him in suspense, mostly because she wanted to take another bite herself. "It's amazing. It's kinda like orange jello, but sweeter and... punchier, somehow."

He beamed, looking far too bright-eyed and bushy-tailed for 7:30 in the morning and no Coke. "Brilliant. We'll get a better feel for what you do and donnae like soon enough so no every meal will be a taste-testing effort, aye?"

She sincerely doubted that. She tended to live on sandwiches, chopped veggie salads, and Chinese take-out when left to her own devices. Tucker had always insisted she make "home-cooked" meals for them both, though he knew she felt like she wasn't a good cook, until she grew to hate cooking at all.

Thus, she didn't tend to experiment much with her food. Pretty much everything would be new if the guys continued sharing their favorites, considering they were from another country.

Which brought her up short, marmalade brioche bite half-chewed. She swallowed quickly and took a slurp of tea to wash it down.

"So what do we do about... ya know... me being American and you guys being not? You say you're supposed to guard me constantly—which I'm still wrapping my head around, if I'm honest—and you've insisted on staying. But what about your lives back home? Am I supposed to go with you, or stay here while you travel, or what?"

Thankfully, neither seemed too worried about the question. In fact, Callum didn't even stop eating, letting Dex do all the explaining.

"My lady, we go where you go." He shrugged. "We've been nomads since we were young, going from one war-torn country to another. It's why bounty hunting has suited us for so long, but now we have a new vocation." He smiled, his eyes warm. "You."

She blinked. "Wait, am I supposed to be paying you, then? Because I cannot afford that. Not for long. And I know you'll get around to this yourselves, but this apartment isn't going to work for much longer. If you both stay and, God forbid, more of you show up, we'll *have* to get a bigger place, and I can't afford that, either. What will we live off of?"

Dex reached over and touched her knee. "No fretting, remember? We protect you. We keep you from harm. We will sort it all out."

"But—"

"Wen."

Her name. It was still so rare coming from either of them that it did as it was intended and gave her pause.

"Leave it with us. We'll find a way. We've made good money for a long, long time. If, at some point, money becomes a real problem, we'll perhaps see about one or the other of us taking more jobs whilst the other stays with you, but that is not a problem right now."

The "right now" caught her attention. He'd given it a strange emphasis. She tilted her head and narrowed her eyes, and Dex sighed.

"Please finish your breakfast, my lady. Not everything must be discussed right away. It's best if we all just get to know each other better and see how we rub along together and let things develop as they will."

If it was meant to sidetrack her, it failed. "What things?"

Another sigh, and Dex looked to Callum for... advice? A distraction?

But Callum merely sipped his tea and shrugged. "Your fortress, for one thing."

She blinked. "My what now?"

Dex grunted, not pleased. "It doesn't have to be a fortress. He's exaggerating. But you do need a safe place that's easier for us to guard than a tiny flat in a large complex in a small city."

She eyed him suspiciously. He sighed.

"Brigid does have a veritable fortress on Culloden Moor, but she's had longer to get it just as she wants it, and she lives in Scotland, where castles are just part of the scenery. She didn't even buy it herself; the government let her have it outright for living there and fixing it up to something of its former glory." He shrugged. "It's been decades since anyone I know had contact with Thea, the other Sister, but last we knew, her home in France was more like a hippie Wiccan commune than a fortress." He again touched her knee. "*You* decide what you want, and we figure out how to keep it safe." He forced a smile that didn't work nearly as well as his real ones. "See? Sorted. No worries."

Stunned, she pictured the balance total of her little nest egg and wanted to cry. She'd had such plans for it. But if she had to build some sort of fortified compound with it, she'd never have enough for what she really wanted.

But Dex was trying so hard to put her at ease, and Callum seemed completely unconcerned about how they were supposed to afford a fucking fortress, so she tried to smile and reassure them. But her mouth didn't want to cooperate, so she probably should have saved the effort.

Such a shame. She no longer wanted to eat any of her first Full English breakfast.

Somehow, miraculously, Wen had stumbled across perhaps the only two (presumably) straight men in existence that actually volunteered to wash dishes. Considering how much she disliked washing them herself, she felt like she'd hit the "new best friends" jackpot.

Callum and Dex stood side by side at her hobbit-sized double sink, Callum up to his elbows in suds, Dex drying with a dish towel she hadn't even known she had. She tended to use paper towels, as she only ever washed for one person, but the proper Brit had looked so scandalized by the idea that she'd gone digging through drawers she didn't remember filling and found one sad, ratty old towel.

She watched, another cup of tea in hand—something herbal this time, mellow and sweet and flowery—while they tidied up the pile of dishes they'd dirtied, listening to them banter back and forth and getting to know them better when they weren't looking at her than she ever would in direct conversation. For instance, Callum loved to cook. Apparently, he was quite the expert and had already planned a spectacular lunch of some sort of fancy pasta and a light salad of mixed spring greens. She didn't even know if her oven worked. Or if she had bread pans.

She shouldn't have worried—fretted, as Dex insisted on calling it—because Callum had, of course, bought his own the night before. According to Dex, the Scot never stayed anywhere without appropriate bakeware.

And Dex was, at heart, an avid gardener. He droned on and on about what kind of plants and flowers he hoped she'd allow him to cultivate whenever she chose a location for her fortress. As if she'd ever tell him no when his eyes glowed like that. Not amber, not as if he were feeling a shift coming on. Just warmth, life, even joy.

Beautiful eyes. He was such a beautiful man, outside and seemingly in.

Callum regaled her with the proper organization of an efficient, functional vegetable and herb garden. Dex suggested rose arbors and ivy-covered benches and overflowing flower beds. Her head whirled with all the possibilities until she simply watched and listened to them, smiling with the closest thing to calm and comfort she'd felt since Mama died.

"Do you have an idea what part of the world you'd like to live in, my lady?"

"Dex. No." Callum flicked suds-fingers at him. "Give her time. Decidin where to put a Probably Forever Home takes a bit of time and thought—"

"Oregon."

They turned to look at her, and for the first time in years, she didn't long to shrink from the sudden, direct attention. It was a good feeling to be able to just grin at their expressions without worrying about how they'd take her amusement.

"We lived there for a few years after college." Her amusement faded. "Tucker and I."

Solemn now, Dex dried his hands and handed the towel off to Callum to do the same. Then they both turned to lean back against the counter, watching her with attention but not with demanding questions. She supposed now was as good a time as any.

"We married right after I graduated high school. I'd always loved pictures of Oregon—all that glorious green forest and miles of gorgeous coastline—so I applied to a college there and was accepted. Tucker hated it. He was bored. There weren't enough people he knew or liked, and he hated that I was making friends at school, especially since I'd always been so shy here in Missouri."

Dex's jaw clenched. Callum looked thundery.

Not at her, though. She was almost glad they didn't know what Tucker looked like. They *were* bounty hunters, after all. If they wanted to find him—

She shivered, not sure if that would be a good or a bad thing..

"Anyway, we moved back after I graduated with a bachelor's, and I never got into the marine biology graduate study program I wanted because... well, Missouri is about as land-locked as it gets. So instead of saving the oceans, I got my job in coding and billing and just stayed. For the benefits and the pay, mostly, but I really did like it at first." She smiled a bit, wistful for a time when she'd held such high hopes for herself. "But I always wanted to go back to Oregon. It felt... I dunno—"

"Like home," Callum said, his accent and gentle tone making the short phrase sound like poetry.

She nodded. "Like home. I've been saving up since the divorce to go back—"

"Oregon, it is," Dex stated.

Could it really be so simple? What would she do there? She knew she could always get another coding job, but that wasn't really what she wanted if she moved back to Oregon. She longed for the ocean, to study the delicate ecosystems being slowly destroyed by climate change and try to salvage them, to swim with animals both miniscule and gargantuan. To see a blue whale and feel microscopic. A giant squid, still alive and cruising for large enough prey.

A narwhal, the only unicorn she'd ever dreamed of.

That's what she'd hidden deep inside herself once she understood what kind of man Tucker was: she wanted to get her Ph.D. in marine biology and save the oceans. It's what she'd always wanted, even when Tucker said she was too scatter-brained and immature to be a scientist. *Silly girl, leave the important work to the menfolk.*

But neither Dex nor Callum seemed to think it was so far-fetched. Admittedly, they didn't know if she was smart enough for more than just coding, but neither of them laughed at her or gave her the "oh, you poor, stupid thing" look that Tucker had always given her.

But she still had to check.

"Really? You guys would help me get to Oregon?"

"Why would we no'?" Callum seemed genuinely curious, as if going with her, helping her, *believing in her,* was a foregone conclusion. "Lass, milady, think of us as ride or die. If you have a wish, especially one as good-hearted as savin the oceans, we lads'll move heaven and earth to help you get it."

Dex nodded. "Whatever it takes."

Oh, not the waterworks again.

Her eyes prickled, and she blinked them as fast as she could, holding the embarrassing emotion back. She just... no one but Mama had ever taken her seriously before. But these men—two strangers who had made her tea, made her breakfast, held her while she cried herself to sleep, and made her feel like what she wanted was actually important, all in less than twenty-four hours—believed in her. Would help her. Would go with her so she wouldn't be scared and alone.

Her heart clenched, and she closed her eyes and swallowed hard. Another "for the first time since Mama died" for her, because it was a *good* sort of hurt. It was a cut to a festering wound that would hopefully let some of the poison out so it could finally heal.

At least, she hoped. Dared to hope.

Opening her eyes, even though they were still watery and hot, she managed a wobbly smile. "I guess I'd better start looking into 'returning to school after an absence' grants, huh?"

Callum grinned and winked as he shoved away from the sink to get back to the dishes. "Better than loggin in for work, aye?"

Yeah. It sure as hell was.

Dex made her tea again at around eleven o'clock—"elevensies", he called it, which sounded like some Lord of the Rings goofiness but was apparently a real thing—bringing her a tray filled with goodies and her new tea set, steaming with Earl Grey this time. It smelled heavenly, tasted even better with a bit of half and half, and instantly became her new favorite thing. She also enjoyed the little, crustless, creamy-cool cucumber sandwiches he'd cut into delicate triangles. She even liked the salmon, dill, and cream cheese triangles he'd also provided, though she'd normally rather starve than even smell salmon. Somehow, he'd taken the stink right out of the fish. A miracle worker.

Dex, though reluctant to share such high praise, graciously admitted that the food was Callum's good work rather than his. She muttered a loud but indistinct thanks toward the kitchen, her mouth full of sandwich.

Then, she returned to her research. The program she'd been interested in over fifteen years before wasn't still offered at her old alma mater, so she'd been searching around for something similar. She was so absorbed that she didn't even realize she needed to pee until her third cup of tea hit her bladder like a tactical nuke and she had to practically run for the bathroom.

Close call. But in a good way.

Unfortunately, now that she was away from her laptop, she caught herself thinking. Questioning. Doubting. Could she really go back to college, *grad school,* after fifteen years? Everyone would be so much younger than her. So much smarter, their knowledge base so much more current.

Would Dex and Callum really go with her? Or would they find excuses to be off on a fascinating and exciting bounty hunting job somewhere and never come back again because they'd discovered she just wasn't a very interesting person? Maybe they'd find another Sister and not need her anymore and just... go.

No. They said there were only ever three Sisters at a time, and if they hadn't already joined the other two, they surely couldn't be called away like that. Which wasn't the kindest reason she could give herself for why they might stay, but it did at least set her mind at ease on that point.

"Milady? You alright in there?"

Callum's jovial Scots burr. She smiled, though she tried to hurry through all the wiping and replacing of clothing and washing of hands as if he'd demanded to know what was taking her so long. Like Tucker.

They were not Tucker. How long would it take her mind to stop comparing them to him? She tried to think back to what her therapist had said way back at her first appointment three years ago, right after the divorce.

*"Recovery isn't linear. Trauma doesn't heal in a day, and sometimes it feels worse even after it's felt better. But recovery, over time, does trend upward. Give it time and remember: **recovery isn't linear.**"*

She hadn't understood at the time, had been too hurt and confused and still gaslit to know what to believe to understand, but she thought maybe she did now.

"I'm alright," she said when she opened the door to find Callum still standing there, waiting for her. "Just thinking me thinks."

He grinned, flashing a dimple. "The loo will forever be the best place for ponderance."

The loo. So quaint. She really needed to Britishize her speech patterns. So many things they said sounded so much more fun than the American equivalent.

Callum had said "a-lu-MIN-i-um" earlier, and she'd laughed even while in the throes of her research. A-LU-min-um. A-lu-MIN-i-um. It was somehow more fun to say it the British way.

And she could listen to Callum's Scots burr all day long. It made her want to purr like a cat.

She paused, looking up at him with surprise at herself. "Can we get a cat?"

He slid his arm through hers, escorting her the few steps back to her desk as courtly as a suitor at a ball. "I've no objection. Would you like one? Or ten? Have you always wanted to be a crazy cat lady, then?"

She huffed and elbowed him before taking her arm back. "Ten is a bit much. I've just never had a pet. We couldn't afford one when I was growing up, and Tucker— well."

Callum's delightful hazel eyes darkened, his forehead going thunderous. "I see."

Somehow, even though he couldn't possibly know the whole story, she believed that he really did see. Tucker had been such an asshole to her, and as lonely and desperate for affection as she had been all those years, she couldn't bring herself to subject a helpless animal to his whims and moods, his shouts and punches to the wall. What if she had a lovely, fat house cat, and Tucker kicked it? Or threw things at it like he sometimes did her, though he deliberately never actually hit her with anything.

She'd have never forgiven herself.

Without warning, Callum lowered his head to lean his forehead against hers, his eyes closed. "Aye, lass. Even if you want ten, you can have whatever pet you want."

She stood frozen, stiff and awkward but unwilling to pull away from the strange intimacy. It was a friendly gesture, nothing more—sympathy for what she'd been through, understanding that she didn't want to say it out loud—but she felt the contact all the way to her toes. How she had missed a simple, friendly touch.

Not sure how to react, she finally made herself huff. "I think we can start with just one. But probably not until we get wherever we're going. I never put down a pet deposit here and don't see the point now."

He finally pulled away, his expression strange enough that she couldn't quite make it out. "Then, by all means, milady, let's get out of this wee shoebox."

She snorted, surprised out of her worry about what that look on his face meant and into sitting back down at her desk in front of her laptop. She'd narrowed down her university options to two: the Oregon Institute of Marine Biology or Oregon State University's marine biology specialty course. The Institute was her first choice, but she needed to look into tuition fees, the housing market, cost of living, etc. Would she need a different car, or would Roger be okay out in the rainy, often cold Pacific Northwest?

Her mind effectively off of both Tucker and Callum's strange expression, she went back to her study, waving absently when Callum announced that lunch would be ready in less than an hour as he headed back into the kitchen. She really was close to a decision between the two.

Oregon. God—Goddess?—she couldn't wait to go back.

6

"I think I'm having a foodgasm."

Unashamed of the statement, Wen forked in another bite of creamy, tomatoey, basily pasta goodness and felt it melt on her tongue. She dragged a bite of homemade bread—which was nothing like any bread she'd ever had in her entire, deprived life—through the sauce not coating the pasta, then sipped at a sweet but sharp red wine of some sort that paired perfectly with Callum's supper masterpiece. She'd never even had wine before, but she was two glasses in already and just getting warmed up.

Lunch's bowtie alfredo with bacon had been good, but this supper feast was sublime.

"Best thing about food, lass, is how few ingredients you actually need to make somethin irresistible." He twirled his angel hair pasta around his fork, expertly using a spoon in a way that made her feel like a child learning how to use chopsticks, and savored a massive bite, chewing slowly. "You can go fancy and have a good result, aye, but few foods have ever paired together better than a grain, a cheese, and a tomato-based product. Especially if you add basil."

She thought about it for a moment, because it seemed like such a weird claim, but... macaroni and cheese with ketchup had been Tucker's go-to easy meal on the rare occasion when she couldn't (or wouldn't) cook. Pizza was basically bread, herby tomato sauce, and cheese and didn't really need meat or vegetables to be delicious.

The ambrosia she currently gorged on certainly qualified. Dex hadn't said a word since he'd sat down with a full plate, and that was a feat in and of itself, what with Callum singing his own praises and all.

So, she nodded and savored another bite, scooping up stray sauce on the heavenly, airy, yeasty bread he'd created out of what looked like a science experiment. Fresh-from-the-oven bread. She could never have guessed how different it was from processed store-bought.

Another sip of wine, and she started to feel drowsy and warm in the cheeks. Her eyelids grew heavy. She tapped her phone to check the time, and it was barely 7:00 in the evening. She couldn't possibly already be sleepy.

To keep herself from floating too far away on a fluffy cloud of food-and-wine-induced bliss, she cleared her throat and asked a question she'd been pondering in the back of her mind almost all day.

"Hey, guys?"

Dex looked up, trailing a strand of angel hair. Callum just raised an eyebrow as he buttered another slice of manna from heaven.

"Would it be possible for me—us—to go see Brigid's fortress?" She eyed them warily, trying not to look like she was gauging their reactions while she absolutely tried to do so. "Just to get an idea of what we should be looking for? Or planning or adding or should forget about?"

Callum sat up and tilted his head. "Why wouldnae that be possible? Sounds like brilliant reasonin to me."

Dex nodded, already twirling another forkful.

She shifted in her seat and toyed with her wine glass. Of course, she'd never even imagined having wine glasses before today. Callum had bought a set of four. She wasn't sure if he was planning ahead for another guardian or if they only sold them four at a time.

"I just— I don't have a passport, so I know it couldn't be any time soon, and I know it's a long trip, and it'll be expensive just when we should be trying to economize for making a place for us all. But…." She shrugged. "I don't have any idea at all what to plan for. I don't know anything about what my... I dunno... moon duties are."

Callum snickered, almost choking on his bread. Dex coughed and finally put down his fork to sip at his wine, likely to hide a smirk.

She'd said something stupid. She always said something stupid.

"We are absolutely referring to them as 'moon duties' forever now." Of course, Callum thought her ignorance was hilarious. "That's going in the lore if we have to write it in ourselves."

Apparently, something in her expression alerted the pair that she wasn't as amused by their hilarity as they were. Callum chuckled once more, then cleared his throat. Dex gave her a look of such understanding that she wanted to get up from the table, leave her apartment, and walk out into the ocean.

Pity she lived in the middle. No ocean to walk into.

"Wen."

As always, Dex's voice flowed like honey. He likely intended it to be a balm to her prickly reaction, but it only goaded her further. She didn't want to be patronized any more than she wanted to be ignorant and foolish.

"We're not having a go at you, my lady." He reached out to touch her hand. She forced herself not to pull away. "It's just that, as far as we know, Sisters of the Moon don't have duties, per se. Their magic is in their very being, allowing shifters to shift as they will, which in turn allows them to be the perfect guardians for the Sisters."

She huffed, unimpressed, and leaned back in her chair, crossing her arms. She didn't want a sweet touch of the hand right now. "That's dumb, though. It's a tautology, not the way the world works."

Callum's eyebrows shot up, likely at her tone. Dex, though, just took his hand back and looked curious.

"What's a tautology?"

Ah. Something the worldly, all-knowing, hundred-year-old shapeshifters *didn't* know.

"A tautology is a repetition meant to explain but, instead, you're just saying the same thing a different way. Like something is what it is because... of course it is."

They both blinked at her. She sighed at their shock, even though she actually felt like she knew something useful for the first time since they'd showed up.

She *had* been to college, after all. Fifteen years ago, but still.

"You're saying that Sisters of the Moon developed the ability to allow shifting at will so you guys could be better guardians. But we only need guardians because we have the ability to allow shifting at will. Otherwise, we're any other human. Nothing special at all."

Like me, she thought but couldn't say. She was finally feeling less pathetic. She didn't want to ruin it by saying the quiet part out loud.

Callum opened his mouth, closed it, and frowned. Dex's lips twisted, his eyes starting to twinkle.

Why was he twinkling? Didn't he realize she was miffed by their snickers at her expense?

But when she lifted one imperious eyebrow at him, he only chuckled and picked his fork back up. "You're right, of course, my lady."

Wait, what?

"I suppose I never thought of it like that. There has to be more to it, or it wouldn't be a thing in the first place."

She felt slightly deflated. She wasn't used to being agreed with on the rare occasion she dared to voice her own standpoint. This was a new sensation, and she wasn't sure yet if she liked it or not.

He didn't reach out to touch her again, though she uncrossed her arms as she lost some of her pique. He only smiled at her, eyes warm and bright.

"It shouldn't surprise me that you're apparently the first person in at least our lifetimes who grasped that essential fact."

She blinked. "Uh. Why?"

His smile tilted. "You have no idea how unique you are."

Suspicion tried to worm back in, but she really did try to keep it at bay. "What's that supposed to mean?"

Damn, but suspicion was persistent.

Before he could respond, Callum butted in. She'd almost forgotten he was there.

"It means someone along the line forgot to write some shite down in the official Sisters of the Moon handbook, because you're fookin right, and none of us ever caught that." He shrugged. "Brigid and her brood never did, anyway. I'm no' sure about Thea, but if she had, she surely would've shared. The Sisters are never in opposition to each other. You're too rare to be infightin."

She considered that, an odd feeling blooming in her chest. It took her a moment to recognize it: yearning. The same yearning she'd felt before at the idea of having a sister, even if it was just the moon.

Maybe... just maybe... she could have more than just these two friends. Wouldn't that be something?

Dex finally reverted back to his usual form and reached out to pat her forearm, giving her a light but warm grasp before returning to his pasta. "At any rate, to answer your original question, no, it wouldn't be at all a problem if you wanted to visit Brigid. I'm sure Callum can ring her up so she can welcome you herself."

That blooming feeling spread. "Really? In Scotland? In her fortress?"

Callum shrugged. "She doesnae like to leave if she can help it. She has it just the way she likes."

Hope. That was it. Not just yearning, but hope.

"A forever home."

The words were almost as good as the pasta. Not a nightmare from which she couldn't escape. Not a place she stayed until she could afford to do something better.

A home. A home forever. With friends and literal cryptids to study at close hand and, apparently, every type of plant known to man at arm's length, if Dex had his way and Callum had his vegetable/herb patch.

It really could be.

Sighing, she felt her eyes droop as the wine and the not-quite confrontation hit her. She *was* sleepy. Early evening or not, she wanted nothing more than a hot bath and bed.

Since she couldn't really have a hot bath, she'd settle for a nap. Or even for just curling up in her chair with a cup of steaming tea, a saucer of biscuits and jam, and her two new guardian friends at her feet, bickering with each other and telling her about themselves and making plans for the future.

That, too, really could be. If she could just stay awake through supper.

She almost made it.

7

The smell of sweet dough cooking—baking? frying?—and a waft of what she happily recognized as the bold scent of Irish Breakfast tea brewing brought her up out of a deep and dreamless sleep. Was it Callum or Dex in the kitchen?

Slowly, she became aware of a hand draped over her midsection. A forearm. The warmth of a long, strong body eased up against hers. Breath on the back of her neck, stirring the frizzy hair there.

Dark Brown #4, that hand, like chocolate velvet. Dex. Must be Callum in the kitchen, then.

She should probably be concerned to find a second man in her bed overnight, but she wasn't. Dex had treated her with nothing but respect, and, frankly, he felt glorious to lie back against. She hadn't wanted to so much as touch Tucker for so long that she forgot how lovely and comforting it felt to be gently held by someone kind. She'd denied herself... *had been denied* simple human contact for so long.

This was sheer bliss.

So she stayed right where she was, letting her eyes drift closed again and sighing, content. Callum would call them when breakfast was ready. She had almost decided between the institute and the university, and she wanted to spend today looking for property around those areas to see if values were prohibitive enough in one or the other to make the decision easier.

After she called in sick again. No way could she log in for work today.

How long until she could no longer avoid putting in notice? It seemed as if all of these amazing things really would happen at some point, which meant she couldn't keep a job that rooted her in Missouri. She didn't care about the little studio apartment she'd inhabited but hadn't really lived in. She didn't have anyone keeping her here.

But her job was security. Financial safety. Her lifeline when her entire life had fallen apart around her. Could she bring herself to quit it?

She had to, didn't she? If she wanted even part of what Dex and Callum promised she would have, she'd have to bite the bullet, jump out of the plane, step off the zipline platform, whatever metaphor she could think of.

Suddenly, she had a flash of the only tarot card she'd ever really studied. Way back at the beginning of her marriage, back when Tucker still took her places to have fun, not just because he needed someone to watch him perform and compliment him later, he'd taken her to a county fair in Oregon. It was a muggy summer evening, kids running around laughing, rickety rides in full swing.

She'd seen a palm reader tent and begged to go inside. Tucker, of course, didn't believe in that nonsense. It was a waste of time and money. The fake psychic inside would just tell her what they thought she wanted to hear.

It was still early days for them, so she insisted. Later, she'd know it wasn't worth the petulance and passive-aggressive bullshit he'd inflict afterward, but then, she was still young and thought he loved her.

He did refuse to go inside with her, but that actually suited her better. Had she known, even then, that something was wrong? Had she secretly been worrying, wanting an outside opinion to tell her that her fears were, indeed, coming true?

She couldn't remember now. Then, she'd been surprised when the bottle blond with all the scarves and blue eyeshadow eyed her for a moment, then reached into a hidden pocket for a deck of tarot cards instead of across the table for her hand.

She didn't remember what the other cards in the reading were. All she remembered for sure was The Fool. A bright-eyed youth, head up and reaching for the sky, blithely walking into his future with his little yappy dog at his feet... one of which hovered over a precipice.

"You see what The Fool does not—that he's about to fall. That he's stepping off a cliff." The lady stared at her with an intensity that had seemed put on at the time, and a little over the top at that. "What you don't see is what he does—you cannot fly off into your destiny if you won't take the first step into uncertainty."

Those words stayed with her for days afterward. She puzzled over them, seeing the card in her head—the smiling youth, the adorable puppy barking at his feet. Trying to warn him or happily trotting along with him? The innocent confidence on the youth's face. The sun shining down as if nothing bad could ever happen on such a beautiful day. The dark tones of the cliff's edge falling so sharply away at the bottom of the card, the dark unknown he was about to fall into.

You cannot fly off into your destiny if you won't take the first step into uncertainty.

She abruptly shrugged out from under Dex's warm grasp—he yawned and stretched, waking up instantly but not as if he intended to hold her back—and rolled out of bed. She didn't care that one pant leg was bunched up around her knee and her old neck-stretched t-shirt hung off of one shoulder. She didn't even bother to run a hand through her frizz to tone it down.

She was on a mission. Whether or not she had moon duties—it *was* a little catchy, she could admit after a good night's sleep—she could take one direct action right here and now.

Picking up her phone, she scrolled to her boss's number, started a text, then shook her head and tapped the call button instead. Two rings, and a groggy, rough voice answered. Clare sounded horrible, like she'd had a rough night.

"H'llo. Uh... Wen? Y'alright?"

Oops. She was supposed to be sick. Well, she could at least try to sound like she had a sore throat.

"Um... better, but that's not really why I'm calling." She took a deep breath and that first, possibly disastrous, step. "I just wanted you to know that something has come up, and I'm going to be moving soon. I wanted you to have as much notice as possible so you can get someone in my position before I leave."

Silence, both on the phone and in her apartment. She couldn't look at Dex or Callum yet. Not until it was done.

After she checked her phone to make sure the call hadn't dropped, Clare finally responded. "Jesus, Wen, this is really sudden. Did someone die or something?"

She huffed, still keyed up. "No, nothing like that. I have a... an opportunity, I guess. And I want to take it. It's time."

More silence.

"Clare?"

"Yes, sorry. I mean, I'm happy for you, of course. I'm just still catching up." A little huff. "It's not even 7:00 yet, girl."

She pulled her phone away to look at the time, and sure enough, it was only 6:47. She never woke up before 7:00 AM. She was usually comatose until at least 7:30.

"I'll— are you logging in today, then?"

Oops. Still supposed to be sick. And she only wanted to look at property values, not billing.

"Uh, no, actually." Cough, cough. She doubted either was convincing. "I just... found out some stuff, so I wanted to get this to you as soon as possible. I'll try to log in tomorrow, though, okay?"

"O-okay." More silence. "Wen, are you sure everything's okay?"

Was that... concern? More than just a boss asking why an employee was quitting? Wen thought it might be.

Feeling strangely comforted by the concern, she smiled a little. "Everything's fine, except this darn sore throat."

Uh-huh. The little pause told her exactly how bad a liar she was. She finally turned around to look at the guys, then melted. They both looked so proud of her, so happy.

She'd done something right.

"Well." Her boss finally sounded fully awake, but not terribly happy. "I guess I'll let you get back to bed. I'll probably grab another snooze or two, myself."

"Okay."

She had no idea what else to say at this point. It almost felt anticlimactic. She'd girded herself up to take that ambiguous first step, and it hadn't been the dramatic battle she'd half-expected.

"Oh, wait." Clare grunted a little, as if she was trying to sit up in bed. "How much notice do you think you're giving? Please tell me you're putting in at least two weeks. Or a month?"

That last sounded almost like a plea. Surely, it wouldn't be that difficult to replace her.

"Uh." She looked at the guys again and shrugged. "Two weeks should be... okay?" She was asking both her boss and her new friends, but when Dex and Callum both gave her thumbs' up, she said it more confidently. "Two weeks ought to be enough time. If I have to leave earlier—" *If I find a place I can't bear to lose and have to go see it immediately.* "—I can still remote in, right?"

"Yes, absolutely. I'll clear it with HR first, but if you can work from home, I don't know why you can't work from the road, so long as you have a solid connection when you're keying."

"Good." That really was a relief. If they left sooner, she wouldn't be leaving in a lurch, which not only would be hard on Clare but might hurt her chances of getting a job in Oregon if she needed references. "Well, I should probably get back to bed. You, too, actually."

Clare murmured a response, still not sounding very happy, but hung up amiably enough. Wen looked at her silenced phone for a moment. Had she really done the right thing? It had felt right, but—

Yes. She felt a little in free-fall now that she'd put in official notice, but all she had to do was look up to remind herself that she wasn't alone anymore and, thus, had a parachute at hand. Dex. Callum. Friends and guardians.

They said they'd protect her, even from herself. That last might be the hardest job of all, but in this one instance, she became surer by the moment that she'd done exactly what she was supposed to.

Now, there was nothing but an open, dizzying, unknown future to fall through.

Belgian waffles were definitely going on the list of things she wanted every single day, if possible. Crispy golden on the outside, fluffy and light on the inside, covered with anything from fresh fruit and whipped cream to peanut butter and chocolate sauce, waffles were clearly a delicacy that only kitchen wizards knew how to create.

Dex didn't seem impressed by this out-loud suggestion. "He just uses a waffle iron. Literally anyone can go to a store and buy a waffle iron."

Callum, much faux-affronted, squared his shoulders. "I'll see you on the green for that, mate."

"Name the date, kilted wonder, and let the trees fall where they may."

"Cabers, mate. Cabers."

"Which are lopped-off trees."

She watched them bickering and smiled. She'd quit her job, she was looking into finally living her dreams, Oregon called, and as soon as she could get her passport, she'd be on her way to Scotland and, if she had her druthers, a trip to Loch Ness. And friends. She had friends. She might even have *more* friends in time. Life was surprisingly good.

Waffles might still be better, though. Would marmalade taste as good on a waffle as it did on brioche?

"Don't you think, my lady?"

Oops. She'd lost track of the bickering, as amusing as it was, in her contemplation of the good life.

"Um...?"

"We should head to Brigid's fortress before we go to Oregon. No sense trying to get your security established, then leaving the country right away."

"Oh." She hadn't considered that, but she didn't want to wait months to start her Oregon dream. "One problem with that: I really don't have a passport. I thought we didn't want to wait that long?"

Dex blinked. "Oh. I thought you were just saying that. Huh." But instead of grumbling, Dex only shrugged. "Don't see why that's a problem, though."

She tilted her head, frowning. "Because I can't leave the country?"

"Why not?"

She blinked, wondering what she had missed. "Because I don't have a passport?"

Callum shook his head. "Donnae listen to him, lass. He's

being deliberately obtuse."

"Never." Dex sniffed, tilting his head up haughtily. "I just don't see that not having a passport means not being able to travel when your guardians are two international bounty hunters with connections, favors to call in, and no need to bother with silly human laws that have nothing to do with magical business."

She blinked again. "Oh."

Callum grumbled. "Well, when you put it that way."

Dex smirked, looking entirely too smug for his usual, stoic self. But it wasn't a bad look on him, so she didn't complain. Plus, he turned his smirk into a grin as he reached out to touch her hand, as was his wont.

"We'll charter a private plane, my lady. We can be there in a day whenever you want to go." He turned to Callum. "You'll ring Brigid and ask for a visit?"

"Aye, leave it with me."

But there were still waffles to be eaten, so all of that part would have to wait. Could she remote in to her work log-in from a chartered plane? From Scotland?

Did it matter? She'd already put in her notice. Not like they could fire her.

Cutting ties was so freeing.

"She wants to speak with you, lass."

Wen startled, deep into her Oregon property searches—by which she meant looking at picture after beautiful green picture of the Oregon wilderness and coastline she so missed. "What? Who?"

Callum stood at her side, offering his phone. He grinned with dimples. "Brigid. Remember?"

"Oh!"

She hesitated to take the phone, though, all her awkwardness and shyness coming back. She didn't know this woman. She wasn't very good at speaking with women, even though she was one.

Who was she kidding? She was terrible at talking with any gender.

"What does she— what should I say?"

He patted her affectionately on the shoulder and put the phone in her hand until she took it from him. "She's no' the bloody Queen, lass. Just talk to her like you talk to us. You'll be brilliant."

She took a moment for a few deep breaths before lifting the phone to her face. "Hello?"

"Wendolyn?"

She raised her eyebrows at the masculine sound of the voice, then shrugged. Maybe Brigid just had a deep voice. Probably sounded amazing singing an old blues song.

"Yes. Brigid? Is it okay for me to call you that?"

A chuckle. "Of course, love. There can be no formalities between Sisters o' the Moon."

She didn't sound like a deep-voiced woman. She sounded like a deep-voiced man. And then it struck her: Brigid was trans. Of course! Wen would've facepalmed if she hadn't had someone else's cell phone in her hand.

And she'd called her "love". It made her feel all gooey, even though they'd never met. And her Scottish accent was much thicker than Callum's.

"Did Callum tell you why we're hoping to visit?"

"He did. By the way, may I say how pleased I am that ye called him? I was so disappointed when we realized he couldnae be one of my Nightwatchers. He's been more of a father to me than me own ever was, and I so hoped— but no."

She hadn't thought of that. Of how sad it would be for the both of them to not be Sister and—

Wait. What had Brigid called them?

"Nightwatchers? Is that what you call your guardians?"

Brigid huffed. "Aye, love. That's what they're all called, no' just mine. Did he no' tell ye? Or Dex? Oi, those lads are a bag o' cats, they are."

A laugh bubbled up out of her at the thought, and she found herself liking her new sister very much.

"They really are." She allowed herself another good laugh—without looking at the guys—before getting herself under better control. "But they *have* told me a lot. Just not that."

"Well, we'll have a nice, long blether when ye've arrived, then. I'll tell ye everythin I know about being a Sister. I came to Light back in the '80s, so I dunno much more than the lads, but Thea did tell me a few things back then before disappearin into the wilds of France. One o' them was about Nightwatchers and how yer magic calls to them even as their shiftin cries out for a Sister's magic."

It sounded so poetic, but that could just be Brigid's lovely accent. Wen could listen to it all day. Maybe she would, and soon.

"That sounds so cool. Nightwatchers. I wonder why they're called that. Is it because of the moon?"

Brigid hmmed. "Thea didnae say. I assume so, but I also go' the feel there was a lot she didnae know, either. I dunno what happened to the Sisters before us—they told ye there are only ever three at a time, aye?"

"Yeah. Not why, but the fact of it."

"Three is a perfect number and very strong magic. Many old depictions of goddesses had three spirals over their bellies. Spirals and the number three have always been potent symbols of magic."

She knew none of this, but she was fascinated. Absently, she left her little office chair and went over to her recliner. Out of nowhere, Dex appeared with her tea service, the pot steaming with the lovely herbal-flowers brew from the day before. He poured her a cup, then backed out of her immediate attention while she listened to her new sister tell her about who she was. Who *they* were.

"Anyhoo, love, Thea doesnae talk about what happened to the two Sisters she originally served with, but I reckon it wasnae pretty. Shifters who were called but refused to serve, mayhap? Humans burnin them at the stake or stonin them or whatnot? Who can say?" Brigid's voice dropped to a whisper. "I think her education from the lore wasnae complete. I cannae see how that woulda happened if somethin awful hadnae happened to the other Sisters, aye?"

Wen dropped her voice to a whisper, too. "That doesn't sound good. Should we be worried?"

"Nay, love." Her voice returned to the normal deep burr, warm and friendly. "I've been around a good, long while now with nary a problem, aye? We should be safe as houses, so long as we take precautions and let our Nightwatchers do their jobs. They're quite good at it, and they ken what an honor it is."

She glanced over to where Dex and Callum were giving her as much space and privacy as her miniscule apartment would allow. They saw her looking and smiled, and her heart melted. They *were* good men. Good friends. Good guardians.

She wouldn't balk at their protection anymore. She hadn't realized it was a point of honor for them, but it made sense now why they'd been so distressed at the idea of her sending them away. It would have been a great dishonor to them both.

She wouldn't make that mistake again. She liked them too much to dishonor them.

"Anyway, m'love, you come right along as soon as ye want. Ye'll always be welcome on Culloden Moor." Brigid's voice warmed toward a smile. "We'll have to take a full moon swim in me black pool, aye? Ye've no' lived until ye felt Sister Moon's light on every inch of yer skin."

Wen blushed a little, but she really wanted to try that. She didn't know what a black pool was—just a regular swimming pool tiled with black? or something more supernatural?—but she'd always wanted to try skinny-dipping. Even when she packed on the pounds as she turned to food for solace as her marriage tightened like a steel trap around her, she'd wanted to swim free, out in the ocean with her beloved sea creatures.

She could imagine doing so at night, the moon above, dolphins leaping around her, humpback whales breaching, life all around her in the darkness, the waves lifting her here and there until it felt like she was flying, soaring between the enormous stone stacks rising here and there in the water as she rushed toward the rugged shore.

She blinked and shook her head. That hadn't been a fleeting thought. That had felt like... a vision? Was she capable of having visions? Was that a Sister of the Moon thing?

"Hey, Brigid?"

"Aye?"

She hesitated. So far, she thought she'd done pretty well not to make a fool of herself with her new sister. She didn't want to say something weird or stupid now.

But—

"Do you ever have... visions?"

"What d'ye mean, then?"

She cringed a bit, but Brigid didn't sound snarky or sarcastic —just curious. So, she gathered her courage and took another step off that cliff.

"I just had— I dunno, a thought, maybe? But it felt... heavy. Like it meant something, not just the normal stray thought."

"Just now?" Brigid sounded excited. That was good, right? "What was it, then?"

Blushing, she lowered her tone to a whisper so the guys wouldn't hear her talking about being naked. She knew they'd hear anyway, but they'd also pretend not to.

"You said we should swim in your black pool naked in the moonlight, and I got this image in my head. I was swimming in the ocean at night, the moon giant on the horizon and glowing across the water, but no stars. It was black otherwise." Now that she'd started, the vision seemed to rush out of her. "Dolphins and whales were breeching, and I knew other things swam below me, with me, but I didn't feel scared, like maybe Jaws was down there or something." She paused, then said the rest. "I felt *right*. Like that's where I was supposed to be."

She waited for Brigid's verdict, but she shouldn't have been concerned.

"That, m'love, is a gift from Gaia. If that's how ye felt, that's where She wants ye to be on Her great and good earth."

Her heart pounded. Brigid believed her. She knew in her galloping heart that Dex and Callum would, too. And she knew something else: she was looking for a home in the wrong place.

She'd been googling images of Oregon land. She needed to look at Oregon beaches until she found the inlet and small cove she'd been swimming in.

A gift from Gaia. The boys had mentioned her—Her—before. The goddess she clearly needed to research. She hadn't realized they were serious, but she knew better now.

"Now, m'dear Wendolyn, I want ye to keep that vision in yer mind until ye find it, aye?" She sighed, sounding regretful. "I feel like we could blether all night and still have more to say, but me First is here telling me there's somethin needin me attention. Aye, Eiji."

Was that a name? With the deep Scottish burr—definitely stronger than Callum's, likely because Brigid still lived in Scotland—it was hard to tell, but it sounded like she was addressing someone specific, so it must be a name.

"I said aye. I'll no' hang up on my Sister until we're proper finished."

Wen heard murmuring on the line but couldn't make

anything out.

"I know, love. A minute more, aye? The chancellor can wait when the full moon isnae until next week."

She blinked, not sure what that meant, but it sounded important so she dared to break in.

"Brigid? We can talk more when I get there, okay? I don't want you getting in trouble because of a phone call or interrupt your life or anything."

"Ah, love, ye're never an interruption. But aye, we'll talk again very soon. I cannae wait to meet ye and hug ye close, dear Sister. I'm so pleased that one such as you has finally come to Light."

Come to Light. It finally clicked. She was coming into Sister Moon's light, which was apparently her magic. She really should have figured that out sooner, but now wasn't the time for self-recriminations.

"I'm... I'm just so glad to know you, Brigid." She swallowed hard. "I dunno what Callum told you, but I've been— well, I've been on my own for a long time, and now I have two friends and a sister, and... just... thank you." Her eyes prickled, but she vowed she wouldn't cry again so soon. "You sound so lovely and warm, and I can't wait to meet you in person."

"Oh, love. Ye'll be very well met indeed."

That sounded like heaven. But she didn't quite know how to respond, so she was glad when Brigid continued.

"Until we meet, dear Sister, goodbye."

"Bye."

She let the phone go dead, looking at the black screen in her hand, feeling wistful and hopeful in equal measures. Soon enough, Dex and Callum came to her and sat at her feet, Dex touching her knee and Callum leaning his head against her plump thigh.

For that one, beautiful moment, Wendolyn Eudora Cheney knew what it was to be whole.

8

"I found it!"

She almost fell out of her office chair trying to leap out of it. Her feet had gone numb from sitting still too long—through elevensies at least, because Dex had brought her the little triangle sandwiches again, this time with olive and cream cheese instead of salmon, and a pot of Earl Grey—and she winced when she realized how stiff and achy she was.

A far cry from sailing blithely through the stacks, borne on the swelling ocean waves with sea creatures all around her and the moon close enough to touch.

"My lady?"

Her guardians—Nightwatchers, which the boys had admitted they knew about but hadn't wanted to put her off by using too much unfamiliar verbiage while telling her about her new path—were of course there to steady her so she wouldn't topple over. She pointed at her laptop even as she rotated her feet at the ankles, trying to get the feeling back and the blood pumping.

The stacks. The shape of the inlet coastline and the small, private, cliff-sheltered cove. The fact that the open ocean just beyond the inlet had been a popular whale-watching sight until the local government banned boats for miles because all the attention disturbed the whales' roaming patterns.

It was the place from her vision. Gaia's gift.

And it was for sale. Apparently, when a goddess sent a vision, She made damn sure her surf and turf was available for purchase.

A hundred acres of coastal forestland, and though the price was insane, Wen knew she was supposed to find a way. It had been a private-owned, protected wilderness preserve for almost a hundred years, according to Google, but the owner had recently died, and her heirs were now short of funds. The only caveat to a purchase was an homage to their mother: the land must stay undeveloped. The buyer could build a house, if they chose, but no more than ten percent of the property could be developed, or the sale would be invalidated, per contract.

Wen had no idea if such a provision would hold up in court, but she had no intention of developing such a pristine natural wilderness any more than her Nightwatchers needed for security purposes. In fact, the very nature of the place should act as a natural deterrent.

It was perfect. It was exactly what she wanted. It truly was Gaia's gift.

"Would you like to contact the sellers, my lady, or would you rather one of us did so?"

Ah. Of course Dex had realized how anxious Wen got leading up to and during phone calls. She couldn't help it. She just knew she'd say something wrong and never be able to talk to that person ever again.

"Either of you, really." She blushed, but if they wanted to help, she would let them. "I don't know how to afford the place, but maybe they'll give us a deal, given I'll be in a marine biology program and will happily promise to keep the area as a preserve like their mother did."

The boys exchanged a look, and Callum grinned. "This might be a moment for diplomacy rather than snark, mate. It's to you."

Dex rolled his eyes but had clearly expected the verdict. He was already jotting down the real estate company's details and the owner information Wen had found. "Don't worry, my lady. I'll have it sorted as soon as possible. I'm sure that, between the three of us, we'll be able to manage a decent offer. And if it's a gift from Gaia, it *will* happen. She wouldn't have shown you otherwise."

She considered that as Callum helped her back into her chair and knelt at her side to look at the pictures she clicked through. Those stacks in the inlet and the sheltered cove. The expanse of ocean beyond. The acres and acres of undisturbed forestland and meadows. Even a secluded freshwater lake.

"I love it." She hadn't expected to say anything, but she discovered that she meant it, so she said it again. "I just— I love it. I want to swim in the cove. I want to swim in the lake. I want to walk in the woods in the moonlight and listen to the night. I want to have a bonfire in a meadow under the full moon."

Callum smiled softly at her—no dimples, just warmth. "You truly are a Sister of the Moon. You're feelin her pull on you, just as the tides do."

She nodded. "I really think I am. I just—"

She turned to look at him fully, and he sat back on his heels, giving her his full attention. It should have flustered her, but she was getting used to having their full attention when she needed it. They weren't gawking at her, after all. They just wanted to make sure they understood what she meant, what she needed, so they could help her.

"I want to do this right, ya know?" She bit her lip and lowered her eyes, her fingers twisting in her lap. "I've never been important before. I've felt like a failure and a fool most of my life. This all feels too big for me, and I don't want to screw anything up. Does that sound stupid?"

"Milady." Callum's expression darkened, but not as if he were angry with her. He touched her hands to stop their squirming. "Wen, you are *no' stupid*. You've never been stupid. You've never been a failure. If you were a failure, you wouldnae be here right now, receivin visions from Gaia, wantin nothin more than to save the ocean and all its wee beasties."

She grinned, unable to stop herself at the term. Callum grinned, too, flashing his dimples this time.

"You listen to me, Wendolyn Cheney."

"Wendolyn Eudora Cheney."

He blinked, sidetracked. "Beg pardon?"

She huffed. "Sorry. Mama always called me by my whole name when she wanted me to really listen and remember something. 'Wendolyn Eudora Cheney, remember that you can do anything you put your mind to,' that kind of thing."

He liked that. She could tell. Maybe she could tell them more about her past, after all. The few good parts, anyway. It was just so difficult to separate them from the bad ones.

"Right, then. Wendolyn Eudora Cheney, you listen to me, aye?" He waited until she nodded. "You are worthy."

The words cut unexpectedly, and she gasped softly.

"You. Are. Worthy." Callum clasped her hands in his own. "The magic chose you. Sister Moon chose you. And no' just now, either."

Her hands clasped tight on his, she whispered, "What does that mean?"

He sighed. "I didnae mean to blurt, lass. Now that I have, though— think about it. You say you started going white around sixteen, aye?"

She nodded, not sure what to feel at this point.

"And you were married, but you're no' now."

Another nod, her eyebrows drawing together.

"You've nothin holdin you here in this place to keep you from Gaia's chosen home." His fingers squeezed gently, then returned to simply holding hers. "And though you were married... lass, you never had children. Sister Moon would never have taken a mother away from her bairns, though She loves it if Her chosen Sisters choose to bear lovely wee ones after they come to Light."

Oh, that hurt. He surely didn't mean it to hurt, but he couldn't know—

Her eyes flooded, and she hurried looked away, but it was too late. He saw. He *understood.*

"Oh, lass— oh, Wen, I didnae mean— oh—"

Of course she'd been pregnant once. And of course, she'd failed to stay pregnant past three months. Her womb was as defective as the rest of her. Or her eggs. Or her DNA.

She couldn't even perform the natural functions of pregnancy and childbirth right. How the hell was she supposed to be this magical moon priestess?

Maybe she was better off alone. At least she didn't cry every damn day when no one was around to stir up her past.

"Dex!"

"I'm on the— oh, shite, mate, I'll have to ring you back." Just like that, he was there before her, squashed up against Callum, big hands clasping both of theirs in his. "What? My lady, what happened? Callum?"

"I fooked up," Callum almost moaned, trying to stroke her hands but unwilling to let them go. "I didnae mean to, but I opened my goddamn mouth and shite poured out. Fix it, Dex, please. Milady, I didnae mean to make you cry!"

"Wen, *Wen,* please talk to us."

But she was beyond speech. She was crying again, stupidly, and she couldn't stop. It hadn't even really been a baby at that point, just a tiny clump of genderless cells, no organs or hands or eyes. She'd tried to remind herself over the years that she hadn't lost a baby. Her body had simply flushed out a defective zygote that didn't have a chance. It was probably a good thing, given her marriage.

But it would've been a Zoe if it had been a girl. Ben for a boy. Not Benjamin, just Ben.

"I'm sorry, lass. I'm so sorry." Almost crying himself, Callum closed his eyes and shook his head. "I told her about how Sister Moon wouldnae take a mum away from her bairns. I just meant to say that none o' this is sudden, that the magic chose her long ago and has been preparin her right along, but—"

Great. Now Dex understood, too. His eyes, so warm and safe, locked with her teary ones until she jerked her head around, unable to meet those beautiful, sympathetic eyes for long. A sob caught in her chest, hurting her lungs, her heart.

Little Zoe or Ben would have been seven years old by now. Her marriage had already been over by that awful, heartsick time, but she could've at least had something wonderful from it.

Dex didn't try to talk her out of her tears. He merely scooted to her side and rose to his knees to hold her close, gently, safe in his arms. Callum did the same on the other side, holding her between them like they had before. It didn't feel better. Not yet.

But she appreciated the gesture. She appreciated even more that they hadn't tried to tell her that it didn't matter to them. It was okay. These things just happen sometimes.

It *should* matter. It *wasn't* okay and never would be. And the process being natural didn't make it hurt any less. She'd heard all the platitudes. None of them had filled the hole in her life where her child should have been. None of them made her feel less of a failure.

"We're here, Wen." Dex's honey voice, his hand stroking her hair, his arms around her. "We're here for you. You're not alone."

Callum's soft burr, nearly a whisper. "We're here, lass. We're no' lettin go."

So, for the second time since they'd all met so strangely, they all huddled together and tried to pretend everything was alright.

It wasn't. But maybe it didn't have to be. Maybe it just had to keep going.

It was Callum's turn to snuggle up to her back in bed, and Wen still wasn't sure how to feel about it. On one hand: cuddly hard-body who wanted nothing more than to hold her close and protect her. On the other hand: *awkward*.

But after her crying fit that afternoon, a subdued dinner of mouth-watering lasagna, wine, garlic bread, and Caesar salad, and a long and thankfully uneventful evening trying not to think about things, it was rather nice to simply be held while she couldn't help but think about things.

Think about little Zoe. Or Ben. Think about how excited and happy she'd been. Think about how excited and happy Tucker *hadn't* been.

Think about the fact that, if little Zoe or Ben had lived, she couldn't be a Sister of the Moon. Had that so-called destiny killed her baby? Was that a fair way to look at the situation?

She didn't know. Callum said the magic chose her, that it had been working to bring her to Light for a long time. Had it reached into her womb and stopped the life growing there so she could be free to up and move back to Oregon? Because if so... fuck that.

Fuck all of that.

She wouldn't do it. Nothing and no one could make her.

She looked toward the one, tiny window in her shitty little apartment, scowling and not trying to hide it in the dark. She'd never really noticed the ring of light around it from where the curtains didn't fully block out the world. Or maybe it was only that bright tonight because the moon was almost full.

Gritting her teeth, she carefully wormed herself out of Callum's warm grasp and slipped out of bed. Dex wasn't lying at her feet—he'd sacked out in the recliner again—so she didn't have to worry about stepping on him. She just needed a minute.

A little chat.

Moving as quietly as she could, she turned the lock, then the doorknob. The door let loose of the threshold with a *sssshhk!* sound she couldn't help, but neither of the guys so much as twitched. She wasn't leaving. She was just going outside at night to stand in the moonlight and have her say.

She tried leaning over the railing around her little stoop, but that didn't feel right. She needed to stand free, feet bare in the cold grass, head thrown back. She didn't know why, but she assumed Sister Moon was pulling her again and went with it, angrier by the second.

Her bare feet made no sound on the metal risers as she hurried down them. Then cold, gritty concrete, and then she stood in the grass, ankles tickled by a light, chilly breeze, the world around her bathed in cool, delicious moonlight. Gritting her teeth, she looked up at that nearly-full eye in the darkness and let her anger and loss fill her.

"How dare you," she whispered, not wanting to be disturbed by someone calling the cops on the crazy lady howling up at the moon. "How *dare* you."

The moon looked down at her, unblinking, unresponsive.

"Did you kill my baby so I could serve you?"

Silence. Cool light, soothing when she didn't want to be soothed.

"Because if Zoe had to die for me to be a fucking moon princess, I'll fucking pass. Understand? I won't take that bargain, even seven years too late."

That cool, unblinking eye shone down on her, bathing her skin in its soft, lustrous glow. Tears filled her eyes, and she could see the moon's reflection on their surface before they trickled down her cheeks. And she felt something tight and clenched like a fist in her heart... release.

That light was so unlike the harsh light of the sun. Daylight revealed, burned, demanded. But the moon's glow cajoled instead of insisted. It was made for dapples of shadow where anything could happen, good or bad. It didn't burn but soothed, healed, softened.

"I'm sorry." She lowered her head, hugging her arms around herself. "I don't know what to think anymore. I just want—"

Her breath hiccupped, but she was done sobbing. She couldn't stop a tear or two, but she couldn't bear the hiccups and gasps and cries. She just couldn't.

Closing her eyes, she whispered the only truth she still understood.

"I just want to be happy. Please."

A flash of her little cove, the stacks in the inlet, the sea beyond, as far as the eye could see. The whales. The less definable creatures below the surface that wanted to swim with her. The moon above, shining that forgiving, comforting, soothing light down on her naked body and not caring about the plump or saggy places because She was the only one looking. And She loved what She saw.

The tears dried on her cheeks. The pain in her heart lessened to a more bearable ache. She wasn't sure that ache would ever fully go away, but maybe she could make room for it instead of trying to squash it deep down inside her. Maybe if she could bring it into the moonlight instead of clenching it deep inside, it, too, would heal in time. A scar rather than an infected wound.

As if a storm had passed, she opened her eyes and looked around in wonder, vaguely surprised that she wasn't standing on a silent, empty coastline in Oregon. She felt prickly, close-cropped grass under her feet instead of rough sea oats scratching against her legs. The scene had been so real she could almost have reached down to touch the long blades, could have cut a finger on their sharp edges.

    Another vision. A quiet vision of her alone, but unafraid and unabandoned. She was alone because she chose to be, because she was safe in her sheltered cove, and the night and the sea awaited her. She suddenly felt like she could swim out into the very depths of the ocean without ever running out of air or being eaten by a predator.

    Was that a vision, too, or just a moonlight fantasy?

    Did that matter?

    She decided it didn't. She also decided that Sister Moon hadn't demanded a sacrifice of her but had only known what it had meant to her and ached for her loss, as well. That it made her able to serve was a sad side effect, not the cause.

    And that was okay. The storm had passed.

    Wendolyn Eudora Cheney was ready to serve.

9

She should've known she couldn't sneak out from under two shapeshifters intent on protecting her without them knowing. Luckily, they weren't mad at her.

Callum, scrambling eggs and shooing Dex away from the thick, ham-like bacon, merely shrugged when she asked why they hadn't stopped her if they were so worried about her safety.

"Why would we try to keep you from Sister Moon? She clearly had a message. We knew you needed to speak with Her."

And that was that. She logged into her workstation for about an hour, but Clare must be taking it easy on her because she didn't have any new billing to enter. Bored, she signed back out with an email to her boss to text her if something for her to do came up.

So, for the first time in recent memory, Wen sat down in her recliner with a book and just... read. Dex brought her tea, brought her elevensies, roused her for lunch. Callum left briefly after lunch and returned with three throw blankets—one Sherpa-style with the fuzzy under layer, one crocheted with tassels, and one a fuzzy flannel. He draped the tasseled one over her legs, and she smiled up at him with simple bliss. She was warm, comforted, entertained, and some of the constant ache inside her seemed to have subsided in the night.

What could be better?

Her cell phone rang, so she put aside her book and looked at the unfamiliar number, unsure if she should answer or not.

"It's Brigid, milady." Callum looked a bit sheepish. "She asked for your number so she could ring you directly, and you lot got on so well yesterday—?"

She grinned. "It's totally fine. I'm glad we have each other's numbers now. Thank you." She quickly swiped. "Hello? Brigid?"

"Wendolyn, m'love, I have very, very interestin news."

She'd been reaching for her teacup, but she paused. "Good news? Bad news?"

Brigid lowered her voice to a dramatic whisper. "Thea just rang me. She wants a meet."

She blinked. "That's unusual, right? I mean, I guess I got the impression she's a bit of a recluse."

Like me, she thought, *but voluntarily.* But she wasn't so much the recluse these days, was she?

"Ye guessed right, love." Still whispering, Brigid couldn't mask her excitement. "I've barely heard from her in all me years in the Light, and here, up ye pop, and she's askin for the same as you: a visit to me humble abode."

Wen wanted to snicker at the idea of a castle fortress being a humble abode, but she didn't want to hurt Brigid's feelings in case she wasn't joking. Instead, she gasped a bit.

"She wants to come to you? That can't be a coincidence, right?"

"I think no!." Finally returning to a more normal—but still quiet and intimate—tone of voice, Brigid hmmed. "Mayhap she wants to meet our new Sister and somehow knows we've already spoken and considers me neutral territory?"

She tilted her head one way, then the other. "Maybe so. You'd know better than me. Maybe she's had a vision, like I have? Have you been having visions lately?"

"Nary a one, love, but I've never had any magic that wasnae linked to me Nightwatchers. I heard once that Thea had some active magic, but no one knows for sure. None of the uncalled shifters or normal humans know more than the basics of our heritage to tell of it."

"This is all so weird. It feels like too many things are happening at once."

"Aye, it does." Brigid huffed. "For decades, the world only spins on, and now, in less than a week, all o' this. It cannae be a coincidence. Ye're right about that, love."

She mulled it all over for a moment, but there was really only one thing to do.

"When does she want to meet?"

Brigid rummaged around for a moment, and Wen suddenly realized that she should probably get some sort of planner if she was about to be thrown into a bunch of moon duty travel. She got up and went to her desk for the next best thing: her work calendar. She'd see if Callum would be so kind as to grab her something suitable the next time he was out.

For now, she signed in and opened her calendar just as Brigid found whatever she'd been rooting around for.

"Right, then. I dunno how soon ye were plannin to visit, but I reckon sooner than later now, aye?"

"Yeah." She considered, then turned to Dex, the make-things-happen guy, according to Callum. "How long would it take us to get to Scotland, given that I don't have a passport so we can't just book a flight?"

He didn't even pause to think. "We can have you there tomorrow night, provided you're free to leave as soon as possible. There's a time difference, of course, so if you're prone to jetlag, you mightn't want to schedule anything important right away."

Brigid, apparently hearing just fine, though Wen had forgotten to put her on speaker—which she did now—hmmed. "How's about ye get here as soon as ye can, and we'll plan a quiet day to for ye to rest, then have the meet with Thea the day after?"

She looked at the boys who looked at each other and nodded.

Dex took out his phone, already on the job. "It will be so, my lady."

As soon as he headed back into the bathroom, likely so he could close the door and be undistracted while he set everything up, Callum snickered. "He's so formal."

Brigid snorted. "Aye, mate, and ye've never had the proper respect for schedulin and plannin that lad has always been aces at."

"Oi, donnae start," he grumbled.

Before they could get distracted, Wen smirked and turned off the speaker, putting the phone back to her ear. "They really are a bag of cats, aren't they?"

"That they are, m'love." Brigid chuckled softly. "Now, Wen, promise me ye wonnae wear yourself to flinders to get here so fast, aye? I heard that ye donnae have a passport, so ye're no' used to travel like this. Water and rest, love. And let the lads take care o' ye."

Surprised and warmed by the concern, Wen melted. "Oh, Brigid, you're really so kind. I don't even know what to say."

"Say ye'll be safe," she responded, a smile in her voice. "And I'll say I'll ring Thea back and give her the good news. The first meet of Sisters in— bloody hell, lass, I donnae even ken!"

"It feels big, doesn't it?" She lowered her voice again, though Callum had already turned to going through her tiny dresser's drawers, like to see what needed packing. "It feels like something's been building. The visions, the sudden trip?"

"It does indeed. I feel somethin in the wind." Her voice also lowered, Brigid sighed. "I dunno if it's good or ill buildin to a storm, but somethin is stirrin, sure'n as we're bletherin right now. Which is why I want ye to be ever so careful, darlin Wen. Get to me safely, aye? And ye'll have a glad welcome waitin."

She smiled, both excited and feeling so cared for. "And tea."

"Oh, aye. Never greet an honored loved one without a pot."

She chuckled, and they said their goodbyes. Callum gave her a look from her dingy little bed area, and some of the good feelings faded. That wasn't a happy look.

"Is this really all you have, then?"

She blushed, trying not to feel defensive. "I don't get out much, so I don't need much."

He sighed, looking at her with sympathy. "Ah, lass, how much you go out has nothin to do with how much you need." He shook his head down at the half-empty drawers. "Mayhap we'll have a wee shoppin trip before we hop Dex's plane."

She blinked. "Dex has a plane?"

"Oi, lass, 'twas a figure of speech." But Callum was grinning with dimples, so he wasn't really exasperated. "But shoppin is in order. What have you always wanted to wear, lass, that you didnae think you could pull off?"

Oh. She was not prepared for that question. She'd never pictured herself in anything but pajamas and jeans. She wasn't sure she even owned a skirt, or would ever wear it if she did.

What *would* she wear if she thought she could?

"Ah, lass." He shook his head and twined his arm through hers to lead her back over to her chair and book and tea. "Here, you go back to readin, aye? Just let it run in the back o' your mind, and let us hammer out some details. When we're all sorted, we'll take a wee trip to the nearest mall and see what you like."

The mall. Everything in her clenched up. Her shoulders jerked up, her hands fisting. Was there ever a more terrifying or mortifying place to go than the mall? Teenagers and pretty people and old folk walking out of the weather and too much noise and too much light and—

"Wen? Wen!" He knelt in front of her, taking her hands in his. "Lass, I didnae mean to worrit you. We donnae have to go, aye? 'Twas just a fancy of mine to kit you out how you always wanted. What you have is more than enough for a wee jaunt, aye? Wen? Milady?"

She managed a tight breath, then a slightly looser one. Her shoulders inched down. He wouldn't make her go. She could say no. They'd both listen to her if she said no.

"There you are, lass." He stroked the backs of her hands with his thumbs, leaning up against her knees. "Had me worrit there for a bit. I didnae think about the mall being such a busy place, aye? We can always hit a few wee specialty stores instead. That might be less stressful."

"No." She managed one word. She could surely manage more. "No, you're right. The mall is smarter. Everything in one place."

Everyone in one place. Horrible over-lighting. Overwhelming people smells. So much noise.

She swallowed hard. "We'll hit a mall." She couldn't manage a grin, but she tried to at least soften her expression. "Maybe a little one."

His grin broke out like a sunrise, and he chuckled. "That's the spirit, lass. And we'll be there with you every step, aye? You wonnae be alone."

No, she wouldn't. That helped immensely, and her shoulders went back down to their usual level.

"Another spot o' tea?"

"Please."

He gave her hands a little squeeze, then stood away and took the tray with him. She picked up the cup she'd been savoring when Brigid called and cradled it between her hands. It still held a hint of warmth. She took a steadying sip and closed her eyes.

What would she want if she didn't care what she looked like? Nothing tight, she knew for sure. She'd always hated tight clothing. It just made her feel wrapped up in a sausage casing. Some people could pull off such a look and be amazing, but she was not one of them. She lacked the confidence.

So, loose things. Sweaters? Perhaps. Skirts? Maybe, though she didn't see herself in mermaid tails or pencil skirts. Maybe something flowy? Loose and flowy? A kaftan, maybe? A mumu?

Robes?

She just didn't now. She rather liked pantsuits—her idols were Hillary Rodham-Clinton and Michelle Obama, who could rock a pantsuit like goddesses themselves—but slacks never looked good on her. They always showed how over-round her thighs were, and her calves were too thick for them to hang properly.

No pantsuits. She'd stick to admiring them from afar.

What did a Sister of the Moon wear? She was tempted to call Brigid back and ask what she favored, but her new sister had specifically told her to rest and hydrate, not worry.

What would Thea be wearing? Callum—or was it Dex?—had said her fortress was more like a hippie commune. Would that suit her better? Especially given how excited Dex was about turning Wen's fortress into a fantasy garden?

Loose, flowy dresses. If she were tall and willowy, she could pull those off, but—

No. Callum asked what she'd always wanted to wear but thought she couldn't. If she wanted to try on some loose and flowy hippie dresses, that surely couldn't hurt. Not like she *had* to buy any.

And she'd always wished she could wear tights, but they never stretched horizontally enough for her fat legs. It was so frustrating. She wanted to wear tights and high boots, but her legs—

No. It didn't matter if she thought she couldn't. Callum said so. And again, it couldn't hurt to try.

Besides, Clare had said many times that she'd given up on tights years ago and only bought leggings now. Plus size leggings were not like tights, and they had all sorts of patterns and designs. Maybe she could try those. And maybe Callum would know where to find boots with bigger calves. He seemed to be pretty fond of shopping, actually. Maybe he already had someplace in mind.

So she could try some loose, flowy dresses. She could try patterned leggings and tall boots with tunic shirts. She could try some hippie skirts with ruffled edges. Oh, and those wide-leg pants that almost looked like skirts. She could try some of those.

And a cloak. A Sister of the Moon should surely have a cloak. Did anyone even make cloaks anymore? Would a mall have a store with cloaks? She'd have to ask Callum. Or maybe she could order one? Surely Amazon had cloaks.

She felt an image bloom in her mind and realized she was having a vision as it happened. She stood in an open space, trees all around, darkness hovering in the depth of the forest but moonlight shining softly all around the clearing. No, she didn't stand on the *clearing*. That wasn't grass under her feet but some sort of smooth stone.

She looked down at a round stone-tiled floor inlaid with three spirals around a central opening for a fire pit. A cauldron—an actual kettle-black cauldron—stood on a metalwork stand over merrily crackling flames, smoke wisping upward, smelling of herbs and burning. It was a beguiling smell, and she followed the trail of smoke up with her gaze, only to realize she wasn't just on a tile circle but in something of an arbor. Metalwork formed a curlicue design overhead, spirals and circles chasing each other around the top edges. The top was completely open, and the brilliant, full moon—so close she felt like she could touch it—hung in the very center of that opening.

It wasn't an arbor. It was... a temple, perhaps. A place for worship or communing or even just for soaking up the moon's glow on her skin. For dancing in that light with her Sisters. Maybe even with her Nightwatchers, if she ever felt comfortable enough with them.

She wore only a sleeveless white shift in that pale glow, flowing in a light breeze around her otherwise naked body. The fabric felt like the finest silk, gauzy and billowy, cool and loose. It made her feel... special. Beautiful, even. The material didn't cling to her rolls but flowed gently around her, accenting her curves without feeling at all constrictive.

She felt like a moon priestess. And she very much liked it.

Wen opened her eyes, and both Dex and Callum sat back on their heels before her, watching her patiently as she... visioned. She needed to think of a better term for that. Maybe Brigid or Thea knew what to call it when she went off into a daydream that wasn't her own.

"My lady?"

"Lass?"

She smiled at them, reaching out to them for the first time before they could reach out to her.

"Guys? I think I know what I want."

Both her boys smiled and clasped her offered hands.

10

Apparently, taking a last-minute trip halfway around the world, a whirlwind shopping trip, and packing an entire apartment up because she probably wouldn't be coming back to it was nothing as long as she had two burly menfolk ready and willing to do all the hard stuff and make all the arrangements. Including finding poor Roger a safe spot in the airport's long-term parking lot so he'd still be there, unharmed, when they returned.

Wen, on the other hand, had little to do besides read, sip tea, and even take a nap, as she'd promised Brigid. Her hardest task had been emailing her boss, Clare, and explaining that, due to unforeseen circumstances, she'd be leaving the country for a few days and probably wouldn't be able to remote in from another country.

Her phone rang almost instantly.

"Wen, are you alright? Seriously, I asked before, but now I'm serious. I'm worried. If you're in trouble but can't say, just say something clever like 'no thank you, I don't want to buy a mattress today' or something, okay?"

She burst out laughing, but immediately felt bad. "I'm sorry, Clare. I'm fine, I promise. Things have just been happening at warp speed these past couple of days, and I'm running to keep up."

Clare huffed. "But why are you leaving the *country?* How can you even do that so fast? Do you even have a passport?"

Settling back in her recliner, she grinned. "Unfortunately, I really can't explain. Just know that I'm going of my own free will, and I'm excited as hell about it. Just... it's a bit sudden, so I couldn't give you the advance notice I would rather have given you."

A pause, then: "You're not coming back, are you? This isn't just for a few days."

Biting her lip, she considered fibbing the slightest bit, then remembered she couldn't act her way out of a wet paper bag. "To the country? Yes. But I don't think I'll be coming back to Missouri, no."

"Seriously, Wen, what is going on? I'm really worried about you."

Not about her ditching work but about *her.* About *Wen.* She hadn't realized Clare even knew her well enough to care other than about filling an office seat. It was... nice.

But, conversely, it made Wen feel worse about having to leave so quickly.

"Thank you, Clare." She felt a little overwhelmed, actually. "That means so much to me. I can't even tell you. But I promise, I'm okay." Maybe she *could* tell her boss a little, just to set her mind at ease. "If it helps, after I take this trip, I'm going back to grad school to get the degree I've always wanted. I'm moving to the state that felt more like home than Missouri ever has, even though I was born here. I swear, it's an opportunity, not a— not something dangerous."

Okay, that last part might not be entirely true, but she hadn't been threatened by anything but her own emotions yet, so it wasn't entirely false, either. And it seemed to set Clare's mind at ease.

"Wow, Wen. That all sounds pretty amazing. I'm actually kind of jealous and wish I could go with you." She sounded much less concerned, so Wen must have finally said something right. "I hate to ask again, but *did* a family member die or something? This is all so sudden."

She considered latching onto that, then remembered again how terrible a liar she was. "Not exactly. It's more— I've been handed a chance to live my dreams, and this time, I'm taking it."

And that was the strict and utter truth. She had a chance at a future of which she'd never dared to dream. All she had to do was keep stepping off that cliff and trust that her little yappy dog—or her black dog and apparently-too-big-for-her-apartment war horse—would tell her when it was time to stop.

"Good for you."

The vehemence in Clare's tone surprised her.

"I mean it, Wen. You deserve better than what you've been given. I know I don't know even half of the details, but I know a 'that man tried to ruin my life' story without having to hear the whole thing, and you deserve better than that."

Warm fuzzies assailed her, and she wondered if, perhaps, in leaving the state of Missouri, she might have finally made a friend here. And if that was a bad thing. It wasn't like she was planning to come back, now that she'd cut this final tie. Now, she could just let the contract on her apartment run out—there were only two more months, anyway, and she didn't mind paying two months' rent to avoid the penalty fees of breaking contract—and... go.

Just go.

Just one more thing to say. "Hey, Clare?"

"Yes?"

"Thank you." She smiled, hoping it would make its way into her voice. "You've been a great boss, and you're being a great friend right now. I just want you to know how much I appreciate you."

"Wen, I'm touched." She sounded it, too. "Be careful out there, okay? I wish you nothing but the best of luck."

"You too, Clare. Thank you."

"I guess this is goodbye?"

She nodded, wondering if she would puddle up again and relieved when her eyes didn't prickle. "Yeah, I guess it is. Goodbye, Clare."

"Goodbye, Wen."

She sat and stared at her phone for a long moment, then looked for the guys. They were, as usual, clustered in the little kitchen area, trying to give her privacy, but when she put down her phone and reached for them, they came to her with smiles and wrapped their warm arms around her. She hugged back.

It was just the three of them now. Come what may.

"That one."

She looked at herself in the full-length mirror, trying to see what Dex apparently saw while Callum rummaged around for more clothes for her to try on. They'd already been to five stores and bought more clothes than she'd ever owned in her life, and she was fretting—against orders—over prices and spending too much when they were blowing coin on a sudden trip to Scotland and how much they had to put down in earnest money to even stake a claim on what she already considered her land and—

She had, however, found pantsuits she liked after all. They were flowy, loose linen with tunic tops and drapey vest-like covers rather than tailored wool, but she was happy, just the same.

Callum, though, wasn't satisfied yet. Apparently, he was a shopaholic. Dex just shook his head and followed the sound of Scottish exclamations, pulling Wen along with him.

But now she stood in front of mirror in a silky, lacy, flowy nightgown and peignoir of deep, ocean-in-the-moonlight teal, wondering what he could possibly see that made him speak up with such finality when it was usually Callum making such aesthetic assessments.

"It brings out your eyes. Makes your hair practically glow. It suits you."

Her eyes? Her hair? She tilted her head, eyeing them critically, not seeing a difference. "My eyes are gray. So's my hair. Boring. I don't really see a difference."

He stepped closer, standing beside her in the mirror. "Trust me. It suits you."

She couldn't help but compare herself—dowdy, white-haired, plain, plump (if she were being kind)—to Dex's six-foot-two of muscle and gorgeous dreads and beautiful, glowing eyes. He looked like a fashion model, despite the usual faded black t-shirt, charcoal jeans, and serviceable black boots. He looked like a dream.

She looked like a middle-aged fat lady in a borrowed nightgown that she'd probably only borrowed because she'd spilled something on her own footie pajamas.

Callum reappeared, muttering to himself, with more night clothes laid over both arms—including something white and floaty that struck a chord within her from the vision she'd had—then came to a sudden stop. "Oh, aye, lass. That one for sure."

"See?" Dex put an arm around her waist and pulled her close. "It suits you."

She still didn't see it, but she was beyond understanding what her boys—her Nightwatchers, she reminded herself—

thought looked good on her at this point. Callum brought her things seemingly at random, always seeming to know just her size. He must have looked at all the tags on her clothes at home, because nothing he'd brought her had yet been too tight or too form-fitting. Nothing uncomfortable.

So, she shrugged and went with the flow, as she'd been trying to do since this excursion began. She'd almost had a panic attack when Dex pulled Roger into the parking lot and she saw all the cars stacked back as far as the eye could see. Too many people. She wouldn't be able to—

"D'you look to see if there's a tea shop in this mall, mate?"

Callum. Saving her from herself again.

"There's a Starbucks. It's the best I could do." Dex, the planner.

"Starbucks? Mate, that's no' a tea shop."

"They have hot tea drinks. I thought a London Fog would suit my lady nicely. It's Earl Grey. She likes Earl Grey."

She did, indeed. As long as it wasn't coffee, she'd trust them to get her something nice, though she couldn't remember the last time she'd been in a Starbucks. She didn't even know they had tea.

But their bickering had got her into the mall and through the first store, and she finally calmed down enough with a bodyguard on either side of her to not feel a migraine coming on each time they had to leave a store and rejoin the shifting mass of humanity in the main aisles. And now, they'd even convinced her to try on lingerie.

Nothing skimpy, though. Callum knew better than to present her with something skimpy. She was nowhere near ready for flashing skin.

Once they'd talked her into at least a week's worth of nightclothes that didn't classify as onesies—she comforted herself that she did have footies at home, and she had insisted Callum pack them along with everything else—they stopped for the promised afternoon tea near the food court Starbucks. Callum ran out yet another load of bags to stow in Roger's trunk while Dex led her to a corner table far away from most of the crowd. There was no way to be completely private, but there was at least a buffer of a few tables between them and the nearest other mall-goers.

"Are you feeling well, my lady?"

Dex, ever the gentleman, sat her down and scooted her closer to the table before choosing the seat next to her and sitting down himself. He unwrapped scones and croissants and a meat and cheese tray they'd also picked up in the coffee shop while she sniffed at the little hole in her cup's lid. It definitely smelled like Earl Grey. And steamed milk. And... vanilla? Something floral?

But the barista had said to let it steep a few minutes before drinking, so she dutifully put the cup down on the table and looked at all the goodies her boys—Nightwatchers—had provided. Any other clothes-shopping trip would've had her vowing to diet for a year so she could actually fit into something from a "normal" store. This time, though, Callum had made sure she only tried on clothes that *would* fit, and it made all the difference in the world.

Besides, those butter croissants looked amazing and smelled even better. She chose one and sat back to wait for her tea and for Callum, and to hell with the calories.

And then she remembered that Dex had asked her something.

"Yeah, I'm okay. Little tired. Might be getting a headache, but I brought my migraine meds, just in case."

Dex frowned. "Do you get migraines often, then?"

She shrugged, picking at the top layer and unrolling it a bit. "Sometimes. Sometimes, I'll go weeks without getting a single one. Other times, it's like I have a headache all day, every day, and they build into migraines off and on for, like, a week. More, sometimes."

His frown deepened. "That sounds awful. You do have medication for them, though?"

She nodded and made a mental note that she'd need to find a new doctor when they moved to Oregon. She couldn't go too long without her migraine meds or she might just lose her mind. The worst one she'd ever had left her bed-bound for three days, severely dehydrated, and down five pounds because she couldn't even get up to eat. The postdrome of that one had lasted over a week, and she'd honestly worried at several points that she'd had a stroke or grown a brain tumor and would die any minute.

She never wanted to feel that way again. Would being a Sister of the Moon help slow the migraines down? Was that a possibility? Even if it just meant spending less time in punishing sunlight?

Callum strolled toward the table, pink-cheeked from the brisk November wind outside, and Wen abruptly realized that several women—and some men—were drinking him up with their eyes. It occurred to her, too, that the changing room lady at the sleepwear store had been awfully keen on helping Dex with anything he might need. *Anything.*

She was with two men who, between them, drew every eye. She was, by no means, used to their handsome looks or their impressive physiques, but she already knew them well enough to look past that to the men they truly were. Their kindness, their good hearts. Callum's shopping bug and brash sense of humor. Dex's quick mind and warmth, his instinctive knowledge of when to reach out and comfort her with a simple touch. Callum's cooking. Dex's would-be gardening.

Their silly bickering that kept her endlessly entertained.

And maybe, just this once, she might let herself feel the slightest bit proud that they were here with her. She may be a frumpy nobody, but they sat at her side like they never wanted to be anywhere else, and they thought she looked pretty in teal silk and lace, and they paid no mind to any of the hungry looks cast their way.

They were here with *her*.

So, when she caught a pair of pretty twenty-somethings switching their attention between the men and Dowdy Wen, she only locked eyes with one of them, lifted her cup to her mouth, and took a sip. Then, she looked away.

It wasn't a big gesture. The girls probably wouldn't gasp or be offended by some cougar giving them the cold shoulder for staring at her young men—not that the situation was anything like that. Not that either of the men with her were even young. But it felt good to tell herself she didn't care what those two nubile, lithe, good-looking girls thought.

Whether it was true or not.

"Well done, my lady," Dex whispered, leaning close to her ear. His warm breath tickled the fine hairs there, giving her a shiver.

"What's all this, then?" Callum asked, pulling out the chair at her other side and flipping it backwards to straddle it. "What'd I miss?"

But Dex only smiled at her as he sat back more comfortably in his chair. "Poise and courage, mate. That's all."

Callum raised an eyebrow, then looked around to see what the fuss was about. He apparently spotted the two girls, for he grinned crookedly, then leaned in to whisper in Wen's ear, as well.

"They donnae have the eyes for deep-sea teal silk, lass. Nor are they flowin with magic, like the light on your hair in that nightie."

Her cheeks heated, as he likely intended, given his dimpled smirk as he pulled away. These guys. Her Nightwatchers.

Defending her even just against a pair of tweeny mallrats. How had she lived without them before now?

Oh, right. She really hadn't. She wouldn't have been able to get past the mall parking lot without them.

"Now then, lass," Callum said, returning to his usual bluff attitude and stowing the flirtation, thankfully. "Was there anythin else you specifically wanted to try? You've been a good sport, but sure'n there's somethin you've a yen for yourself?"

She did, actually, but she didn't know if it would be possible. So, picking at her croissant, she shifted in her seat. "I thought I might like to try... some knee boots with those leggings you found. But my calves—?"

To her surprise, Callum only nodded. "I know just the place."

Her eyebrows rose. "How on earth—?"

He grinned with dimples. "Dex isnae the only planner of the lot. I've my ways, don' I?"

But Dex only grunted. "He memorized the mall map before we left the flat. He didn't want you worrying about wandering around, trying to find things."

She melted. That was so much sweeter than anything she could imagine. She reached out and touched his hand.

"Callum. Thank you."

His eyes widened, but he nodded, his face reddening. "It's my honor, milady."

Dex touched her hand, and it was as if he'd completed a circuit. "Our honor, my lady."

She felt so connected. Whole in a way she'd never felt with Tucker. These men, without ever having touched her in a sexual way, made her feel more wanted and loved than her own husband had in twenty years of marriage.

She didn't know what to do with such a complete feeling. So, for now, she put it aside. No way could she deal with treacherous emotions in public. She had a hard enough time in private.

Instead, she dug into the croissant and let herself forget about the twenty-somethings watching them. The London Fog, as Dex had called it, was delicious, sweet and somehow floral while still tasting obviously of Earl Grey. Dex promised to learn how to make it the same way so she could have it any time she wanted.

And then the shoe store. She hated shoe stores. She hated that the store people wanted to "help" her into and out of shoes that may or may not fit, touching her never-once-pedicured hobbit feet. She hated trying things on.

But her old tennis shoes were worn through in patches, and the left one had the nagging tendency to come untied despite her best efforts. She'd even double-knotted them once, but then couldn't get back out of them and was too embarrassed to try again.

She hesitated on the threshold of the store, though her shoulders rose at the idea of leaving her back open to the mass of humanity moving behind her. Dex and Callum both took a step further but immediately stopped and came back to her. They didn't say anything. Just waited for her to be sure.

Swallowing, she stepped inside The Dreaded Shoe Store.

No associates rushed over to demand what sort of shoe she was looking for. No one looked at them at all, in fact, though the three workers she could see surely noticed two men such as hers walking into their store.

Her eyes narrowed, and she looked at Callum to her right. "What did you do?"

But he only smiled, dimples digging deep, and threaded his arm through hers, leading her toward the back of the store where all the boots were stashed. Dex, without missing a step, went directly to a pair and ran a thumb down the line of boxes until he found a size he approved of. He passed it off to Callum, then moved to another pair, doing much the same. Another.

Had— had they studied ahead of time? When? Maybe they'd

shopped online while she'd been distracted with debating what to pack and what to put in storage (like one of Mama's quilts to come with her, the others left in storage, though wrapped up in sachet to keep them safe).

But *why?*

Callum sat her down on one of the ugly upholstered chairs, then knelt at her feet and reached out a hand, palm up. She blinked for a moment, then understood.

Only if she was okay with it. He wouldn't touch her without her okay, even just to help her try on a boot.

Touched in a completely different, non-physical way, she managed a wobbly smile and dutifully lifted her foot up. Her awful hobbit foot. Did her sneakers smell? Her socks? She never made a point of scrubbing her feet or trimming her toenails, though she obviously washed them regularly. What if—

But he only stripped off her gross old tennis shoe, leaving her sock in place. Cupping her heel gently in his big hand, he eased one black boot onto her foot, then eased her jeans up over her calf to pull the shaft into place and zip it.

It fit.

It *fit.*

The shaft of the boot didn't cut into the top of her calf. She didn't feel like her leg was in a sausage casing. The foot part itself was perhaps a little too roomy, but... the boot *fit.*

And it finally hit her. They hadn't just shopped ahead. They'd made sure this store had boots that fit her so she wouldn't be upset or feel bad about herself. They'd done so all day, but for some reason, with her foot and calf literally in Callum's hands, it suddenly meant so much more.

I will not cry in public. I cannot cry in public!

Firming her lips so they wouldn't quiver and betray her, she forced herself to speak up, even if just in a whisper. "The foot part's a little big. I can tell just sitting here."

He smiled. "Well, then. Shall we try a size down, or d'you like these others better?"

She closed her eyes and thanked whoever was listening—Sister Moon, perhaps—for sending her these Nightwatchers. These specific ones. She wasn't sure she even wanted anymore when she had two such wonderful friends at her side already.

Then, she smiled and said, "Do they have any in brown?"

11

Wen was exhausted. It was only seven in the evening, and they hadn't even started the actual trip yet, but the mall had exhausted her despite all of her Nightwatchers' careful plotting. Luckily, they'd also planned for just such an eventuality and had made sure the private jet had a bed berth where she could sleep away as much of the trip as she chose.

A private plane. What kind of world was she even living in now? She reclined in luxury on expensive sheets, wearing silk pajamas, pillows piled all around her and Dex and Callum playing paper-rock-scissors for dibs on sleeping at her back. A pot of tea—not her yellow and daisies, unfortunately, as her set was packed safely (wrapped in one of Mama's quilts) in the storage box they'd rented until the move to Oregon—steamed close at hand, a tray of her newly favorite goodies also within reach. They'd even provided her with the book she'd been reading earlier.

Talk about luxury.

And she was going to Scotland. Any minute now, this flying wonder of luxury technology would lift off and carry her to the other side of the planet, where she'd meet Brigid (wonderful) and Thea (intimidating). Her new sisters. Or Sisters. Would she get along with them? Would they like her? Would they hate her timidness and anxiety?

Goddess, had she packed her anxiety meds? Where would she have—

"Your carry-on." Dex, practical as always, as he brought it to her. "What were you looking for?"

Oops. She'd almost climbed out of bed in her worry. She leaned up on her elbow and rooted through the new baggage they'd bought specifically to bring into the cabin, while the rest of her new gear languished in the cargo hold. Her regular meds—migraine and anxiety, ibuprofen for everyday use, and the generic allergy pills she took to keep her sinuses in check pretty much year round—nestled in the back zipper pocket.

She debated not taking one; she already felt better just knowing they were there. But she hadn't flown since coming back from Oregon, and then she'd been trying so hard not to cry and annoy Tucker the entire flight.

She took one of the pills with a sip from the bottle of water Dex offered next. Flying with a migraine would be a special sort of hell, even if she wasn't weeping her heart out this time.

The whine of the engine revved higher still, and the boys moved to their seats to buckle in. She wondered if she should do the same, but where would seatbelts be in a bed? Before she could again reveal her ignorance, the jet taxied forward smoothly and they were on their way, joining the small airport's flow of traffic to the runways.

To Scotland. To Brigid. To Thea. Hell, toward her whole future.

No pressure.

She leaned up on her elbow again, wanting to watch the earth fall away through the little portholes lining the shell of the plane's cabin. Land sped by, rushing away, and then, with a short lurch of weightlessness, they were airborne, and all sensation of motion stopped. The little jet felt as still and solid as the ground; the earth was moving away from them.

Her stomach rolled, and she swallowed hard as she eased back down. The pillow felt cool against her cheek, settling her a bit. She wasn't motion sick, usually. Maybe the nausea was because she was lying down?

"Alright, milady?"

She forced a smile, though she still felt a little green about the gills. "I probably should have sat up all the way if I wanted to watch take-off."

Callum grinned and unbuckled, though the pilot hadn't announced cruising elevation yet. "Where'd that bottle o' water roll off to, then?" He searched around a moment, then found it under her covers where they brushed the floor. "Here, lass. Have a wee nip and you'll feel better."

She did as suggested, and the cool water did settle her stomach. Callum's grin dimpled, and she smiled back much more easily.

"There's your color back. Had me worrit there."

"I'm good now. I haven't been on a plane in—"

"Fifteen years?"

Her grin twisted. "On the nose."

He reached out and ran his fingers into her hair, then pushed a stray strand back behind her ear. She shivered, her expression freezing on her face, but he didn't touch her in any other way.

"Seems as though you've no' been allowed much at all in fifteen years, milady."

His voice was low and not quite teasing. The intent expression on his face wasn't the usual bantering charm, but it wasn't entirely serious, either. She could interpret it several different ways, if she wanted.

She didn't want. Her stomach was still too whoopsie for contemplation. For now, she chose to take the most literal probability and run with it.

"Once he got me back here, Tucker had no intention of letting me spread my wings ever again. He'd worked too hard to clip them."

Surprised at her sudden eloquence, she almost winced at the truth of the words. If only she'd seen it then. If only she'd sent him back to Missouri on his own and stayed on in Oregon. Had that been a possibility at the time, or was that hindsight talking?

Callum didn't seem to have any answers for her. Just that enigmatic little smile that wasn't quite funny and wasn't quite serious.

"He didnae clip your wings, lass." He shook his head, his hazel eyes intense on hers. "He thought he had. *You* thought he had. He wounded you, aye, but he could never break wings as strong as yours forever. You'd have always flown away from him, Wen. Remember that."

She blinked as he touched her hand where she still held the water bottle, then stood up and strolled back to his seat. Where had that come from? What had it even been?

She didn't know. She was tired. Her stomach still felt uneasy. Another sip of water didn't really help, but she told herself it did. She told herself she was just tired.

And she told herself she didn't like that enigmatic little smile.

But oh, sometimes—only to herself—she lied.

"Sure'n it's no' me best work, mates, but at least it's no' airplane food."

She turned away from the window—her face had been practically glued to it for the past hour, watching the world spin by below her—and twisted in her seat to see what the master chef had managed to whip up in a tiny private jet galley. To her surprise, Callum presented her a plate of lasagna, fresh and piping hot, sauce and cheese melting down the sides and spilling out between the layers. She blinked up at him as she accepted the plate, astonished and not bothering to hide it.

He grinned even as he tried to pout. "Only leftovers. It wonnae taste as good as last night, lass. The pressurized air affects your tastebuds, which is why airplane food always tastes so flat, but it'll be still good for all that, aye?"

She grinned and turned around fully to sit properly and unfold the little tray from beside her. It was just big enough for the plate, a fork and knife, and a glass of something. This time, the something was a crisp white wine in a tall flute. Not champagne, he explained with a smirk. That only came from a certain region in France. Everything else was "sparkling white wine".

She rolled her eyes. "Why do I feel like that's just France thumbing their nose at the rest of the world and laughing at us for falling for it?"

Dex grunted, switching his first mouthful over into his cheek. "You're thinking Australians, my lady."

Callum huffed and nodded, then shrugged. "Or the Germans with that town they donnae admit exists that very obviously does." He paused. "Oi, mates, maybe the French *are* just fookin with us."

He rode the wave of chuckles back to the galley, and Dex dug right back into his food with vigor. He wasn't quite as intent and protective as an actual dog would be, but he did tend to shovel as if he thought someone—or something—else would come along and snarf up his portion if he didn't eat it fast enough. Maybe he'd been part of a big family. Litter. No, he'd said shifting didn't run in families.

She tilted her head to one side, still cutting her lasagna into bite-size pieces. "You never have told me about where you come from. Your family or friends, besides Callum, that is." When he looked up from his plate, she grinned. "I feel like I know everything about what you want to be as a Nightwatcher, right down to how many colors of rose bushes you'll plant and in how crazy a tangle. But who *were* you?"

He chewed slowly, and she suddenly worried that she'd somehow offended him. He'd been in multiple wars, by his own admission. Maybe he had PTSD, and that's why he didn't want to talk about his past. Maybe she was being an absolute jerk for asking again when he hadn't answered the first time.

Then, he swallowed and shrugged. "I didn't realize I had dodged the question, truly. I reckon it's because I find my own past so boring that I don't feel it's noteworthy."

She blinked, putting down the knife but not quite ready to use the fork yet. "Dex, you've been in wars that killed hundreds of thousands—even millions—and drove so many others to awful fates for years afterward, and you not only survived but seem to have thrived. How is that boring?"

His mouth quirked on a knowing smirk. "You survived the loss of your mother, an abusive marriage, a tragic miscarriage, and decades of loneliness. Yet you offered us hospitality when we were merely strangers with an unbelievable story to sell you. How is that boring?"

Damn. He had a point. Sort of. But damned if she'd admit it out loud.

"Seriously. If you don't want to talk about it, I get it. Believe me, I do. I'm just curious about you both and if we're going to spend time together for however many years in the future, I think it's a good idea to actually get to know each other."

His smirk softened to his more usual smile. "Fair enough. Although, I warn you, you might wish to lie back down and have a pillow handy in case you fall asleep."

"Ha ha. You're hilarious."

But she grinned and finally took a bite of leftover lasagna. Even on a pressurized jet flying tens of thousands of miles above the Earth's surface, Callum's cooking tasted like heaven.

"Right, then. The life and times of one Decimus Braxton Talmadge. Chapter One. My mother and father owned the only bakery in our little village in the lovely but rugged Peak District countryside. We were simple folk—"

"Dex."

He smirked again. It looked just as good on him as literally any other expression. He just had that kind of face. Beautiful in all weathers.

"Just speaking truth, my lady. My parents were bakers, and they did own the only bakery in the village. They were successful, and I was raised in relative luxury with plenty of freedom. They knew what I was, of course, and they lived in fear that someone would find out and, out of ignorance, try to harm me. My black dog would fight back, no question. It would be a nightmare for everyone involved." He shrugged. "But other than that, nothing interesting ever happened. We truly were simple people with simple lives."

"Time to make the donuts, huh?" She grinned.

"I already made the donuts," he intoned solemnly, then snickered. "Early mornings, yes. Sticky bread-related chores, absolutely. But none of it was terribly interesting."

"Until you went to war at sixteen."

He shook his head and poked his fork at his still half-full plate. "Oh, that was even less interesting. Action-packed, yes. Full of blood and horror. But not interesting in the slightest. Even as an inhuman, I find human suffering the least fascinating topic on Gaia's green and good land. Unlike your fellow humans."

She sighed. "No argument from me. My wildest dream as a kid was to live in an underwater research station, preferably alone, so I could feel like I was a sea creature instead of a mere human. My childhood was bloody 80s action flicks, constant fear about nuclear attacks destroying the world, the end of the Cold War, and more depictions of cocaine use than a kid like me could begin to comprehend."

He burst out laughing. "Perhaps you have exactly the right attitude, after all. That particular decade was lived with the nihilism of a thousand decaying societies' decadence."

She laughed, too, and shook her head. "If nothing else, there had to be some sort of fallout from the sheer amount of coke snorted. How many people my mother's age are walking around with no septum because they sniffed a hole right through it?"

"It doesn't bear thinking about." He shrugged. "But no particular generation has been more or less noble than any other. Mine is known as the Greatest Generation, but were we any less reckless with our lives and others'? Were we any less arrogant about our place in the world? Did we become any less jaded by the death all around us in a war against enemies instead of a war against disease and addiction?"

She started to respond, then paused, mouth open. It took her a moment to gather herself. "Are we really having a philosophical discussion about the cyclical nature of humanity's compulsions and the illogical practice of assigning sweeping generalizations about entire generations of people all across the globe?"

He tipped his fork her way before refilling it. "Of course. What did you think we were doing?"

Eyeing him wryly, she sighed. "Getting to know you."

His wicked smirk twisted his mouth again. "And aren't you so glad you now do?"

She closed her eyes and shook her head. "Hush, you. I'm eating. Can't you tell?"

Still smirking, he played innocent. "Yes, my lady."

"Wen."

"Yes, my lady Wen."

"Jerk."

And they laughed, though the subject of pasts was dropped

in favor of better topics, like how the constant looming threat of world-ending war so frequently led to the urge to party hard and live life to the very hilt.

Light table fare, indeed.

Wen was nervous about landing. Not nervous enough to take another anxiety med, but nervous enough that when Callum moved to sit beside her and take her hand in his, she clenched down hard on that offered hand and clung like he was a lifeline.

She wasn't afraid of crashing. The flight had been uneventful in the best possible way, and she'd long since put her trust squarely on the pilot's shoulders. He seemed experienced, the weather had been excellent for a flight of great length, and everything had gone well.

She was, however, afraid that they'd end up in some turbulence as they drifted down for a landing and she would lose her shit. She hated turbulence. She tried to suck it up and be a big girl because Tucker had hated nothing worse than a sobbing, hysterical woman clinging to him, but the swoops and dips between pockets of air scared the hell out of her. She'd be a fool to try and hide it, but how could she not? The last thing she wanted was to fireball herself out of the little jet the second it touched down and fall face-first onto the tarmac at her new Sisters' feet.

It could happen. She was still wearing her old sneakers with the slippery tie, and she was perhaps the most naturally gifted klutz she'd ever known outside of a slapstick comedy.

Unfortunately, it wasn't as funny when it was *her*.

She just didn't want to make a fool of herself. She didn't want to look gauche. Nor did she want to be the entitled, ignorant American that gave her home country such a bad international name. She didn't have the kind of American dollars that would excuse her from mortifying behavior.

And these two women were important. Important to her own future, but also important to the world. To a whole race of shifters, even if only for the special few that were affected by them directly.

Her Sisters. She'd never had a sister. The thought had been running on a circuit in her head for days now. She wanted loving, supportive sisters that she could gratefully support and love in return. She didn't want snarky, hateful, jealous sisters because she had absolutely nothing worth the jealousy in return. She had nothing either of them could possibly want, except perhaps her Nightwatchers, and they weren't really hers. Not like that, anyway.

Callum's thumb brushed the back of her hand, sliding slowly back and forth in a soothing gesture. It was somewhat effective, but only somewhat. She happened to catch Dex's eye as her own darted around the cabin, looking for... what? A crack in a window that would explosively decompress them? Sharp things flying around the cabin as they thumped down on, hopefully, a runway?

She didn't even know, but her eyes would not stop roaming the jet's interior, searching, restless. Scared.

Until they met Dex's and clung. He radiated warmth and compassion. He may not understand exactly what had her spooked any more than she did herself, but he was there for her. Even sitting across the cabin from her, he was there. Callum was there.

Everything would be fine. She'd lived through a good handful of airplane landings before and likely would again. Nothing to worrit about, as Callum would say.

The airstrip loomed closer and closer, and she tore her eyes away from the windshield, then closed them entirely as the engines whined higher.

Big thump. Little thump. Smooth running, the engines reversing to slow them down, the brakes squalling. Easy as pie.

Not that she'd ever made a pie. It always looked too damn hard.

"There we are, then. Nary a hair out o' place."

As if to prove it, Callum reached over and ran his thumb along her cheek to tuck a stray strand of hair behind her ear. If there even had been a stray strand. At this point, he'd become easily as touchy-feely as Dex. He seemed to enjoy any excuse to touch.

Maybe they'd been as lonely and touch-starved as she'd been. Maybe that's all it was. Probably.

Shaking the tension out of her shoulders, she tried to relax. She had no idea if either Brigid or Thea would be waiting for them, but she doubted it. Callum said Brigid rarely left her castle fortress, and as far as she knew, Thea wouldn't even arrive until the day after tomorrow. What time even was it in Glasgow, which Dex had informed her was only the first leg of their journey to Culloden Moor? What day was it, for that matter?

But she didn't have time to ask. As soon as the little jet taxied to its designated square of tarmac, the guys got up and began gathering bags to sling over their broad shoulders and tidying up as if they wanted to leave no trace that they'd been there.

Oh. Oh, shit. Maybe they didn't.

How had they even gotten this flight? Did the owner of the plane know it was being used to technically-illegally transport an undocumented guest into a foreign country?

Anxiety washed over her again until she realized she was nearly crushing Callum's hand and hadn't let him far enough away to rescue himself. She abruptly let go to an almost rubber band effect where they sprang apart and nearly fell on their asses.

Dex snickered, then straightened his expression. "Sorry. Not funny. But the look on your face, mate."

Callum's face. Not hers. Bless Dex to the moon and back.

"Nothin wounded but my pride, and I've precious little of that left, mate. Give us a hand, aye?"

Dex dutifully offered assistance and pulled Callum to his feet. "I'm sorry. Did I just hear you call yourself humble?"

"Never." Indeed, the Scot looked almost scandalized at the accusation. "I said I've very little pride left."

Dex blinked, then winked at Wen, which helped lower her shoulders again until she could reach under the little bed berth for her carry-on bag.

"Mate, what do you think humility is?"

"What am I, a thesaurus?"

"A dictionary. Goddess above and below."

"Aw, that's sweet, mate. You think I'm a walkin dictionary. I'll cherish that one to the grave, I will."

She finally cracked a smile, and that seemed to be the reaction her boys had been waiting for. They each offered her a hand, so she stepped between them and took both offerings. Their big hands gently clasping hers as if she were something priceless made her head lift, her chin tilting back the slightest bit. Her shoulders squared, and she walked as bravely between them as she could.

With men like these at her side, what on Earth could she possibly fear?

She was, however, a little disappointed that no one was there to greet them. Neither of the boys seemed put out, so they'd clearly expected to drive themselves to Brigid's fortress, but it was a little anticlimactic. She was used to that, though. If anxiety had taught her anything, it was that very little was ever as bad in reality as it felt in her head. The worst-case scenario was reassuringly rare.

So they traipsed down the narrow little stairway to the

tarmac, airport people already unloading their cargo into an equally reassuring, boring minivan that awaited them. She'd been a little worried that they'd book something showy for the trip, so it was a huge relief that they'd gone for practicality over flash.

She should've known better and trusted them. They wouldn't want to draw any undue attention, and not just because they didn't want anyone asking for passports. They were her protectors. They wouldn't want anyone noticing they had something worthy of such protection.

Callum's words rang in her head: *you. are. worthy.*

Not yet. But maybe she could be, if she did Sister of the Moon things right.

Dex handed her into the middle row of seats, and she buckled herself into the middle seat in the row. She wanted to be able to look out the windows, yes, but she also wanted to feel like she was still safely between them. She wanted to see them equally, converse easily. Plus, she had a feeling they'd be excellent tour guides as well as guardians. They were, after all, back on home turf. Callum, especially.

Dex scooted into the driver's seat to her right, which threw her American sensibilities off a bit. Callum plopped down into the passenger seat with an exaggerated sigh.

"Ready, lass?"

She clutched her carry-on bag with her regular meds tight and nodded. "Ready."

Dex started the minivan, and they were on their way.

12

Scotland's scenery was everything Wen could ever have hoped for. Green everywhere, like her beloved Oregon. Gardens full of color. Craggy tors sprawled around like a giant child's toys. Rugged cliffs and peaks, misty with enchanted fog. Heeland coos, as Callum called them, straining his accent to the breaking point but making her laugh every time.

She loved the heeland coos. They looked like stuffed toys with their scruffy, long coats and their wide pink noses and their horns. She wanted to pet them, cuddle them. They looked like pets rather than stock animals.

Maybe some other time. Maybe Brigid had a few she'd allow to be smothered with cuddles. If they were tame enough. Wen was more used to sea creatures than farm animals.

Either way, she enjoyed the trip immensely. Callum and Dex acted as if they were driving across half the planet, insisting on stopping for "petrol" and road snacks and loo breaks as if they'd been driving for hours, and Wen wanted to laugh. Mama had taken her on a several-day Route 66 driving tour when she was still in single digits, and they had driven for four and five hours at a time, only stopping for "last gas for X miles" signs to top off the tank and cheap motels for a decent night's sleep. Scotland wasn't large enough to make such an epic trip necessary or even possible, but it was fun to watch the boys fuss and plan.

Especially since their main concern was for her. Did she need to use the loo? Was she hungry, thirsty, too tired? Did she need to step out for a moment to stretch her legs? Was she getting a migraine?

It was sweet. Totally unnecessary, but sweet.

And the countryside they drove through was well worth a slower pace. She filled herself up with the misty mystery of the place, the calm greens, soft grays and purples, and bright pops of color, the wild nature of the open areas, the quaint buildings of the villages they passed through. It was glorious. She'd never thought to see such wonders in person, to feel the sense of timeless age that America often lacked. And for the short but satisfying span of the trip to Culloden Moor, Wen allowed herself to be enchanted.

It was a heady distraction from what awaited her at Brigid's fortress. She looked forward to the meeting, but she also dreaded it. Would she say something impossibly crass? Would she trip and fall face first into a pat of heeland coo poop? Would she be unbearably gauche and gawk at everything like the worst possible example of an American tourist?

She didn't want to be a disappointment. Unfortunately, it seemed the entire shapeshifting world had been waiting for a new Sister of the Moon for over forty years. She was bound to be a disappointment.

She wasn't worthy. Callum was just being kind.

You. Are. Worthy.

She clung to the words as the miles—kilometers—passed.

"What is a moor, anyway?" she finally asked, unintentionally breaking the companionable silence. She hadn't actually meant to ask out loud.

But Callum grinned like a sunrise and turned in his seat to

face her more on the level. "D'you want the scientific explanation, the dictionary definition, or poetry?"

She couldn't help but grin back. "Poetry. Obvs."

His expression shifted from a grin to a wistful smile, his eyes suddenly far away. "A moor is an unknowable expanse of constant change that nearly always looks the same, lass. It is life and nests and lambs and kids, covered by gorse and heather that looks drab and foggy until that one, brilliant moment when they're in bloom, where the eggs hatch and fly away as birds, where the kids hop to the top of the tors and the lambs grow their first fluffy coats and look like low clouds."

Enchanted as much by the imagery as by the look in his eyes, she sighed. "It sounds so beautiful."

"'Tis."

That didn't sound wistful so much as... lonely. Did Callum miss his home so much? Would he ever really be content anywhere else?

Her eyes met Dex's in the rearview mirror, and he spoke, likely to ease her mind. "Bollocks. A moor is just a patch of scrub where you trip through overgrown bushes and hidden rocks and step into a bird's nest only to get a faceful of angry mama bird, my lady. Don't believe his Scottish fairy tales."

Catching the hint, Callum brightened. "There *are* fairies in Scotland, though, lass. Or there were. And Ireland, too. They floated about the moors like fireflies that didnae blink and haunted the hollows and gathered around the tors to worship the moon and the sun and the changing o' the seasons."

Her smile came back. "And what happened to them? Are they really gone forever? Back to— oh, what'd you call it?" She racked her brains. "Underhill, right?"

"Aye, lass, well done." He seemed genuinely pleased that she remembered. "No one knows what their home place is really like, but legend refers to it as Underhill or Elfhame. Mayhap another dimension, mayhap a world the darker, mirrored reflection of our own. No one who's never been there can know. And most as goes there never comes back."

She played along. "Because they're trapped there forever after they eat something? Like in Queen Mab's court?"

She did love a good fairy tale.

"Because they donnae want to, lass. Why would anyone want to come back from the enchanted realm?"

Huffing, she looked out across a sea of grayish-green lowgrowth dotted with stacks of rock. The moor? Tors? Were they close?

"I don't think I'd ever feel right among the fair folk. They're unearthly beautiful, after all. Even the awful ones can be pretty."

Oops. She probably shouldn't have said that part out loud. But it was true. She'd never imagined herself in a fairytale before because— well. She wasn't meant for happy endings, and she'd be an absolute nightmare on an adventure, having to stop the hike every few hours to take an anxiety med or hiding under a rock during a migraine or, Goddess forbid, being caught without either her allergy meds or a box of lotion tissues.

No. She wasn't meant for such fanciful daydreams, and she'd never had them. Not really.

But both Dex and Callum looked sad at her admission, so she smiled. "Can you imagine me meeting a fairy queen? I can't even brush the frizz out of my hair."

Dex started to respond—she watched his mouth open in the rearview—but, suddenly, his expression changed. "We've got a tail."

Callum immediately craned around in his seat, a hand on her thigh, either as a comfort or to brace himself to turn around so fully. "Could be just a local, mate. We're no' to even Culloden yet."

"No." Dex kept flicking little glances at the rearview, looking behind her rather than at her. "I saw that same car at the last petrol station. A bloke driving. Dark hair and eyes, tanned or naturally brown skin, your height."

Wow. Wen hadn't even noticed anyone specific during their last stop, but Dex could probably have a police sketch drawn from his description. They really were amazing guardians.

"Oi, I did see that one." Callum craned around again. "Best stop. We're less than an hour from Culloden, and I wonnae lead a bounder right to Brigid's front door."

And just like that, to her surprise, Dex pulled the minivan over, then leaned back to touch her hand.

"No matter what happens, you don't get out of this vehicle without our okay, my lady. He may be a local chappy on his way to Culloden proper, but he may not be. Let us do our jobs."

She nodded, eyes wide and biting her lower lip. Surely, it was just some random guy. Surely, no one was after them. How could anyone even know—

Oh. Maybe it was her. Maybe she was calling someone somehow. Another Nightwatcher? Or one of those shifters who would just kidnap her away and use her so-called power?

If there were ever a time for an anxiety med.

Dex and Callum both climbed out of the minivan, Callum moving around to Dex's side, then down the car to stand in front of Wen's door. Always one as a last defense, he'd said that first night. Apparently, he hadn't been exaggerating.

All the things that could go horribly wrong shot through her mind, and she dragged her carry-on closer to dig for her meds. She had a bottle of water, thankfully, so all she had to do was unzip, unzip, take the cap off, and— but the first zipper stuck. Because of course it did. She turned to look behind the minivan since Callum took up her window, and the car that had apparently been following them—a sedan of some sort; she didn't know much about cars—slowed and pulled over, parking perhaps thirty feet behind them. Ten meters, her mind translated, and she wanted to laugh, though none of this was funny.

The first zipper finally opened, and she shoved past all the crap she'd thought was so important, trying to get to the back zipper pocket. A man got out of the car, tall and broad, dark curly hair and, as Dex had said, honey-tanned skin. She couldn't see his eyes, but she already knew they were dark. Dex had said so, and he hadn't been wrong yet.

The second zipper gave with absurd ease, the dangly bit yanking back so hard she almost pulled it right off the tracks, and she fumbled around in the pocket for the right bottle. A migraine med wouldn't do a damn thing for her right now. There, the slightly taller bottle. The lid popped off on the first twist, and she poured half the bottle into her hand, which was shaking. *Damn it.*

The man walked closer but stopped well out of arm's length and put spread his hands out wide. No weapons in hand, but his eyes went to the back of the car, as if he could see her in there. He *was* called. But to help or to hurt?

The little white pill caught in her throat, dry and scratchy, and she gulped down half the bottle of water in an attempt to flush it down. It went, but reluctantly. In her worry and fear, she forgot how long it would take to work, so she tried to remember what her therapist—she would definitely have to get a new therapist in Oregon when they went, provided they all survived the current situation—had drilled into her about calming her panic.

Grounding. She needed to ground herself. Be in the moment.

"Hail, fellow Nightwatchers."

Oh, shit. Not that kind of moment! Five things she could see: the bottle of water, her carry-on, Callum's butt (nice indeed), the folded-down rear bench seat of the car. The strange man standing back there, looking at the back of the car and seemingly seeing her there.

Not. Helping.

"Hail, sir." Dex sounded solemn, rather than angry or wary. "I'd ask your business, but you've already answered that question."

Instead of answering, the stranger crouched, looking through the window and definitely seeing her this time. His eyes glowed—now she could see a color, but the fiery red wasn't reassuring—and his features... changed. Flowed. Shifted.

One minute, a strange man crouched behind the minivan. The next, an enormous, shaggy, charcoal-colored wolf with glaring red eyes and steaming breath stood on all fours, hackles ruffled, growling.

Dex and Callum both changed their stances, Dex's hands already shifting into paws, though Callum didn't seem to change at all. Animal growls rumbled, even through all the minivan's glass and metal. Wen clutched her open carry-on to her chest, her heart in her throat, spilling useless junk everywhere because she hadn't rezipped the top.

The giant wolf—clearly not the average, run-of-the-mill wolf, though she knew even regular ones were damn big—sidestepped closer to the vehicle. Callum stayed put, one hand on the window as if to reassure her, but Dex mirrored that sidestep, stooping down until his hands (paws) touched the pavement. And just like that, he was his black dog, an enormous, hulking Hound of Baskerville with those haunting amber eyes and an eerie, glowing sheen to his black coat.

This. Was. Bad.

Four things she could touch. The bottle of water, again. The upholstery of the car seat. The cold metal of her carry-on's zipper tab. The fingernails on her free hand digging into her palm.

Why was this a therapeutically recommended tactic? It was stressing her out worse!

The wolf closed in on the minivan, continually looking between her inside, Callum standing guard at her window, and Dex, who neared even as he widened the space between himself and her.

Five feet away.

Four.

Callum crouched, and she tensed. If both of them shifted, she could only imagine the worst-case scenario, but she was pretty sure a giant war horse and an equally huge black dog could take on a monster wolf with relative ease. Surely.

Three feet. That ghastly, monstrous muzzle raised, steaming as if the fires of hell were banked in the creature's gullet. The heavy-fanged mouth opened.

A pink tongue flattened against the window, giving it a good, steamy, saliva-coated lick.

Callum relaxed entirely and stepped away just enough to open the car door. She didn't budge. Dex had told her to stay inside unless they said otherwise. She had no intention of—

Dex, still in dog form, looked right at her and ruffed softly. When her eyebrows shot up, he nodded and ruffed again, not quite barking. It was... okay?

So, dropping her carry-on to the floor and spilling the last of its contents everywhere, she scooted over and took Callum's offered hand. The monstrous wolf stayed at the back of the car, even going so far as to sit back on its haunches, tongue hanging out, breath still steaming in the chilly air. Maybe it wasn't smoking like a banked fire. Maybe it was just cold out.

And a little damp, now that she was out in it. She hadn't considered that the misty atmosphere meant the air would be wet. Admittedly, she had other things on her mind, but she could feel her hair both frizzing worse and sticking to her forehead and cheeks. Gross.

She pressed closer to Callum, and without her having to ask, he wrapped an arm around her waist. She didn't want to cling to him, but she did want the comfort of his strong bulk at her side. The wolf started to stand to all fours, then caught itself and sat back down. It would wait for her to come to it. Him. Did werewolves have pronouns?

Not the time.

Dex trotted closer, and she stepped away from Callum to run her hands into the thick black fur over his haunches. His tongue—pink and black spotted—lolled out, his breath steaming. She couldn't resist. She scratched him behind the ears and grinned at the resulting happy puppy noises he made.

She could do this. She could walk over to the giant wolf monster and... make friends? What did it—he—expect from her? Ear scritches?

She was starting to appreciate how Dex had handled her from the start. While he'd accidentally scared her, he hadn't hit her with the supernatural right from the first moment. The giant monster wolf was *scary*.

But she could do this. Straightening her shoulders, she fisted her hands and walked away from Dex and toward the new creature. It really wasn't a wolf, she realized as she neared it. The haunches were much narrower than the broad chest and shoulders. Its head was blocky but somehow more angular than she expected. And those eyes. What red eyes you have, Grandmama. What monstrously huge teeth.

"Um. Hi, there."

She put her hands out to her sides, then slowly brought them around in front of her to show that she was completely harmless. Helpless, in fact. If he wanted to tackle her and rip her throat out, she couldn't stop him.

Not helping!

"I'm gonna step closer now, okay? And give you my hands to

smell. I dunno if that makes a difference or not, but I don't know what else you might want me to do, so...."

She did as she said, creeping forward with her hands out, palms up. The wolf waited for her, twitchy and obviously eager to stand, his thick, brushy tail swishing behind, but he stayed in his position by the back of the minivan. Closing in, she slowed even further, giving him plenty of chance to betray her while there was still a chance for Dex or Callum to get to her if he pounced.

Closer. A few more steps.

The wolf stretched out his head and whuffed hot, damp breath on her hand. She stopped instantly, fear trying to choke her. Another good sniffle, and he lolled out his tongue and licked her palm. It tickled. And was sort of gross.

"Is that good?"

He growl-whuffed. Was that a yes?

"Okay. I'm— is it okay if I pet you now?"

Instead of whuffing, the giant animal shoved up and at her before she could flinch back, bumping its huge head into her stomach and burrowing against her. But he didn't disembowel her. Didn't bite.

In fact, she'd swear he was snuggling her, though he didn't have arms.

Her breath coughed out of her—she'd been holding it, apparently—and she ran a still-shaking hand over the wiry, dark gray fur. The ruff around his shoulders and chest was thick and warm, a little oily and not quite soft but still nice to run her fingers through.

"What's your name, then?"

Right under her hands, he shifted back, and suddenly she held an adult human male against her, her arms around his shoulders, his face pressed against her stomach paunch, on his knees before her.

"I am Florin, my lady. I am yours."

He had a completely different accent from either Dex or Callum. If she had to guess, she'd pick some sort of Slavic heritage. Maybe Romani? That might account for his dark hair and light brown skin, right? Or was she thinking Italian? No, that was olive-toned skin.

And none of that mattered, because she was holding an adult human male against her, and she hadn't so much as touched another human being in years before three days ago. Or was it four? She'd lost count without having to log in for work every day.

"Oh. Okay." Feeling like an idiot, she looked to Dex—who had transformed back, and it really must be a magical transformation because neither shifter had to take off or put on any clothing to do it—and Callum for help. "I guess... I'm glad to meet you? I'm Wen. Uh. Wendolyn. Wendolyn Eudora Cheney."

Just saying her whole name gave her back a slight measure of confidence. Mama had always used Wen's full name to buck her up, to help her feel better or more empowered. It helped now. She was able to let go of the new man and step back as Callum and Dex stepped up beside her. He, Florin, stayed on his knees on the damp pavement, not seeming to care about his jeans getting soaked through.

He was casually dressed, the damp jeans paired with a dark green, plush sweater and some sort of trench coat that kept the weather off his clothes. Oilskin? Had she heard that word before on some British mystery drama she'd seen? It sounded familiar, anyway. But so did "great coat", and that just sounded like the person was really proud of their coat.

It didn't matter. She waited for Dex or Callum to introduce themselves, but neither seemed inclined. And Florin stared at her, drinking her in with his dark eyes. She looked closer, trying not to stare in return, and realized those eyes were a dark, deep blue. Like the ocean at night blue. Gorgeous eyes, and he was a gorgeous man.

Why were all these shifters so damn pretty?

"Um." *Do better, Wen.* "This is Dex, and this is Callum." She thought it best to follow Florin's lead and just give first names. If the boys wanted him to know their last names or Callum's shifted shape, they could tell him themselves. "I guess— I don't know what happens next."

But the new stranger didn't seem fazed. "You are American?"

She nodded, hesitant. Was that a bad thing? Would he reject her because of it?

"If I may ask, my lady, what brings you to the U.K.?"

She couldn't believe this conversation was happening with him kneeling on wet pavement in the middle of Scotland on her first trip out of the United States. Well, she could at least do something about the wet pavement part.

"You can stand up. I'm not— I don't—"

"She's not so formal," Dex explained, coming to her aid finally. "She only discovered who she is a few days ago and is still getting used to everything."

Why couldn't she sum things up like that? It would've taken her half an hour of mumbling and "um"s to get that out. So frustrating.

But after another long, deep look, the new shifter slowly stood and brushed at the wet patches on his knees. His eyes only left hers for the briefest of moments before returning to drink her up again. It was... disconcerting.

This time, Callum came to her rescue. "And she's here to meet with one o' her Sisters, mate. We didnae expect to find another Nightwatcher so soon."

The new guy, Florin, took a slow step forward, extending his hands toward her. She hesitantly reached out in return, managing not to jerk her hands back when he took them gently in his own. He sighed and closed his eyes for a moment.

"My lady, I have long given up the hope of a Sister calling

me. I am two hundred thirty-seven years old and perhaps the last living dire wolf, shifter or no."

Her jaw dropped, leaving her gaping like an idiot, but she couldn't help it. She couldn't even imagine— and a dire wolf? They existed? Or used to, if he was the last one? How horrible to bear the burden of being the very last of an entire species.

At least it explained why his wolf was so monstrous and intimidating. Even when licking the window.

He squeezed her hands slightly, then lifted one to touch to his forehead. She blushed, desperately uncomfortable but hoping he was at least getting what he needed from the touch.

"I go where you go, my lady. Now and forever. I am your loyal wolf for whatever time I have left."

She blinked, suddenly worried. That sounded like he was dying or deathly ill. He didn't look old. He certainly didn't look two hundred thirty-freaking-seven years old. Not a speck of white intruded on the dark curls around his face. His deep-set eyes weren't bracketed with crow's feet. No laugh lines.

Then again, maybe he wasn't much for laughing. She knew literally nothing about him.

"Are you— I mean, okay?" Goddess, why was she so awkward? "Just, whatever time you have left sounds—?"

He tilted his head for a moment, then brightened. His whole aspect changed as a smile lit his face. It was an almost magical transformation.

"You worry for me. You truly are a Sister of the Moon. It will be my pleasure to guard such a precious gift from the goddess." Another hand squeeze, and he backed away and turned his attention to the men bracketing her. "Fellow Nightwatchers, may I join your ranks?"

Callum and Dex exchanged looks, then looked to Wen for confirmation. What could she say? She had no idea how anyone could just stop what they were doing and join someone else's cause with such certainty and finality. She couldn't begin to imagine doing so herself.

But if that's what everyone wanted—

She nodded to Dex. Callum reached over and gently squeezed her hand. And it was done.

Just like that, their trio became a quartet.

13

Wen missed Callum. He'd volunteered to drive Florin's car so Florin could ride with Wen and Dex and catch up on everything that had been happening. It was kind of him, but she still missed the snarky Scot. She'd only known him a few days, but she felt the separation as if he'd been her constant companion for life.

"I agree," Florin said, responding to whatever Dex had said. Unfortunately, she hadn't been listening but had craned around to make sure Callum was still right behind them. "A change is definitely on the wind if all the Sisters are meeting together for the first time in perhaps a hundred years."

Oops. Maybe she should've been listening. Last she heard, they were talking about Florin's travel photography career, which had taken him literally all over the world and explained how he could just pack it in and join them. He worked freelance.

"Brigid feels it. I think we all feel it." Dex shook his head. "I worry for my lady. She's had so much to absorb in just a few days. She isn't ready."

She really *hadn't* been listening if they were talking about her like she wasn't there. Sighing, she turned around again to make sure Callum was close, waving at him to be sure. He waved back, smiling sunnily even in the misty murk.

"There are three of us now," Florin said, his tone grave. "We will keep her safe." He abruptly turned to look at her, to drink her up with those dark blue eyes. "She is a miracle."

She blushed, fiddling her fingers together in her lap. She'd managed to gather up all the stuff that had fallen out of her carry-on earlier, but she almost wished she had something to occupy her attention like that now. He was so intent. Like the weird occasions where Callum would look her directly in the eyes, seemingly trying to tell her something without words. Even Dex did so once in a while. As if they were trying to help her understand something she didn't even know she didn't understand.

Ugh. She hated silent signals. She'd much rather someone just tell her what they wanted to say. Sure, she might be embarrassed (understatement) but at least then she'd know what was expected of her. All this guesswork and fretting was exhausting.

Or maybe that was the jetlag.

"There it is, my lady," Dex said, gesturing toward the road ahead. "Brigid's fortress."

She sat forward as far as her seatbelt allowed, surprised when Florin took her hand the second she was close enough. But that was a secondary sensation to the awe she felt as the castle—a literal stone-walled castle—grew large ahead of them. Turrets, towers, stained glass windows. Everything a castle needed to be grandiose and forbidding at the same time.

Her breath left her. She wasn't dressed for a castle. She wasn't even wearing the new pair of sneakers exactly like her old ones. They'd been packed in the cargo hold with all her new things and now were on the bottom of the pile in the back of the minivan. The boot, Dex had called it.

And Brigid lived here all the time. No way Wen could meet

the owner of a literal castle without being a complete mess. What had she been thinking?

But the castle grew ever larger in the windshield, the gray expanse of Culloden Moor spreading off into every distance, and she could only try to tamp down the sense of impending doom inside her and remember that Brigid was expecting her, Brigid was kind and open, and she, Wen, was a Sister of the Moon. Even if she still didn't know exactly what that meant.

She was welcome here. At the castle.

They came to a low-slung rock wall across the moor that bookended a simple iron gate. Beside the gate stood a bald Asian man in dark jeans and a heavy sheepskin coat. He waved them closer, then came around to Dex's side to speak to them. Dex obligingly rolled down the window.

"Who seeks the Sister's wisdom?"

Wen blinked, a new fear overtaking her. Was she supposed to be wise? No one had ever accused her of being wise. What on earth was she supposed to know?

But Dex was unfazed. "A fellow Sister." He turned to smile at her, and the Asian man leaned down further to peer at her through the window opening. "Wendolyn Eudora Cheney, from the States. She's expected."

To her surprise, the stern expression on the Asian man's face softened to a not-quite smile. "Welcome, Sister. I am Eiji, my lady Brigid's First, and I bid you welcome. Please, enter and be at ease here in your Sister's home."

It all sounded so formal, but Dex merely tipped a two-finger salute and drove in when the other man—the one Brigid had spoken to while they were on the phone together?—flung open the gate. She turned to watch Callum come through, too, just to be sure, but Eiji only waved him on, then shut the gate behind them.

For better or for worse, they were in. The castle loomed large, even more forbidding as the fog rolled in from the moor.

But the stained glass in the larger windows shone with merry color, lit from within, softening the harsh stone face of the edifice. Brigid awaited, and she'd promised a glad welcome.

And tea. Wen wasn't sure which she wanted most right now.

And then, there she was: Brigid, Sister of the Moon, friend and hopefully soon-to-be family. And Wen had to laugh at herself at all her fears and worries of not being fancy enough for a castle, because Brigid was dressed like a cross between Cindy Lauper and Stevie Nicks, her skin pale and her hair black—

Wait. Black hair?

As if sensing her confusion, Dex sighed. "She dyes it to match her old color. And because she's a wee bit Goth at heart. Generation X, goddess help us."

Much more confident at the actual sight of her new sister, Wen only waited for the minivan to stop—not even for Dex to put it in park—to scoot over and practically jump out. To her relief, Brigid squealed and ran down the steps toward her, and they met somewhere in the middle in a big, cuddly hug. They both laughed, and Wen felt tears spring to her eyes, though she couldn't imagine why. Were these the fabled happy tears?

"Ah, m'love, 'tis wonderful to see ye in the flesh!" Brigid squeezed almost too hard, then sniffled. "I didnae know how happy I'd be, but ye're as welcome as the first star o' the night during the harvest moon!"

Wen had no idea if that had Sister significance or was just a really sweet way of welcoming her, but for once, she didn't care about all the possible interpretations and pitfalls. The hug they shared was warm and kind, and that was enough for her. She'd come halfway across the world and had somehow still found a friend.

Two, apparently. Oops.

"Oh! I'm so sorry, Brigid! I haven't introduced everyone." She reluctantly pulled away, but they still held each other by the wrists. "You know Dex and Callum, but we met Florin on the way here. Florin, this is Brigid."

Florin bowed at the waist, but Brigid didn't let Wen go to do the same. Interesting.

"Pleased we are to have another Nightwatcher on our side, lad." She gave Wen's wrists another little squeeze. "Now, love, I promised you a spot o' tea, and I aim to deliver. Ye look damp to the skin. Will ye all come inside and get settled? We have ever so much to blether about, aye?"

She grinned. "Aye."

They both laughed, Wen still a little high on the better-than-expected greeting and not feeling like a complete frump, despite the castle setting. Another hug, and Brigid finally let her go so Wen could take the carry-on Dex had grabbed for her. Eiji walked up as Brigid took her by the hand to lead her inside.

"I could take that for you, my lady."

Her eyebrows went up. She didn't expect Brigid's man to wait on Wen like her own seemed to want to.

"Oh, thank you, but I can manage. Eiji, right?"

He nodded, climbing the stairs at Brigid's side, a hand on her elbow in case she slipped. Which was possible in the platform, knee-high combat boots she was wearing. Wen could never manage such a badass look, but Brigid had the height to carry it off beautifully.

She stopped at the top of the steps to look back at her boys. Callum had joined them in unpacking the boot, and she felt her heart settle at the sight of them all together. She didn't know how she knew, but just looking at them, she knew that Florin belonged with them. With her. He glanced up from the suitcase he'd hefted and caught her eye, gifting her a small smile. Callum grinned cheerily and waved with his free hand. Dex, calmly and masterfully directing the unpacking like a military campaign, paused to give her one of his warm, beautiful smiles, his eyes glowing amber for a bare moment before he winked the glow away.

Her boys. Her Nightwatchers.

She followed Brigid's gentle tug and smiled at her new sister as they finally stepped inside Brigid's castle fortress.

Callum was right. Clotted cream was truly a gift from the Goddess. From all of the goddesses. Wen was sure she could never go back to plain old butter, even Kerrygold, now that she'd tried such bliss.

"Aaron makes it himself every mornin, love," Brigid said, slathering a bit on a light, fluffy, cheesy scone. "You havenae met him yet. He's often out with his coos, whisperin them into givin him their sweetest cream."

Wen hadn't met the rest of Brigid's Nightwatchers yet, but she felt she knew them already, thanks to Brigid's bright chatter. Aaron, the fellow Scot who tended her heeland coos. Halvor, the big Norse blacksmith with icy eyes that Brigid compared to the underside of a glacier from the coldest waters on Earth. Gerhardt, the German cook who considered himself the finest chef to ever come out of Europe. She found it fascinating that they all had vocations—jobs, even. Brigid explained that they hadn't truly had to guard her since she first came to Light, so they'd decided to pursue their various interests, most of which were comfortably practical and saved a load of money. Having a fortress as a first line of defense had its benefits.

And then there was Eiji, who stayed at Brigid's side as if he suspected Wen of the most nefarious plots possible.

To be fair, he was perfectly polite and solicitous. As far as Wen knew, he suspected no such thing. She just didn't know how to act under such a stern eye, and with Dex and Callum up in guest rooms unpacking, she had only Florin, her newest

Nightwatcher, to keep her from acting a complete fool. And Florin, bless him, was too busy staring at her hair to keep her from sticking her foot in her mouth.

His attention was distracting, in fact. He looked at her like an oasis in the desert, like she would sprout magic sparkles and fly away at any moment. Or like her hair would. She couldn't help running a hand over the frizz any time she caught him staring, which only increased the frizz. The misty murk outside hadn't helped, either. She was fairly certain she looked like she'd stuck her finger in a light socket.

And none of that counted the drying effect of the fire roaring in the massive stone hearth off to one side of the sitting area.

"Was the flight nice, then?"

She shook herself, afraid she was being a bad guest, letting Brigid do all the talking. She probably should've taken an anxiety med before trying to have tea with the new sister she wanted to impress, but everything had happened too quickly, and Brigid hadn't wanted to let go of her until they sat in her exquisitely Goth parlor, waiting for Eiji to bring the tea things. Shades of blood red and black surrounded them, roses both red and black, black lace, and red velvet covering every surface. Antique silver frames that might actually be antique silver held pale, solemn faces from the past, all probably dead by now, given the patina on the sepia-toned photos. The old stone walls were dark with both age and smoke from the hearth.

Honestly, Wen could've just looked around the room in total silence for an hour and felt much less awkward. But Brigid, bless her, was trying, so Wen should, too.

"I slept through most of it," she admitted, a tea cake slathered with clotted cream in one hand and a cup of some brisk Scottish brew in the other. "Probably a good thing, but I feel like I missed a day somehow."

"That'll be the jetlag, love." Brigid nodded. "I'm glad ye were able to sleep, though. It'll help. And ye've all day to rest and hydrate, and we'll have a lovely meal tonight to keep yer strength up. Ye'll be right as rainbows and able to enjoy the company."

Oh, she hoped so. If only she could relax. If only Florin wasn't staring at her instead of skillfully guiding her away from being a dolt.

"Well, these tea cakes will surely help."

Mama's rule: when in doubt, compliment the chef. It had only failed her once when the food had actually been burned and awful, and her so-called compliment came out like the worst kind of obvious lie. Tucker had been furious.

And Brigid brightened. "Gerhardt will be so pleased to hear that. He and Callum have a long-standin rivalry in the kitchen."

Wen's eyebrows went up. Callum was, indeed, a gifted chef, but she hadn't considered he might consider his hobby rivalry-worthy. How serious was this little controversy?

Brigid smirked. "Ye realize the irony, aye?"

She blinked. "Um... no?"

Snickering, she leaned close and lowered her tone. "German food and Scottish food are generally considered the least 'cuisine' o' national foods, but they're both absolutely convinced they're top chef and will hear nae argument on the subject."

Wen bit her lip, not sure if she should smile or not. "I mean, Callum does make a mean lasagna. Even just leftovers on the flight over tasted like a mouthful of heaven."

"Ah, so ye've thrown yer lot in with the likes of him, aye?" Grinning, Brigid sat back and tossed her long, black hair back over her shoulder. "I promise no' to tell Gerhardt. He'll feed you naught but wurst if ye give him half a reason and half a rhyme."

Wen chuckled, her shoulders unwinding some of their tension. A food rivalry, especially if no one was terribly serious about it—and from Brigid's response, she guessed everyone but Callum and Gerhardt thought it was hilarious—was just her speed. She opened her mouth to retort in Callum's favor, but Florin beat her to speech, speaking out of nowhere, given he'd been silent until now.

"My lady Brigid, have you a boar bristle hairbrush anywhere?"

Brigid stilled, eyebrows raised. "Er— aye, I do, actually. Have ye need o' one, lad?"

To Wen's surprise, he smiled softly. "I do. May I borrow one? It doesn't have to be yours."

Brigid batted her eyelashes at him. "And what makes ye think I use one meself?"

His smile widened, his dark eyes twinkling, and Wen felt her heart skip a beat. Uh-oh. He was damn pretty when he really smiled. Hopefully, that wouldn't be a problem.

"My lady, no one can grow hair as long, as silky and glossy as yours without the touch of natural boar bristle."

Talk about pouring out the butter boat. Wen stared in surprise, but Brigid only tittered like a schoolgirl and waved a hand at him as if shooing him away. Eiji dutifully headed for the doorway, gesturing for Florin to follow, which he only did after taking Wen's hand in both of his and pressing an actual kiss on her knuckles. Warm, soft lips. Those deep blue eyes on hers. Curly, dark hair she wanted to run her fingers into.

Oh, no. Maybe it *would* be a problem. She couldn't afford to develop a crush. She was already in too deep with Dex and Callum, considering how much she missed their company and guidance at the moment. What on earth was she thinking?

Flustered and blushing, she tried not to eye Florin's backside as he walked away, but she couldn't quite look Brigid in the eye, either. Somehow, she knew her new Sister would *know*.

As soon as the menfolk left the room, Brigid put down her tea and leaned over the narrow table between them to touch Wen's hand. "How are ye holdin up, m'love? Really now."

The genuine care in Brigid's dark brown eyes just about did

wen in. She drew in a deep breath and let it out slowly, the exhale a little shaky.

"Honestly? I don't even know. This is all so crazy, but here I am. I just saw two men shapeshift into a giant dog and a giant wolf and face off, ready to fight. Over *me*." She huffed. "I'm in Scotland with two—three!—men I've only known a few days, and I have a sister for the first time in my life."

"Oh, love." Brigid's eyes were huge with concern. "I wish ye'd had so much more time to get used to all o' this. It's a lot to take in, aye? And in a country such as America where magic is laughed at and looked down on—" She shook her head. "At least here, we still believe in the old ways, in the Good Folk and the Veil."

Wen sighed. "I just wish I knew what I'm supposed to do. I feel like we should be capable of more than just allowing shifters to shift, ya know? What even is the point of that if they're only able to shift at will to protect us but we wouldn't need protecting if we couldn't allow them to shift?"

Patting her hand, Brigid smiled wryly. "M'love, I have asked the same thing many a time over the years. But for all my efforts, the closest I come to magic is readin tarot, and nearly anyone can do that if they're willin to study, both the cards and the people."

Her eyebrows rose. "You read tarot?" She thought of The Fool, of taking that potentially deadly first step, and wondered if she was falling or flying. "I've only ever had mine read once. Tucker—" She swallowed hard and looked down at her hands, at Brigid's beautifully Goth-manicured fingernails over her short, no-nonsense ones. "My ex. He didn't approve."

Brigid's grip tightened, and Wen looked up to see a hard look on that sweet, pale face. "Would this Tucker bastard approve o' you bein a Sister o' the Moon and hangin about with shapeshifters and would-be witches, then?"

She had to laugh, though it was a weak one, at best. "Oh,

Goddess no. He wouldn't believe a word of it. He'd have called the cops and gotten poor Dex shot before I could even talk to him in the grocery store parking lot."

Snorting, Brigid let go of her hand to stand up and go rummage in a carved wooden box—painted black, of course—on the hearth's mantle. "There ye are, then. He's yer ex for a reason, love. Ye donnae need his approval, do ye?"

"No." She shook her head and said it again, more firmly. "No. But I think it's why I'm having a hard time with being this magic person in a way I can't see or feel and not being able to do anything with it. To prove it, ya know? Even just to myself."

Her eyes widened. That was it. That was the vague feeling of wrongness she'd been feeling about the entire situation. Her magic, if she had it, was passive. Maybe Dex and Callum and Florin were perfectly capable of shifting any time they wanted, but they'd concocted this whole story for some bizarre reason of their own. And roped Brigid and Eiji in. And her other Nightwatchers she hadn't met yet.

In fact, she had no proof that Callum or Eiji or any of the others could actually shapeshift at all.

She didn't feel any magic inside her. She didn't feel capable of doing anything new or magical. She felt like a fraud.

Brigid sat back down across from her, regaining her attention, a deck of large cards in her hands. "Ah, lass. He tried his best to ruin ye, did he?" She shook her head. "Lucky for yer lads, he didnae succeed. Ye're here now, Wendolyn. Ye're allowed to be happy, aye?"

Wen's eyes puddled up, but she blinked rapidly, trying to keep the weepies away. She'd cried far too much in the past few days, and she was tired of it. Tired of the headache, the stretched-face feeling, the burning eyes and stuffy nose. Crying wasn't cathartic. It was a pain in the ass.

Looking down to give Wen some space to get herself together, Brigid shuffled her cards three times, then put them on the table between them and ran her right hand in a swoop from left to right, spreading the cards into a neat arc.

"What's yer question, then, love?" She smiled softly. "Yer most urgent one, anyway?"

Wen huffed. "I can only pick one?"

"For now, love. Only for now. We can do as many readings as ye like, but no' until ye've been fed and had a nap."

Now, she chuckled, feeling absurdly sheepish. And she considered. What did she want to know the most? What did she think the cards could tell her?

What did she need to know?

But she'd already asked that.

Shrugging, she asked again the question that bothered her the most: "What am I supposed to do?"

Brigid closed her eyes, hands hovering over the cards. She hmmed under her breath for a moment, the crackling fire the only other sound in the room.

"Choose three cards, love. Focus on the question. Focus on yer past, what ye *have done,* for the first."

What had Wen done? She'd failed, mostly. Bad marriage. Lost future. Well-paying but ultimately unrewarding job. Lost house she hadn't wanted in the first place. Half her retirement savings.

She still didn't like thinking about the past. So she reached out and pulled a card out of the swoop with one finger, instead.

"Good. Now focus on right now, lass. What are ye doin right now?"

She assumed Brigid didn't mean having her tarot read. Right now, Wen was... trying to place herself. Trying to learn this new destiny. Trying to make friends. She traced her finger down the arch of cards and touched another. Drew it out with one finger.

"Right, then. Now, the future. What will ye do once ye have yer answers?"

Oregon. Dex and Callum and Florin. Her fortress, which hadn't yet taken shape in her mind other than all the flower and vegetable gardens and a big kitchen and now, probably, a dark room for Florin's photography. Although he might shoot digital and not need all of that. She'd have to ask.

Another card, this time from the very beginning of the arch.

"Lovely." Brigid opened her eyes and smiled. "Let's see now, aye?" She turned over the first card. "Oh, love. The past. Seven of wands, inverted."

"What does that mean?" Wen whispered, not sure why but feeling that doing so was important.

Brigid's eyes were warm when they met hers. "It means ye've lost yer confidence. Ye've felt too weak to defend yerself, to fight for what ye want. Ye need time to rebuild your self-esteem from all the wands that have beaten ye down in yer life."

She blinked, eyes wide. She almost felt like when the psychic lady had explained The Fool to her. Import. Significance.

And damn if that explanation wasn't spot-on.

"Now the present. Oh, lovely!" Brigid said as she flipped the second card. "The Star! That's a major arcana. Ye know big things are happenin when ye have a major arcana in yer readin, love. The Star is optimism, hope. See how she stands shinin in the night sky, banishin the darkness and rejoicin with her sister stars? She's tellin ye that a bad time in yer life is drawin to a close. Clear skies lie ahead for ye."

Wen's heart fluttered. Could it be true? It certainly seemed like things were on an upswing at the moment. She had friends. She was on the trip of a lifetime. She was planning big things for her future, regardless of whether or not she had some mission as a Sister of the Moon.

Maybe—

Brigid flipped the final card. "The future. Oh, love, I just got the shivers, I did." She tapped the card where a bunch of rods—wands?—seemed to be trying to skewer the central figure. It didn't look particularly good. "Eight o' wands, m'love. The wands in motion bring much energy, vitality, and combined with the import o' The Star, a major arcana, it suggests that now is the time to act. Somethin big is comin; ye can either use the energy to dodge it all, or ye can ride the energy to overcome it." Brigid rubbed at her upper arms, chafing at the black lace covering them. "I knew it. I sensed somethin on the wind, I did, and now the cards confirm it."

Scrubbing at her own goosebumps, Wen stared at the cards in wonder. Perhaps Brigid really was magic. Or psychic. Or one hell of a cold reader. Any way she sliced it, that reading was a goad in her side.

I sensed somethin on the wind.

Now is the time to act.

"Wendolyn, some sort of storm is comin. We Sisters have a choice: take shelter to wait it out or go out in it to face our fears and our destinies. I feel it. I *know* it."

Hands shaking, Wen reached out across the table. Brigid reached out, too, her hands also shaking. They clasped together in the middle, right over the arc of cards. After staring at each other for a moment, they both burst out into too-loud laughter, standing as one to hug one another over the table.

"Brigid, my love?"

"Yes, Wen, m'love?"

She laughed again, shaking her head but not letting go. "You really are magic."

Brigid laughed and pulled her closer still. "Aye, lass. I might be at that."

14

They'd just settled back into their seats, Brigid pointing out features on the cards and what they meant—especially The Star—when Florin and Eiji re-entered, Florin with an ornate silver-handled bristle brush in hand. She looked at him curiously, but his hair didn't look any different from before. If he'd used it, she couldn't tell.

And she had a sneaking suspicion Eiji had been giving them time to themselves, likely at Brigid's request before the opportune moment.

Her thoughts derailed as Florin came to her and knelt at her feet. Again, she didn't particularly like the idea of anyone kneeling to her, though she'd become used to Dex and Callum sitting on the floor because she didn't have any chairs for them. At least, that's why she'd thought they did it. Now, she began to wonder.

"My lady." He presented the brush like a sword, lying across his open palms. "Would you be so kind as to allow me to attend to your hair?"

Wait, her hair? He hadn't wanted the brush for himself?

She looked over his head at Brigid, who was smiling behind

her hand, and Eiji, standing stoic at her side, his expression impassive. Then, at Florin again, his deep ocean eyes earnest and, yes, adoring.

He really, really wanted to brush her hair. Was that a testament to how bad it looked? Or was it sweet?

"Uh... I guess so?"

His face brightened on a smile. "Yes? I swear to be gentle. I only wish to bring out the glow I can see in the firelight."

Glow, huh? Well, Wen's hair did tend to reflect some serious light, but she'd never considered it a glow before. But if he was game, she couldn't think of a reason—other than her own awkwardness—to deny him something he so obviously wanted.

"Okay." She nodded, reaching out a hand in case he needed help up. He didn't, of course, but he took her hand and kissed her knuckles as he stood just the same. She blushed. "Do you need me to, I dunno, sit on the floor or something?"

"No, my lady. Don't mind me. Please, enjoy your tea."

And he came to her side, kicked one leg up onto the settee, and slid in behind her, sandwiched between her big butt and the back of the settee. He settled, his groin very much squashed up against her ass, hands on her upper arms until he settled.

Brigid's face was red, her hand pressed over her mouth now and her eyes dancing. Oh, yes, this was so, so funny. Hilarious.

Gentle fingers stroked her hair away from her temples, tangling almost immediately in the frizz but not pulling. He simply stroked over the curls a few times, then plied the brush.

"This isn't a detangling brush, my lady, but I vow you will not feel a single pull."

Eyes wide, face on fire, stiff as a board with her teacup—a very fancy jet black exterior with a blood red interior—clutched so tightly between her hands that she feared it would break any second, Wen tried to get over the shock of sudden closeness and make sense.

All she could manage was a strangled "Okay, Florin. Um,

thanks?" that had Brigid coughing to hide a snicker. Even Eiji's stoic expression twitched at the corners of his mouth and eyes.

Where were Dex and Callum? Would they laugh to see the new guy straddling her ass, brushing her hair? Or would they see absolutely nothing wrong with it? Or would they laugh, not at Florin, but at her being so damn flustered that she could barely speak?

The door opened. "Oh."

Speak of the devil.

Callum cleared his throat. "Forgot to tell you, mate: she's a wee bit shy o' physical contact yet, aye?"

Brigid chuckled, unable to help herself, and Florin's brush paused, his fingers not quite tangled in the hair at the nape of the neck.

"My lady? Am I making you uncomfortable? I will stop this instant."

Dex knelt in front of her, studying her face. "My lady? He will quit if it's making you nervous. We promise. Are you alright?"

Brigid's expression changed from dancing amusement to concern. Had she not realized how awkward Wen was? How unused to bodies pressed against hers? Especially virtual strangers' bodies?

At least no one was laughing now.

She swallowed hard, trying not to bite her lip. "No, it's... totally okay. I just... wasn't expecting it, is all."

Which was true, but not the whole truth. The truth was that she'd *get* used to it. Her Nightwatchers seemed to be a touchy lot, and she didn't want to deny them something that gave them comfort just because she wasn't used to it. She'd get used to it.

She just needed a little time.

"If you are sure, my lady—"

The brush hesitantly touched her head again, drawing slowly down from roots to tips. She stayed still, eyes locked on

Dex's. Callum came to sit beside her and took her freehand, starting up a bright chatter with Brigid that distracted everyone from her long enough to get the conversation rolling around her again.

Another brush stroke, slow and careful not to pull. It was... soothing, actually. Florin's hands were so gentle, so careful, and clever at working through the many tangles without ever yanking the brush or her hair. And patient. He brushed her hair as if he had the rest of his life to do so and was in no hurry to finish the job.

Slowly, brush stroke by brush stroke, she relaxed, even closing her eyes at one point and letting her head loll with his movements.

"Wendolyn, m'love?"

She opened her eyes, finding herself lying sideways, curled up on the velvet settee, a tasseled throw blanket—red and black, of course—drawn up to her shoulders. What on earth? She'd only closed her eyes for a moment.

Sitting up, she ran a hand through her hair, then paused in wonder. It felt silky, not crinkly like pubic hair. The curls didn't seem quite so tight. What magic was this?

Confused and tired and not sure what was happening, she looked at Brigid for an explanation. She sat down beside her and took her hand.

"Ye fell asleep, love. You were knackered from the trip and our talk and all the—" She waved her hand eloquently, and Wen understood exactly what she meant. The drama, the kerfuffle, the embarrassment, everything. "We wanted to let ye sleep as long as possible, but ye really ought to eat somethin before beddin down for the night, lass. Ye'll be starvin in the mornin otherwise, aye?"

Asleep? When had she fallen asleep? The last thing she remembered was swaying slightly with Florin's brush strokes. Was it possible he'd brushed her to sleep? Was that humiliating, or just evidence of how much she'd been hit with the past few days?

Blinking the sleep out of her eyes, then rubbing them with the heels of her hands, she yawned hugely, almost falling over. Brigid chuckled and helped her stand, keeping an arm around her waist as she led her slowly toward the smell of food from further inside the castle.

Oh. Right. She was in a castle. Scotland. The Star. Big things coming that she needed to take action on. Apparently, she'd needed a nap first.

But she was awake now, and she smiled sheepishly to see her Nightwatchers all seated around a food-heavy table—*briefly* seated; they rose when she entered the dining room—and smiling at her. Apparently, they didn't mind that she'd been out cold for who knew how long, leaving them to their own devices. Florin, especially, lit up at the sight of her, his eyes going to her hair. She ran a hand over it again, then clasped them together to stop herself. It only ever led to more frizz, and she couldn't see herself, but it certainly *felt* like he'd managed to tame the worst of it.

An heroic feat, indeed. Hercules would have paled at the challenge.

Shaking her head at her own weird thoughts, she started to sit by Callum, only to pause as Brigid cleared her throat and gestured toward the seat at the opposite end from herself. Luckily, even though the end of the table was a focal point, she found herself seated between Dex and Callum with Florin just next to Dex on his other side, so she didn't feel so exposed.

She wouldn't be able to eat if everyone was watching her. She'd choke on every single bite.

The conversation, which must have been going on for a while, picked back up as she made herself comfortable and accepted a saucer stacked with clotted-creamed bread rolls from Callum. He winked, carrying on with a tale of Brigid from their shared past. She listened, discovering as she took the first bite that she was absolutely ravenous.

How long had she slept? What time was it? There were no windows in the dining room, and she must have left her cellphone— no. It had been in her pocket and should still be there.

Dex silently put it on the table and scooted it over to her, tipping her a wink. Except it wasn't her old, battered cellphone but a brand new one, almost like his.

But this one had a deep teal cover, the slight variations in the color looking like underwater currents. They'd bought her a new phone? When could they have possibly found time to buy her a new phone?

She pushed the home button. 8:37 PM. Was that home time or Scotland time? She had to assume it was current Scotland time, but she couldn't quite connect it to how she felt. It felt so much later, but also so much earlier. She'd arrived in early afternoon, after all, and had only been talking with Brigid for perhaps an hour or two before passing the hell out. It shouldn't be that late in the evening.

But it also felt like she'd been up until the wee hours of the morning, so it really shouldn't be that early. How confusing. Was that jetlag, or was she just not good at international travel?

Dex poured her a cup of tea and a filled a silver goblet—highly decorated, as she should have expected from her Goth Sister—with a blood-red wine. "It's a bit strong, my lady, but you may like it. If not, Brigid has a chilled white standing by, as well."

She looked across the length of the table, and Brigid smiled and raised her own goblet. Eiji sat to her right, Aaron to her left, and Halvor next to Aaron. Gerhardt was nowhere to be seen, and Wen wondered where he could possibly be until she remembered that he was, for all intents and purposes, the cook. Had he made the amazing bread rolls?

Speak of the devil. The bottom half of a Dutch door opened

behind her—the upper part already thrown wide—and a tall man in chef's whites and an actual chef's hat strode in, a silver tray hefted up onto his shoulder.

"Dinner, honored guests."

Definitely a German accent. The words were harsh and blunt, Gerhardt's expression underlying their sternness. They would like his food. He commanded it.

With a grunt, he tipped his head as much as his burden would allow, then handed off a plate of some sort of creamy pasta dish. It smelled like heaven, and she ignored the salad he also put down to lean over her plate and inhale deeply. So good. Was that ham in the creamy sauce? Some sort of vegetable? She couldn't tell. She still wasn't used to more than basic foods, except for what Callum had already made.

As if he knew she was thinking of him, her ginger Scot sniffed warily at the dish Gerhardt plunked down on the table before him.

"Is that fig?"

"Of course is fig." The German accent seemed even thicker when aimed at his cooking nemesis.

"Why not truffles?"

Gerhardt's chest puffed up. "Why you don't eat and enjoy?"

Brigid and Wen locked eyes across the length of the table, then Brigid tore her gaze away and took a sip of wine to cover a snicker. Wen, a little alarmed, took comfort from her Sister's amusement.

"Mate, I know ye've access to truffles." His accent had thickened a bit since arriving at Brigid's castle. This time, though, he might be doing it on purpose just to annoy. "A creamy pasta dish practically begs for them. Why've ye no' used them, then?"

Dex took a sip of wine, effectively bowing out of the conversation. Florin, though he looked from one to the other with speculation, soon shrugged and went back to his bread roll.

Gerhardt hadn't served him yet, and it didn't look like the poor guy would be eating pasta any time soon.

"Fig is better. Is sweeter. Changes whole soul of dish."

"Oi, but who wants sweet pasta? Sounds revoltin, mate. Truffles are *earthy*. Umami. Ye cannae get that from figs—"

Gerhardt abruptly slung a bowl of pasta across the table, where it fetched up against Florin's wine glass, nearly knocking it over. "You want umami, you eat dirt. You want fine cuisine, you eat fig and be happy."

A smaller bowl of salad shot across the table, too, but Florin was ready this time and intercepted it without batting an eye. He merely picked up his fork and began eating as if nothing else of interest was happening. Wen still hadn't managed so much as a bite. Sure, it was all pretty damn funny, but she couldn't help but worry.

Sure enough, Callum wasn't done yet. He put aside his napkin and stood up. "I'll be havin yer kitchen, mate."

Gerhardt whirled around, scandalized, thankfully not losing any food off the tray. "No."

"Look, I saw truffles in there earlier, mate. I ken ye have them. I aim to sort this mess for milady."

She blinked as he reached over and snatched up her pasta bowl. She hadn't even eaten any yet. Probably a good thing?

Giving up on being the dutiful server entirely, Gerhardt practically threw the tray down on the table near Halvor's elbow and turned his full wrath on Callum. "When were you in my kitchen?"

"Not the important bit." Callum snorted. "I'm usin those truffles."

Gerhardt skirted the table and ran toward the Dutch door, bracing himself in front of it. "Truffles are mine. You are not allowed in my kitchen."

Unimpressed, Callum strolled casually around Wen's chair

and headed toward a possible fight. "It's my cousin's kitchen. Mate."

"Nein! Ist meine Küche!"

To Wen's amused discomfort, Callum actually moved to shove Gerhardt aside. The two scuffled, flailing enough that she seriously worried about the bowl of pasta ending up in someone's face, and then disappeared back into the kitchen, the Dutch door thumping closed behind them. Dex continued eating. Florin stood briefly to take Callum's pasta bowl and hand it to Wen so she wasn't just sitting there, watching everyone else eating.

Brigid and her remaining Nightwatchers had already divvied up the rest of the food from the tray and were eating merrily, as if nothing untoward had happened. As if one of the guests hadn't just had a slap fight with the chef and invaded the kitchen.

She glanced at Dex, seeking his... okay? approval?... to go ahead and eat, but he only winked at her and gestured with his fork. Apparently, it was okay to eat Callum's portion.

Or maybe Dex meant— well, the bickering duo might just be a while.

Sighing, she twirled her fork in the sauce and dared to take a bite of fig pasta, no truffles.

Wen really did try to stay awake after supper, but the heavy, creamy pasta and the ridiculous amount of bread she consumed mopping up all the sauce left her feeling droopy. The wine probably hadn't helped. She hadn't liked the red, but the white— a Moscato, Dex explained as Florin poured her another glass— was spectacular, and she'd had three glasses before realizing how sleepy it made her.

Thus, within ten minutes of slumping on the velvet settee

beside the fire, she already leaned against Dex's broad shoulder, Callum warm at her other side and Florin sitting on the floor, his back against her legs. She knew she should try to converse sensibly, but it was so much easier to let her boys do the talking for her. She could just close her eyes for a moment and rest. Not sleep; just rest.

She did awaken when Dex picked her up in his arms. "No, Dex, you'll throw out your back," she muttered, nuzzling closer and tucking her head under his chin. "Give yourself a hernia."

Callum, so near she could feel his warmth, whispered reassuringly. "'S alright, milady. We're made o' stronger stuff than that. Dex could haul me war horse without breakin a sweat."

She took sleepy comfort from that and sighed, letting them take her where they would. Even half-asleep, though, she wouldn't call the upstairs room they entered a simple bedroom. No, this was a bed *chamber,* large and drafty with high, heavy-beamed ceilings, a merrily crackling hearth fire, and a bed big enough for three or four of her. Or herself and three Nightwatchers, though the thought made her chuckle down in her throat.

As if she'd sleep with all of them. She hoped there was another bed or some cots or comfy furniture or something, though. She'd hate any of them to have to sleep on a stone floor. What would it do to their backs? Would they be too cold? Was there a bearskin rug? Hopefully not a wolfskin rug. Florin would surely be offended. Or maybe sad, which would break her heart with those blue eyes of his.

A huge yawn almost pitched her out of Dex's grasp, but luckily, he'd reached the bed and swooped her down on it.

"Pajamas, my lady?"

She blinked her reluctant eyelids open, and for a moment, all she saw was deep, dark teal. *That* one. *That* nightdress and peignoir set with all the silk and lace. Or was it satin? She didn't remember.

"Do you need help getting into it?"

Her eyes opened much more decisively this time, and she shoved to her feet, wobbling a little as she did so. "No, I can manage. Um... bathroom? Loo?"

She should brush her teeth. She should take a bath or a shower. She should ask Florin how that boar brush worked so she could get it all shiny again, like he had. She should definitely not let three men she'd known less than a week altogether change her into her new lingerie, even though it covered everything and then some.

So, despite Dex's small, wry grin, she took the fancy nightwear in hand and dragged feet over to the en suite bathroom. There, she stopped still, her jaw dropped, the nightgown dragging the floor.

This was no mere bathroom. This was a luxury spa with all the amenities. The bathtub was enormous—big enough for at least three people. Glass bottles and black marble containers of varying heights and widths cluttered the long, two-sink vanity. Red towels hung over brass rungs, setting off the black and white checkerboard tile that ran halfway up the wall, covered the floor, and formed a separate shower stall with a frosted glass door.

"My lady?"

Oops. She was still standing in the doorway, dazed by the opulence, staring like an idiot. And her brain, tired from all the everything, coughed up only one thing. "What's black and white and red all over?"

Callum piped up, and she heard the dimple-grin in his voice. "Yer loo?"

She huffed and turned her head to look at him. Sure enough, dimples. "Me, when I slip and fall and bust my ass on all this tile."

Her boys laughed, even Florin, who stood to help her until she waved him off, grinning wryly at herself. She could do this.

She'd take a shower or even a fancy bath in the morning. Right now, she just wanted to brush her teeth, put on the new nightwear, and go the hell to bed.

Her reflection in the wall-sized mirror behind the vanity brought her up short again, though. Her hair. How'd he get it so smooth? It glowed in the big, round lights surrounding the mirror, still in curls, but not springy, crinkly curls, like before. Another good brushing might even have it down to waves, which was all she'd ever wanted from her hair. Just nice, smooth waves she didn't have to bother with.

Blinking, she finally let herself run a hand over the smoother mass. Her fingers twiddled with the looser curls. No frizz anywhere. Just soft, luminous hair. No wonder Florin couldn't look away.

Shaking her head, she stripped, went to the bathroom, washed all the fold-over bits with a warm washcloth, brushed her teeth, and carefully pulled the nightgown over her head. As it settled into place, she again gawped at herself in the mirror.

Who even was she? That wasn't frumpy old Wen in the mirror. Not with her grey eyes reflecting the teal, her white hair glowing like the full moon on a clear night, her stout build teased to curves under the flowing silk and lace.

That was Wendolyn Eudora Cheney, perhaps. Sister of the Moon.

She was briefly reminded of The Star, the tarot card Brigid had gushed over. She didn't have the serene dignity of the lady on that card, but she wondered if she didn't feel a bit of the magic of it changing her perception of herself. Optimism. Coming to the end of a bad season.

Maybe... just maybe...

But not tonight.

Sighing, she pulled the wispy fabric of the peignoir on over the nightgown and tied the flimsy cord into a bow. She had no idea what the extra garment was supposed to hide, given that it was only held in place by that one tie, but whatever. She felt slightly more clothed, anyway, with the long, full sleeves instead of the spaghetti straps on the nightgown.

And when she walked out of the bathroom, her Nightwatchers all stood and stared, as one, for a long moment. They seemed enraptured, which was just crazy. Wen wasn't the enrapturing type. It was, though, more than a little flattering.

So she allowed Dex to take her hand and lead her over to the enormous bed. Allowed Callum to crawl in beside her from the opposite side. Accepted Dex's kiss on the forehead and Florin's lingering press of lips to her knuckles. She watched as they both went to large, red velvet chaise lounges covered with pillows and blankets and relaxed, knowing they'd be almost as comfortable as if they were in the bed with her and Callum.

Weary from the long day and everything she'd learned already, Wen closed her eyes and let herself drift off to dreams of The Star standing overhead, dancing with Sister Moon.

In her dreams, The Star wore a silky teal gown and had gleaming white hair.

15

A knock at the huge, dark wood door woke her in the wee hours of the morning. She lay on her back with Callum's big, muscled arm thrown over her ribcage. Sighing, she scooted out from under him, detangling the long nightgown from the equally silky sheets, then wincing as her feet found the cold, stone floor.

But the boys were out cold, and she didn't want to wake them. She actually felt much better after such a deep sleep, so she tiptoed over to the door and opened it a crack.

Aaron? What on earth—?

"So sorry to disturb ye, milady Wendolyn, but milady Brigid mentioned hoo much ye adored our heeland coos. Thought ye might like to come with me to milk them this fine mornin."

Wide-awake and thrilled with the possibility, she smiled brightly and nodded, then held up a finger before closing the door just to the jamb. Heart skipping at the idea of being close to the shaggy, adorable beasties, she didn't even bother going to the bathroom to toss off the fancy nightwear and step into old jeans, her old sneakers—given her luck, she would absolutely step in a cow patty—and two warm shirts. She'd grab her coat downstairs.

She did, however, tiptoe back to the bed and gently touch Callum on the shoulder. His eyes fluttered open, ginger eyelashes batting at her until he really saw her and started to sit up. She pressed lightly against him, and he subsided, looking sleepy and confused.

"Aaron's taking me to see the coos. We'll be back with fresh milk before you know it."

Relaxing completely, he nodded and grinned sleepily, even managing a wink before rolling over and going back to sleep. He was so adorable. She wanted to scruff his hair but resisted.

Instead, she joined Aaron in the hallway outside her room and carefully, quietly closed the huge door behind her. Then, grinning like children, they hurried to the ground floor where Aaron stopped her and pointed at a row of boots along the wall just inside the main entrance.

"Wellies," he whispered in response to her curious look. "Wellington boots. Rubbers. One wrong step, and the muck will suck those shoes right off yer foot, lass."

She snorted, trying to laugh quietly, and kicked off her old shoes to find a pair that fit. The ones she chose were still a little big, but she wore thick socks against the chill, so she should avoid any blisters or chafing. He even helped her into one of the heavy, sheepskin coats hanging from pegs jammed between the stones of the wall above the boots. She managed to wrap the thick wool scarf he handed her around her neck by herself, but she spared a thought for how much static and frizz she was inflicting on hair that had looked so good last night.

Oh, well. Heeland coos awaited.

Following Aaron out the front door, she was immediately swallowed up by a thick, dense fog. She could see the Nightwatcher walking a few feet in front of her and a small circle of grass around her, but everything else was reduced to dark shapes in the murk. It was like walking through a cloud, cold and damp enough to have her sniffling in less than a minute, but she loved it.

The uneven shape of the barn finally loomed ahead, and they sloshed through a muddy, puddly corral to reach the huge double doors that were already thrown open. Aaron turned to look at her just on the threshold, grinning and pink-cheeked, his green eyes sparkling.

"I took the liberty o' bringin in the milkers already. They're lined up in a row. They're patient as lambs, lass, so long as ye don't startle 'em. They wouldnae hurt ye for all the hay in the loft. Would ye like me to show ye how to milk, or would ye rather watch and maybe scratch behind their ears?"

Smiling, she stepped over the threshold and waited for him to lead the way. "Can I do both? I'd like to say I've milked a heeland coo, but I don't want to miss out on ear scratches, either."

He stopped beside a shaggy ginger cow, patting it gently on the rump. "Sure'n yer a good lass. I reckon ye'll be brilliant at both, aye?"

And thus began the funnest and most interesting morning of Wen's life.

When Wen re-entered the castle, pink-cheeked and starry-eyed with a pail of frothy milk in each hand and a gasp at the difference between the cold outside and the warmth inside, it was through the kitchen instead of the front door. Gerhardt glanced up from where he stood at a butcher block island, chopping meats and vegetables with a bowl of eggs near to hand. When he saw her, his eyes narrowed, but then he gave her a considering look up and down.

"Milk is early today, yes?"

"I helped milk the coos!" she said, too excited to be subtle or answer questions. "We did the whole row!"

Aaron, grinning beside her, nodded. "Sure'n she's a natural, she is, with a gentle touch 'n a way with the beasties." He plunked his two cans down on the floor near the island and shoved his cold hands in his pockets to warm them up. "Would that I had such help every mornin. Ye'd never have to wait for yer cream again, mate."

Nodding, Gerhardt went back to his chopping, apparently done with the chitchat. Aaron eyed her and smiled.

"Care to try yer hand at churnin, lass?"

She narrowly resisted clapping her hands together and jumping up and down like a kid at Christmas. She couldn't stop the "yes yes yes!" from pouring out of her, but she managed to keep at least some dignity.

He chuckled. "Right, then. Let's get out o' this heavy shite, and we can get started. Gerhardt, might we ask for a spot o' tea for milady? She's more than earned it."

The chef grunted agreement and left his chopping to put the kettle under the faucet. Aaron gestured for Wen to follow him back to the main hall, where they shed their coats and toed out of the Wellies. Wen put her old sneakers back on, while Aaron shoved his heavy-socked feet into an old pair of hobnail boots. She'd never seen hobnail boots before, but she'd be very disappointed if that's not what they were.

Then, it was back to the kitchen, where Gerhardt had done something to separate the milk from the thick cream and had made her a lovely pot of tea with some of the cream in the little pitcher. She gratefully stirred some into a steaming cuppa and watched as Aaron poured the rest into... a barrel. An old wooden barrel with a crank handle. Weird.

But he clearly knew what he was doing, and when he gestured for her to come closer, she put down her cup and did so.

"Here ye are, lass. Just crank this handle like so. Hear that sloshin? When it starts to sound thicker, I'll show ye what to do next. Get to it, then."

So saying, he poured his own cup of tea and watched as she dutifully cranked the handle. It was fairly easy, but her arm tired quickly, not used to the motion. Hell, she spent more time typing than anything resembling physical labor. But it was strangely soothing, cranking the handle, watching the barrel swap ends, listening to the sloshing as it changed in tone. Aaron paused her to check it at one point, bringing over a wooden paddle and giving the barrel's contents a few good swipes before shaking his head, closing the top, and gesturing for her to continue. And pouring himself another cup of tea.

"Aye, lass, that ought'a do it."

He waved her back over to the tea tray and took her place, opening the barrel to peer inside. He attacked again with the paddle, grunting occasionally as he whipped the churned cream inside. After a few sips of cooling tea, she couldn't resist going back to peer over the rim of the barrel at whatever was happening inside.

Separating. That's what was happening. It was as if the paddle pushed the more solid parts together, pressing out a cloudy, liquidy stuff in a way that wasn't at all appealing. And then, like magic, the solid parts formed a recognizable clump of real, fresh-churned butter, and delight took over once again.

"There we are, lass." He scooped a bit onto the paddle and held it out for her. "Slather it on one o' them scones and taste the fruits o' yer labor, then."

She did as suggested and— oh. Clotted cream. From milk she'd gathered and cream she'd churned. It was the finest-tasting food she'd ever eaten. The scone wasn't bad, either.

"There ye are, Gerhardt," Aaron went on, scooping out the rest of the butter, then pouring the liquid leftovers into a tall, glass pitcher. "That's the buttermilk. May be a bit sour on its own, but it's the best thing in the world for cookin. Gerhardt'll put it to good use. Nothin goes to waste."

When the seemingly-grumpy German reached for the pitcher, he paused long enough to give her a short, sharp nod. From him, that was clearly immense praise, and she felt herself glowing with a good morning's work. The things she'd seen, and it wasn't even 7:00 AM yet.

When she was sure Aaron was done with her, she scurried back upstairs to her room, ended up in the wrong one, and had to retrace her steps from earlier in the morning. When she finally found the right chamber, she tiptoed in and closed the door behind her. Callum sat up a little, realized it was just her, and went right back to sleep.

Grinning, she shook her head and headed for the immense bathroom. The giant shower beckoned. The oversized tub did, too, but she'd fall asleep and drown if she tried to use it now. But a shower would soothe muscles unused to such work and clean the light sheen of sweat off her back and the dusty-hay smell of the coos off her hands. It was amazing, really. She had just milked cows. Churned her own butter and eaten it right out of the churn.

She was a badass.

The first hot spray took her by surprise, but only because it came from practically every direction, and she was only expecting the overhead. However, once that good, hot water started pounding all her achy bits, she sighed with bliss and relaxed. She definitely wanted a shower like this for her fortress. Although she didn't think she wanted a castle.

Maybe milk cows. And a barn. She loved the barn smells, the sounds of the coos lowing and shuffling in the hay, the dusty rays of pale light cutting through the fog that had followed them in. The barn was a magic place, a happy place. She definitely wanted a barn.

When she felt all loosey-goosey, she took up a poofy and a

bottle of shower gel and scrubbed all over. Brigid had even thought of shampoo and conditioner, so Wen took advantage of trying something new that smelled like milk and honey and vanilla. When she stepped out onto the fluffy (red, of course) bathmat, she felt like a million bucks.

Damn good morning.

Smiling with simple good cheer, she put the teal nightgown back on, though she forewent the peignoir, and climbed back into the huge bed under the covers. Callum immediately rolled over onto her before she could get comfy, but she didn't mind. He was warm and solid and comforting, and after such a fun but strenuous morning, she wanted a little cuddling and perhaps a quick nap before breakfast.

So, pleasantly tired, Wen did just that.

Breakfast was a jolly affair with everyone complimenting the clotted cream until Aaron looked put out and muttered about beginner's luck. Wen was worried until she caught the wink he snuck her. After that, she went back to being proud of what she'd accomplished.

"Guys," she said moments later, suddenly solemn, "I hate to tell you this, but I'm gonna need a to-scale replica of that bathroom in my fortress. No matter what. I need the shower. I need the tub. I need all the little bottles of soaps and salts and sugars and lotions and, hell, poisons, for all I know." She tried to keep the solemn expression on her face, but she was trying too hard not to smile. "We can talk about the colors if you want, but I want everything else, as is."

Brigid piped in with an amused, "Oi!", and everyone had a good laugh. It was, by far, the most relaxed and least worried Wen had ever been in a room full of strangers, and she reveled in it. Was this what The Star meant for her? Because if so—more, please.

After breakfast, the boys all went outside—even Eiji, though he gave Brigid a long, slow look before doing so; Wen had to wonder exactly what their relationship entailed, given the heat in that look—leaving the Sisters to talk Sister business. Or gossip. Dex and Gerhardt paired off for the German to show the Brit his much-loved and well-tended kitchen garden. Callum followed Halvor to his smithy shack; the Norseman had offered him a pair of custom daggers the last time he'd visited, and Halvor had finally finished them not two weeks before.

Florin and Eiji opted to stay in the castle but not in the same room, though they both ended up sitting just outside in the uncomfortable, straight-backed wooden chairs in the hallway and eventually even struck up a conversation. At some point, Wen discovered later, Eiji revealed that his shifted form was a kitsune, an ancient and loyal fox spirit, and Florin begged permission to take a photo. He had to swear on his lady's—Wen's—life that he would never show a living soul outside the Sisters of the Moon and their Nightwatchers, but soon enough, both men were searching the castle grounds, looking for just the right place for a magnificent photograph of a four-tailed fox spirit.

Wen worried about Aaron going off on his own until Brigid explained that it was his way. He liked people well enough, and he and Wen seemed to have hit it off, but he much preferred his own company when his lady was otherwise occupied. Relieved, Wen settled in for another good chat.

Kicking her socked feet up on the velvet settee, Wen sipped her tea and grinned. "If I didn't know better, I'd say Eiji had a crush on you." She winked. "And you might have one back."

Brigid tilted her head, smiling but with a hint of confusion. "O' course he does. He's me First."

Wen, who had expected some light banter and a lot of hand-waving, blinked. "Um. What does that mean?"

"Wendolyn, m'love." Brigid sounded as flustered as a Southern damsel in distress, her hand fluttering at her throat. "Please tell me they explained everythin to ye by now. How it all works."

Worried now, despite the excellent morning, she put her cup down. "I thought so, but the way you say that makes me think not. How what all works?"

Brigid considered her for a moment. "Why would they no' tell you?" She shook her head. "Have ye no' noticed that sometimes... the lads are a bit... keen?"

Wen waited, but that seemed to be all the prompt she would get. So, she answered honestly. "No? What does that mean?"

"Keen on *you*, love."

"Uh." She simply did not understand. It felt like they weren't even having the same conversation at this point. "I mean, I guess I'm lucky they like me, right? We surprisingly hit it off, though I'm not sure Florin isn't only with us because of my hair."

Laughter bubbled up out of Brigid's throat, but it wasn't mocking at all. Just sheer enjoyment. "Oh, Wendolyn, I do love ye. Ye're a breath of fresh air."

Completely lost now, Wen huffed, smiling crookedly. "Thanks. But I still don't know what all of this is about." The smile faded. "Honestly, I'd rather you just say it right out. Whatever it is can't be as bad as what my anxiety is imagining right now."

She wasn't kidding, either. She was less than a minute away from five things she could see, four things she could touch, three things she could hear, two things she could smell, and one thing she could taste.

"Fair enough." Sighing, Brigid leaned forward, pinning her with her gaze. "Lass, it's traditional—not required, but definitely traditional—for Nightwatchers to be the Sisters'... lovers."

What.

"Aye. The lads get a bit intense because they're— well, I reckon they're waitin for ye to be ready. I donnae what's holdin 'em back, but if they havenae made any moves, that'll be why: they think ye're no' ready yet." She shook her head. "As for why they havenae even told ye, I've no clue."

Seriously. What.

Lovers? None of them had even hinted they wanted anything like that. Sleeping in her bed for protection's sake, sure, but...?

What even.

"Oh, Wendolyn," Brigid crooned, coming over to sit on the edge of the settee by Wen's legs. "What's happened to keep them from ye? Can ye tell me, or is it too much?"

She huffed, the sound a bit choked. "It's not even that bad. I just— bad marriage, bad husband, bad divorce. It's probably more my anxiety and general state of fluster keeping them from wanting me more than anything else."

"Oi, now," Brigid said, narrowing her eyes. "Who said anythin about no' wantin ye? Yer lad Florin nigh to made love to yer hair last night. Callum is easier and, honestly, funnier than he's been in decades. I pity poor Gerhardt, tryin to keep up with his blether and keep him out o' the kitchen. And Dex...." She shook her head, smiling softly. "Dex, m'love, is over the moon for ye. I've never seen him so devoted. How ye donnae see his love for ye every time ye look at him, I'll never know. That bad marriage must've been some sort of nightmare to blind ye so."

Tongue-tied, Wen could only stare. Florin just really liked her hair, right? Maybe because it symbolized her Sisterhood and his ability to shift at will. And Callum— well, he'd been snarky and fun right from the start, hadn't he? And Dex.

Dex.

Lips numb, she almost sounded shot full of Novacaine when

she managed to speak. "What does First mean? When you say Eiji is your First. Is it, like—?"

Because if that were the case, Tucker was her First, and she couldn't stand the sight of him anymore. He definitely wasn't devoted to her in any way. He hadn't been in marriage, so there was even less chance of such a miracle in divorce.

But instead of blushing, Brigid only tilted her head one way, then the other, hmm-ing. "Hard to say, love. Which one o' your lads do you go to first with questions? Which do you look to first for comfort, for reassurance?"

Her eyebrows drew together. "Dex, probably. He's the get-shit-done guy, ya know?"

She nodded. "Then, like as no', he's yer First. The one ye trust the most, even though ye trust 'em all. Notice how Eiji hovers about, waitin for me to need somethin? He's my First. I love all my Nightwatchers. It's no' about how much ye love them. Just... somethin about Eiji makes him the first one I turn to, no matter what."

Dex was her First. The phrase tinged like a tiny silver bell in her mind, feeling *right* somehow. He had been her rock from the second she allowed him into her heart, even just as a friend. And yes, he was beyond lovely and, if she allowed herself, she could form quite a crush on him without even trying.

But... *all of them?*

"I— Brigid, am I really supposed to sleep with *all* of them? Is that what they're expecting?"

"Expectin? No. Hopin?" She shrugged, a smile flirting with the corners of her mouth. "I'd say hopin, sure'n certain."

She blinked. "And you... with all of...?"

Now, finally, Brigid blushed, though she smiled outright as she did so. "Yes. Well, Aaron doesnae want sex with anyone, but he's a first-rate cuddler, he is."

Blushing herself, Wen tried to open her mind to the idea and hit a wall. Even one of them would be— They couldn't actually want her, could they? She was still frumpy, dumpy Wen. Nothing had really changed, even with new clothes and a new future.

Who would want her, let alone three gorgeous men who could have anyone they wanted?

Or was that Tucker the Fucker talking? Surely not. But what about her could they possibly want?

The door opened, blowing in a rush of cooler air to rustle the fire in the hearth. She shivered. It felt like an omen. Of doom, of course.

"My lady." Eiji looked as if he'd just run from a mile away. "My lady Thea Deschamps is here. I just let her in the gate. She is in the drive."

Wen went blank. The white-out hit her before she even knew it was coming. It was as if she blinked and, suddenly, Dex was at her side, holding her hand, tenderly thumbing curls away from her cheek. Nothing in between. Had she passed out?

"It's all right, my lady. We're here. You're not alone. You are safe here."

She was supposed to be having sex with this man who looked like a superhero right out of a Marvel movie. And Thea, the eldest Sister who had practically disappeared for decades, was at the door.

Five things she could see: red velvet. Dex's warm, brown eyes. Callum's concerned hazel ones peering over the back of the settee. Florin's dark blue eyes, darker still with concern, down near where her feet were up on the settee. Brigid's pale face and black hair, her worry—not about Thea, but for Wen. Her good heart.

Not enough.

Four things she could touch: the smooth skin of Dex's hand clutching hers. The velvet of the settee she'd collapsed on. The stubble on Callum's cheek. The dark curls crowning Florin's head.

Better, but still not enough.

Three things she could hear: the crackle of the fire. Eiji murmuring softly to Gerhardt, likely about moving preparations up to now instead of tomorrow. Dex's low, warm honey voice, telling her he was there for her, they were all there for her, and everything would be alright.

He *was* her First. The tinkling of that bell in her mind hadn't lied.

And he cared for her, whether he wanted her or not. The current moment was all the proof she needed.

She didn't need two things she could smell. She finally felt better.

Sitting up, she felt a little light-headed and touched a hand to her temple. The side of her head felt— oh. She should have expected. With all the shocks of the day combined with jet lag and excitement and the early morning, even though she went back to bed later, she had all the makings of one hell of a migraine. Where were her meds?

"My lady? What?"

Damn. It was almost like Dex could read her mind. But with Thea at the door, she didn't waste time doubting it. That was a problem for Later Wen.

"Migraine coming on. Probably explains a lot. My meds—?"

He nodded, but before he could direct either of her Nightwatchers, Callum sprang away from the back of the settee. "On it. Hold tight, lass."

He vanished out of her line of sight, so she focused on Dex and Florin, both looking at her with concern but not with dismay or disgust. Or lust, for that matter, but perhaps now wasn't the time.

Goddess, but she was supposed to be having *sex* with these men. How—?

No. Wen didn't have the energy for that train of thought right now. She needed to get her shit together. What would

Thea think of her? The newest, obviously weakest Sister everyone had been waiting for. Forty years, they'd waited, and this was what they got?

She closed her eyes. As if reading her mind again, Dex reached up and rubbed the back of her neck. It felt heavenly, gentle and firm at the same time, warm fingers soothing muscles already tightening up. And then Callum was back with a glass of water and two medicines for her to choose from. She took the as-needed one and popped the little pellet out of its protective coating, put it on her tongue, and let it melt there. Twenty minutes, and she could take on the world.

Or meet her newest, most intimidating fellow Sister of the Moon. Yikes.

For now she lowered her eyelashes and looked first at Dex, then at Callum, and finally at Florin. Beautiful men. Concerned men. Smitten men?

Surely not. Not smitten with *her*.

But her eyes went to Brigid, who smiled with sympathy and nodded. *Yes,* that nod said, *they **are** smitten with ye. Give 'em a chance to prove it, love.*

But Wen wasn't sure she could do that. She couldn't bear to feel the shame of knowing her lover didn't find her sexually attractive at all. Not again. She couldn't stand the failure of another relationship, let alone three at the same time.

Goddess, she couldn't do it. She just wasn't that brave.

A knock at the door had her jerking away from Dex's massaging grip on her neck, almost falling to the floor as she tried to get out of the settee without kicking one of them in the head. She had to get herself together.

Thea was at the door.

16

"Oh, merde. What have I done?"

Those were the first words Thea Deschamps had spoken to a fellow Sister since the eighties. Wen looked the eldest Sister of the Moon up and down, too stunned to speak. Thea was a goddess in the flesh. Her hair was ghostly white, coiled into dreads so long they brushed her thighs. Her skin was polished dark chocolate, glowing with vitality. Her features were so beautiful that statues would weep with joy to be compared to her.

And her arms were so tightly muscled that she looked like she could take on a champion boxer and win. Thea Deschamps was *tough*, and even with the apologetic first words, Wen could tell from the start that this was not a woman who took any shit. Her anxiety started to crank back up again.

The emerald green of my new leggings. The faux-worn brown leather of my new knee boots. The ivory satin of the poet's blouse Callum picked for me. Callum's stubble that I sort of want to rub my palm over. Florin's deep-set eyes that just flicked my way to make sure I'm okay.

Better. Thea still stood, tall and statuesque and stunning, in the doorway, her purple wool pantsuit looking both ravishing and devastatingly business-like flowing around her. She truly looked like what Wen assumed a real goddess would.

She wondered briefly how old the woman could possibly be, then pushed the thought away. None of her business unless Thea Deschamps *said* it was her business.

"Brigid, ma belle, have I mixed up the days?" Now that she wasn't cursing, Thea had a charming French accent that made Wen think, absurdly, of croissants. "I see I have surprised everyone. Your poor Eiji had to run ahead of the auto."

Brigid, who had been uncharacteristically silent, shook off her surprise and went to Thea, offering both hands. Thea took them both, smiling like the first rays of dawn in the dark, and leaned forward to kiss each of Brigid's cheeks. Would she do that to Wen? Should she be expecting that, or was it only because Thea and Brigid had already met decades ago?

"Ye're a day early, love, but yer here now, so we'll make it right. I'd like you to meet our new Sister, Wendolyn Cheney."

"Wendolyn Eudora Cheney," Wen corrected, feeling as if she needed every ounce of Mama's confidence to make this acquaintance. "Pleased to meet you, ma'am. Er— my lady? Madame?"

Flustered already, she made herself stop and smile tightly, her hand out rigidly in front of her. Thea looked her up, looked her down, and tilted her head to one side. Wen froze inside, the already tight smile going brittle.

"Tu es très belle, ma sœur. Bonjour." Thea leaned down from her towering goddess height and placed a gentle kiss on Wen's right cheek, then her left. "Is such pleasure to meet you, my Sister. I hope I have not caused the distress?"

She wasn't sure what all the French meant, but she was pretty sure the first part was "you are very beautiful". She couldn't help but give this impressive new Sister the side-eye. To her surprise, Thea brightened and laughed softly.

"Oh, I like this one. She has the spirit." Her strong hands squeezed Wen's briefly, then let go only to sweep her into an all-encompassing hug. "Yes, Wendolyn Eudora Cheney of the beautiful name and opal eyes, you are précisemént what we need. For you see," she continued, pulling back enough to take in the whole room, her expression sobering, "I have nearly lost my magic."

Brigid tilted her head. "Ye have magic? Why've ye never said?"

Wen watched like a tennis observer, unable to even begin to be part of the conversation.

"I say nothing because I am never sure if magic is what I learned in New Orleans with all the wonderful hoodoo and voodoo queens or if it comes from Sister Moon." She made an evocative gesture toward the ceiling with an elegant hand. "But I see now that the loa do not speak to me because my power is failing. And it is important, yes, because of what it means for us all."

Wen frowned, but Brigid asked the question. "But how do ye know, then? If yer power is failin— I don' ken much about voodoo, but if the loa donnae speak to ye—?"

"Non, non. You see, I did not know how much I had failed. I think I grow old. I think it is time for this old Sister to pass away. The circle of three is already broken, yes? Perhaps it is the end of the Sisters of the Moon." Thea sighed somewhat dramatically. "But then what happens? Days ago now, the loa, they speak to me. After so long, they speak! And they say the time is come to plow the fields, to ready the land. The earth changes, yes, and we must meet the change strong and united." She turned eyes so dark they were nearly black to Wen. "They say a new Sister has come to Light, and it is time."

Lips numb—that was almost verbatim what the last tarot card from her reading said—Wen could only whisper. "Time for what?"

Thea reached out and took Wen's left hand in her right, then reached to take Brigid's right hand in her left. Without consulting, Wen and Brigid reached out and joined hands until they stood in a circle of three, like Thea had said. It felt... powerful.

They felt powerful. Wen felt like her hair was standing on end.

"Time, my darlings, for this." She looked at them each in turn. "The loa, they say they cannot speak because the Veil is thick. When you came to Light, chéri, the Veil thinned enough for me to hear them. They say if the Veil is too thick, no magic comes through to this world. Earth will have no magic ever again. No Sisters, no shifters, no spirits, no hoodoo, no Wicca, no religion, no miracles. All will be lost to us."

Wen's eyes widened. Brigid's did, too, just as worried as Wen, for once. That sounded way too serious for someone who just happened to have white hair and a divorce in her past. And a miscarriage.

"We must find a way to thin the Veil. That is what I learn. The loa did not, cannot say how. Only must."

Thea finally stopped, though she didn't release their hands. It felt as if their circle existed outside the rest of the world, as if they weren't standing in the castle anymore with their Nightwatchers all around them but in some space, some liminal space. Perhaps in the Veil, now that they three were together.

Wen gulped. Did she believe any of this craziness? Talk of loa and Veils and fading magic?

Yes. Yes, she did. Maybe this was why she had come to Light, finally. She'd known that allowing shifters to shift at will was too passive a magic to exist in a vacuum. There had to be a reason for the magic in the first place.

And this? This was it. She felt it through to her bones.

Brigid squeezed her hand, catching her eye and nodding, her pale face resolute. They both looked to Thea, who smiled on them with misty eyes and trembling lips.

The circle of three, complete at last, and in accord with one another.

After a moment spent savoring that sense of connectedness, of a perfect joining together, Brigid sighed and released both Wen's and Thea's hands.

"Glad we got that sorted, m'loves. Now, who's for elevensies?"

There wasn't a single naysayer in the bunch.

Elevensies passed with exchanged stories and with the menfolk coming and going with goodies or throw blankets or wood for the fire, etc. While her Nightwatchers were on a snack run, Wen explained why she'd been so out of it when Thea arrived—panicking over intimacy issues and the sudden knowledge that she was supposed to be intimate with not just one but three men she'd only just met. Brigid reached out to her and clasped her hand as she told her stupid story, then quickly reminded her of the tarot reading from the day before.

"Ah, so that is your gift, mademoiselle." Thea nodded and Brigid blushed. "Do not be embarrassed, chéri. Reading another's energy is perhaps the eldest and most personal of magicks. It is a noble gift from the Mother."

Wen's eyebrows went up. "The Mother?"

"Gaia, the earth goddess, the embodiment of all life and substance on or of Earth." Thea gestured, again somewhat dramatically. "She who gifted us with magic so we could hear Sister Moon and do Her bidding on this, Gaia's green and good earth."

"Wow." It sounded stupid, but it was all Wen could think to say. "I mean, I guess I need to do my research. I'm into cryptids, not goddesses."

Thea frowned slightly. "What is this 'cryptids'?"

"Oh. Uh." Now it was Wen's turn to gesture, but hers weren't nearly as dramatic and about three times as flail-y. "Cryptids are... monsters, sort of. Non-human creatures that most people don't think exist. Shapeshifters, for example. Chupacabra. Sasquatch. Nessie. The Jersey Devil. That kind of thing."

Thea's eyebrows rose. "Our wonderful Nightwatchers are these cryptids? Then you have studied well, indeed, ma petite."

Wen wasn't sure, but she was pretty sure "petite" meant "small", and she was anything but that. Although she *was* the shortest of the Sisters. She barely reached Brigid's nose, and if the top of her head reached Thea's chin, she'd be surprised and likely standing on her toes.

So maybe "ma petite" was an okay nickname, after all. Sure as hell beat Wendy.

A knock on the door derailed her train of thought, and Eiji cracked it open and poked his head in. "My ladies, lunch will be served shortly. Gerhardt has made every French dish he knows."

Thea's right eyebrow rose in a withering stare. Eiji could only shrug while Brigid snickered and elbowed Wen. Wen could only hope that Callum and Gerhardt would shelve the rivalry, as fun as it was, in recognition of the gravity of the situation.

They made their way to the dining room, and Wen gladly offered Thea "her" chair at the opposite end from Brigid. She could still sit between Callum and Dex that way with Florin directly across from her. Brigid's Nightwatchers were all present, including Aaron, though Gerhardt only came in to bow low over Thea's hand and welcome her with all the charm he possessed. Surprisingly, there was just enough for Thea to smile and pat his pale cheek.

And then, there were Thea's Nightwatchers. Wen had received a cursory introduction during elevensies, but she wasn't sure yet if she had them all right.

They seemed to come from all over the world, including a breathtakingly beautiful Native American man whose long, black hair swept in a curtain every time he turned his handsome head. His name was Catahecassa, which she unfortunately had to ask for twice so she could pronounce it without being rude. Maya? Aztec? Cherokee? Even Anasazi, since time didn't seem to be an issue for shifters? Wen had no idea, but the man was stunning and soft-spoken. Simply beautiful. Perhaps it was no surprise that he shifted into a buffalo, though he kindly didn't demonstrate the gift and accidentally destroy an entire room of Brigid's castle. Callum raised his glass in silent solidarity.

At his side sat Brody, a dark-headed Irish bloke who seemed unimpressed with the fancy French food and stuck to the braised venison and thick slices of bread. Aaron piped up and explained that Wen had churned the butter herself that very morning, earning her a reassessment and a somewhat impressed nod before the bloke returned to his bread and meat. It didn't seem a stretch to discover that he shifted into a huge Irish wolfhound. Unfortunately, she also discovered that he didn't care for ear scritches, at least not from strangers. Shame.

On Thea's other side sat Samuel, her French-Canadian First who proudly announced that he shifted into an elk. When Halvor, who shifted into a polar bear, boasted that venison was indeed on the menu, Samuel eyed him, unimpressed, and asked if he'd ever seen an elk in person before. The "conversation" nearly devolved into a shifter showdown, but Brigid and Thea rolled their eyes and told their men to compare shift sizes later.

Wen nearly choked on her Moscato.

Finally, next to Samuel sat Phaeton, a gorgeously olive-toned Greek nonbinary with startlingly light green eyes that seemed to glow even when they weren't feeling the shift. And, much to Wen's delight, they shifted into a pegasus. It took everything in her not to beg for them to shift then and there. They did, however, promise to shift for her as soon as it was convenient, winning Wen over completely and causing Callum to grumble about how she hadn't even seen his war horse yet.

"You're the one who wouldn't shift to show me," she reminded him, spreading her own clotted cream on a slice of bread.

"Aye, because I'd've destroyed yer wee shoebox of a flat if I had. War horses are straight massive, lass."

Samuel, unimpressed, rolled his eyes. "My elk could take any horse."

Dex piped in, smirking. "Not a Shire horse, you couldn't. Stupidly huge, he is."

"War. Horse." Callum glared around Wen, who leaned back out of the line of fire. "Ye do that all the time, mate. I am no' a Shire horse. Ye cannae just strap me to a wagon and haul yer ale, can ye?"

Dex shrugged. "Might be more useful if we could. How many times have we ended up with destroyed furniture because you couldn't find a good enough vault during the full moon?"

Phaeton smiled charmingly. "Now add wings to that, and you'll have a real problem."

Samuel nodded, mock-solemn. "Antlers. They destroy everything."

Wen, both amused and slightly worried that she'd started either an argument or a support group (she wasn't sure which) tried to change the subject. "Why do you think some of your shapes are cryptids and some aren't?"

Silence. Oops. What had she said wrong? Clearly, she'd said something either insulting or outright taboo because an entire table full of people now stared at her with varying expressions of disapproval.

Then, perhaps to save her, Florin spoke, his clear, deep voice and crisp accent breaking the increasingly uncomfortable silence.

"Our numbers used to hold *only* cryptids, my lady. Unicorns. Sea monsters. Minotaurs. Elementals, like Eiji's fox spirit. Even dragons." He smiled softly, but the expression held quiet pain. "I said when we met that I am perhaps the last living dire wolf, yes?"

She nodded, mortified and fascinated all at once.

"We are dying out, my lady. Losing our more magical shifted forms is only the start. Too soon, we will be unable to shift at all and merely be... human. A few generations, and there will be no more shifters."

What could she even begin to say to that? Thankfully, she was spared a response by several other shifters—and Brigid and especially Thea—becoming alarmed by the dim prognosis.

"How do you know?" and "And who are you to say?" and "Oh, bollocks!" and a few expostulations in other languages that could only be curses all erupted. Thea talked over them all.

"Pardon, Monsieur Fleur, but you must explain, s'il vous plaît."

"Florin, my lady." But he didn't sound annoyed. Just so sad. "I remember when you came to Light. I was already more than a hundred years old then, Sister. I do not even remember my own surname anymore. I have watched and waited, I have captured the passage of time on film, and I have seen." He looked at Wen and softened. "I waited for you, my lady."

Blushing, she wished he would stick to the explanation and not look at her with those gorgeous eyes of his while she was still reeling internally from the idea that she should be having sex with him. With all three of them. Now was so not the time.

Thankfully, most of the tumult in the room calmed after his admission. It appeared Florin was easily the eldest shifter present—older, even, than the eldest Sister of the Moon. Who could argue with his experience?

Thea didn't even try. "What again is your shape, monsieur?"

"Dire wolf, my lady."

Her right eyebrow rose. "Ma déesse. One of your kind terrorized my birth region more than two hundred and fifty years ago, savaging children and shepherds, tearing out their throats and eating their organs."

His eyebrows rose, as well. "Gévaudan?" When she nodded, he grinned wryly. "No relation."

Dex and Callum chuckled. Actually, several around the table chuckled, and the mood lightened considerably.

"So you have seen much, monsieur. I believe you." She nodded, serious but not so severe. "I have felt the magic wane over my lifetime. I cannot imagine what you have experienced in yours."

Wen couldn't, either. Hell, she was a spark in her ancestors' eyes compared to his span of years, though he looked a good ten years younger than her. How had he stayed alive so long? How did it feel to be the last of his kind?

No wonder he looked so sad.

She reached out her foot and leaned her ankle against his under the table. She wasn't playing footsie; she simply couldn't reach across the table's width. Her arms weren't long enough. He looked at her, and some of the sadness left his ocean-deep eyes.

Suddenly, Catahecassa, who had been all but silent since introducing himself, spoke. "I am descended from the ancient Puebloans. We used to be called Anasazi, but we do not own that name and do not want it. I only tell you so you know my truth." He turned his attention to Florin. "You, too, speak truth, friend. I am buffalo, but I remember when my people shifted into the great spirits of the land. We have only the buffalo now, the coyote, the wolf, the eagle, the mustang." He looked at Thea and nodded. "I have seen it, my lady. He speaks truly."

Thea nodded, deep in thought. Silence filled the room without the clink of silverware or the slosh of drink. Finally, she nodded again.

"The loa want us to thin the Veil. You, Wendolyn, thinned it enough for them to speak, enough for Brigid's cards to speak to her, when you came to Light."

She blushed, again finding herself under scrutiny. So, she blurted. "I may have also had something of a chat with the moon. Sister Moon, I mean. Er— not so much a chat as... an argument? Things were said—"

She trailed off at the array of looks, ranging from interested to appalled, around the table. *Why, oh why can't I just be normal?*

Aaron was perhaps the only person who looked amused. "Ye shouted at Sister Moon?"

The blush traveled, covering her from hairline to shoulders. "It was the middle of the night, and I didn't want anyone calling the cops. Of course I didn't shout."

He looked as if he knew better, but Thea again took over. "But you heard Her in return, yes?"

She thought back to something that had, at the time, felt almost like a religious experience. She'd been so angry, and then she'd felt... soothed. Felt something broken inside her mended but not removed entirely, like one of those kintsugi vases stuck back together with gold to show the beauty of the repair instead of hiding it.

"Not in words," she finally said. "But I just... knew."

It was the best she could do to describe what had happened. But was that magic, like Thea's voodoo and Brigid's tarot? Weren't they all Sisters of the Moon, which should mean the moon would always answer them?

Maybe she didn't have any talent of her own. It seemed likely.

Thea nodded—not as if she were privy to Wen's depressing thoughts but in understanding of what she'd tried to say. "The magic *is* coming back. I knew it when the loa spoke. But how are we to thin the Veil? This, we do not know."

A little quiet fell, though not a full silence. This lull was filled with shuffling feet, the gentle clink of silverware, a few gulps of beverages, and a faint humming from Gerhardt in the kitchen. Before anyone could come up with any sort of answer, the bluff German backed through the Dutch door and turned around with what looked like a fluffy cloud on an enormous silver tray.

"Ta-da! Behold, my pièce de résistance!"

French spoken with a German accent made for an interesting hodge podge, but that was Gerhardt. And apparently, he'd made them... dessert?

Whatever it was, he elbowed between Florin and Aaron to place it close to the center of the table, then struck a dramatic pose. "En flambé!"

With that, he snapped his fingers and made a tossing gesture, and the dessert caught on fire. Wen, jumpy at the best of times, leapt away from the table amongst the oohs and aahs, pulling part of the tablecloth with her, which only brought the flaming death even closer. Shouts erupted, along with the screech of almost a dozen chairs scooting away from the table. She closed her eyes and flung her hands out before her to shield, and—

Sudden silence.

Deathly silence.

She froze, eyes squeezed shut, wondering what on earth she'd done now. Goddess, how could she embarrass herself even further?

"Reckon it's a good job we none of us were sippin whisky, aye?"

Aaron's voice, but Wen had no idea what he meant until she opened her eyes. The so-called dessert was a soggy, smoldering, melty mess. Gerhardt looked stricken, and she made a note to apologize if he'd ever speak to her again. And if she could ever look him in the eyes again.

Every single glass, goblet, flute, cup, or mug on the table was tipped over, empty.

What.

What had happened. What had— had she done something?

Thea, hand over her heart, stared at her in... wonder? Shock? "Ma petite. How?"

Lips numb, the white-out threatening—five things she could see: the elaborate mess she'd somehow made, Dex and Callum and Florin staring at her, everyone else gawking like she was a freak, Gerhardt's broken heart over his ruined dessert, the smoke curling up from said ruined dessert—Wen could only shake her head. She didn't even comprehend what had happened, let alone how.

"You— all the water— all the drinks— ma petite...?"

All those empty glasses, cups, goblets—

Dex laid a warm hand on her shoulder. "My lady, you drowned the fire."

But she hadn't touched anything. It wasn't like she'd picked up every liquid receptacle on the table and flung them on the fire, one by one. That was crazy.

"Yes." He leaned closer, moving his light grip from her shoulder to around her waist. Probably worried she would faint, and she couldn't blame him. "You put out your hands, and all the drinks flew out of their cups and onto the Baked Alaska. You put it out, Wen."

Baked Alaska? So that's what the dessert was. She'd never seen one before. Probably never would again, if Gerhardt had anything to say about it.

"But I didn't."

Callum leaned in, too, slipping his arm around the middle of her back. "Ye did. We all saw. Ye have a gift, milady."

And suddenly, there was Florin, pressing up against her back with his big, strong hands on her shoulders, burying his face in her hair as he'd probably wanted to from that first moment on the damp road in the middle of nowhere.

"My lady, you are truly blessed. Sister Moon shines in you. She has given you great power."

Thea picked up her goblet and Brigid did the same.

Solemnly, all the remaining Nightwatchers not currently attached to her mirrored them, raising their glasses and cups in salute.

But they're all empty, she couldn't help but think, the white creeping over her vision.

All the cups are empty.

17

A panic attack wasn't like passing out, although that sometimes did happen. For Wen, she just went away for a while. Sometimes she even kept walking around or working or otherwise functioning with no memory of doing so afterward. Sometimes, she sat in her recliner for two hours without moving or thinking or comprehending the passage of time.

This time, she passed out, and when she came to, she was in bed in the bed chamber, Dex wrapped around her from behind, Florin burrowed against her from the front, and Callum lying across the head of the bed, leaning up on one elbow, looking down at her while he curled a lock of her hair around his finger over and over again. When he realized she was awake, he grinned.

"Sure'n ye know how to make an exit, lass."

"Oh, no." It popped out before she could stop it. "What did I do this time?"

"No fear, milady. Everyone understood. We none of us have seen anythin like that before. We were all a wee bit shaky afterward."

She started to sit up, but Dex and Florin clung to her more

tightly, and she took the hint. "But what did I even do? It didn't feel like anything. I just—" She sighed. "Panicked."

Dex sighed into her hair, and the nape of her neck tingled. It suddenly struck her that she was in bed with three men. That she was supposed to be having sex with.

Oh, well. She was too tired to tense up.

"My lady, I have seen more magic in the past week than I have in the past hundred years. Thea is right; the circle is complete, and all the Sisters' powers are growing. You're only just now discovering what they are, so you won't know what you're capable of until you do it."

Florin nodded against her neck. "I have not seen such magic since the last two Sisters vanished. When I was a child, I saw a Sister stand in the middle of a field and call down so many birds that they blotted out the sky." He cuddled closer. "I thought that magic gone forever, my lady. You have brought it back."

She shook her head. "But I haven't. I didn't do anything. And if I did, I don't know how."

Callum shrugged, still twiddling his fingers through her hair. "Doesnae matter, lass. Ye have the magic, and ye used it in a moment o' stress. That means ye can learn to use it whenever ye want."

Florin nodded again. "The legend in my time was the Sisters of old grew stronger as the moon waxed and weaker as the moon waned. That's why they needed Nightwatchers—to protect them during the new moon, when their magic was at low ebb."

"Okay, see, now that makes so much more sense." She again moved to sit up, but her guys still held her down. "That at least would explain the whole Sister-shifter relationship, why it's even needed."

Callum grinned. "So it's no' a tautology, then?"

She blinked. "You actually listened to that rant?"

He leaned down, suddenly serious with his lovely hazel eyes

only inches above her own. "I listen to everythin ye say, milady. I know hard-fought wisdom when I hear it."

Sighing, she closed her eyes and shook her head. "I'm sorry about that. I'm just so damn sensitive—"

"No." Dex's voice left no room for argument. Everyone stilled. "Wendolyn Eudora Cheney, you had every right to be vexed with us. We behaved like children, and you rightly called us out on it."

She opened her eyes and finally turned her head to look back at him. "You two were just having a good laugh, and I ruined it by getting huffy and lecturing you."

Callum sighed. "Then you taught us two valuable lessons for the price o' one, lass."

A little hush fell between them, and Wen tried not to tense up or think about anything but the moment. Not grounding, per se, as she wasn't currently panicking, but more avoiding thinking too much and winding herself up. Everything happening around her was too important for her anxiety to keep holding her back. She needed to think clearly, not obsessively.

She had (according to everyone else) moved water. Had reached out her hands, swiped all the liquid from all the glasses and doused it all on the flaming dessert. Without thinking about anything but not wanting to be burned by the flaming cloud thing following her away from the table.

Or had she just moved the cups? Simple telepathy?

No. If she had moved all the glasses and whatnot, they'd have fallen all around the Baked Alaska and shattered or spilled everywhere. And if she'd simply tipped them over, none of the liquid would have made it to the dessert to put it out.

The liquids. She could somehow affect liquids. Her eyes widened.

"The tides." Shaking her head, she finally sat up despite the initial resistance. "The moon pulls the tides. That's why it's the liquid instead of the glasses. I moved them like the tides."

She turned to face them, and all three looked impressed. She blushed.

"Sorry. Just thinking out loud. I was trying to figure out... ya know... so I can do it again, maybe?"

Even now, with all three of them in her bed, she was hesitant and awkward. She should be used to it by now, but at the moment, the awkwardness was a waste of time and energy. She just wanted to be able to say things right out, dammit.

This time, it was Callum that saved her, his accent no longer as heavy as when Brigid was around. "Quite right, milady. You should practice, aye? Perhaps in the bath?"

She reached out and cupped his cheek, enjoying the tickle of stubble on her palm. It had been so long since she'd touched a man's face, felt that prickle against her skin. She'd missed it.

"Callum, you are brilliant. Let's go."

Nothing. Half an hour of trying everything she could think of, and she hadn't created even a ripple in the enormous tub's waterline. What was she doing wrong? Dex and Callum had called dibs on sitting on the long vanity, while Florin had put the toilet seat down and was googling Goddess knew what on his phone, clearly bored with the whole disaster.

"Why isn't this working? Ugh!"

Irritated, she flung her hand at the tub as she turned away, and... *slosh*.

She paused. All four hopped to and drew nearer, collectively holding their breath. The waterline waved gently against the tub's sides, slowed, stopped.

Tingling all over, she whispered, "Do I have to be angry or scared or something?" She frowned and crossed her arms. "I don't want to only have power when I'm overloaded. That's a recipe for disaster."

Dex hmmed. "Florin, you said the Sisters used to draw power from the phases of the moon?"

He nodded. "That was the legend, yes."

Nodding, Dex frowned, considering. "Perhaps it's not overloading you need but energy. Energy from the moon, which is almost full, energy from being scared, energy from being irritated—"

"Energy from fire!" Wen supplied, suddenly excited. "Anybody have a lighter? Matches? With all these damn candles, there surely has to be a fire source somewhere."

After much rummaging, Callum finally slapped himself on the forehead and snatched up the cache of kindling sticks on the fireplace mantle, then ran down to the sitting room, where the fire had been stoked up in preparation for afternoon tea. When he returned, he'd ditched the tin of kindling somewhere to cup his free hand in front of three lit sticks.

Wen quickly met him halfway to the bathroom with a candle, in case the punks went out. Then, she went to stand by the tub, the candle held before her, and concentrated while Callum handed a glowing stick to Dex and one to Florin. All three immediately began lighting every candle in the bathroom while she tried to focus.

Nothing. Not one ripple. If only she knew what she'd done before. Maybe she was thinking too hard.

Maybe the flambé disaster had been a fluke. Wouldn't that be just her luck?

No. She could do this. She had already done this.

She closed her eyes. Held the candle with one hand and reached the other toward the tub. Stilled her thoughts. Grounded herself.

With her eyes closed, she couldn't list five things she could see, but she could list four things she could touch. The smooth glass of the candle holder. The warmth of the tiny flame. The slight chill that came from the stone walls. And almost, just almost—

—the surface of the water. She could feel it, cool and wet beneath her fingers, and she dabbled them lightly, then smiled as she heard the sound she expected: the slight trickle of droplets and lap of slow ripples against the edges of the tub.

It wasn't the fire, though that had certainly goaded her panic response before. She just had to settle herself. Be grounded.

She opened her eyes and smiled. Three wide-eyed, impressed men smiled back at her.

Callum put up a hand. "Well done, lass. Up high."

Grinning and feeling giddy, she hopped up to slap him a high five, and for that moment, everything was absolutely awesome.

"Répéter," Thea ordered, smiling. "C'est magnifique!"

Wen's bathroom had seemed enormous until she tried to crowd her three Nightwatchers, two Sisters, and their eight Nightwatchers into it for a demonstration. The crowd and close quarters threatened to lock her up, but she closed her eyes, thought of three things she could hear—the low hush of quiet, anticipatory breathing; the shuffling of feet; her own heartbeat as it threatened to crawl up her throat—and felt her hand slip into the cool water. A bonus thing she could hear: ripples and dabbles.

She did that. She made that happen.

Beaming, Brigid threw herself into Wen's arms. "Ye're amazin, m'love! A marvel! How on Gaia's green and good Earth did ye sort it out?"

Blushing, she pulled back and hunched her shoulders, then made herself straighten them back up. "Anxiety, actually." She huffed and shook her head. "I thought maybe the fire gave me the energy to make it happen—"

"Oi, is that why Callum came thunderin in on me readin time in the sittin room?"

"Oh, sorry!" She blushed, but Brigid only chuckled and waved her on. "Anyway, I lit a few candles, but that didn't seem to do anything, and I started to get all wound up again and did one of the grounding techniques my therapist taught me. Worked like a charm."

"C'est ingénieux, ma petite." Thea stepped in when Brigid backed away and wrapped Wen in those strong, badass arms. "You truly are the one we have waited so long for."

Her eyes started up the traitorous prickles, so she closed them and hugged her Sister tight. It felt so strange, but also so wonderful, to be around so many huggy people. She'd barely had any physical contact since the divorce, but she'd so quickly become needy for touch now. She loved it.

It felt like family. Like home.

After a moment, she made herself huff and pull away, wary of being too needy. "I dunno about that. All I did was—"

"Discover a method that will surely aid the mission given us by the loa?"

She pressed her lips together, caught without a ready disclaimer for that one. She *had* figured it out. She didn't know how it would stop the thickening of the Veil, let alone thin it down enough to *save all of the freaking magic on Earth*, but hey. Baby steps.

"Well, anyway. You guys should try it. I just closed my eyes and thought of four things I could feel, and the last thing was the water I wasn't even touching, and it moved like I *had* touched it."

Both Thea and Brigid tried, but the water stayed still.

Frowning, Wen crossed her arms and considered. "Maybe it worked for me because it's what I always try to do when I start to panic. Maybe it's different for each of us, and you guys just need to find what makes it work for you?"

"Perhaps so," Thea agreed, but not as if she was terribly happy about it. "I wish this were a problem with plants or crystals or even plain soil. Those are things I am used to with my voodoo and hoodoo. They have symbolism and inherent properties that I understand." She smiled tightly. "Or perhaps that is only because I was taught by those who already knew the magic. Je ne sais pas."

Brigid tried one more time, then grunted. "I've no knack for it, love. I feel nothin when I get to that last step." She grinned wryly. "Mayhap if ye sort out how to fly, I'd find a knack for that. Always had a yen for watchin birds in flight."

Phaeton spoke up, also wry. "It's not as easy as it looks."

A general hubbub of laughter echoed off the black and white checkerboard tile, and people started filtering out. Wen stayed behind a moment longer, smiling to herself. Dex came to stand beside her and take her hand. She squeezed it, smiling at him now.

"You truly are a wonder, my lady," he murmured, warm eyes on hers. "Thea is right; you *are* the one we've all been waiting for."

She blushed, then startled as Florin took her other hand.

"I have waited for you for two hundred years, Wendolyn Eudora Cheney."

She melted. He didn't even know the story about why her full name was so important to her. She'd have to tell him so he'd know how happy he'd just made her.

"Every moment was worth being here with you now, watching you bloom into your power."

She gasped, then squeezed his hands, beyond words. Callum bent down to let the water out of the tub, then stood before her and leaned down to touch his forehead to hers.

Connected. It wasn't just physical contact she was starting to crave, but connectedness. Her guys. Her Nightwatchers.

"Milady, if you ever again doubt your worth, remember this: you leave even me feelin humbled, aye?"

She chuckled, and shook her head gently, so as not to dislodge their connection. "You are such a brat."

He snickered, then pulled back so suddenly that she took a step forward to catch her balance. She hadn't realized they'd been leaning so hard together.

"Milady Wendolyn Eudora Cheney," he intoned, sounding far too formal for the dancing light in his hazel eyes and the dimple flirting with his cheek. "I've an idea."

"Ye wannae do what now?"

"Non. It is too dangerous. An unnecessary risk, ma petite."

Wen's Sisters didn't seem to like Callum's suggestion. Maybe she hadn't said it right.

"I don't think it's unnecessary. Callum says the full moon is just two nights away. I should be able to draw on it tonight, right?" She hurried on before they could protest again. "And what better test run than trying to clean up the ocean, which is what I've wanted to do since I was a little girl? Hell, I'm even looking into getting a degree in marine biology. It's perfect!"

Brigid shook her head. "Ye wannae take a wee boat out onto the actual ocean to see if ye can shift a trash island back toward the coastline what caused it. And ye don't see how that could possibly go wrong?"

She sighed. "Don't say it like that. The moon controls the tides. I can move water. I bet if I have enough oomph behind me, I could figure out how to raise a few waves to break up the junk, then direct it against the current back to where it came from. Easy-peasy."

She was not, in fact, sure it would be at all easy-peasy. But she was trying to feel confident, and she really wanted to try something a little bigger than bathwater.

"Look." Wen pulled out her phone and tapped it on, bringing up the picture she'd googled earlier. "The North Atlantic Gyre swirls between the west coast of Europe, including the British Isles, and the east coast of the States. I did a Google Earth search to see where the nearest North Atlantic garbage patch was, and it's cruising northwest of Portugal." She brought up the screenshots she'd taken of the search results. "See? If we can charter a good enough boat, we can be there in a few hours. Just in time for a nighttime test run. Dex has already run the numbers."

"Oi, love, that doesnae mean ye should do it." She turned just enough to thwap Callum on the arm. "Why'd ye go gettin her all wound up, ye bad lad?"

"Oi!" He rubbed at his arm. "If ye're to fix the Veil, ye'll need more than a wee fire extinguisher, aye? Milady wants to try, and I support her. We all do."

Dex and Florin both nodded, though Dex looked fidgety, an obvious change from his usual stoicism and despite his complete willingness to help her get where she wanted to go. She reached out and took his hand, appreciating that he would go to bat for her despite his misgivings about her safety.

Thea sighed, then smiled wryly, that right eyebrow going up again. "Of course, you will go, ma petite. No one tells you what you do. Non."

She blushed but nodded. Dex squeezed her hand lightly.

Sighing again, this time with a touch of drama, Thea rolled her eyes. "And we will go with you. Even for the small trash, we must all try together, mais oui?"

Her eyes widened. "Oh, that's not— you guys don't have to come if you don't want to. I don't want to endanger anyone else, if it's really so dangerous."

Brigid snorted, not having it. "Ye cannae leave us behind, love. We'd only follow after. We're all in this together now, aye?"

"Aye," Thea said, dark eyes gleaming like jet beads.

Her mouth twisting wryly, she sighed. "Aye, I guess. If you insist."

"Bien sûr, ma petite."

"Aye, we insist."

Thea held out her hands to either side. Brigid took her left, and Wen let go of Dex so she could take Thea's right and complete the circle with Brigid.

The circle of three. Complete. Coming into their power. Mission: save the planet's magic.

No pressure.

But this time, Wen wasn't alone. She'd take those odds any day.

18

"Dex, you are a genius." Wen stood in the prow of the charter boat, leaning forward into the rush of the cool, damp sea breeze. It blew her hair back, ruining the careful, shining waves Florin had again coaxed it into. She'd apologized for that at first, but Florin had only smiled and said not to worry. It meant he could brush it again later.

Dex, of course, stood beside her, though Callum and Florin hung back with the other Nightwatchers. "You will go where you will, my lady. I swear to it." He softened and grinned. "Even if I could take a right whack at Callum for suggesting this."

This nonsense, she finished for him, knowing he'd never say it out loud.

They had made amazing time with Halvor piloting the ship and Phaeton navigating. The pair worked well together, which Wen hoped boded well for future endeavors. If all their Nightwatchers could get along, pretty much anything was possible, surely.

If she could really do magic, of course. And if Brigid and Thea could find theirs. She had no doubt that they *did* have magic, now that their circle was complete. Just... what was it? Why could she move the water but they couldn't?

But they were less than an hour away from the last Google Earth's positioning of the nearest garbage patch. Wen caught herself thinking ahead, but she didn't think she was obsessing. If this worked on one of the smaller, newer-formed Atlantic garbage patches, maybe they could start picking away at the island-sized Great Pacific garbage patches. Do some real good.

So long as she didn't accidentally disrupt the big currents. She couldn't possibly have that kind of power, but those currents pretty much controlled the weather of the entire planet, not to mention the temperature and delicate balance of the oceans' ecosystems. She'd have to be careful to not make things worse by being clumsy now.

Even though she was the Queen of Klutz.

Please, Sister Moon, guide me as You do the tides.

It was the closest thing to a prayer she'd said since the divorce. That prayer had been that she not buckle under the depression and loss and anger. This one felt a lot less devastating. More hopeful, perhaps. And more likely to be answered.

Smiling, she closed her eyes and let the fresh, salty ocean air fill her lungs. She had missed the ocean more than anything besides Mama. She'd only been able to go on a few excursions while she'd lived in Oregon, but she never forgot that endless, boundless feeling of looking across the great expanse or closing her eyes and feeling the ceaseless motion, the rise and fall, the rush of the waves, the cool sting of the spray.

She loved it. She wanted to savor every minute.

She had to admit to a small worry, though. The sky had clouded over the closer they came to Portugal, and Sister Moon was only visible in flirty little flashes. Would the cloudy sky impede whatever energy the moon gave her? Or did it matter so long as the moon was near full, whether she could see it or not?

The possibilities started to circle, and she closed her eyes.

Five things she could— no. Maybe four things she could hear? The whoosh of the wind. The ceaseless rush of the waves. Quiet chitchat from her fellow seagoers—

A sudden spurt off to starboard had her jumping half over the port railing before she caught herself and realized there was nowhere to go but into the drink that way.

A whale! A whale had surfaced not fifty feet away and blown a plume from its blowhole.

"Oh my Goddess!" she shouted, elated. "I think it's a humpback! Look at that!"

It didn't resurface, but just knowing one of the majestic sea creatures swam nearby filled her with an inner peace unlike she'd ever known. Humpbacks had been brought back from the brink over the course of the years, and what a salvation for the planet. Gentle giants. Beautiful.

Three things she could touch, though she didn't need the calmness now. She needed focus.

The metal railing in her hands. The cool sea spray on her cheeks and forehead. The glow of moonlight as Sister Moon peered out from behind a cloud.

Spsssh!

Another whale spout! And this time, the humbpack actually breached, flashing its fins. Another one joined in, splashing an enormous fan of spray with its fluke. Her breath caught. Magnificent.

And dolphins! A pod of dolphins began popping up off to port, swimming along with the boat and chittering to each other. She could hardly believe her luck.

"Can we slow down? I know we want the garbage patch, but—"

She gestured toward all the ocean life happening around them. Halvor touched a finger to his watchcap and cut the engines, letting them coast in a gentle slowdown, allowing the helm to drift where the ocean wanted them to go.

A squadron of spotted eagle rays sailed past, just below the surface, some of their flappy fins breaching the surface enough to draw her attention, and she tilted her head to one side. They'd been at sea for hours and hadn't seen a single living creature until now. What were the odds?

Another whale breached, the black and white unmistakable. That was a freaking orca. Orcas wouldn't usually be near humpbacks without a tussle. What was happening?

Brigid crept closer to the prow, though Wen got the feeling she wasn't too keen on boating. "This isnae normal, is it."

It wasn't a question, so Wen didn't bother answering. Something strange was happening here. If she could see a little better—

The moon disappeared behind a cloud, and she huffed, annoyed. "I wish Sister Moon would come back. I can't see what might be below the surface without Her."

"Aye, love. We donnae want to run aground on the trash pile, I expect." She glared up at the sky, eyes narrow. "If only the clouds would— oi!"

Though the moon had disappeared behind a solid wall of cloud only moments before, it suddenly sailed into a completely clear patch and shone brightly around them. Thea gasped from where she leaned over the port railing and looked out across the illuminated waves.

Wen leaned as far over the railing as she dared and gasped, too. A huge circle of sea creatures—fish, rays, jellyfish, turtles, dolphins, the pair of humpbacks, the orca, even a few sharks— cruised serenely around the boat. She followed them with her eyes until the cabin cut off her view, then ran to the starboard side to confirm what she already knew.

They were circling them. Circling *her*.

"Ma petite, you are calling them."

Like the birds, she thought, looking to Florin for confirmation. *He said she called so many birds they blotted out the sky.*

Goosebumps raced up and down her arms, and she took a step back as she looked out over the crazy gathering of creatures she had somehow gathered together. Fortunately or no, Dex was there to bump into, and he wrapped his arms around her, being her physical support. He wouldn't let her white out. He wouldn't let her fuck this up.

Gaining confidence when the creatures only circled serenely, she stepped out of his grip and back up against the prow railing. Again, she leaned over as far as she could. She even laughed when one of the humpbacks spouted close enough that she caught some of the spray—enough to dampen her shirt and hair.

And then she felt something on her hand. Something... wet. And cold. And a little... rubbery?

She looked down and blanked. What could that possibly be? A coral red thing with a spatulate shape and suckers on the bottom. Suckers that were winding the thing around her wrist.

A tentacle, of course. A tentacle had come up out of the ocean to wrap around her wrist, and the tentacle was actually thicker than her forearm. Interesting.

"Jesus Christ," she murmured, unsure if anyone would even hear her. "Did I just release the Kraken?"

Before anyone even realized the danger, the tentacle gave a mighty tug, and over the prow railing she went.

She didn't scream. She hadn't drawn in enough air to do so before she hit the water with a stinging slap and came face to face with perhaps the greatest cryptid-that-was-real ever.

A giant squid.

Things seemed to happen very slowly underwater. She had time to see the creatures circling the boat, to pick out the species she knew. She had time to appreciate that, while the suckers did sting a bit, the tentacle wasn't trying to cut off circulation. The squid was, however, pulling her deeper into the nighttime ocean, drawing perilously near the furthest reach of the nearly-full moon's range.

She probably shouldn't go down there. Even if she didn't drown, she would probably explosively decompress. It would be messy. The last thing she wanted from this trip was to be the shortest-lived Sister of the Moon of all time.

And then she saw something flitting in the shadows just at the edge of the moonlight's reach. It moved in a vague circle—nothing as regimented as the great conflagration above—and the giant squid headed right for it.

Her ears tried to pop. It hurt. This was not good.

And then the something left its pseudo-circling and swam directly toward her. Her first thought was how interesting it was that a baby blue whale—the smallest one in existence—was flowing toward her. She had always wanted to see a blue whale, even the runt of the litter.

And then it finally rose up into the moonlight and she realized it wasn't a miniature blue whale. That had been a trick of the light, the blue-gray sheen to its skin, and the length and shape of its tail.

It was a mermaid. A merperson. She couldn't tell, even this close. The features were only rudimentarily human, with two eyes facing forward, two holes for a nose, gills on the neck (though that aspect wasn't so human-like), and a wide, full-lipped mouth. Sharp teeth in that mouth. Good for ripping into other fish, she presumed, her scientific side kicking in as her head pounded and her lungs screamed for air.

It was all very interesting.

The squid abruptly let her go. She should probably try to swim for the surface, but she felt like she could barely move her arms and legs. It was cold this far under the surface. And she was tired. And her head hurt. Her lungs burned.

The merperson reached out to her, and she managed to raise her arm enough to count as an offer. The creature took it, then gaped in surprise as it... changed.

Shifted.

How the hell had she found a shapeshifter in the depths of the Atlantic Ocean?

Unfortunately, she realized right away that something was wrong. The merperson didn't shift into another creature. It shifted into a man. A human man.

Who apparently couldn't swim, as he started to sink, his hand clutching hers as he flailed his other arm and his legs, trying to coordinate them. She realized in that moment that he would drown. He'd likely been a merman his whole life, only to be drawn to the one person who could allow the shift into a human form that could not survive underwater.

She had to save him. She had accidentally done this to him. She had to fix it.

Some of her strength returned with her resolve, even in the deeper cold, and she clutched his hand in hers, dragging him up to her. Once he was in reach of the other hand, she pulled him into her arms and started kicking toward the moonlight.

Sister Moon, guide me.

Another prayer, but she was almost out of breath, and the man clutched her almost too hard, as if trying to squeeze out what little air she had. This was bad. The squid had dragged her further down than she thought. They were both going to drown.

No. She could still kick. She could still get them both to safety. The boat couldn't be that far away. She was still inside the ring of lazily circling, unconcerned sea life. She briefly considered trying to ask one of the animals—maybe a dolphin; they were supposed to be friendly, right?—for help, but she had no idea how to go about that and no time to figure it out.

They were running out of time.

Another heave upward, kicking mightily and perhaps even using some of her new ability to manipulate water, and she finally broke the surface, sucking in a huge, salty breath and choking it back out as she sank again, the man a millstone around her neck. That one breath had revived her, though it burned her lungs from the salt. She kicked like mad and breached again, this time managing to keep bobbing on the surface. Shifting her grip, she wiggled the man until his back was to her front—though he then grabbed onto her arm like a vise and nearly sent them under again—and lolled his head back against her shoulder.

"It's okay. We're gonna be okay. The boat is—"

She looked for it, turned in the water, looked again, then heard a splash. Hoping for a life preserver or, better still, another swimmer who could help her get her new friend over to the boat, she turned toward the sound and nearly sank again in astonishment.

An enormous polar bear, white coat glimmering in the moonlight, dog-paddled over to her from the direction of the boat. Halvor, bless him.

When the bear neared them, he turned around and glided in close enough that Wen could heft the new man over his back. He eyed her, and she could only guess that he'd meant for her to hitch a ride, not some random dude. But without the former merman's weight dragging her down, she found she could swim just fine.

Though the man refused to fully release her, so she had to swim at the same pace as the bear whether she wanted to or not.

When they finally reached the boat, the anticipated life preservers made their way over the edge, and several ropes as well. The polar bear transformed back into Halvor and rolled the new man around to heft him up for Dex to get a grip under his shoulders.

One problem solved.

He reached for her, and she gladly let him pull her closer. "Thank you, Halvor. I don't know if we could've made it without you."

He grunted as a reply but seemed pleased by the thanks. Then, as if she weighed about as much as a cup of ale, he hefted her up for Callum to catch and reel in. Her Nightwatcher held her close, chafing her arms and shivering himself. She was soaked and soaking him in the process.

"Please never do anythin like that again, milady. My goddess, we thought ye were gone forever and we couldnae do a damn thing about it. Lass, me heart—"

Dex wrapped her in a rough blanket from behind as Brigid's men hauled Halvor up and over the side of the boat. He barely even got the blanket around her shoulders before pulling her out of Callum's grip and into his own, nearly crushing her with his too-strong arms.

"Never again. I'm not letting you out of my sight ever again."

She sighed and let him fret, finally feeling somewhat warm again. "Sounds good to me."

Better still when Florin glomped onto her from behind, shivering as Callum had, and Callum joined back in. Connected. Safe. Warming up.

And saving some poor sea creature she'd unwittingly turned into a human.

Oh, right.

"Uh, guys?"

They didn't let her go, but they did ease their grip enough for her to look around and find the new man, also wrapped in a blanket, looking around like... ha ha... a fish out of water.

Awful. Just an awful thought to have at a moment like this.

"I think that's my new Nightwatcher."

And the kerfuffle started up all over again.

19

It was perhaps inevitable that the latest commotion would only be stalled by Gerhardt presenting everyone with an elaborate (for being on a boat out to sea) midnight tea. Wen silently blessed him for his foresight, even as she couldn't stop glancing at the new man she'd accidentally caught, because she also couldn't stop shivering. The blanket was warm and scratchy, but her soaked clothes clung to her clammy skin and she still felt so, so cold deep in her bones.

He was pale, for one thing. Deathly pale, like he'd never so much as seen the sun. Where his skin had been the sleek blue-gray of a blue whale in his other form, it was now so ghastly white that it was almost translucent. His hair was also incredibly pale with just the slightest tinge of blonde to it, again as if it had been bleached out by the salty ocean water or had never seen the sun. Perhaps it hadn't. Why would a merperson bother bobbing to the surface?

But it was really his eyes that drew her attention. Halvor had, as Brigid had so poetically described, eyes as light blue as the ice on the underside of a glacier. New Guy's eyes were lighter still and seemed to glow in the moonlight. Mesmerizing.

"My lady, you are still shivering. Florin, another blanket?"

She hated for him to leave for even a moment, taking his body heat with him, but she couldn't deny Dex's assessment. She *was* still shivering. Shuddering, even. Was New Guy as freezing as she was?

She glanced over again just in time to see Phaeton offering him another blanket. To everyone's surprise, the man opened his mouth and spoke.

"Όχι ευχαριστώ."

To everyone's further surprise, Phaeton's eyes widened and they responded in kind. "Είσαι Έλληνας?"

"Όχι." And then a word Wen recognized. "Atlantean."

"Did you just say Atlantean?" She squirmed around in her Nightwatchers' grip to see him better. "Phaeton?"

Eyes wide, Phaeton nodded. "I asked if he was Greek. Those first words were in Greek, so—"

She blinked at them, then looked at New Guy. Atlantean. As in, from the lost city of Atlantis. Could it really be?

"Any chance you speak English, sir?"

New Guy eyed her, more as if he was debating whether or not to answer than as if he didn't understand her. Then: "Some. From books."

The words were so heavily accented in a way she couldn't define that it took her a moment to catch what he said, then another to realize what he meant. He'd learned some English from books. It made some sense; Atlantis had disappeared some nine thousand years before Plato's time, although most scholars thought that a generic "a long time" like the Christian Bible's "forty days and forty nights". But either way, who was speaking English that far back in the past?

And it didn't explain the books.

She frowned. "Where did you get books in English?"

He frowned, too, then seemed to struggle to express himself. Finally, he said, "Sunk boats?"

Light dawned on her poor, tired, frozen brain. "Shipwrecks?"

He nodded, then looked suspiciously at the cup of tea Phaeton offered him. They conversed a bit in Phaeton's native tongue, New Guy seeming much more comfortable with Greek than English, and Wen racked her memory for everything she knew about Atlantis as Florin returned and tucked another blanket around her. Advanced society, bit conquer-y, fell out of favor with the gods for sacking Athens and failing and thus was sunk in the ocean for their hubris.

She didn't remember anything about Atlanteans being merpeople, though.

Phaeton must have finally convinced New Guy to try the tea, though he didn't seem to enjoy it much. He sipped, squinched up his nose, then sipped again, possibly just to be polite. Plenty of ancient societies found it unforgivably rude for a guest to refuse something a host offered.

"He says he came to the Sister's call, but he would like to shift back now, please."

She blinked. "I called him? I'm sorry. I didn't mean to." She paused and frowned. "Wait, he said Sister? As in, Sister of the Moon? He knows about us?" She looked to Thea and Brigid, but they looked as confused as she did, even with a cup of tea in hand. "How is that possible?"

He spoke up again, looking to Phaeton to translate.

"He says there were Sisters of the Moon for centuries even before Atlantis sank, though they weren't always called that." They paused to listen, then continued. "No Atlantean has been called since. He was curious, so he came to see who had finally penetrated the depths." Another pause. "He sent the giant squid to you, but he didn't mean for it to almost drown you. He didn't think about your human state. He is sorry."

Gobsmacked, she could only blink at him for a moment. Then, she shook herself. How was this any weirder than anything else that had happened to her this week?

"Oh. That's okay, actually. I didn't mean to turn him human, so maybe we're even?"

New Guy smirked and nodded, spoke again.

"He's never been in human form before and panicked. He should have changed back and rescued you, but you rescued him instead. He is grateful. And to you, Halvor."

The big Norseman only nodded, seeming untouched by the chill that still racked Wen's bones.

More Greek. "He asks if you're as curious about him as he is about you."

She huffed. "Obvs."

New Guy tilted his head, confused, and Phaeton smirked. "Yeah, I don't know how to translate netspeak, my lady."

She rolled her eyes. "Okay, okay." Her eyes met those lighter-than-ice blue ones again. "What is your name?"

He smiled. "Tarquin."

Her eyebrows rose, and she looked to Phaeton for a translation. They looked back, waiting, then startled. "Oh, no, that's his name. Tarquin."

She blushed. "Oh. My bad. Um... Tarquin, I'm Wen. Wendolyn." She didn't bother with her whole name, since he'd only given one to her. "But you can just call me Wen."

He stood shakily, the lone blanket held together in a fist, and bowed his head. "Wen, my lady."

"Oh, you don't have to—" She stopped herself and forced a smile. "Thank you. Any chance you can tell us what happened to Atlantis? An entire internet of enquiring minds need to know."

He rattled off a lot more Greek, and Phaeton nodded along. "He didn't understand some of that, but he says nothing happened to Atlantis. They decided it was easier to stay merfolk than to deal with petty human concerns anymore, so they lowered their island into the ocean, deep down where the Veil is always gossamer thin." They grinned. "I'm editorializing a bit, but that's the gist of it."

Brigid, who had been wide-eyed and drinking her tea, huffed. "Centuries o' debate, and just like that—"

Thea shook her head. "And there have been Sisters for millennia, only to have nearly died out now. Ma déesse."

Tarquin's attention snapped to her, and he barked a harsh question. Phaeton obliged. "What do you mean, nearly died out? You three are standing right here together."

"Ah, non. He does not know." She sighed. "We are only now, after a century, a complete circle, Monsieur Tarquin. Our dear Wendolyn only came to Light this past week. Lovely Brigid," she said, gesturing toward her, "four decades ago. And I—"

She trailed off and closed her eyes. It seemed an entire boat full of people held their breath.

"I had only just come to Light when my Sisters, they were slaughtered." Her lips trembled. "Animal attack, the papers say, but I know better, yes. My beautiful Sisters were murdered. The animals that attacked were shifters."

A collective gasp of horror and outrage seemed to suck all the oxygen out of the open air. Wen and Brigid exchanged knowing, wide-eyed looks. Brigid had expected as much and had told Wen of her suspicions during their first conversation. But the confirmation... brutal.

"So you see, monsieur, we Sisters were all but dead, and it has taken a hundred years to complete the circle once again."

Stunned, Tarquin sank back down into the deck chair. His tone gutted, he murmured a long string to Phaeton, who looked far too grim for it to be anything good.

"He says the Sisters of the Moon guard the Veil, the portal between our world and what he calls the Night Realm, from which all magic flows. He should have realized when he couldn't change back immediately that the Veil is much different on the surface, that it has thickened, blocking the flow of magic." They listened again, then frowned. "He asks why you haven't spoken to the Folk to stop them closing the portal."

Silence. A lot of wide, confused eyes.

Finally, Callum spoke for literally everyone, his Scottish accent a caricature in his shock.

"What the fook is rrreally goin' on then, lads?"

It turned out that being part of an ancient, isolated civilization far removed from the tribulations and destructiveness of mankind made Tarquin a font of useful lore. Thea, having been cut off from her elder Sisters before learning more than the rudimentary basics of what her Sisterhood meant, hadn't been able to pass that information to the new Sisters. So much had been lost.

And then... Tarquin. And Phaeton to translate for him.

And Gerhardt to serve them all another tea, because damn if they didn't need it to get through a story so long and convoluted.

"Millennia ago, there was no Veil. Earth and the Night Realm intermixed freely. Denizens of the Night Realm (the Folk he mentioned earlier) who exist only as pure energy (I'm guessing here; his Greek is a lot older than I'm used to hearing) could enter the Day Realm (that's Earth, by the way) and gain material bodies. It gave them all sorts of new sensations they had never experienced, and in return, they allowed material beings from the Day Realm to experience the spirit form of their pure energy state in the Night Realm."

Callum, still flustered, huffed. "Everyone got that, aye?"

Wen elbowed him. "Ssh."

Tarquin reeled off another lengthy bit of Greek. Phaeton nodded, eyebrows furrowed as he tried to keep up.

"When humans began to industrialize—I'm editorializing again; he said something about working metal, but I didn't catch all of it—the Folk begged them to stop, as the pure ores made it difficult for them to work their magic. The humans wouldn't listen; worked metal was too useful and durable, and most of them— oh. Huh." They blushed. "Intermixed seems to have been... ahem... a sexual term. That's how Wen's cryptids, especially shifters, came to be. Well."

There was suddenly a lot of foot-shifting and throat clearing. Tarquin ignored them and spoke on, growing more and more agitated as he went.

"Right. Sorry. Most of the humans didn't feel the blocking of magic because they had none of their own. The mixed bloods—cryptids—were caught in the middle and didn't know who to side with. The Folk, furious and a little scared, declared they would close off their Night Realm and take all their magic with them if humans didn't stop." They paled. "Oh. It seems that would have killed the cryptids off entirely, as we can't survive without magic in our world, but we also can't survive without our material bodies in the spirit realm."

Brigid reached out and took Eiji's hand. Thea gripped onto Catahecassa and Brody, Samuel crowding up close to her back to hug her from behind.

Wen's three non-Atlantean Nightwatchers were already crowded around her to stop her shivers, but they clutched her tighter, and she clutched back any way she could. She didn't want to lose them. She didn't want their dual natures to tear them apart. She just met them.

Hell, she hadn't even slept with them yet.

Tarquin, eyes on her as she held her cryptids tight, narrowed his icy eyes and spoke again.

"The cryptids decided to act as peacemakers between the two realms, but humans didn't fully trust them, as they were just as Folk as they were human. So they bartered for three of their own kind to— oh. Oh, that is—"

Brigid groaned. "What, lad? Just tell us, aye?"

"They chose three men to act as go-betweens to keep the

peace between human and Folk. The Folk, not trusting them, demanded that the go-betweens be women, who they found... heh... less volatile and more likely to seek compromise and fairness."

Callum opened his mouth, and Wen held up a single, commanding finger. "Callum, I swear that if you try to 'not all men' this one, I will never speak to you again."

Brigid snickered, but Thea hushed them all. Tarquin continued.

"Anyway, the Pact was struck, and to preserve it— ah. The go-betweens, called the Sisters of the Moon (because even then, the female menses were tied to the phases of the Moon), were then granted the power to walk between the realms to keep them separate but not cut off interaction entirely. They vowed to preserve a balance between the two worlds, to communicate between the Folk, who didn't trust humans, and the three human men who'd been elected to delegate before women were chosen."

Wen huffed, fascinated despite all the implications. "I'll be damned."

Dex tightened his grip. "No, my lady. You were blessed."

Thea hushed them again, and Tarquin continued.

"He says he doesn't know why the Veil is failing, but it's slowing the flow of magic, and the Sisters are supposed to be protecting it and keeping the balance. He suggests contacting either the humans or the Folk to learn more and to figure out how to fix it."

Callum grunted. "Aye, and sure'n that'll be easy as a meat pie, then."

Tarquin speared him with an icy glare and rattled off something that sounded unbearably snarky. Phaeton snorted.

Everyone waited.

They shrugged. "I'm not saying that. I like my head right

where it is, thanks. There will be no killing of the messenger today."

Another bit of Greek, this time sounding a lot less volatile. Phaeton's amusement faded.

"Oh."

More Greek.

"Are you sure?"

Tarquin nodded, then looked directly at Wen. She had no idea what he was thinking, but the look in those should-be-cold eyes made her heart suddenly ache with dread.

"He says he's sorry, but he can't accept your call, my lady. If he doesn't warn his people and the Veil fails, they will turn into humans at the bottom of the ocean and drown. Thousands of people dead, just like that. And that's only if the sudden loss of magic doesn't kill them outright. He has to warn them." Phaeton sighed. "He can't go with you."

Her eyes closed. Here was the rejection she had always expected, rearing its ugly head now that she'd just gotten used to acceptance. It stung.

But, surrounded by three men who wrapped themselves around her, it didn't hurt as much as she expected. So, she made herself smile and open her eyes.

"I understand. You go help your people, Tarquin." Her faux smile tipped sideways. "Sounds like I need to help mine, too. I get it."

He stood, less shaky this time, and tossed aside the blanket. Her eyes widened—she vaguely heard several whistles and catcalls, but her mind had apparently shorted out at the sudden naked man—and she froze as he strode toward her, all lean muscle and quick agility.

When he reached her, he cupped her face in his hands and kissed her, long and deep. Time stood still.

Goddess, she had missed kissing. She hadn't even realized....

"Oi, I've been waitin' me moment all bloody week, and this wanker just strolls over and—"

"Callum!"

The shout came from several sides, but Wen was too dazed and breathless—literally breathless, as she hadn't taken a breath since the kiss started—to count how many. When Tarquin finally pulled away just enough to lean their foreheads together, she was pretty sure she would've collapsed like a bunch of broccoli without her Nightwatchers supporting her. Her knees were weak, her spine like jelly. She was a mess.

Tingly, though. And she was no longer cold to the bone but uncomfortably warm.

In careful English, Tarquin spoke only to her. "I would go with you, my lady. If you succeed—"

She nodded, understanding what he didn't have the English to say but didn't want translated by a third party. He *had* to go. She wouldn't make him stay. Couldn't.

So, she smiled softly. "Tell Atlantis Wen says hi."

He pulled away to eye her, not sure if she was serious or not, then kissed her forehead and stepped away, over to the port side of the boat. His eyes on her, he shifted, slithering down to the deck with his blue-gray skin and long, thick tail with its whale-like fluke at the end. Still those eyes, though. Lighter-than-ice blue and focused only on her.

And then he was gone, hefting himself over the rail and into the water.

She gave herself a moment to feel rejected. When she didn't feel rejected but only saddened by the loss, she sighed and turned back to the crowd gathered on the deck with her.

"So... what now?"

No one answered.

20

"Well, then," Brigid said after a long pause to allow Wen to adjust to losing a Nightwatcher the same day—almost the same hour—she met him. "Looks like we have ourselves a choice, lads an' lasses: human or fairy?"

Wen blinked, shaking off a growing melancholy. "Wait, fairy? I thought they didn't— ooooh."

Spirit forms. Pure energy. Back and forth through the Veil, which would be why there was little to no evidence of them outside of hearsay.

"Sorry. Carry on."

Brigid gave her an understanding look as Gerhardt poured her a fresh cup of tea. "I only meant that it seems we Sisters havenae been told what to do, so we havenae been doin it, have we?"

Thea shook her head. "I should have told you. I should not have kept that awfulness secret all this time. But it was so horrible—"

Samuel, her First, gently touched her cheek. "You had to hide, ma belle, or they would have killed you, too, just in case."

She huffed bitterly. "Non, they left me to die alone with so little magic it might have been my imagination. It would have been better—" She cut herself off, her eyes sparkling with tears in the moonlight. As if she heard a distant call, she looked up and focused on the nearly-full moon. "Forgive me, Sister. But it is hard, yes? So hard to be alone."

Brigid stood, and Wen slipped out of her Nightwatcher's grasp, and both went to Thea to join hands, the three taking comfort from their small but complete circle. Thea closed her eyes and settled herself, then raised her head and squared her shoulders. Just like that, she was ready for action.

"It would seem logical to find the human half of the Pact, yes? But I find I would rather search for the Folk. What about you, mes chéris?"

Wen didn't hesitate. "I wanna meet fairies." She then, of course, blushed to the roots of her hair. "Sorry. Just sayin."

Brigid chuckled. "I'm with Wendolyn. The Folk havenae been seen for perhaps a century. We need to find out why."

Thea nodded. "Then we agree. The Folk."

"Agreed."

"Aye, agreed."

Wen sighed. "Only one problem: how do we get to them? If the Veil is a portal—?"

Brigid hmmed. "And we dunnae how to cross it—?"

"The Giant's Causeway."

Everyone turned to stare at Aaron, who lounged in a deck chair with his hobnail-booted feet kicked up onto the railing. He seemed unfazed by the sudden attention.

"Aye, miladies. Ye'll wanna go to the Giant's Causeway." He winked at Wen. "That's in Ireland, lass."

She blustered. "I know that!"

But he smirked and looked like he knew better. But before he could say anything, Brody gruffly broke in. "It's long been storied as hidin' the door to the Kingdom Under the Hill. And if we're on about fairies, that's the place to go."

Wen blinked. She hadn't heard the man speak so much in whole day she'd known him.

"Aye, my lady?"

Thea nodded once, sharply. "Then that is where we go."

Considering, Wen shrugged. "Maybe they can tell us who their human counterparts are, since I have no idea where to even begin to look for them."

Brigid touched her arm. "That's brilliant, love. I've been rackin me poor, wee brain over that bit."

Halvor hmphed, drawing all eyes. A hmph from someone that big sounded a bit like an avalanche. It tended to draw attention.

"So we go now, yes?" His English was heavily accented with his native Norwegian tongue.

Brigid smiled. "Aye, m'love, we go now. Quick as can be back to the Isles."

Beaming, Wen put up her rock fist. "We have a plan. Why does it always feel better when there's a plan?"

"Because, ma petite," Thea said, coming back from her own bout of melancholy with a small smile, "it feels like moving forward."

Wen lifted her cup, though the tea inside had long since grown cold. "Here's to moving forward, then."

Wen still stood at the prow, even hours later as they neared Ireland's coast, trying to process everything that had happened. She had called sea life. Whales, even. Hell, she'd scrounged up a cryptid with her call. Who could have ever known that mousy ol' Wen would have such power?

And that kiss—

Dex came to check on her again. He'd mostly left her alone to think, sensing that she wasn't quite settled about the night's events, both big and small, but he had checked on her every half hour or so. Probably to make sure she didn't call up any more giant squid to haul her overboard again.

She grinned at the thought and bumped her shoulder against his upper arm affectionately. She appreciated his thoughtfulness more each day.

He leaned on the railing next to her. "You should see your hair, my lady. Beach waves. Florin will be in ecstasies."

She huffed and ran a hand over the defined, wind-blown curls. "I doubt it. Beach waves may look nice, but they feel gross. It's the salt. Uck."

He chuckled, and then a gentle quiet fell between them. She'd become used to the cold sea wind, though she still clutched the two blankets around herself. It was peaceful up here in the prow. Most of the others had either crammed into the cabin or sat scattered around on the rear deck, out of the direct chill, so she had the place to herself, other than when her First came to check on her.

Because he was her First, and she now knew what that meant.

"It's alright to miss him, you know."

She startled and gawked at him. How could he know? And how silly was it to miss someone she'd known for an hour or two, at best?

But she kept seeing those icy eyes. And that moment where he dropped the towel. Dex and Callum were big, strapping lads, and she liked that very much now that she was used to it, but Tarquin had rocked a swimmer's build. Probably not surprising, given his nature.

"He was intended for you, and now, one of your pillars is missing."

She frowned. "Pillars?"

He side-eyed her. "Have you not wondered why Brigid and Thea both have four Nightwatchers?"

Huh. She'd never even thought about it.

"They represent the four directions, so you can be safe from every side—north, south, east, and west."

Blinking, she considered that. "So does that mean that I'll always be missing a pillar, or is there another shifter out there who'll answer my call?"

She wasn't sure she wanted that. Tarquin had felt like hers, just like the others. He'd been familiar in a way she couldn't put her finger on but was the same way she felt about Dex and Callum and Florin.

She just... missed him. She didn't really want another shifter to replace him. It shouldn't be that easy to yank off a part of her edifice and slot in another generic part.

Tarquin wasn't generic. None of them were.

But Dex only shrugged. "I honestly don't know, my lady. I only know that Sisters have four Nightwatchers."

She swallowed hard, then bit the bullet. "And have sex with all four of them?"

Okay, *that* got his attention. He eyed her incredulously, then sighed and looked out across the ocean rolling under and around them.

"Brigid."

She didn't answer.

"My lady, Wen, we didn't want to pressure you. You've been through so much, and Callum and I agreed the first night that you weren't ready for such entanglements." He darted a sheepish look at her, then looked away again. "We told Florin when we got to the castle. He'd already literally thrown himself at you. We had to make sure he knew why you weren't ready for that yet."

"And why was it your decision?"

She wasn't mad, exactly. Just uncomfortable and unsure how to feel about the whole mess. Embarrassed that they hadn't told her and she'd only found out by accident. And, as always, awkward as hell.

He turned to her, standing away from the railing. "It is only ever your decision, Wendolyn Eudora Cheney, and never let anyone tell you any different."

She sucked in a deep breath and felt a quiver through her at his intensity. At the promise in that uncompromising tone.

She could trust that. She could trust him. He wouldn't whine about blue balls or demand she do her wifely duty like Tucker the Fucker had. He wouldn't allow Callum or Florin to do so, either.

And it sort of explained why Tarquin felt no qualms in kissing her like he was trying to taste what she ate for breakfast. No one had a chance to tell him before he had to leave.

Her heart twisted at the reminder of his absence.

Dex sighed and leaned on the railing again. "If it helps, I think he would have stayed if the Veil weren't in danger."

She sighed, too, leaning beside him, arm to arm. "He probably wouldn't have liked the Pacific anyway. He's been in the Atlantic his whole life."

He grinned and bumped her. "Maybe he'd like it better not freezing his gills off."

Chuckling, she rolled her eyes. Then, feeling better, she dared to turn her head and look at him in profile. To see him, entirely. He was a beautiful man—proud, chiseled features, that velvety black skin, the dreads, once again pulled back so they weren't blowing in his face.

She waited until he looked at her and paused at what he saw in her eyes. He wouldn't push her, he said.

So she'd just have to push herself.

Closing her eyes, she leaned in and kissed him. His lips were full and warm, opening to her without prompting. He made a soft noise in his throat, but didn't press for more. She wasn't ready for another good tonguing at the moment, but she did want that feeling of connection. Of intimacy.

She ended the kiss and leaned their foreheads together because she liked that it felt as though they were still connected. "When this is all over...."

"Yes. When it's over."

Feeling the first flickers of both nervousness and impatience, Wendolyn Eudora Cheney smiled.

21

The Causeway Coast filled the horizon, stretching over the northern shore of Ireland. The legends about the place were easy to understand when she neared it in person, the interlocking, hexagonal, basalt columns forming such an alien landscape that it was hard to believe it wasn't a movie set. If any place on earth were to house a portal to another world, the Giant's Causeway was that place.

Dex had informed her that most of the Causeway was public property, owned by the National Trust, but the part they needed to see, according to Brody, was privately owned, so Dex had phoned to seek permission. The seagoers unanimously agreed not to step foot on private land until they had the owner's okay, so Halvor had been ferrying them up and down the coast through false dawn and well into real dawn, waiting for Dex's phone to ring.

Wen was starting to wish she'd at least taken a token nap, like most of the passengers, but she'd wanted to enjoy the sea for as long as possible. Who knew how long it would be before she could be on it again? She'd even seen another pod of whales just after false dawn, though she was pretty sure she hadn't called them. Nothing else leaped out of the water, anyway, and likely wouldn't, now that the moon had set.

Nonetheless, she couldn't stop the occasional yawn from stretching her face and was fairly certain she was carrying Samsonite luggage under her eyes. As the sun parted ways with the sea, Dex brought her a cup of tea and her carry-on, in case she wanted to take her anxiety meds before they went ashore. She did, and she was grateful she didn't have to go searching for her little bag amongst all the other "little bags" that had joined them on her spur-of-the-moment experiment trip.

Yes. Brigid was an obsessive packer. Wen probably should have expected that from all the Goth gear, but she hadn't. Fully half the below-decks was stuffed with the woman's luggage, as if she thought they were going on a cruise instead of a day trip. Well, more of a night trip.

Just as she popped a pill into her mouth, Dex's phone finally rang. He looked at the number, then held up a finger and stepped away to answer. She didn't try to hear the conversation, mostly because it was so short. Within two exchanges, Dex turned to give a thumbs-up to Halvor, who dutifully turned the boat to head for the port nearest the area they needed to search. It took another few exchanges to wrap up the conversation, but soon enough, Dex joined her at the prow to watch the Giant's Causeway, in all its alien splendor, grow in their field of vision.

"He's a shifter."

She raised her eyebrows, though she couldn't tear her eyes away from the curious stacks of hexagonal rock. "Who is?"

"The owner." He sounded vaguely troubled. "Neither Aaron nor Brody mentioned that. I wonder if it's changed hands since last they knew."

She shrugged. "Maybe they didn't know. Do you guys often announce yourself to each other?"

Dex eyed her. "We know, my lady. We can't not know." He pointed to his nose. "Animal senses, remember?"

Oh. Right. Black dog. War horse. Dire wolf. Etc., etc.

She grinned sheepishly. "Anyway, does it really matter if he's a shifter? Shouldn't that be a good thing, considering why we need to be on private Causeway land?"

He was quiet a long moment—long enough that she finally managed to tear her gaze away from the stacks.

"What?"

"It's only— what Thea said about it being shifters who killed her other two Sisters."

That gave her pause, too, now that he mentioned it. "Oh. I mean, there's nothing to say it's the same shifter or shifters, right? What are the odds?"

He eyed her as if he knew she knew better. "The odds of a shifter who owns a private part of the Giant's Causeway, apparently fairly well known as being a portal to the Night Realm, could have anything to do with the murder of two women known at the time for being the go-between for both worlds?"

She bit her lip, then shrugged. "Anything sounds bad when you say it like that."

He snorted. "It sounds bad because it looks bad. And it looks bad because it may actually be bad. We won't know until we meet him. At least there should be more of us than of him."

She chuckled because, yes, it suddenly occurred to her that she was on a boat with three hopefully powerful Sisters of the Moon and eleven shifters, the least powerful of which was Aaron, who shifted into a sheepdog. Of course, that sheepdog was about twice the size of a regular sheepdog and could easily bite a human leg in two, but hey. Sheepdog. Protective but rarely aggressive.

Feeling better, she turned back to the coastline, watching a lone dock come closer and closer. This must be it. Three men in business suits stood at the end of the dock, waiting for them. The tallest one waved, smiling broadly when he saw her. Them.

Her?

She felt her forehead wrinkle. Why would he smile specifically at her?

Dex, stone-faced, reached down and took her hand, squeezing it twice. It was a signal, but she didn't have to be told for what. The man smiling at her was the shifter. Of course he was; he was easily eight inches taller than either of the men beside him.

Just great.

She didn't wave back as Halvor maneuvered the big boat into place at the end of the dock, but she pretended to be busy tugging at a likely-looking rope to cover up the fact. Dex did a better job, finding the right rope and tossing it to Business Suit Shifter, who caught it with ease and did a quick figure-eight knot around one of the weird metal bits bolted into the wood at his feet. She should probably learn what all this stuff was if she wanted to be out on the ocean more often once they moved to Oregon.

For now, she waited for Callum and Florin to join her and Dex, then realized everyone but Halvor was ready to hop out with them. Better and better. Show them their numbers and maybe they wouldn't try anything sketchy.

She almost wished Dex hadn't put the idea of a rogue shifter in her head, but she knew he only did it as a protective measure. Damn. She could take another anxiety med, even though she'd just taken one.

Five things she could see—

"Well met, travelers!" Business Suit Shifter smiled, showing off perfectly-spaced, gleaming white teeth, and she was again reminded of Little Red Riding Hood's fake grandmother. What perfectly-capped teeth you have, Grandmama. And what a quaint, lilting Irish accent, but that was beside the point. "Please, come ashore with me blessin. Ye're all very welcome here."

Nothing suspicious about that, but she still moved aside, her guys moving with her, to let Thea's Catahecassa step off the boat first. He turned and held his hand out for Thea while Samuel held her from behind to make sure she didn't slip. They were so careful of her, in fact, that Wen knew Dex was right; they knew Business Suit Shifter was a shifter without having to be told, and they weren't letting their Sister of the Moon out of their grasp even just to disembark.

Brody followed directly after Samuel, and then it was Brigid's turn. Thea's group shook hands and greeted the smiling shifter with stone faces, like the other two suits wore. Wen watched it all with narrowed eyes, wondering why the shifter had bothered bringing two humans along with him. They couldn't be bodyguards. They weren't big enough, compared to him, and... *shifter*.

He could take care of himself.

Maybe they were lawyers? Something about allowing people on private property maybe assuming liability if something happened to one of them? That made sense. Maybe that's why they were here.

Less suspicious with a reasonable explanation, she let go of Dex just long enough for him to step onto the dock, then allowed Callum to pick her up (princess style, much to her amusement and embarrassment) and pass her over the bobbing edge of the boat to him. Callum quickly followed, Florin hot on his tail, and just like that, the shifter smiled even brighter and stepped closer, hand out for a shake.

Hand out to *her*. Not Dex, who had made the call. Not either of her other men. *Her*.

Could she be calling him? Surely not. She'd just called Tarquin, and her heart was already set on him, whether she could have him or not.

"Milady, may I say how great an honor it is to meet the Sister o' the Moon who has finally completed the circle?" He took her hesitantly offered hand and bent low over it, brushing his lips across her knuckles. "If I may serve ye in any way, dear lady, ye only but say the word, and it is done."

His eyes, a dark brown to match his shoulder-length hair—an odd match with the clearly expensive business suit, but she was no one's fashion expert—bored into hers as if he wanted her to understand some secret message he dare not impart in front of the humans. Unfortunately, unless he'd been called, she had no idea what that message could be. And if he *had* been called, she didn't want to receive the message. She already had four pillars, even if only three were present.

Dex finally stepped in and wrapped her hand around the inside of his elbow, leading her away from the smarmy shifter gripping her other hand so intimately. "We've been at sea all night, Mr. Flanagan. Would it be possible for our ladies to refresh themselves before we make for our destination?"

She did feel a bit grimy after her dip in the ocean. Salt water always left a grit behind. If refreshing herself meant a hot shower and a change of clothes, she was prepared to be as polite as possible.

Thea and Brigid had already reached the shoreline and stood on the crazy hexagonal surface, waiting for them and eyeing the interaction with narrow-eyed interest. She wondered if they suspected what she did—that this shifter might be called to her to replace Tarquin. She hoped they understood that she wasn't interested, that they knew her well enough, even after just a day, to know no one could take his place.

The shifter—Mr. Flanagan, Dex had called him—obligingly widened his attention to include them all as he preceded them off the dock. "Of course. Come with me, miladies, and make yerselves to home. I've had the guest house cleaned and readied for yer comfort. It truly is such an honor to host the Sisters o' the Moon in me humble home."

Okay, the smarminess was surely just camp at this point. Mr. Bountiful Host was laying it on a bit thick. Rolling her eyes when he turned to lead the way, she gave her full attention to navigating the weirdly geometric landscape and let her guys listen to all the pandering. Thus far, neither of the other two suits had said so much as a word, and that made her feel suspicious again, but at the moment, that wasn't her problem.

Those damn hexagons jutting up at all heights were a bitch to walk over without tripping for the Queen of Klutzes. It was a good thing Dex had taken her by the arm. After the third misplaced step nearly turned her ankle, Florin rounded to her other side to help, too. She felt like a little old granny being helped into the local Golden Corral by her handsome young nephews who'd been guilted into the job.

How embarrassing.

Finally, the house came into view over the awkward stacks of basalt, and she had to stop and gasp. That wasn't a house. That was a full-on mansion, and the guest house a short distance to the east was only slightly smaller, though equally grandiose. Neither was quite up to Brigid's castle standards, but seriously. Mansions. Who *was* this guy?

Beaming at their jaw-dropped reactions—only Brigid and her Nightwatchers didn't look impressed—Mr. Flanagan gestured for them to head for the guest house while he dropped back to walk with Wen, despite the hulking shifters flanking her and helping her along.

"I hope milady will find the place to yer satisfaction. Please know ye're welcome any time ye wish to come to Giant's Causeway."

She blushed, hobbling awkwardly over the uneven ground, being practically carried along by two strong men. "Oh. Uh, thanks. I dunno that we'll need to come back, but I guess you never know."

If they were supposed to be go-betweens and this was the only place to go between, they might indeed have to come back to interact with the Folk. She hadn't thought of that. Maybe she should return the smarminess, after all.

Just then, a giant golden eagle took off into the air, and she gasped at the majestic sight. She'd never seen a bird so large, let alone an eagle.

Then, she saw the look on Flanagan's face, and it wasn't all that impressed. In fact, he looked downright narrow-eyed and jaw-clenched. She looked around, confused, and realized Gerhardt had disappeared.

Gerhardt was the golden eagle. Brigid must have sent him to scout out the portal for them. It was genius.

Why wasn't Flanagan pleased with that idea? Was he hiding something from them?

All her suspicions came rushing back, and she tamped down any ideas about being more accommodating just to facilitate easy access to the Folk. There had to be a better way than this freakin guy.

Thankfully, the guest house's expansive lawn had been leveled and grassed over with a neat garden on either side. If there was still basalt around, it was neatly covered, so she didn't have to worry about tripping anymore. However, neither of her guys let go of her arms. They continued to escort her across the yard and inside the massive house, not letting Flanagan get close enough to her to touch.

Surely he wasn't called. Callum had kept himself together pretty well, but even Dex had been moved to follow her around a grocery store, staring at her, when he was first called. And Florin had shifted right in her arms, his face buried in her stomach paunch. If Flanagan was called, he was doing a damn good job of hiding the fact.

Was he that good an actor? Was it just the perfect, toothpaste commercial teeth that made her wonder? Again, she thought, *My, Grandmama, what perfect teeth you have.*

Her Spidey senses were tingling. Or her magic was talking to her. Either way, she had no intention of ignoring the warning. Flanagan was trouble, somehow. She did not want to find out the hard way.

The shifter showed Thea to the master suite on the bottom floor, then led Brigid and Wen upstairs to the two huge guest suites, one on either side of the grand, sweeping staircase. Brigid gave her an intense look, which she responded to with a single, short shake of her head and a cut of her eyes toward Flanagan. She got a sharp nod in return before being directed toward the other suite.

"Here we are, milady. Remember, if there's anythin ye need, anythin at all, just say the word, aye?"

Nothing could compare to an old castle bed chamber, but this suite came damn close. Goldenrod yellow wall panels and cream plaster moulding, a sumptuous yellow-draped bed with about a thousand pillows, a sitting area with cream and yellow striped upholstered furniture and a massive cream marble hearth, a dressing table with an enormous trifold mirror, and an en suite bathroom she couldn't see the far side of made the room appear to be an entire apartment of its own.

All it needed was a kitchen. For all she knew, there was one in the bathroom.

Abruptly, she realized Flanagan was staring at her, expecting a verbal response. She also realized the other two suits had disappeared at some point, perhaps downstairs. She'd been a little distracted with all of the everything.

"Uh." *Great start, Wen.* "N-no, thanks. This is... more than enough. I'll—we'll be just fine here. Thanks."

Smooth. She wanted to smack herself on the forehead. She hadn't been this tongue-tied since first meeting Dex and Callum. And Florin, of course.

"Wonderful. I've suggested to the other Sisters that perhaps we should meet at the main house for a nice supper, then a good night's rest for the lot of ye, then to the Gateway in the mornin. Does that suit ye, milady?"

Why was he asking her? Thea was the obvious choice for discussing schedules. Or Dex, since he'd made the original call to ask permission to come in the first place.

Practically crawling with suspicion now—though that could be her salty skin itching with proximity to a hot shower—she did everything in her power to not narrow her eyes at him.

"Yes," she said, her voice cool. "That should be just fine, provided it's all right with my sisters."

A subtle reminder that she was not the sole decision maker. He must have got the hint because he smiled tightly, then bowed at the waist and backed out of the room, closing the heavily-draped French doors before turning to stride away.

"I don't like him," she murmured, hoping he was out of earshot, even with shifter hearing.

"Sure'n he's a slimy one, lass. You're right about that." Callum held out a hand, grinning when she took it without hesitation. "Now about those beach waves your sportin."

Florin hopped to, brightening. "Yes. Will you allow me to assist you, my lady?"

She balked, hanging back against Callum's light tug. "With a shower?"

"Oh, no, lass." The Scot smirked. "We're all havin us a bath, aye? Four birds with one stone, ye know."

She wanted to facepalm. Dex must have told them that they'd broached the sex conversation. She was in for it now.

But she stopped dragging back and allowed Callum to lead her to the sumptuous bathroom, also decorated in sunny yellow and gentle cream colors. Dex and Florin followed eagerly behind, shedding grubby, day-old clothing as they went.

This... would be interesting.

Wen and Tucker had never taken a romantic bath together. Tucker hated baths, calling them a waste of good hot water because it inevitably cooled off well before Wen was ready to get out. And he hated sitting still for so long with nothing to hold his attention.

Clearly, Wen was unable to do so.

Thus, finding herself in an enormous jacuzzi bath with the jets on and three men crowding in with her was a new experience in more ways than one. She wasn't sure if her face was hot from blushing like a fire engine or from the heat of the ever-circulating water.

Or from the awkwardness of lying back over Dex's arm, sitting across his naked lap, while Florin lovingly washed her hair with rose-smelling shampoo and Callum shaved her legs with delicate, careful strokes. He had asked if he could, and she saw no reason to tell him no besides her own awkwardness. Now, she would've been kicking herself if he didn't have a gentle hold on her legs.

And after kissing Dex—

Well. Sitting on his lap after that was an experience.

"Such lovely, silky hair, my lady." As usual, Florin was totally absorbed with her tresses and oblivious to her discomfiture. "I am glad you have left it long. If we treat it right, it should grow to your knees. Would you like that?"

"Uh."

Always with the witty rejoinders. She groaned internally and closed her eyes. Freaking. Awkward.

"You do not have to, of course, my lady. I only thought—"

"No, no," she said quickly. "It's not that I don't want to. Just, it's never grown much past the middle of my back, even when I trim it regularly."

He hmmed softly, massaging an equally rose-smelling conditioner into her hair and scalp. It felt heavenly, despite her awkwardness.

"Hair such as yours needs nourishment, my lady. I am sure Callum would help add the proper nutrients to your daily intake. Perhaps some supplements." He sighed blissfully. "Such beautiful hair already. We are blessed."

She opened her eyes and accidentally caught Dex smirking down at her, his eyes dancing, and blushed to the roots of said hair. If anyone asked, she would blame it on the heat.

To her great relief, she heard a knock at the French doors. "Hey, we should get that."

Of course, Callum had already stood up. She was pretty sure he deliberately stood with his backside toward her so she couldn't help but admire the taut curve of his ass. She'd never much appreciated a man's ass before, but she couldn't help but want to drool over this one. All of the guys had proved to have beautiful butts, but Callum's—

She sighed and tensed to sit up. Florin reluctantly rinsed the conditioner out, tut-tutting about not giving it long enough to penetrate the hair's sheath, and Dex helped her to scoot off his lap without making a water mess.

That reminded her; she wanted to try something.

Florin stepped out and offered a hand, and she took it to stand up. Then, she just stood there, her eyes closed.

Four things she could feel: the gentle circulation of the jets moving the water around her ankles, her eyelashes clumped together with wet, the warm porcelain under the soles of her feet, the stray bubbles trailing down her stomach and thighs as she willed the water to stream off of her and rejoin the rest of the bath.

Just like that, she was dry, except for her feet still in the water. Even her hair had dried as she directed the water to simply leave it.

She opened her eyes and smiled at her guys' impressed expressions. She then promptly slipped trying to step out of the tub and had to grab onto slick, naked man bodies to keep from bashing her skull into the edge of the tub.

Queen. Of. Klutzes.

Now and forever.

"Gerhardt is back." Callum wasted no time helping her into a fresh pair of leggings, a tunic top, and her new boots, though Florin knelt to tie them for her. "He says he scouted the area, and there donnae seem to be any more shifters on the property. And he thinks he found the Gateway, as Flanagan called it. Brigid suggested we sneak out tonight and go alone instead of waitin for that wanker in the mornin. What say ye?"

She pushed her hair back over her shoulder for Florin to brush. It already felt thicker and smoother, but that could've been because she'd taken the water out instead of allowing it to air dry and frizz.

"If Thea's okay with it, I think that sounds like a good idea. I dunno why, but I don't trust him. I get the feeling he's making a play for me, but why? There's nothing to gain. He may or may not be called, but I'll be damned if I take him as a Nightwatcher."

"I would never trust him with your safety, my lady. You are right about him. My black dog's hackles are up."

"My dire wolf wants to tear out his throat."

She smiled back over her shoulder. "Florin! Please tell me you weren't really the Beast of Gévaudan all this time!"

Surprise pulled a hearty laugh from him, and he hugged her back to his front, leaning their temples together. "I said nothing about eating their organs, my lady."

Feeling better with both a plan and a laugh, she skipped looking at herself in the mirror and left the room to meet Brigid on the landing so they could both go down together. Her Sister looked amazing in a Stevie Nicks black dress and heavily-embroidered, fringed shawl thrown over her arms. Thea waited for them at the front door, tall and elegant in a slinky coral dress that brought a lick of flame to her dark eyes. She had unwound her dreads and wore her gloriously white hair natural, still so long that it reached the curve of her lower back.

Wen could never compete with either of them. Luckily, they held out their arms to her, and she joined them with the glad realization that she would never have to. They were a complete circle, and nothing could change that.

Smiling with their arms linked together, the three Sisters of the Moon headed out the door to the bigger mansion, heads held high as the sun sank further in the west. Soon, it would be one night closer to the full moon.

Soon, it would be *their* time to shine.

22

"Miladies, ye shine like the full moon on a cool, spring evenin."

Was that a compliment? Wen supposed it must be, but when she looked from Brigid to Thea, she saw the same polite confusion she felt on her own face.

Hurrying past the potential blunder, they allowed their guys to lead them to their chosen seats. Thea sat across the table from Flanagan, her men crowding around the head of the table with Samuel at her right hand. Wen and Brigid sat across from each other in the middle of the length, their men fanning out on either side of them, their Firsts also at their right sides. The two suits Wen assumed were lawyers sat at Flanagan's sides.

Then, she realized Gerhardt was missing. Had he flown off again? She shot a questioning look at Brigid, who only smiled.

"Donnae worrit about him, love. He insists no one prepares me food but him. He's a picky one that way."

Flanagan did the closest thing to grumbling as they'd seen yet, unrolling his napkin with a little more force than was surely necessary. "I do hope, milady, he doesnae think my chef would harm ye in any way."

Brigid's face betrayed nothing but polite interest. "Of course not. I've convinced him over the decades that I'm a picky eater, so he thinks he's the only one as can please me with food."

Now that was smooth. Why couldn't Wen be a badass under pressure like that? Because she doubted if Flanagan's chef would try anything sneaky with one of the Sisters' Nightwatchers in the kitchen with him or her. They should all be safe with Gerhardt looking out for them.

Plus, she was getting used to his cooking. After this was all over, she planned to goad Callum with compliments on Gerhardt's food. It would be such fun to watch him fume and sputter and stomp off to the kitchen in their Oregon home to cook some insane delicacy.

She wished they were already there. But they had things to do first.

Gerhardt himself brought out the soup course, spooning from an enormous tureen into each individual bowl. That told her he knew exactly what had gone into it and he trusted at least the one course. Thus, she relaxed and stirred the chunky, creamy potato and corn chowder-looking stew before taking a small bite.

Heavenly. She loved creamy potato soup, but she never ate it. She had no idea how to make it for herself, and most places that sold it pre-made were out of her usual circle of less awful places to go. She hated restaurants, too—eating alone in them, anyway, and feeling everyone stare at her and pity her—so those were out.

So good. So starchy and creamy and herby. Whoever made it certainly had a gift. She could fill herself up on soup alone.

But then Gerhardt brought out two baskets full of differently shaped loaves and bread rolls, and she snatched a large wheat roll out almost before he put it down. He eyed her but made no complaint, so she searched for the nearest butter and felt her first disappointment of the evening.

No clotted cream. A pity.

Sighing, she pulled open her roll and slathered on the butter. It would just have to do.

The actual dinner course—salad, an enormous roast that must have come from a freaking buffalo, and a creamy pumpkin-and-gnocchi dish that made her eyes roll back into her head, plus more potatoes, roasted this time—passed like a dream, and she found herself eyeing Callum meaningfully as she sampled each item. He ignored her very carefully the entire time, but she had no doubt he got the hint.

She wanted creamy pumpkin gnocchi for every meal from now on.

Lastly, a thankfully-not-flaming dessert that she didn't have to destroy the table to enjoy. At first, she thought Callum might remind everyone what happened last time they tried to enjoy a dessert, but then she remembered that no one likely wanted Flanagan and his goons to know what the Sisters were capable of just yet. She could relax. Her overreaction was safe for now.

"What is this, anyway?" She rolled a bite of the rich dessert around in her mouth. Coffee, but not terrible bitter coffee? Cinnamon? Some kind of creamy filling? What was the cake part? It seemed like a bunch of separate pieces all smooshed together. "I mean, it's great, don't get me wrong—"

Callum put his fork down abruptly.

"—but I've never had anything like it."

Dex, smirking and knowing exactly what she was up to with Callum, answered her. "It's tiramisu, my lady. Coffee brandy, lady fingers, and whipped mascarpone cheese."

She looked down at the elegant cube of dessert with one bite missing and frowned. "That sounds revolting. How can it possibly be this good?"

"Depends on the chef," Dex said, far too innocently to actually be innocent. "A bad chef would curdle the cheese or oversoak the lady fingers until they're soggy. The cut pieces would be a mess." He turned to tip his glass to Flanagan at the head of the table. "Your chef is excellent, sir."

Callum muttered and shoved his dish aside, and Wen hid a smile with another decadent bite. Sheer bliss in food form.

Eventually, Flanagan put down his fork and played the bountiful, generous host again by offering coffee and brandy in the salon. "There's a lovely grand piano there if anyone plays. It's been eons since I stretched me fingers, so I'll gratefully bow out to a more seasoned artist."

No one volunteered. Wen looked at Brigid and raised her eyebrows.

Brigid shrugged. "I play cello."

Wen grinned. "That's better than me. I haven't played a musical instrument since one of those recorder things in, like, fourth grade. I sucked at it then, too."

Chuckles abounded, but for once, they didn't set her anxiety to spiraling. She knew most of these people by now and knew they wouldn't laugh at her in a mean way. If nothing else, they'd consider it rude to ridicule a Sister of the Moon, even if she was an absolute fool.

But they all stood up from the table, anyway, as dinner was clearly over. Brigid called to Gerhardt and asked for tea for all the Sisters. The guys all put in their drink orders with Flanagan, who sent the two suits into a different room for the various whiskeys and brandies required. Wen made a note to remind them all to be wary of what they were offered if it didn't come from Gerhardt.

Just in case. Couldn't be too careful in a shifty shifter's house.

Once they were all seated around the richly-decorated room —gold tones and chocolate browns, leather and metal studs, elegance and class and a huge price tag, Wen would bet— Flanagan moved to the middle of the floor and held up his glass.

"I'd like to propose a toast." He smiled benevolently at Wen, then belatedly widened his gaze to the rest of the room. "To the Sisters o' the Moon, whole once again."

What a lame toast. He was really milking the whole "it's an honor, Sisters" thing.

"The world has been waitin for ye, miladies. Glad we are that ye've returned to us. Happy days are ahead."

It took everything Wen had to not roll her eyes and look to Brigid for the droll, blankly polite expression on her face. She glanced at Thea instead and almost spit out her tea at the bored look there.

And yet, Flanagan went on, even though everyone had already taken a token sip. "Please know how glad I am that ye've come to the Gateway that we've kept safe for ye."

Dex stiffened almost imperceptibly beside her, and she made herself pay better attention. She noticed a flicker in Thea's eyes that said she'd sharpened her focus, too. She still didn't dare look to Brigid yet, though.

He now tipped his glass toward the two suits standing beside the elegant grand piano. "Stuart. Berenger. We lads go back a long while. Proud I am to have such loyal compatriots in this important duty that falls to me."

Was he really praising himself in a toast to the Sisters? Again, Wen felt her eyes trying to roll and did her best to stop them. She felt a headache coming on, and this was not the time for a migraine to disable her. They had plans tonight, dammit. Important ones.

Ugh. She sounded like Flanagan now. Gross.

He lifted his glass higher still, that toothy smile plastered on his smug face. "Here's to a united front. Cheers, lads and ladies!"

Finally, he threw back his entire drink in one go, then went to the credenza where the suits—Stuart and Berenger, apparently; were those first names or last names? She hated when she couldn't tell what was a first name and what was a surname; it was the worst part of the billing side of her job—had stashed the booze, and poured himself another one.

Goddess, she thought, *he isn't about to make another toast, is he? He can't be that pompous!*

And no, he wasn't. He was much worse, for he strolled over to her side and inserted himself between her and Florin, which neither appreciated.

"Milady." He smiled with those teeth again. "Wendolyn. May I call you Wen?"

Dex stiffened against her other side, and Wen could almost feel Callum's attention zeroing in on this schmuck.

"I wondered if I might have a moment of yer time, lass."

That was way, *way* too forward. Who did he think he was? He spoke as if she would just blithely go with him. Be grateful for the offer. Look at him with stars in her eyes.

Fuck that.

"Thank you for the kind offer, Mr. Flanagan, but I'm still very tired from the sea voyage. I almost drowned, you know."

Oops. She hadn't meant to blurt that, but once her mouth took off—

"So I think as soon as I've finished my tea, I'd like to head off to bed. Big day tomorrow, and all that."

Big night tonight. But he didn't get to know that.

"I'm sorry to hear that, Wen." He didn't sound at all sorry. He sounded annoyed and impatient. "Perhaps we could steal away for a moment before breakfast in the mornin. I'd really like to speak with ye." He leaned in. "Alone."

She leaned back, eyebrows rising. "I guess we'll have to see how I feel in the morning, then. But I'm very tired now, Mr. Flanagan."

"Please," he said, reaching for her hand, which she whipped behind her back to casually scratch as if she didn't notice his gesture and had a sudden itch, "call me Sean."

Sean Flanagan. Was that some sort of joke? He might as well call himself Irish McIreland.

She forced an unconvincing smile. "I'll do that. Sean."

At least it had fewer syllables to waste her time on. Whatever he wanted to say couldn't be at all important to her. He wasn't called. He couldn't be. He was too damn smarmy to be called.

Finally, *finally*, he moved away to circulate around the room. She caught Brigid's concerned look, her eyebrows rising when their eyes met, and shook her head. Not now. The encounter had worsened her headache, and she wanted nothing more than one migraine meds and a cool, dark, quiet room. Worse, one of the suits had lit up a cigarette, sending an ice pick through her sinuses and into her brain.

She hated cigarette smoke. It was one of her worst migraine triggers.

"My lady," Dex said, taking her arm again. "You look pale. Are you well?"

She smiled, but it felt more like a wince. And she only showed that much because Flanagan had left her alone finally. "Migraine."

"Florin."

But Florin was already on the move as soon as he heard the dreaded M word. Callum started making polite goodbyes while Dex led her along by the arm, encouraging her to lean on him if she needed to. Thea started to stand, but he shook his head, so she stayed put, though she looked concerned.

"Milady Wendolyn?" Flanagan asked, all polite and respectful now that everyone would hear him. The snake. "Ye're leavin already?"

Dex answered for her, throwing the response back over his shoulder without bothering to stop. "My lady is tired. She's sorry for leaving the party early, but she *has* had a trying day. Good night, all."

Murmured good nights and sleep wells followed them out

the door. She couldn't help but take a last peek back, only to curse herself when she realized Flanagan was still watching her, his eyes narrowed, his face red. Tucker had looked at her like that when she didn't perform as expected at one of his parties. He hated looking unpolished or unprofessional in front of his business contacts and friends.

Well, fuck him. And fuck Sean Flanagan, too. He was nothing but a stepping stone to the Gateway for her, and he'd damn well better learn that.

As soon as they started up the stairs, she put her free hand to her head and groaned. This one had come on fast. Conveniently, but too painful for her to be grateful for the handy escape plan. Dex, without missing a step, swept her up bridal style and carried her up the steps. She thought about fake-fighting against him, like Scarlett O'Hara, but she just couldn't do it.

Instead, she lay her head against his chest, listening to his heartbeat and letting it soothe the thunder brewing in her brain. She had a mission tonight, dammit. She didn't have time for this nonsense, but getting all worked up over possibly being the one to pooch their plans to go to the Gateway early wouldn't help. It would, in fact, make the migraine so much worse. No way could she work any kind of magic if she couldn't think straight.

She needed to be sharp. She needed to be able to focus.

She needed to be able to get out of bed, for the goddess' sake.

Callum ran ahead and opened the French doors, where Florin was waiting just inside with a full glass of water and her as-needed migraine pill already in his palm, ready to melt on her tongue.

These men. These wonderful, thoughtful, ridiculous men.

How had she ever lived without them?

23

It was dark when Wen awoke suddenly, covered in men. Dex and Florin cuddled up on either side, and Callum lay over her, his head on her chest. She tried to sit up, and they sleepily jostled around to let her, though Callum muttered darkly as he did so.

The migraine was gone, faded in the hours of sleep she'd managed, but a new urgency grew in its place, filling her head with a buzzing feeling and rang like a clarion call. It was time.

She went to the nearest floor-to-ceiling window, her footie pajamas—seriously, her men knew her and pampered her far too well—warm as a hug on her skin, and drew aside the curtains. She expected to see moonlight illuminating the scene like a spotlight, but the world outside was dark and blowy. She looked up at the sky, covered in angry storm clouds, and felt the first moment's doubt.

Could they do this without Sister Moon? Could they still draw on Her power if She was hidden behind the clouds?

Maybe Brigid could move them. Wen was pretty sure it had been Brigid who conveniently moved the clouds on their sea journey, but those had been wispy, floaty clouds, not this roiling mess about to loose its quiverful of thunders and lightnings upon them.

The buzzing in her brain increased, and she knew the storm brewing outside didn't matter. They had to go to the Gateway tonight. That sensation urged her to go, go, go, and whether it came from the Gateway itself or from Sister Moon hidden behind the storm, she had no intention of ignoring it.

Florin had thoughtfully packed her a pair of jeans and a thick sweater, and she stripped out of her footie pajamas and put them on, glad for the warm clothing on a night like this, then pulled on her boots under the jeans in hopes of minimizing twisted ankles with their support. She wound her messy hair into a lop-sided bun and pinned it in place. She didn't have the patience to deal with it tonight and wanted it out of her face. Then, she checked the window again to see if the weather had let up any and sighed. It didn't look any worse, but it didn't look better, either.

Didn't matter. She woke up her guys, shushing their grunts and yawns and solicitous questions about how she felt. When they finally woke enough to sense her urgency, they quieted and dressed in a hurry, ready to go much faster than she had been. They didn't have to deal with their hair.

They crept out the French doors and over to Brigid's room, but it was empty, so they tiptoed down the sweeping staircase to Thea's room, where they found everyone crowded into the master suite, waiting for them. It didn't look like they'd been waiting long, and Wen sighed a quiet thank you to the buzzing that had awakened her and got her moving.

"How's yer heid, love?" Brigid asked, wrapped in a black velvet, hooded robe, her Goth make-up impeccable even in the middle of the night. She looked like a metal album cover.

Dammit. Wen should've bought a cloak when she had the chance. Why hadn't she insisted on buying a cloak?

"Can ye—?"

"I'm good." Wen gestured toward the windows and the roiling clouds outside. "Can you maybe shift some of the clouds so Sister Moon can shine on us?"

Her eyes widened. "Me? I cannae do anythin like that."

Wen tilted her head to one side. "Pretty sure you did it last night. It wasn't me who moved those clouds away. Thea?"

They both looked to their elder Sister, who was clad all in black but didn't have the sweeping robe Brigid rocked. Wen was the only one wearing colors, and she felt like an idiot for not packing more black. She'd thought a single carry-on would be easier to deal with, and now she'd be the most easily-spotted liability in the group. Dammit.

But Thea only shrugged. "Was not me, mes chéris. I have packed some herbs and crystals and other ingredients tonight in case we need the help of the loa, but I have no power over the sky."

Brigid blinked, trying to grasp this new idea. "Power over the sky." She looked at Wen. "Power over water." Now, at Thea. "Power over earth and plants."

It clicked for all three of them at the same time. Earth, air, water. But there were only three Sisters, so who had power over fire? It didn't make complete sense.

Maybe that didn't matter right now. Maybe they could ask the Folk, if they actually got to the Gateway. That buzzing in her skull hadn't abated, even though she'd joined her Sisters. If anything, it amped up in urgency until she wanted to thunk the heel of her palm against her forehead to shake it loose.

"Ladies, I think we need to go now." She shrugged. "Something tells me we need to book it."

"I feel it, too," Brigid admitted. "Like wasps in me heid."

"Yes!" Relieved, Wen could hug her. "That's exactly the feeling."

"I, too, mes soeurs." Thea looked gravely at each of them. "We must go now."

Brigid flipped up the hood of her cloak. Thea slung a stringed backpack over one shoulder, likely her spell components. Wen grumbled internally. She didn't even have a bottle of water, which she might have thought of if she'd been thinking instead of just moving. She'd have to hope for puddles or maybe a hard rain to give her something to work with.

As geared up as they could be, the Sisters of the Moon crept out of the guest mansion and followed Gerhardt across the smooth expanse of the lawn. When they reached the small fence that marked the boundary, the Nightwatchers helped the Sisters over and steadied them on the uneven basalt on the other side. Now that they were out of sight of the main mansion, Brigid took a deep breath and looked up at the sky, letting her hood fall back. She closed her eyes.

Thunder rumbled as if in warning.

After a moment, she groaned softly. "I cannae do it. There's too much happenin up there."

Wen moved closer and took her hand. "Don't focus on the clouds. Focus on the sky, the air. Then think of four things you can feel or touch, the last one being the clouds as you wipe them away. Say them out loud if you need to. Really focus on them."

Brigid pressed her lips together and closed her eyes more tightly. "Yer hand tight on mine. The velvet of me cloak. The damp chill in the air. The clouds movin aside as I wipe them away with me hand."

She made the gesture as she spoke the last sensation, and a single ray of moonlight shone down on them. They all looked up and gasped. Sister Moon peered down at them through a small hole in the gray. It was as if Brigid had pushed one of the storm clouds off to the side, just as she'd said.

She looked at Wen, her eyes wide and almost scared. "Wendolyn Eudora Cheney."

Wen, elated, squeezed her hand back. "Brigid Maureen McLaughlin."

Because of course they'd exchanged full names during their long conversations in Brigid's comfortably Goth sitting room. They'd told each other all about themselves. It's what Sisters did.

Thea joined them, holding out her hands to them, smiling when they eagerly took them. "Althea Alciénne Deschamps."

The clouds overhead whooshed away, and they all gawked upward to watch as the nearly full moon filled the sky with Her gentle light and glowed on the basalt columns of the Giant's Causeway.

They did have power. It was all true. They were Sisters of the Moon, and Goddess help those who tried to stop them from learning their true purpose.

Gerhardt led them over the rocky, alien terrain, harshly beautiful in the moon's serene glow. They moved, slowly but surely, toward the cliffs rising up into the night sky, and Wen began to worry that they'd have to find some way to climb those hexagonal basalt columns. Unless they suddenly learned how to fly—or Phaeton offered them each a ride—they'd be up the creek if they needed to reach the top of those sheer, intimidating walls.

Thankfully, as they stumbled and clambered ever closer, they began to see a strange pattern forming along the base of the cliffs. A cave of sorts, the basalt columns making the opening look like an open mouth with uneven teeth. It wasn't the most comforting impression, but if they were headed for the cave, they at least didn't have to climb the cliffs.

Sure enough, Gerhardt led them up to the cliff face and stopped, gesturing toward the cave mouth. They all looked around, curious, but saw nothing magical. Nothing to indicate this was the fabled Gateway.

Brigid eyed her Nightwatcher, not doubting so much as

genuinely confused. "What makes ye think this is the place, then, love?"

But Gerhardt didn't seem doubtful in the least. He simply gestured inside the cave. "Him."

The Sisters drew together, joining hands without thinking about it. Inside the cave, a glow began to bloom in the darkness. It almost matched Sister Moon's luminous, gentle light. Perhaps they were one and the same.

A hobbled-over little man stepped out of that light and out of the cave, a tall crook keeping him steady on the uneven terrain. His scraggly beard hung to the ground, his clothes were patched and scruffy, and he was missing more than a few teeth and one eye. But when he finally spoke, his voice was rich and full, not at all the crackling wheeze expected.

"Who approaches— ah. Sisters. Ye've finally made it then, have ye?"

He didn't sound terribly welcoming, and Wen and Brigid exchanged glances, then looked to Thea for guidance. She'd been around the longest, after all. Surely she knew—

"We were unaware we had a scheduled visitation, monsieur," she said coolly, seemingly unimpressed by this little man who'd appeared out of thin air.

The lone eye narrowed, the other side of his face crinkling on a scowl. "Aye, lass. Ye have." His tone sharpened, almost accusatory. "And ye're about a hunnert years too bloody late."

Thea raised that devastating right eyebrow. "Pardon, monsieur?"

He reeled off a line of French too fast and angry for Wen to even begin to understand, and Thea answered him right back, then caught herself and stood tall. Statuesque as a goddess, she lifted her chin and spoke English again so they could understand.

"We understand, petit homme, that we know very little about our duties—"

Moon duties, Wen thought and almost brayed nervous laughter but somehow managed to remain silent.

"—but we lost the Sisters before these two, and I had not yet been taught in our ways. Forgive us if we have failed somehow, but how were we to know?"

His eye narrowed again. "Lost how?"

Thea's head lowered. "They were murdered, their throats torn out."

The little man's eye popped wide open. "Aye? Well, then, lasses, come with me. The Queen needs to hear about this, and ye cannae do yer work without a bit of instruction." He finally considered them on the level, rather than with belligerence or suspicion. "Though ye've managed to sort a few things out for yerselves, aye."

He could sense their magic? Or see it somehow? Wen fidgeted, wondering what that lone eye really saw. Or perhaps he saw with the missing one. Stranger things were currently happening, after all.

"Come on, then," he barked, impatient as he gestured with his free hand. "In ye go." But when the entire group moved toward the cave, he paused and glared, this time at all the Nightwatchers. "Where d'ye think ye're goin, then?"

They looked at each other, and then Samuel—perhaps the most senior of the group, given that he was Thea's First—stepped foward to speak for the group. "We go where they go, monsieur."

The little man snorted. "No, ye don't. We're travelin to the Night Realm, me lad, and only the Sisters are allowed. Ye'll have to wait here."

"But—"

The light grew until it engulfed the little man, and Wen watched as the wide-eyed group of Nightwatchers was suddenly snatched away from them like the snap of a bungee cord. Moonlight surrounded them, and they no longer stood at the mouth of a cave.

No. They stood in a field of exotic wildflowers, glowing various shades of blue and violet and white, sweeping as far as the eye could see. She looked up, feeling sick to her stomach at the sense of displacement, and saw Sister Moon, looking the same as always, if perhaps a bit closer. Almost close enough to touch.

She did not test that theory. She had no idea how she'd react if she could literally touch the moon.

"Here we are, then, lasses. To the Hill we go, aye?"

Thea, sounding as breathless as Wen felt, asked the question that hovered on all of their tongues.

"Ma déesse, where are we?"

The little man eyed her. "Plenty of names for this place. Faerie. Underhill. Elfhyme. Álfheimr. Tír na nÓg." His craggy old face split into a gap-toothed grin. "Ye're in the Night Realm, lass, and ye're the first material bodies to enter this plane with the ability to leave since the Pact was struck."

Wen blinked and finally managed to speak. "What Pact?"

He rolled his eye and turned to hobble with his crook through the glowing wildflowers toward a flat-topped hill rising into the night. "If ye truly know nothin about it, lass, ye need to speak with the Queen. I cannae tell ye the whole bloody story with a pack o' rabid folk millin about the Gateway. I'm the bloody Gatekeeper, and I've no time to tell ye a wee bedtime story, do I?"

After a shared, wide-eyed look, the Sisters of the Moon—their hands still linked, their grips almost painfully tight—hurried to follow the Gatekeeper through an enchanted field of glowing flowers toward a fairy mound in another realm of existence under a moon they could almost reach up and touch.

Wen again wanted to laugh hysterically.

All in a day's work, apparently.

The Gatekeeper wouldn't allow them to simply walk up the side of the hill once they reached it. Oh, no. They had to trudge clockwise around its circumference nine times to reach the top. When Wen asked why, she received nothing but a one-eyed glare in response.

She didn't ask again.

At the end of the ninth rotation, even though they'd only been about halfway up the hill by that point, they somehow stood on the flat top, where a nighttime banquet was laid out on a table surrounded by beings of every sort. They all had a faint, luminous glow about them. Fairies? Or the Folk, as Tarquin had called them?

Her heart ached. Tarquin.

Not the time.

At the furthest end of the table sat a woman in floating gossamer robes, her hair strawberry blonde and drifting like seaweed about her head, a crown of moonlight tucked amongst the mass. She was unearthly beautiful with sharp, harsh features and tilted electric green eyes.

Queen Mab? Wen supposed not, or not exactly, anyway. Like the Night Realm, these beings likely had a million humanized names that weren't who or what they truly were. She didn't know how she knew that, but she did.

None of those names for the Queen would be quite right.

"Sisters of the Moon." She didn't sound impressed, but that could be the somehow hollow tone of her voice. Unlike the Gatekeeper's, hers seemed to come from far away, as if through a wall or a window. "You have failed our faith in you."

Probably not the best way to start a conversation. All three Sisters bristled, their hands clenching down. Perhaps obviously, Thea was the first to recover.

"Madame, you wound us. You do not have the information."

She drew herself up, as tall and glorious as any fairy queen. "My Sisters were slaughtered when I came to Light, and it has taken a hundred years for more to rise into their place. We did not know we had obligations to fulfill. We were only told that our magic allows shifters to shift at will, rather than being bound to Sister Moon."

The Queen rose, her glow intensifying. "Slaughtered? How can this be? We provided guardians to keep them safe to work their will on my sister Gaia's green and good earth."

Thea shook her head. "Rogue shifters, madame. Perhaps even their own called Nightwatchers, the guardians you sent them. We do not know. We only know they are gone."

Wen was still an exchange back. The Queen was Gaia's sister? Was that, like, a biological thing, or like the Sisters of the Moon, a sisters-of-choice sort of thing? And the Folk had set up the Nightwatcher arrangement? That seemed... to make sense, actually. The tautology finally had a source. Nice.

Then, without warning her first, Wen's mouth opened. "What is the Pact?" All eyes turned to her, and she gulped, withering inside. "Um. Your Majesty?"

"You are Sister of Sea, yes?"

"Um." *This is not the time for um!* "I do seem to have some power over water?"

The Queen's eyes moved to Brigid. "Sister of Sky." To Thea. "Sister of Soil. Is it true? You, none of you, know about the Pact?"

Unanimous, they all shook their heads. The Queen sighed.

"Come. Sit. We have much to discuss, and unlike your fellow mortals, you may take refreshment here and still move through the Veil."

Well. That was a lot.

In a flash, all the other beings at the feast vanished, leaving only the Queen and the three Sisters. They finally, reluctantly released hands and moved to sit at the near end of the table until the Queen impatiently waved them closer. Wen didn't particularly want to be in arm's reach of the sharp-faced, sharp-eyed Queen of the Night Realm, but it didn't look like she had a choice. She sat at Her Majesty's right side, and Thea and Brigid sat to her left. Smart women. They at least had each other.

Wen was on her own. Dammit.

24

"You humans are so troublesome." The Queen shook her head, pouring them each a glass of glowing wine. "We've had no end of bother with you."

None of the Sisters spoke, but Wen caught herself wondering why the Folk continued to bother with a race so problematic if they didn't have to. If there was some sort of pact here, that meant each party had something the other party needed.

Don't let her pretend she has all the power.

"With your earth metals and your brutish natures, you've caused no end of strife to my good people. We made the Pact to protect ourselves without cutting off the energy flow completely, as we knew the lot of you that had interbred with some of our Folk would die without it. But that did not satisfy you, did it? Your greed is perhaps your least desirable trait."

Wen found herself feeling affronted. She hadn't done any of that. She'd just lived her life the best she could, even if that meant fighting her way out of it and hoping for something better down the line. She hadn't been greedy. Tucker had been, but that was different.

"And your lack of respect for my sister's gifts of Nature. You pollute your blue skies and burn your green fields and put poison in your clear, precious water. Do you have any idea how much of our energy has been twisted and perverted by your carelessness? Your planet is a delicate balance of natural resources, and you defiantly exploit and destroy them all. You will be your own undoing."

Brigid put down her wine glass with a thump that spilled some of the glowing wine on her hand. "Oi, milady, did we come here for a lecture or a history lesson? I ken which I'm hearin now, and it isnae the most useful one."

The Queen glared with those tilted, electric eyes, but Brigid failed to wither. Wen felt a burst of hero worship and wanted to highfive her for her courage. Probably wasn't the time for that, though, so she kept her hands in her lap and didn't touch the wine. Just in case.

"Fine. History, then. Humans began working their precious earth metals, which drove us to the corners of the wilderness, despite all we had done for them. They knew our physical bodies could not bear the touch of silver, of iron, of copper or bronze, but they used that knowledge against us and tried to enslave us. That, I would not allow. So I took my power—my magic, as they called it—back and formed a barrier between us." For the first time, she softened. "I did not know it would create such havoc on your world. So many died. It was a catastrophe. I finally realized that Gaia had created her picturesque world with our magic and it could not exist long without it."

Wen racked her brain for what she could possibly be talking about. If the Queen was talking about the Bronze Age, what with all the griping about humans working earth metals and such, perhaps she meant the Bronze Age Collapse? Hadn't that been more about powerful civilizations crumbling than natural disasters?

"War and death. Volcanoes and drought. Fire and flood. It was a disaster for all of your world, but I could not have foreseen how it devastated the population of the interbred half-Folk we left behind there. They could not survive without our magic. But when we collapsed the barrier and brought them to the Night Realm, their physical bodies could not survive in this world of spirit energy. They began to die in both realms, as they were creatures of both and needed both to survive."

Wen's eyes widened. "The Pact. You promised not to close the Veil completely so they wouldn't die."

She nodded, but impatiently. "I created the Veil between our worlds instead of a solid barrier. We refused to speak with any but a chosen delegation of humans and set the Gatekeeper at the thinnest part of the Veil to limit who could enter our realm with the knowledge that they would not be allowed to come back." She poured herself more wine, and Wen noticed her hand shaking. "The humans elected three men to fulfill the delegation duties, but I refused. Men are volatile, stubborn, unwilling to compromise. I chose three women, instead, and the Sisters of the Moon were given power over the elements to protect my sister's creation from the excesses and destruction of human civilization. I gave no one the use of fire, which is a man's element. Destructive and hard to control. Hurting instead of healing."

Why was her hand shaking? Emotion or nervousness? Was the Queen upset, or was she lying to them? Or simply omitting information, like what their side of the Pact was?

They might never know if Wen didn't ask. She wasn't sure the Queen would ever tell them, otherwise. The tale thus far had been entirely one-sided.

"What do you get out of it, Your Majesty?"

Those green eyes weren't just electric as they speared her in her chair. They burned now, almost like laser beams. Wen felt her breath shortening, but she fought it back. She didn't have time for a panic attack. Dex and Callum and Florin weren't here to hold her and tell her everything would be alright.

Five things she could see: those laser green eyes, the bountiful table with all the glowing food, the perfect flatness of the hilltop they sat on, the glint of moonlight that was the queen's crown, Sister Moon overhead, Her rays seeming to stroke at Wen's cheeks and soothe her to quiet.

The Queen's eyes narrowed as she drew back from whatever change she saw in Wen's manner. Better.

"I don't know what you mean."

Brigid hmmed, seeming to catch Wen's meaning. "She means why would a queen of magic such as yerself be so benevolent as to leave yer realm even somewhat unprotected from such destructive creatures as ourselves if ye didnea have to, lass?"

Thea frowned, then smiled as she understood what they were asking. "Yes, madame. What is it you need from Gaia's good and green world?"

Pinned from both sides, the Queen bristled, her hair flowing back as if caught in a riptide current. "You dare."

Wen, greatly daring with her Sisters on the same track, leaned forward and dropped an elbow on the table. Mama would have swooned at such disrespect.

"History, remember? Not a lecture. What do you need from Earth that made you willing to leave even a trickle of magic flowing to us? If you didn't need something, you would have shut the door completely and damn the cryptids."

Green eyes narrowed again. "What is this word?"

Wen rolled her eyes. "Cryptids. The ones you talked about before that had interbred with your people and created beings of both magic and physical bodies—" She sat up and slapped a hand on the table. "That's it. Physical bodies."

The Queen flinched.

"That's why you didn't slam the door. This is a spirit realm, energy only. None of this on the table is real. It's just magic."

Closing her eyes, she thought of four things she could *really* feel: the sweater's warmth on her shoulders, the tight but comfortable fit of her new boots up to her knees, the rough denim of her jeans, her hand swiping through air as she slammed it right through the illusory table she'd pounded on moments before.

She opened her eyes, and there was no table. There were no chairs. They four stood on an empty, flat hilltop, the moon above and the Queen naked, bald, and genderless before them, though they still wore their crown of moonlight.

"Damn you humans," they murmured, though they no longer sounded impatient and angry. "The most persistent of you always see through our illusions."

Brigid looked at her hands, at the ground where she was standing instead of sitting in a chair. Thea brushed at her clothes, but there was a desperation to the gesture, more like she needed to feel the fabric against her palms than that she worried about dust or dirt or wrinkles.

The Queen— no. The Sovereign of the Night Realm lifted their head and looked at Wen, still unearthly beautiful but less intimidating now that all the glamour had vanished.

"My people found the pleasures of the flesh too much to give up entirely." They shrugged one shoulder as if this meant nothing, but Wen knew better. "I am not immune to the pure sensation that can only be felt in a physical body. But I was not willing to allow humans to destroy my entire world just to have it. So I compromised."

"The Veil. A curtain, rather than a wall."

They nodded. "And a Gatekeeper to protect us from unwanted guests. And three Sisters to act as... as—"

They gestured vaguely. Wen made a guess.

"Diplomats?"

"If you like, yes." They again shrugged a shoulder. "You are the go-betweens who guard the balance of Nature. You speak for the human envoy that protect and disperse the gold that symbolizes the Pact between us."

She blinked. "What gold?"

Brigid blinked. "What human envoy?"

Thea still scrubbed at her clothes, her expression pinched and worried. Wen wanted to go to her and take her hand, but even though they were all standing, she still stood at the Sovereign's right while Thea and Brigid stood to their left.

It was the Sovereign's turn to blink. "*The* human envoy. The three men originally chosen to be the diplomats you mentioned, the go-betweens for our two realms. I would not have them, but the humans demanded non-magical representation, so we entrusted them with a chest of gold that never emptied to use for the Sisters' material needs, for ensuring you can be where you need to be for tending to the planet. It placated them enough to agree to the Pact."

Wen thought of Oregon, her worries about how to pay for the property Gaia wanted her to have and the education she wanted for herself. Of Brigid's simple life, despite living in a castle that she had earned rather than paid for, where her Nightwatchers all had tasks that ensured they didn't need money. Of her non-magical tarot readings for pay when she found she did need to pay for something.

Thea's hippie commune in the French countryside, where they grew all their own food and made all their own clothing.

None of that should've been necessary, though her Sisters had made it work for them. But they shouldn't have had to.

Wen shook her head. "I think there's something else you need to know, Your Majesty. We don't know anything about this human envoy, and we certainly don't know anything about any never-ending pot of gold." She looked to her Sisters and grinned with absolutely no humor. "Ladies, I think we've been had."

The Sovereign glowed like an angry moon, their power rising with their temper. "Come with me, my Sisters of the Moon. Retribution is at hand for those who would dare break a Pact with the Folk."

They started off down the hill and, without another word, the Sisters followed.

25

Wen stepped out of the cave mouth and stopped, her jaw dropping. Were they in the right place and time? Because it looked to her as if a battle was taking place where they had left only their Nightwatchers behind. Perhaps she really had joined the Wild Hunt, but the cryptids were all hunting each other.

Wolves and leopards and wild boar howled and screeched and bellowed as they attacked the shifted Nightwatchers. Everything was cacophony. Gerhardt's golden eagle dive-bombed attackers from above. Phaeton's pegasus leaped from fight to fight, wings spread and hooves deadly. Samuel's ancient beast of an elk simply swept its ludicrous antlers side to side, repelling attack after attack and gouging any time it got the chance.

Halvor's polar bear roared and stood up to its full height, then lunged at a brown bear that rivaled his size and ferocity. Florin's dire wolf duelled with a large, strange, foul-smelling dog/wolf hybrid with a dark stripe of black down its back. They each had teeth in each other's throats, and she started forward to help, forgetting in her haste that she had no water to use as a weapon.

A shot rang out. She patted at her chest and stomach, but she didn't think she had been shot. She looked desperately at Brigid and Thea, but they, too, seemed unharmed. She turned her head further and— oh. Oh, no.

The Sovereign, now a queen again with a solid mortal form, touched the wound in her chest from which blood as red as wine poured in a gush. Her hair, a long and lustrous strawberry blonde, drifted down around her body from where it had been floating moments before. She sighed, and a trickle of blood drew a line from her left nostril to the corner of her delicate, pouting lips.

Still those green eyes, though they didn't glow here. Not in a mortal form. A *wounded* mortal form.

The Queen collapsed daintily, seeming more to swoon than to fall gracelessly, as Wen would have done, and Wen tripped over a basalt hexagon to get to her side and catch her, laying her down gently on the uneven terrain.

"Your Majesty, what—?"

The Queen smiled, despite the blood rushing from her material form. "Treacherous, you humans."

Thea knelt at Wen's side, her string bag swung around for her to rummage in. "Go. I will pray to the loa and do what I can. Find whoever has that gun and take them out, however possible."

With that, Thea shoved at Wen's chest, and Brigid grabbed her arm to help her up. They turned to face the melee, and while Wen wanted to search out her black dog and heard her war horse screaming a challenge into the night—Callum had finally found room to transform and the war to prove he wasn't just a Shire horse—she instead looked for the two suits that had been with Flanagan earlier.

There they were, across the battlefield, one with a gun out, the other hurriedly building a pile of sticks and twigs. A bonfire. Goddess, were they going to try and burn the Queen?

She couldn't let that happen. She grabbed onto Brigid's arm and pulled her close.

"You have to make it rain."

Brigid stared at her, uncomprehending.

"Honey, you control air, which means you control weather. You made the clouds go away earlier. Bring them back." She smiled, but it wasn't a happy expression. "Make it rain."

Brigid's eyes widened, but she nodded. "Yer grip on me arm." She closed her eyes and lifted her free hand toward the sky where Sister Moon looked over the battle in progress, shining so brightly that every detail stood out too clearly to miss. "The velvet o' me hood. So damn much fear I'm nigh to wettin' me knickers. The cool damp o' the rain against me face."

And just like that, it was raining. Wen let her go and put her own hands up, then flung them toward the two suits and their would-be bonfire. The black-striped creature let go of Florin's flank and leapt up to intercept her water bomb, soaking itself to the skin but also knocking it back several feet where it wiped out at the feet of the two scrabbling bears. Halvor gave the brown bear a shove, then reached down to bite at the wolf-dog thing's neck, but it scrambled away, turning its attention on Wen.

Three things I can hear: a bedlam of baying animals, Brigid's scared breathing beside me, the pattering of the rain on the basalt—

She flung out her hands again, changing her intention from a wave to horizontal raindrops. Sure enough, the wolf-dog leapt up to intercept again, but she closed her hands into fists and hardened the water droplets.

Hardened them like bullets. Dozens of tiny water droplet bullets.

They drove into the wolf-dog's side, neck, and face, and

blood erupted. The creature howled and collapsed in a heap. Though she had no idea if shifters could regenerate like the legends, she had no silver with which to finish him off, so she eclipsed him from her thoughts and looked at the two suits. The one with the gun had it pointed at her.

The other one had a lighter in one hand and a gallon of gasoline—petrol, her mind irrelevantly substituted—in the other. They really were going to build a bonfire. They'd planned ahead for it.

That did not bode well.

She clenched her teeth together and shoved both hands forward at them, her palms shoving water droplets at them with all her might. The suit with the petrol dropped to the ground and covered his head, but the one with the gun took the full brunt in the chest, stomach, and face. He looked like she'd leveled him with a shotgun blast as he fell over backward, dead before he even hit the ground.

She'd just killed someone. Sure, someone who'd been trying to kill her and the fucking Queen of Faerie, but still. She'd never even thought about killing anyone before.

"Wen!" Brigid yelled next to her ear. "He's lightin it! Ye have to douse it, love!"

Her arms felt weary. Sister Moon again hid behind the clouds, and Wen felt her power wane without Her light. The rain slowed.

Just as she groaned and raised her arms again, this time determined to come in low and at least take the suit's legs out in case he ducked again, she saw, as if in slow motion, the stripe-backed wolf-dog leaping toward her. He still bled from dozens of tiny buckshot wounds, but they didn't seem to be stopping him. Instead of attacking with exhaustion weighing her down, she used her energy to shove Brigid clear of the immediate danger, then crossed her arms over her face as the full weight of the enormous creature flattened her.

The horrific stink of the thing washed over her as it slavered at her face, then chomped down on her forearm, nearly biting all the way through. Growling, snarling, the wolf-dog dragged her toward the melee. As it approached, a path seemed to form as if by magic, the battle forming into two halves of chaos instead of a united whole. It dragged her down that path by her bleeding, ruined forearm, and she screamed.

Bloodthirsty baying answered her. Dex. Dex would find her. He would save her.

The wolf-dog hauled her faster, its filthy teeth savaging her flesh, and dragged her to the edge of the bonfire. Heat flared against her skin, and she winced away, pulling at her arm, even though the motion savaged her worse. She had to get away from the fire. She didn't have the energy to put it out.

She was fucked.

With a flick of its awful, misshapen head, the wolf-dog threw her in. She landed face first against the blazing pile of sticks and screamed. Dex's black dog bayed into the night again, this time in rage and terror.

Everything stopped.

She... wasn't burning. The flames didn't seem to touch her. Hell, the sticks she'd fallen on hurt worse, jabbing into her cheeks and tearing at the already-destroyed flesh of her arm. Stunned, she lay there a moment, then rolled over and sat up.

In the middle of a roaring bonfire.

She looked across the suddenly still battlefield where an entire fucking menagerie of animals gaped at her to where Thea stood next to the standing Queen, her gossamer gown soaked with blood but her chest no longer spurting. A greenish brown poultice was pressed over the wound—some of Thea's hoodoo magic, Wen guessed.

She stood up, trying not to bump her arm, the flames blazing all around her, though they still didn't touch her.

The Queen scoffed. "As if I would ever allow one of my witches to burn."

And Wen could only laugh, even though it wasn't at all funny.

The Queen extended her hand, and all the shifters suddenly stood in their human forms. Every single one was bleeding at least a little bit. The one that had thrown her into the fire, the smelly wolf-dog, turned to face her, and she felt a complete lack of surprise to see Flanagan, his face pockmarked with bloody holes, glaring hatred at her.

With Thea and Brigid to help her on either side, the Queen picked her way through the convenient aisle through the silent, bloody battlefield and right up to the bonfire, which she extinguished with a wave. Wen stepped out of the smoldering pile of sticks and, before she could stop herself, threw herself into the Queen's arms. She wasn't even sure why; it just felt like the thing to do.

Brigid and Thea released her, and the Queen wrapped her own arms around Wen, stroking her messy, fallen-down, filthy hair and murmuring soothing nothings. Embarrassed now, Wen pulled away and bit her lip, but the Queen only smiled at her, blood on her beautiful face, her hair also goddamn mess that somehow still looked magical.

"You did very well, Sister of Sea. You have fulfilled your side of the Pact, as have your Sisters. We will continue to honor ours and return the full measure of your magic to you. The Veil will thin again. Your realm will be saved with the Sisters' good work."

She turned her piercing green eyes on Flanagan and the remaining suit. "Who are you? I allowed no shifters in the human envoy."

Flanagan spat blood at her dainty bare feet. "Exactly, witch. We shifters had no representation when it was our very lives at stake in yer stupid argument with the humans. Did ye think we'd sit idly by and let ye squabble us to death?" He turned his glare to Wen. "I tried to talk to ye. I tried to warn ye what was at stake and offer to be yer Nightwatcher, but ye wouldnae—"

Wen laughed. Right in his face. Which then turned purple with fury.

"You don't know the first thing about Nightwatchers, then, *Sean*. Do you really think I'd accept one that I couldn't trust with my life when that's their sole purpose?" She snorted with considerably less amusement than before. "I have more faith in my pillar that's absent than I could ever have in you."

He growled. "Enough! I donnae even care about that now! That money is ours by right! We are the children of the Night Realm in this world, and we deserve our due!"

The Queen, however, seemed unimpressed with his aggression. "How did you seat yourself in my envoy?" She looked to the remaining suit, who paled and literally wet his pants at her attention. "You are a Thatcher, from the one of the original lines chosen to support my Sisters. He is not. How did you allow this betrayal to happen?"

Flanagan spat blood again, his voice rasping now as the wounds sapped him of his strength. "He did nothin. I killed every last Fletcher male and seated myself. They do as I say now, witch. And yous can do nothin about—"

He stopped abruptly and looked at Wen, who stood with her hand outstretched parallel to the ground, her palm down and her fingers pressed together. He blinked. His head slid, slid more, then fell off entirely, his body collapsing after it.

The remaining mist of rain stopped. Silence reigned.

She shrugged at the numerous sets of eyes on her. "Bad guys." Feeling detached from everything, she lifted her hand toward the last man standing, even though the rain had stopped. "You can't kill just one."

"I surrender. I surrender! He bugged the guest house when you wouldn't let him separate you from the group. I didn't mean for any of this to happen. No one was supposed to die! We were just after the infinite money!"

Wen lowered her hand.

26

The Sisters of the Moon stood with the Queen of the Night Realm at the mouth of the cave, the Gateway between their two worlds.

"You will come see me again soon, my Sisters?"

It sounded like both a command and a question. All three nodded in return.

"You have all done so well. I am sorry that I did not pay closer attention to this world. This uprising was my fault, not yours." She smiled softly, still bloody but healing by the minute. Thea did good work. "We must meet to install a new human envoy. Women, this time. No men allowed."

Wen tilted her head, then smiled. "I think I might know just the right woman for the first spot."

She wondered if Clare might be up for a career change. She suspected she might if it came with unlimited pay.

"I will trust your judgment, then." The Queen looked at the Gatekeeper, who bowed his head respectfully and lifted his hand toward the cave, where soft light bloomed. "The money of the Pact is yours. The responsibility to heal the damage humans have wrought is yours. Gaia needs you, as do humans and Sister of Sea's cryptids alike, though they know nothing of it."

Wen lifted her head, feeling the weight of responsibility but also the pride of having such an important calling. An *active* calling, rather than just existing so her Nightwatchers could shift to protect her.

She'd known that was stupid. She'd called it back at the very beginning of this whole mess.

After teasing Florin about calling the French government to collect the six thousand *livres* promised by King Louis XV to whoever verifiably killed the Beast of Gévaudan, Thea attended to Wen's arm, touching the ground and calling forth the plants she needed to make another healing poultice. Sister of Soil, indeed, to grow tender, new plants from basalt. Then, she'd wrapped Wen's from wrist to elbow in a long strip of gossamer from the Queen's dress, which glowed faintly until it seemed to sink into her and numb the pain.

Nice. It was good to be a Sister.

Brigid obligingly cleared away all the clouds, so they couldn't help but notice as the sun peered up over the horizon, brightening the sky and the land alike. The Queen sighed and looked that way longingly, then stepped further into the shadow of the cliff.

They were Sisters of the Moon, not the sun, and she was the Queen of the Night Realm, not the day.

"I must return to my people now, Sisters. We will not allow what happened a hundred years ago to ever happen again. We will be vigilant. That is our new Pact to each other. I will discuss a Pact with the humans when we have set the new envoy." She touched Wen's hair, then took Thea's hand, then leaned down and kissed Brigid's forehead. "Until then, my Sisters of the Moon."

Saying goodbye would have felt odd, so they only waved as the Queen and the Gatekeeper entered the portal to the Night

Realm. As one, Wen and Brigid and Thea turned back toward the "real" world and winced at the bloody battlefield being illuminated by the harsh rays of the new sun.

But their Nightwatchers, their beloved shifters, waited for them, too, so they went to them and allowed them to enfold them in safety, in comfort. In love.

As the sun rose, the Sisters of the Moon went about getting on with the rest of their lives.

Saving the world was surprisingly anticlimactic.

Three Sisters and eleven Nightwatchers sat crowded in Brigid's ornate sitting room, mostly watching the fire in the hearth. Wen couldn't look at it, though. Not after being thrown face-first into one. It might be years before she could find comfort in flames.

Oh, and she'd killed two people. There was that. One, Flanagan, with such calculated coldness that she couldn't bring herself to move away from the fire, even if she couldn't look at it. She felt cold to the bone, colder than when the giant squid had pulled her down. She knew her Nightwatchers were worried about her and wanted to help, but they couldn't protect her from what she'd done.

Yes, killing Flanagan had been necessary. The shifter admitted to terminating an entire family just to steal their spot on the human envoy. That wasn't counting all the humans he'd slaughtered and partially eaten as the Beast of Gévaudan or the countless deaths he must have caused in the two hundred fifty years since. He wasn't going to stop on his own, so someone had to *make* him.

But did it have to be Wen?

In the moment, Wendolyn Eudora Cheney hadn't seen another option. In retrospect, Wen could've let the Night Realm

Queen deal with him. Or, hell, her own shifters. That was their job, after all—keeping her safe, guarding and protecting her. They would've been happy to spare her the death on her conscience.

It had been her choice, and she chose to kill without mercy or chance of failure. She had to own that choice.

"I've an idea," Brigid suddenly said, hesitant and quiet, though she still sounded loud in the hush of the sitting room.

Wen tried her best to shake off the funk she'd been sitting in all the way back from Ireland so she could pay attention. She glanced at Thea, only to find her Sister looking at her with a patient, kind concern that almost brought tears to her eyes. Somehow, Thea understood, even though her contribution had been healing and helping, rather than destruction and death.

Wen quickly looked away.

"Wendolyn, m'love, d'ye remember when I talked about me black pool the first time we blethered?"

The slightest hint of a smile touched the corner of her mouth. "I do. Swimming in the moonlight."

Naked, she thought but didn't say. Not in front of eleven men, even though three of them had already seen her naked and one had even shaved her legs.

Brigid nodded, smiling softly. "Seein as Sister Moon is full tonight, and we three could all use a bit o' de-stressin, I thought mayhap we could have a midnight swim?"

Thea brightened. "Ma sœur, but that is a wonderful idea."

Wen, though she felt far less enthusiastic, tried to look just as excited. "Sounds good to me." She couldn't help but suggest one possible negative to the plan. "Won't it be a bit cold for skinny-dipping tonight, though?"

But Brigid waved this off. "Not in me black pool. 'Tis hard to explain, lass, but it doesnae get as nippy there as the air temperature suggests. Or mayhap a full moon keeps us from feelin the chill?"

She tried to grin. "I'm just saying that I'm not keen on taking another deep dive into the Atlantic, ya know? Pretty sure there's still a little ice around my spine from that one."

There were a few chuckles, but not from Brigid or Thea. And not from her Nightwatchers who had been unable to help her as she'd been dragged down. It was still too fresh for amusement.

Thus, Brigid's expression was fully serious when she leaned closer to look Wen directly in the eye. "I swear ye'll not feel a moment's chill in me pool, but we'll never make ye jump in." Now, she grinned softly. "If ye dip in yer toe and it's too cold, ye can point and laugh at us sufferin our folly, aye?"

This time, Wen's grin was a bit more successful. "Aye. Can I suggest that we should all get some sleep after lunch? I dunno about you, but I feel like I've been up for a week straight."

That got more ayes than a call for a round of beer, and Gerhardt hopped up and headed for the kitchen. Aaron left to milk the likely-cranky coos. Halvor headed for his forge, and Thea's group left for her chamber to retwist her hair back into the more usual dreads.

Not before a kiss each on Wen's and Brigid's foreheads, though. Thea would never leave without a personal goodbye. Not anymore.

Then, even Brigid left after a lingering hug and a murmur that everything would be alright now. And it would. Wen knew they'd make it right. That was their job.

Finally, it was just Wen and her Nightwatchers, and they gently helped her stand without bumping her bad arm. Thea's magic kept it from hurting, but none of them knew how long that would last or if the painlessness would survive a direct bump to the afflicted area. Flanagan's disgustingly filthy teeth had pretty much destroyed the flesh of her forearm, savaging her down to the bone. Wen did *not* want to feel the full measure of agony she should be in. Not at all.

After a few steps, Dex gave up on restraint and swept her up in his burly arms to carry her up to her chamber for a hot soak and a change of clothes. He didn't even have to ask. He just knew. Florin fussed until her hair was freed from between her back and Dex's arm, and Callum busied himself with making sure the blanket she was wrapped in stayed warm and snug around her.

Her Nightwatchers. Her men.

Her lovers. Maybe it was time.

And then she was naked before them and still trying to hide the worst of her rolls and stretchmarks and she realized... no. She wasn't ready yet.

Tucker the Fucker's voice in her mind was still too loud.

27

Well after dark, Callum helped Wen into a filmy white nightgown, gossamer-fine and floaty in the scant drafts of her chamber. Florin had spent what felt like an hour after lunch brushing her hair until it shone and fell in waves around her face. Those lustrous waves had lasted even through a six-hour nap, supper, tea in the sitting room with the group, and now a strangely meaningful changing from regular clothes into something easy to take off and put back on for skinny-dipping.

Dex brought her the equally-filmy peignoir that went with the nightgown, holding it out for her to poke her arms into the delicate, ruffled sleeves. He then drew it up her arms and over her shoulders, and Florin moved in to tie the single ribbon into a bow that sat just at her collar bones while Dex gently moved her hair out from under the fabric.

She felt like a princess. Like something out of a—

A fairy tale.

Her breath caught, but she pushed the thought away. Not all fairy tales ended in tragedy, but the statistics there were pretty bleak. She didn't want to think about bleak tonight. The moon was full, she was heading out for quality time with both Sister Moon and her fellow Sisters of the Moon, and she wanted to enjoy herself before her real responsibilities kicked in and took all her focus.

After her nap, Dex had informed her that, though Brigid had asked them stay as long as they wanted, they really needed to get back to the States and put in their offer on the Oregon property. With the gold from the Pact returned to them, she'd be able to buy the place outright and start plans for their forever home as soon as they arrived back on American soil. All of those dreams were coming true, and Wen felt a wave of gratitude for that, if for nothing else.

She would gladly accept Gaia's gift. She would also become a marine biologist to determine the best course for healing the oceans with her magic, especially if that meant sending trash islands back toward the countries they came from. She still really wanted to enact that justice.

But for now— Brigid's black pool. Wen still wasn't sure what that meant, but a good day's sleep had put her mind at ease. No matter how cold, she could stand it. She could jump in and have fun with the girls.

Hell. She'd been to the depths of the Atlantic and lived to tell the tale. She'd even saved a man in the process.

But that reminded her of Tarquin, which threatened to suck the joy out of the moment, so she hurriedly put aside such thoughts.

She went to the door, then turned around to say something witty, but her words dried up in her mouth as she caught the expressions on her men's faces: desire, appreciation, longing.

For *her*.

She didn't deserve those looks. They looked like professional athletes in their prime. She looked like exactly what she was: a forty-year-old frump in a princess nightgown.

She lifted her chin. She was also a Sister of the Moon. She

had power over water—had even killed with the normally peaceful element. While she wasn't proud of the fact that she'd done so, she *was* proud that she had the ingenuity to try it and the determination to make it work. That was her strength, and if that's what drew those looks of desire and longing, she could handle that. She didn't need to be beautiful.

Or so she told herself.

So, with a last half-smiling look back at her boys, she left the chamber and went downstairs to meet Brigid and Thea at the main door. She'd snuck out this door to go milking with Aaron —an activity she'd enjoyed immensely— and now she would sneak out with the mistress of the castle for a midnight skinny dip, which ought to be just as fun.

They giggled like schoolgirls as they danced across the back garden and hurried through the brush path toward a cliffside rising up out of the moor. Wen had thought, from a distance, the cliffside was part of an extremely large tor, its sheer face all but glowing in Sister Moon's full radiance, but as they drew nearer, she saw a crack running up the face of the rock, and she could see inside. The interior of the formation was bowl-shaped and overflowing with trees and vines. It was as if a jungle grew inside a rock wall on the otherwise flat moor, a lush, magical pocket of verdant life.

Brigid waved them on as she slipped through the narrow crack, then ran, fleet-footed as a deer, through the close-packed trees. "C'mon, m'loves! We're nearly there!"

Wen had a bad moment where she feared she wouldn't fit through, but somehow, she didn't even catch a bit of gossamer gown on a jag of rock. Magic? Or was she just being claustrophobic about the size of the gap?

It didn't matter. And it didn't matter that she usually couldn't run without being a bull in a china shop. She flew, as fleet as Brigid, along with Thea, holding hands and catching up with their Sister, until the woods abruptly stopped on a short, rocky beach.

Brigid took Wen's other hand so they all stood connected and looked out across the expanse of the enormous pond. The water looked shiny black, as if carved from pure jet, and lay flat and still, not a ripple marring its surface, with the brilliant moon reflecting back into the sky like a beacon.

Nothing else reflected. No stars. No wisps of cloud. No blinky satellites or flashing airplanes.

The pool was entirely black except for the moon directly in the center.

"Brigid, how—?" Wen didn't even know what to ask.

Brigid squeezed her hand. "Magic, love. Now that we know more, I think this is a liminal space, a place where the Veil is naturally thin. Remember there were no stars in the sky in the Night Realm?"

Wen thought back. She remembered the moon being large and low in the sky, almost close enough to touch. She hadn't noticed any stars, but she could've just been overwhelmed by the enormous moon. But it was definitely possible there had been no stars, and she decided to take Brigid's word for it.

"I think the reflection is a mirror image of the Night Realm sky."

Awed, Wen looked from the black pool—the title made much more sense now—up to the "real" sky and gasped. The sky above glimmered like a bucketful of diamonds splashed across black velvet. She looked at the pool again. No stars.

Magic.

And then Thea clapped her hands together. "Last one in is the rotten egg!"

With a loud, combined shout, the Sisters of the Moon ran over the rocks, throwing aside their night clothes and house shoes, to leap full-body into the glistening black pool.

After all the splashing and laughing and swimming and sitting on submerged rocks to braid each others' hair, Wen finally floated, dead-man style, on her back in the pool, staring up at the miraculous sky above. Sister Moon hung low like an enormous opal, and the stars scattered around Her gleamed and winked like a masterwork jewelry setting. It was glorious, and Wen felt glorious in Her light.

She'd unbraided her hair to feel it floating about her face in the warm, smooth water, and she felt like it was absorbing the moon, surrounding her in a halo of pale, luminous light. She felt strangely lovely in that light, as if her stretchmarks didn't matter, her cellulite didn't matter. She felt... *emblazoned* with glow.

She felt beautiful.

And when she looked at her sisters—Thea still sitting on the rocks, one foot drawn up so she could wrap her arms around her shin, Brigid with her head thrown back, treading water and watching the stars—she saw that they were beautiful, too. They glowed. They *shone*. When they looked at her, they saw the moon in her, as well.

Beautiful Sisters. Blessed Sisters.

Sighing, Thea stood to find her slinky red-violet satin nightgown and pull it over her head. Her dreads hung in a loose plait down past her butt, and she looked like something out of a gilded art nouveau painting. Brigid slowly swam toward shore, then walked over to where she'd ditched a piece of clothing at a time all the way back to the edge of the forest. She, too, looked like a painting, perhaps from the Renaissance period, what with her velvety Goth robe and all the ruffles and her smooth, black hair.

Wen, not sure what sort of picture she painted, slipped on the first stone her feet touched but found purchase on the next and stood up out of the pool, expecting to be immediately embarrassed by her stomach paunch, her sagging breasts, her thick thighs, and her jiggling butt. But she didn't feel embarrassed at all. She still felt beautiful.

In fact, once she'd pulled her nightgown back on and swept her hair out from under the peignoir, she felt surprisingly like The Star from Brigid's tarot deck: shining, hopeful, beautiful.

The Sisters didn't run or dance back to the castle, but they did hold hands the entire way. Wen couldn't help but think she'd finally met and exceeded squad goals with her beautiful, magical Sisters, which made her smile. Then she remembered the men awaiting her upstairs in her chambers, and her smile tilted slightly, her eyelashes lowering.

It was time. She knew it. Blessed by the light of the full moon, Wendolyn Eudora Cheney finally felt worthy of her Nightwatchers' admiration and love.

Because they did love her. She knew it like she knew her own name. Callum had told her all along, but she hadn't understood what he meant.

You are worthy, he'd said.

Yes, she thought, relief and joy blooming through her like an exquisite moonflower. *I am worthy.*

So she left her Sisters at the foot of the stairs and climbed slowly to finally, truly call her Nightwatchers.

28

Dex saw her first, and his breath left him. Florin next, and he actually put a hand to his heart, as if he could feel her presence there.

Then Callum, who had been dozing across the head of her bed, sat up straight, eyes alive with want, body already responding to the sight of her in her full power.

It wasn't magic, that power. It was confidence. Wen *felt* beautiful, and so she was. Her men had seen it all along. She'd only needed to see it in herself.

Dex came to her, though he hesitated to touch her. It was as if he thought she was a goddess and he a mortal, unworthy to stroke her skin. She smiled at the thought, and his eyes heated.

She untied the peignoir's bow and let it fall to the floor as she stepped toward him. She pressed against him, against his warm, solid, beautiful body, highlighted and heated by the flickering firelight, and tilted her face up for a kiss. With the softest sound deep in his throat, he obliged, kissing her softly, reaching up to cup her face.

When she heard the door open, she pulled away languidly

and, without looking, sighed. "Where do you think you're going?"

Callum and Florin, eyes wide, looked back at her from where they stood outlined in darkness from the hallway outside.

"To give you a moment alone?" Callum half-said, half-asked.

"No," she murmured, leaning up to brush her nose against Dex's chin. "I want all of you, unless any of you has a problem with that."

She didn't think they would. They'd spent time in both her bath and her bed without any issue, but it might be different during sex, and she didn't want anyone doing anything they didn't like. She knew without doubt that they would never make her do anything she wasn't comfortable with. She could only return that respect in kind.

The door closed, and Callum pressed against her back, his hands on her hips. He, too, was warm and solid and beautiful, so she turned her head without turning away from Dex and kissed him long and deep. Florin slid in against her side, and she wrapped an arm around his waist to pull him in.

Connected. Held. Loved.

Hands—she didn't know how many or whose—swept the gossamer gown up and over her head, then stroked down her body, which still held a glow from the black pool. Florin's hands in her hair, Callum's hands on her breasts from behind, Dex's right hand on her face, his left stroking down her hip and around to cup her butt and pull her closer.

Oh. He was hard. Instead of pulling away from the erection jutting against her stomach, she allowed him to slide his hand down to lift her thigh, then reach down with the other hand to do the same. He held her off the ground, her most vulnerable, secret area exposed to him, and then her three men moved in tandem to take her to bed, kissing and stroking as they went.

Dex lay on his back, his hands on the tops of her thighs now, and she straddled him, bending low to kiss his beautiful lips, his strong throat, his pecs. He pulsed against her as she flicked her tongue at his nipple, so she did it again. Callum molded himself against her back, kissing the nape of her neck and across her shoulders, his erection grinding against her inner thighs and probably against Dex's, though neither man seemed to have a problem with that fact. Florin lay beside Dex, one hand in his dreads and one hand in Wen's hair, his lips nibbling at her neck and ear.

Dex arched up against her, so she shifted just enough to take him inside. Callum drew back, but only to move his erection out from between them and press it against her lower back, moaning at the sensation of sliding against the top of her crack. It was heavenly. It was flying and falling at the same time. And being gently caught by loving hands, cradled close, and held cherished.

Rocking his hips, Dex started up a smooth rhythm, not too fast or too slow. Callum groaned as she moved to match, shifting her hips forward for Dex's thrusts and backward to grind against him. She felt Florin thrusting against her thigh and twisted her head away from Dex's kiss and toward his. He eagerly, reverently touched her face as he kissed her, murmured beautiful nothings in his native tongue, then kissed her again more deeply.

Connected. Close. Loved. Wanted.

Soon, Dex sped his thrusts, grunting deep in his chest as he drove up into her. She ground down against him, breathy little sighs leaving her that she'd never once uttered during Tucker's so-called love-making. Nothing had ever felt like this before, like turning into a delicate dragonfly and flitting up to touch Sister Moon's shining face, like falling back to earth only to be caught in a pair of gently cupped hands. This was exhilaration. This was love and want and need all wrapped up in sweat and sex.

And then he arched against her and stiffened, crying out and gripping her thighs almost hard enough to bruise. But he would never harm her in any way, even at his most vulnerable, so she leaned down and kissed his parted lips as he came, stroked his face as he coasted down, stilled against him until he wasn't so sensitive.

And then Callum lifted her up off of him and entered her himself. She cried out at the different angle, briefly wondered if she was a slut for wanting this dick, too, and decided she didn't fucking care all in the space of a single stroke of him inside her. Dex reached down to stroke her most sensitive flesh while Florin turned her face to his for a searing, mind-stealing kiss. Callum thrust almost lazily, though with a little jerk of his hips at the end of each stroke.

That little jerk would be the death of her. And his size. She allowed herself to think *hung like a horse* for a split second, then shoved the image away before she broke into breathless laughter and gave him the wrong impression.

Florin's hand found her breast, his other hand fisting in her hair as he continued to kiss her hard and long. His touch combined with Callum's insane thrusts and Dex's genius fingers playing her like a harp to push her closer and closer to an orgasm that might just blow her head off. She felt raw. She felt open and vulnerable. She felt powerful as Callum growled between his teeth as he thrust faster and harder.

And then, she felt *everything*. She came apart in a million stars, coasted in Sister Moon's loving glow, drifted down into her lovers' arms.

They held her, her lovers, until she shifted to slide out from between them. When she finally found herself on her back against the cool, mussed sheets, she reached out to Florin and smiled, slow and sensuous. He smiled back the same way and came to her, sliding between her thighs to fill her up. Dex and Callum stroked all the skin they could reach, kissed her ears and neck and breasts, stroked her arms and thighs, while Florin drove her slowly but steadily back to the top of that plateau, holding her there until her face flushed with sweat, her body crying out for release.

Dex stroked her once, twice, and she came apart again, Florin coming with her, and they all coasted down together, tangled up in each other's arms, falling asleep in a heap.

Wen had one last thought before she let her consciousness float away to sweet dreams.

If only Tarquin were here, too.

And even though her thoughts turned bittersweet, she still fell asleep with a satisfied smile on her lovely, moon-limned face.

EPILOGUE
FOUR MONTHS LATER

"I don't like you going alone," Dex said, gently touching her scarred forearm, which hadn't healed for more than a month after the showdown and still ached if she (or one of the guys) lay on it for too long. "I know you can protect yourself, but I worry."

Yes, Wen *could* protect herself. She'd killed two men with a light rain. It still kept her up at night, even though she also went to her inlet cove every evening to practice long into the night in case she had to do it again.

It was her duty. Her moon duty.

Her lips quirked. It was still funny.

"Try doing what I do." She leaned into his space, and he obligingly put his arms around her, but only after taking off his dirt-caked gardening gloves. "Five things you can see, four things you can feel, three things you can hear, two things you can smell, one thing you can taste. Or, hell, mix 'em up. I sometimes do. It's the grounding to the moment that's important."

He hmmed against her hair—her shiny, glossy, several-inches-longer hair, thanks to Florin's special brushes and conditioners and serums and Callum's special additions to his regular cooking that Florin swore would improve her hair from the scalp down—and she grinned, feeling that hmm against her cheek. Dex always gave the best hugs and made the best noises.

She warmed, thinking about just how many noises she could wring out of him and how many he got from her in return. And Callum. And Florin.

But for now, she needed to practice, and she needed to feel the rush of the waves on her skin. She needed to wade out into the cove and turn her face up to Sister Moon and feel Her gentle power on her naked skin.

Yes, she practiced naked in the cove. It was her property and no ships were allowed for miles around, and she'd made Florin promise on pain of a broken camera to never photograph her while she was naked. And though the sea life population in and around her little cove had increased greatly since she moved in and started working her magic close to home, she wasn't worried about some dolphins and manta rays getting an eyeful.

Okay, maybe the dolphins. She'd learned they weren't always as nice as she'd thought.

Besides, Brigid was right: nothing matched the feeling of swimming untethered in the moonlight, Sister Moon's benevolent light working magic on her skin and turning back the clock. She was still forty years old, still overweight, still too anxious to go to the grocery store by herself, and still got migraines at the worst possible times, but she had the skin of a twenty-something now, and she seemed to glow everywhere she went.

Some of that could be all the sex.

Eventually, Dex let her go, and she left the shell of a house that was still being built (and the huge garage where Roger waited for Callum's next trip to town) and walked toward the coastline. She passed the arbor she'd commissioned from Halvor to the specifications she'd seen in her vision. Triple spirals on the stone tile floor. Halvor's ironwork open at the top for framing the full moon and to hold the cauldron up off the coals. Open spot for a firepit and the cauldron full of herbs and crystals she would burn according to Thea's instruction as a celebration of their fully powered time of the month tomorrow night. Which, it turned out, was *not* during their periods, but when the moon was completely full.

And she'd already enrolled in her first college class in over fifteen years, set to start in the summer. She was living that part of her dreams, too. Plus, it would help to know best where to direct her water-clearing powers. Work smarter, not harder.

Speaking of Clare, Wen's former boss had leapt at the chance to take over Flanagan's ridiculous mansions and be the first member of the human envoy. She already had feelers out about the other two. One of them, at Wen's suggestion, was the nice old black lady who had tried to help her when Dex stalked her in the grocery store.

We ladies have to look out for each other, she'd said, and she was right. It was exactly what the world needed at the moment.

And she had a cat. Zoe was a cranky, fluffy-white, hauty thing rescued from the local pound, and Wen loved her beyond reason. She was the only person Zoe would allow to pet her, no matter how many treats the boys offered her.

Smiling to herself, feeling whole and right with the world she protected, she walked further still through the densely-packed woods until she reached the rocky beach, then strolled out over the headland and stood with her feet in the water. It lapped gently at her ankles, welcoming her, asking to be used.

But she couldn't immediately answer that call. Her breath had caught in her throat and refused to budge.

Out in the cove, swimming toward her and flipping its distinctive tail above the surface of the water, was the world's tiniest baby blue whale. Then the blue-grey humanoid head. Then the tail.

And then Tarquin stood up out of the water in his ghostly-pale human form and put out his arms, and she ran into them, spraying water everywhere with her graceless galumphing against the waves and grateful that the flying droplets surely hid her tears. She kissed him over and over again, her fingers clenched in his platinum hair to hold him close as if she'd never let him go again.

Maybe she wouldn't.

Because just like that, even though the contractors were still weeks away from finishing, her house was complete. All four pillars stood in place. She was whole.

And Sister Moon smiled down.

Thank you for reading Sisters of the Moon!

Molly is a self-styled cryptozoologist, a rabid reader, an inveterate crafter, and unapologetically Aquarius. She loves writing with her beloved sister, autumn, being a hermit, sipping hot tea, and heavy blankets. She also sometimes wears haunt make-up for no earthly reason. Hit her up on her facebook page, Molly Burkhart, or her website, mollyburkhart.net.

Made in the USA
Coppell, TX
11 May 2021